CROSSWINDS

CROSSWINDS

MARTHA CHEAVENS

PEOPLES BOOK CLUB · CHICAGO

To the Memory of My Father

CROSSWINDS

1

LET US TURN BACK a few pages, let us look again at a lost time, a bewildered and dissipated and wrecked period, now mislaid and almost forgotten because of the importunities of the present. Yet perhaps not too unlike the present, if only we should stop to think.

The year was in the early twenties, but it still held hands with 1918, trying to pull away from the grasp of World War I. The month was late August. The hour about three in the afternoon. The one train a day that shuttled between Donde, a little Texas town on the Mexican border, and Yucca Junction, had gone up as usual and was at this moment coupling on a box car containing household goods, domestic animals, a minister from Connecticut, the Reverend James Calvert Bronson, three of his four sons, and a cowboy named Fred Werck.

Ninety miles to the southeast of the junction, Donde awaited the train. Because of the blistering heat the town was more dead than alive. The leaves of the pomegranate trees, the cottonwoods, and the oleander bushes hung motionless in the copper-colored air. They were grizzled with dust.

In homes, offices and shops, people moved about, if they moved at all, like sleepwalkers, their senses dulled by the languor of the heat. The temperature stood at 116° F. in the shade. Window blinds were drawn, electric fans whirred in still, darkened rooms. People who had the leisure lay languidly on beds

1

that had been made earlier in the day by Mexican servants, or reclined in tubs of cold water, pillowing their heads on folded bathtowels, reading, refreshing themselves with iced drinks placed conveniently near at hand. Everybody drank iced drinks, iced tea or beer or even water but always plenty of ice in everything. Yet it was impossible to get cool no matter what one did.

From time to time all eyes strayed toward clocks and watches, waiting for evening with its promise of relief from the heat, waiting for the whistle of the train due to arrive at six o'clock, bringing the mail and sometimes a few passengers. The arrival of the mail was like a social event and after supper everybody went to the post office to get it. But now it was too early for the train, even too early for its tinny whistle. Plenty of time for another drink, another magazine story, another hour or two of idleness.

People who had to work, like the sentries on the International Bridge across the Rio Grande or Mexican laborers at the rock quarry, sweated until their clothing became dank and stiff. Servants sweltered in hot kitchens.

In Yucca Junction, which lay in the adjoining county, there was plenty of exertion despite the heat. The train from San Antonio had arrived, railway mail clerks flew into a burst of activity. The train crew backed down the yards and prepared to pick up the boxcar that had been waiting on a siding since morning.

Only the conductor was not busy, as there were no passengers for Donde, to his knowledge. He was glad. It was hard work, on a warm day like this, to have to punch holes in tickets. Clad in overalls and a railroadman's cap, he settled down in the empty chair car and opened a window, letting in a blast of fiery air from the desert. It would probably be cooler with the window closed, he figured, but maybe when the train got under way, if it ever did, its moving would create a breeze. Half asleep, he looked out at the landscape. Beyond the bleak station buildings stretched nothing but desert, cactus, mesquite, sunburned grass, sky. He saw heat devils dancing in the distance. Near-by, to the right, a whirlwind of dust spiraled upwards, carrying with it a few dry leaves and bits of paper. He fanned himself with a San Antonio paper, and frowned in annoyance when the train quivered and began backing off down the yards.

Abruptly there came a violent jolt when it coupled on to the freight car, such a jolt that it sent him halfway out of his seat and almost into the aisle. This was followed by a second similar convulsion, but shortly thereafter, the train began jerking its way southward and the conductor settled down for a good sleep. He did not know that the impact of the Bronsons, like the coupling on of their boxcar, was usually in the manner of a jolt of some kind, although the family themselves would have denied it, especially Mr. Bronson.

At the moment the boxcar had been coupled to the rest of the train, the minister, his three sons, and Fred the cowboy, who had attached himself to them in San Antonio, had been leaning over a map spread out on one of the two bedsteads which had been set up in the boxcar for the family to sleep in on their long journey from the North.

As soon as the jolting had ceased, Mr. Bronson picked himself up from the floor where the impact had thrown him and smiled benignly. He brushed himself off and began peering about on the straw-littered floor for his glasses.

"Oh, Father, are you hurt?" cried his son Matthew, a shy, slender, dark-haired, fourteen-year-old boy.

But Mr. Bronson said, "Why, no, Son, of course not," in such a lofty and surprised way that he gave the impression that he was in the habit of frequently being pitched on his face in a freight car. Mr. Bronson was always like that, impervious to minor inconveniences, especially physical ones.

"The only thing is," he murmured, "my glasses." He groped aimlessly about in the straw. "I can't see to find them."

Mark, Matthew's brother, did not resemble his twin either in looks or personality. He had merry blue eyes and a way with the girls. "You'd better sit down on that old trunk and let *us* look," he admonished. "Since you can't see, you'll be flung out of the car the way this train is going. Get away from the door, Father. Here, sit down."

"Thank you, Son."

Submissively, he sat down.

Mr. Bronson was a tall, thin man, stooped a little from bending over his study table and many pulpits. There was something of the ascetic about him, an air of detachment. When his feet, owing to the law of gravity, perforce clung to the ground when he walked, one felt that he himself soared in some higher, purer air, unconditioned by such laws as gravity. One felt a strange envy, a longing to share with him these lofty regions of the spirit. His eyes were gray and set far back in two deep caves beneath his high and jutting forehead. There was an expression in them of complete innocence, like a child. But it was an innocence so candid, so honest, so penetrating that it was disturbing, because they were also wise, they were mystic, there lay in them some secret.

This afternoon, sitting on a round-topped tin trunk, Mr. Bronson merely looked baffled as his three sons and Fred scrambled around looking for his glasses. Without them everything had become a blur. The desert outside the opened door flowed past, a gray-green and sand-colored river. Inside, the furniture and barrels, the cow, the horse, the dogs, the crates of chickens, everything, all mingled vaguely together before his vision, stirred only by the moving of the train. He longed for his wife, Nora, without whom he was helpless. She always told him he should own an extra pair of glasses, and she was right. But he invariably forgot to buy them. He thought also of his youngest son, John, aged four.

He could not understand why, at this particular moment, impotent and blind because of his lost glasses, the stray thought should come into his mind that he had been married only sixteen years. At the time of his marriage he had possessed only the suit of clothes he wore and this round-topped trunk on which he was now sitting, then containing only a change of underwear and a few precious books. Now he had a wife, a carload of furniture, a horse, a cow, countless chickens, a dog who had had eight puppies on this trip, four sons, and a daughter on the way (or at least, he hoped it would be a daughter). Sixteen years . . .

Suddenly, above the noise of the train, Luke, ten years old and redheaded, gave an ear-piercing shout, followed by shrieks of laughter from all three boys and guffaws from Fred.

"Father! Your glasses! Look where we found them. Look! Hanging on the cow's horn.—Duchess! Be still.—She's trying to switch them off with her tail. Cows *are* stupid! So-o-o, Duchess . . ."

A faint smile raised the corners of James Bronson's mouth. Well, God had taken care of his glasses after all, had hung them neatly on the cow's horn where one of the boys was already plucking them off. The Lord could just as well have flung them out the open door.

"Here, Father," Mark staggered across the lurching train and handed the glasses to his father. Mr. Bronson accepted them, cleaned them with the corner of his handkerchief, put them back on again and with a polite "Thank you, Son," smiled serenely around him. Everything sharpened into focus again. He took out his watch, held it to his ear to see if it was ticking, showed it to Fred and then put it back in his pocket.

Fred was a cowboy and not, he had assured Mr. Bronson, a hobo. To prove this he had showed his ticket. He had been in San Antone to visit his old ma that was sick in a hospital, he explained. Warn't no hospital no closer. He didn't like trains but the boxcar was better than the chair car.

"It's so sorta homey," he said.

The boys had been disappointed at first to find out that the first actual cowboy they met was not at all like the ones in the movies. Fred's lips were wind-peeled and he had a fever blister. He wore no chaps or fancy shirts. He had on a pair of overalls turned up at the bottom, a plain blue-and-white bandana, not too clean, around his neck, a sombrero, and hand-tooled high-heeled boots. The boots somehow made him convincing. In fact, all three boys secretly longed for a pair exactly like his. Thus Fred was initiated into the charmed circle of the Bronson family. At night he rolled up in a blanket on the straw on the floor. In the daytime he helped with the animals, answered questions, and told tall tales. Now with Mr. Bronson's glasses retrieved, all five once again gathered around the map.

Mr. Bronson's reaction to the map was almost the same as it had been the first time he had studied it, before starting out on this trip. Once again his eyes sought the county and the town toward which they were on the way. It seemed impossible that in the whole county there was but one town. He mentioned this to Fred who pushed his hat farther back on his head and grinned.

"Some counties, Parson," he said, "don't have no towns, least, none of the size of Donde."

"How big *is* Donde?" asked Mark.

Fred settled back against the head of the bed. "Looks like a speck of dust on that there map but I reckon they's five, six thousand people live there," he answered. "Hard to tell. Them Spicadees, they don't never know how many kids they have when the census man comes around. Besides, in Donde, people sorta come and go."

"Spicadees?" asked Matthew. "Who are *they?*"

Fred told him they were Mexicans. Usually they were just called Spics. The name was coined from the Mexicans' saying, "Me spicadee English."

Lukey mischievously nudged his father with an elbow. "Hey, Father, do you spicadee English?"

Mr. Bronson looked down at him reprovingly. "To us," he said, "they are Mexicans, not Spicadees. Do you understand, Son?"

"Yes, sir."

Matthew pointed to a small line on the map. "What's this?" he asked.

"That's the bridge acrost the Rio Grande," answered Fred. "They's two bridges, but one don't show on the map. It's just a ore trestle down by the rock quarry."

Back and forth went the questions and answers. Fred, proud of such a receptive audience, embroidered his answers more and more. It was quite a place, Donde, he told them. It had everything. It had a fort, a regiment of United States soldiers, two picture shows, an elegant hotel, a dandy newspaper, the *Eagle,* a boulevard paralleling the river, good country club, golf links, a fine high school, Indians, Chinese, and bad men.

"Bad men?" cried Luke in a transport. *"Bad men?* You mean real bad men like you see pictures of in post offices and places?"

"Yup," said Fred, " 'MEN WANTED BY THE U.S.' I knowed one real well oncet, name of Mr. Rogers. 'Course he lived on the Mexican side of the river but his boys and me, we went to school together. They came acrost the river every day and then went back. One boy, Dan, was my age. He was the one carried a gun."

"A gun?" asked Mark. "To school? A real gun?"

"Sure," said Fred. "What's a gun? He kep' it in his lunch box, hid it in his locker. 'Course when he got acrost the bridge again he stuck it back in his holster in plain sight. *But not in Texas!"*

Mr. Bronson watched the look of enjoyment on Fred's face as he talked and opposite him the thrilled eagerness and curiosity of his own sons. He wondered how much of this they were believing, he wondered how much of it he believed himself and whether or not he had done right to bring his children to such a place.

Fred paused, his imagination having momentarily run dry, and Matthew, the quiet twin, turned to his father and said, "Do you remember, Father, in Robert Louis Stevenson's *Child's Garden of Verses,* that poem you used to read to us? It was called, I think, 'Travel.' "

Mr. Bronson was pleased. "Yes, son, I do remember."

"I remember the way it began," murmured Matthew:

> I should like to rise and go
> Where the golden apples grow:—
> Where below another sky . . .

The boy paused, "I don't remember the next line," he said, "but I feel that Donde is also 'below another sky.' Don't you?"

"Yes," replied his father, "there is something about the poem that has always stirred the vagabond in me, I don't know why. Toward the end I recall another line or so:

> Where amongst the desert sands
> Some deserted city stands . . .

"Oh, yes!" interrupted Mark. "And another place, too:

> Where the Great Wall round China goes,
> And on one side the desert blows,
> And with the bell and voice and drum,
> Cities on the other hum.

Maybe Donde is one of those *cities on the other hum.*"

Fred reached a long forefinger inside the top of his boot and began to scratch, but he could not take his eyes away from this circle of faces bending over a map which had suddenly come alive. This family seemed to be drawn together by some magic, he knew not what. He wished he, too, had read that poem, but he had never heard of Robert Louis Stevenson, having quit school after he finished the third grade. Just then the train whistled and the spell was broken.

"We're almost there, boys," Mr. Bronson stated, "if the train's on time. I'd like to have all the chores attended to before we arrive."

The boys sighed.

"Whose turn is it to milk Duchess?" asked Mark, purposely looking out of the door at the desert.

Fred got up. "I'll milk her," he said. "That's sure *one* thing I can do."

"I'll feed the dogs," said Lukey and walking out of his father's earshot he began to sing to himself softly, "Spicadee, Spicadee."

"Feed 'em good," said Fred. "Don't fergit you folks give me one of them pups. The one with the black spot on his left ear."

Thereupon followed an hour of brisk activity. Luke attended to the dog and the eight puppies. Traveling with the new-born puppies across the burning desert had proved a problem, but an engineer, interested in the minister's menagerie, had offered a solution. He had contrived a sort of air-conditioned incubator by making a nest of ice-cold beer bottles amongst which the puppies rested and thrived. As soon as the beer bottles warmed up the engineer would put them back in the icebox in the caboose and offer a fresh supply. Mr. Bronson would have preferred soft drinks, but it had worked out beautifully and now the trip was nearly over. In fact, the Bronsons and all the workmen on the various trains sooner or later became quite chummy by the end of a run. The gallons of fresh milk supplied by Duchess were exchanged for hot meals in the caboose and hours of companionship, not to mention the ice-cold beer incubators.

Now, the chores over, there was a mad scramble to freshen up, to wash ears and clean fingernails, to slick down hair and exchange overalls for more respectable attire. "I want all of us to get into town looking like gentlemen," said Mr. Bronson, smiling, "even if we did come by freight."

By the time the train came to a spasmlike stop at Donde they were all curried and combed, even Fred. Perhaps a little straw and hay did stick to them here and there and no doubt Nora would have straightened their ties or sewed on a button or two had she been there, but, nevertheless, the boxcar passengers looked pretty good. Their excitement was tremendous. They had come a long distance. Now they were about to embark upon a new adventure, to begin living in a new town, meet a whole set of new people, encounter new customs. Moving about as the Bronson family did was enchanting. They finished at one place and were off to another. It was like reading a book, shutting it with a bang, and opening a new one. When the train stopped the boys made a rush for the door, but Mr. Bronson called them back.

"Before we get off, boys," he said, "we must offer thanks."

"What for?" asked Luke.

"For getting here," replied Mr. Bronson.

"But how do we know we are going to like it?" persisted Luke. "Maybe we oughtn't to thank God until we are sure. Besides if we kneel down, we'll get hay on our knees."

Mr. Bronson appeared not to have heard. He pulled up his trousers slightly and knelt on the hay- and straw-covered floor, his hand resting on the tin trunk.

"Let us pray," he said.

Already in the station could be heard the sound of cars, of voices, intoxicating noises which are a part of the arrival of any train in any station.

"I hope he makes it short," whispered Luke to Mark.

Matthew reached over and put his hand over Luke's mouth with an imperative "Sh-sh!"

Mr. Bronson did make it short. Without knowing it, he had knelt on a board with a nail sticking up, concealed by the straw. He was not worried about the pain but about his trousers, his second-best ones. Nora would not like a hole in the trousers of this suit. She tried so hard to keep her family looking neat. Nevertheless, James beseeched God to take care of her, of little John, and of the daughter who would be born in January. Then he arose with dignity and inspected the torn place in his trousers, brushed himself off and announced that they were ready to investigate their new home. The boys leaped from the door, but the brakeman came up and placed a little ladder upon which Mr. Bronson and Fred descended more sedately.

They said good-bye to the brakeman and other members of the train crew and finally to Fred. They were sorry to say good-bye to Fred but he had explained to them earlier that on Saturdays the wagons came to Donde from the ranch where he worked, for the week's supply of food and for the mail.

"Where is the wagon?" asked Luke, now, looking around.

Fred said, "Reckon at the Feed and Grain Store, or at Tasman's Grocery. That's where they unhitch and wait, mostly. Maybe I better look for it so we can set out as soon as today's mail is sorted. The ranch is a long ways off. But I'll see you again, boys," he added warmly, sharing their disappointment. "And you, too, Parson. I'll take you all hunting with me."

"Deer-hunting?" asked Matthew hopefully.

"Why not?" said Fred. "When the season starts. I'll sure look you all up."

Once again he shook hands with them and then made off across the tracks. The Bronsons felt lost with the disappearance of their new friend. They certainly hated to see Fred go, but there was no help for it, so they, too, crossed the tracks, walking four abreast along the cinders, dividing up when they reached a sidewalk.

Luke pranced ahead, unable to keep in step with anybody, his dancing eyes missing nothing. Behind him walked the twins. Although a shade less tall than Matthew, Mark held himself so proudly erect that nobody noticed it. The late afternoon sun glinted on his crisp, dark-gold hair, on his handsome features. Matthew was unusually quiet, self-conscious, and ashamed of his new corrective glasses. It was too bad he had to start off in a new town wearing glasses. Behind the boys walked their father, deep in thought.

All of them were different but the same fever possessed them, the fever of new surroundings, of undiscovered territory. They had come from a gentle little New England town, a rolling country, the hills on summer evenings gauzy with a lilac-tinted haze. Here the leaves of the trees were a dingy green. All the plants, covered by a film of dirt, had the same parched look. The grass had long ago been scorched. The air was acrid with the smell of alkali and dryness and dust. The houses looked hot and ugly. As they neared Main Street they passed a few homes where Mexican gardeners were finishing their day's labor. They heard the lisping of lawn sprinklers and, like small artificial oases, one or two yards looked fresh and pretty.

"Where are we going first, Father?" piped up Lukey.

"First," he answered, "we'll get oriented and then we'll eat."

"Oriented?" asked Luke. "That sounds like sailing away on a ship somewhere. Maybe to China."

"No," answered his father patiently, as they walked along. "It means finding out about the town, where the streets are, where the post office is—we might have a letter from your mother, you know. Then, maybe if it doesn't get too dark we shall take a look at our new house. I'd like to find a drayman, if possible, and see about unloading the boxcar, but it's Saturday afternoon and late. We may have to stay in the boxcar until Monday."

"Oriented," repeated Lukey, slowing down so that the twins almost tripped on him.

"Get going," muttered Mark. "Oriented simply means getting the lay of the land. Look, Father, here's Main Street. Fred said to turn left when we got to Main Street, and then keep walking."

This they did. They walked down the length of Main Street. The boys were entranced and time and again Mr. Bronson had to urge them to make haste. Matthew wanted to stop in a saddle and leather-goods shop where he saw in the window a pair of cowboy boots like Fred's. Mark stopped in front of the gaudy picture show, the Montezuma Palace, and Lukey sniffed thirstily at the open door of Stirling's Pharmacy with its soda fountain. The first stop they made was at the post office, where Mr. Bronson found a short letter from Nora saying to meet her on Tuesday afternoon and that she and Johnny were fine.

But even the cowboy boots and all the rest of it were forgotten when they reached the end of Main Street and saw the International Bridge spanning the Rio Grande.

"Can we cross it?" asked Mark eagerly.

His father said, "We can walk only as far as the United States ends. We have no tourist cards yet."

"As far as the United States ends!" said Mark. "It's funny, Father, I didn't realize the United States ended anywhere. Now here we are."

"Smack at the end," said Lukey.

"In a way, though, the United States doesn't end anywhere," murmured Matthew dreamily. "The world can't get along without us. Look how we won the war in Europe. And not even our war, either. They started it."

"Nobody wins in a war, Matt," said his father. "Nobody ever wins. Step up, lads, step up. It's getting dark. There are no long twilights here, like we have at home."

Across the bridge they marched, their eyes unable to hold so much at once. They saw American sentries passing back and forth, Mexican women in black shawls walking rapidly carrying beautiful woven baskets filled with food, carriages and horses rushing past, well-dressed Americans with a Saturday-night gleam in their eyes. Near the center of the bridge stood the customs building, the tollkeeper's shed, and a bronze plaque announcing that here ended the United States. Even Lukey was impressed. Matthew read the words aloud and the little boy looked down at the planks that the bridge was made of.

"If I stood here, Father," he said, "with my left foot on the plank that belongs to the United States and put my right foot on the next plank would I be in Mexico? Would I be in a 'city on the other hum'?"

"Don't you dare do it, Lukey," warned Matthew, "or you'll be on the other hum with Father."

"Would I get arrested?" asked Lukey, intrigued. "What if I lost my balance and fell over the other side? Would I be arrested for that? Just for falling down? Would they put us all in jail?"

The prankish little boy was standing with his left foot as far as it could possibly go on the American side, holding the other foot up in the air. He leaned over, as far as he dared.

"Come on, Son," said Mr. Bronson, "that's enough."

"But would I, Father," he insisted, "would I be in Mexico if I just put one toe on the Mexican plank, would I be in Mexico? Just one toe?"

As he asked this a car drove up and the customs officers and the tollkeeper provided a distraction for the twins and Mr. Bronson. They turned away from Luke who, unobserved, quickly put one foot down on the other side and then drew it back. He sighed happily. One of these days he'd tell the family but this was not the opportune time. Mr. Bronson had walked over to the railing and was looking across at the Mexican side where the sun was setting in a red glory. He saw the buildings of the town in Mexico and he saw, far up the river, the willows and other trees whose names Fred had told him about, trees he did not recognize. Above the noise of the traffic on the bridge he could hear the raucous chattering of the hundreds of birds which were settling on the trees. Most people called them magpies, Fred had told them, but they were really grackles. Under the bridge the Rio Grande flowed and he could see undercurrents pulling and swirling as the water hurried toward the sea. Suddenly it was dark. There would be no time now to see the house they were to live in, Mr. Graham's house. That would have to wait until tomorrow.

"Come on, boys," he said, "it's dark. Let's go to the hotel we saw on Main Street and have a good hot dinner."

Reluctantly the boys, who had been talking to some foot passengers, obeyed him. They had just learned, they told their father, that there had been a shooting in Donde that afternoon. The sheriff had been killed. Probably just hearsay, Mr. Bronson reassured them. Look how Fred had elaborated! They turned their backs on Mexico and this time the twins walked ahead while Luke walked quietly and demurely by his father's side. Inwardly, Mr. Bronson smiled. Luke, he thought, was never as angelic as this unless he had done something forbidden.

2

RIO GRANDE BOULEVARD paralleled the river, extending on through the town and petering out when it came to the desert. At one time it had been the most fashionable promenade in Donde, and the most beautiful homes had been built there, facing the river.

But as it happens in many towns, another section gradually became the more desirable. The vicinity became outmoded, real-estate values dropped, a different type of people began moving in.

A country club was built, the Casino, on the opposite side of Donde, on a slight rise of ground which the townspeople fondly called "The Hill." This now became the élite neighborhood and Rio Grande Boulevard became merely a thoroughfare. Some of its fine old homes were torn down, others became boardinghouses and a few, a very few indeed, were still kept up and lived in by their wealthy owners. But it was certainly not a desirable locality. Mexican Town was stepping on its toes. An ice factory was built on the riverbank, blotting out some of the view. Across from the ice factory lay the Thorpe mansion. It was built of red brick and the grounds covered about an acre of land, enclosed by an ornate iron fence.

On the Saturday afternoon of the Bronsons' arrival the house and grounds seemed deserted. The midday meal was over. The servants were taking their siesta. Actually no one was awake but the little girl, Cenci, who propped her thin face in her hands and looked without ambition or interest out of the window toward

15

Mexican Town. Her governess, Miss Manners, was off for the weekend to visit some relatives in Del Rio, leaving Cenci to the servants.

Cenci was eleven years old, very slender and frail-looking. She was not pretty. Her eyes were large and dark in her small face, her thick black hair was long and straight. Her parents were dead, and she had a guardian, a Mr. Graham, whom she had never seen. Several times a year he dutifully sent his business partner, Mr. Derrick, who lived in Austin, to make a trip of inspection to Donde. Prior to these visits there would be a buzz of activity in the Thorpe household, the gardens would be pruned and tended, Cenci would be outfitted with new clothes, her governess would get a marcel wave, and on Mr. Derrick's arrival everything would appear to be perfect but as soon as his perfunctory visit was over things would fall back into their usual routine of neglect and carelessness.

This Saturday afternoon she looked off into Mexican Town with a feeling of boredom close to despair. She looked at her clock. She looked at a letter she had just written but had not sealed. Her fingers were ink-stained. She looked at the clock again, then washed her hands, gathered up her pocketbook and her letter, and stepped out into the hall. She walked out of the house unobserved, crossed the grounds and went out of the gate, headed for Main Street.

The sidewalks were so hot they almost blistered her feet through the thin soles of her patent-leather slippers, so she stopped in at Stirling's Pharmacy to cool off and consume two banana splits. She wondered why it was always cooler in a drugstore than anywhere else. Then she got up, paid for her refreshment, and stepped out on the sidewalk again, walking toward the post office.

Cenci rented a box at the post office which she paid for out of her allowance. The little key to the box, tied on a red ribbon, was to her a magic thing and nobody knew about it except, of course, the clerk at the post-office window. She would think of the pretty gilt key with its red ribbon and the thought gave her a warm quick excitement. Cenci's box had a neat little gilt number on it, 99, and every Monday it had a thick letter in it for her, written to herself on Saturdays.

Sometimes she had other mail. She cut coupons out of magazines and sent for samples of things, free cook books and swatches of wool and booklets on house-decorating. Sometimes Box 99 was quite stuffed. What a thrill! Opening it up, and having all of those letters burst out at her. Oh, there was nothing like it! Frequently she ordered things from the mail-order house. *That* was something. Days of waiting and wondering. At long last, looking anxiously into the box, standing on tiptoe, for P.O. Box 99 was a bit too high for her. Finally the card saying in bold letters, "PARCEL TOO LARGE FOR BOX." Oh, the trembling fingers, the standing in line at the parcel post window, and at last the parcel in her hands. The feeling of it! The smelling of it! The shaking! Finally, in her own room, the cutting of the string, the stripping away of the wrapping papers, like peeling a fruit, the falling out of the invoice, the order itself!

Well, today she was not expecting a package. In the pocket of her dress, the letter she had written to herself lay heavy, bumping against her legs as she walked. It wasn't sealed yet. She might add a postscript later on; she had not decided. It was too early for the evening mail but, nevertheless, she went to the post office. One never could tell. The box was empty. Through its glass window she could see a clerk moving back and forth, his face appearing and disappearing in the lighted interior.

She crossed the street and stood for a moment under the sign, "The Donde Eagle," and looked in. Mr. Brett Lindley, the editor, sat at his desk as she had often seen him, his hat on, his face ruddy and hot under the bright light of an unshaded electric bulb over his head. With his rusty mustache, his great beak of a nose crisscrossed with red veins, his huge hairy hands holding a book, the sight of him filled Cenci with fear. He looked angry. He looked as though he might eat a little girl up, swallow her at one gulp.

Cenci deliberated. Within, the presses rumbled. The linotype machine gossiped away, clattery-clack. There was a funny smell coming out of the door, a queer, hot smell, like cannibals cooking, maybe, Cenci feared. She trembled. Maybe she'd better not go in after all, even though she had come on an important errand.

Then she saw the cat. He was an enormous fellow, entirely black except for the tip of his tail, which was white. He lay curled up on an opened dictionary on its stand, sound asleep. Only the white tip of his tail was awake. It flicked delicately and sensitively back and forth, surveying the room. "I see you, little girl," the white flag seemed to say. "Don't be afraid. Mr. Lindley does not eat little girls, not really."

Although he was the ugliest cat she had ever seen, Cenci loved him. Poor thing, she thought, what a lot of fights he has been in! One ear was almost gone, the other in shreds. He bore the scars of many midnight brawls. Poor thing, Cenci said to herself again, and walked in. Her footsteps were so light that they were like a fluff of *barba-de-chivo* blown across the floor. Mr. Lindley did not even look up. The presses rumbled very loudly. The black cat opened his yellow eyes. He yawned. He arose, standing on all four feet, arching his back like a great inverted U. Then he jumped lightly to the floor, walked across it indifferently, rubbed against Cenci's slender ankles. He was purring so loudly she forgot all about her errand. Stooping, she looked at him and said gently, "Hello."

She did not touch him at first. His purring increased and he rubbed against her until she could feel electric sparks from his fur tingling against her bare ankles. Then she held out one forefinger and scratched him between the ears, not hard.

"Hello," she said again, "have you got a name?"

A voice boomed into the room.

"Of course he's got a name," said Mr. Lindley, "it's Nevermore."

"Nevermore? I certainly never heard of a cat named *that* before, sir."

"Didn't you ever hear, 'Quoth the raven, "Nevermore"'?" shouted Mr. Lindley.

"No, sir."

"You need educating," commented the editor.

He towered above the little girl, but she looked up at him out of lucid brown eyes, clear and frank.

"He's such a beautiful cat," she said.

"Beautiful?" The editor's face softened. "Well, I don't know that I'd call him beautiful," he said, "but he *is* remarkable. He likes you, too. He doesn't like everybody."

Cenci stood up. She looked wise. "Cats *know*," she stated. "People either like cats, or they hate cats. One or the other. Cats either like them, or hate them. I'll bet Nevermore is extra smart. Cats are smarter than most people think. And they're all different, every single cat."

Brett Lindley began walking around the messy office. "Certainly Nevermore is smart," he said. "He sleeps on the dictionary. He won't sleep anywhere else. Did you know, child, that in this dictionary"—the editor thumped it soundly—"between the two backs of this one book, lies all the literature in the English language? The same words. But arranged differently. Naturally. That's the trick. But the same words. Did you know that?"

"No, sir." Cenci was impressed.

"Well, this cat knows it."

"What else does he know, or what else does he do that's smart?"

"He likes pencils. He has a favorite pencil. He will take it between his teeth, and hide it, and pretend he doesn't know where it is. He will look and look. Suddenly, he will act very surprised, and rush to the spot where he has hidden it, and pick it up between his teeth and lay it at my feet, like most cats do a mouse."

Cenci smiled. And when she smiled, her smile began slowly, and grew around her mouth and down to her chin, and into the corners of her eyes, and all over her face.

"Naturally," continued Brett Lindley, "he has to be in the mood to do these things."

"I know," nodded Cenci, "all cats have to be in the mood." Slowly the smile faded from her face. Her brow clouded.

"I had a little cat once," she said. "He used to pick up a marble and carry it to the top steps of the servants' stairs and then drop it. Bounce, bounce, bounce. Down to the bottom step. Miss Manners is a little deaf. But she could always hear that marble. Bounce, bounce, bounce. It was such a cute trick, but then the cat ran away."

Mr. Lindley looked at her with camaraderie. "What was the cat's name?" he asked.

"Kitty. All my cats are named Kitty. I never have one long enough to give it a proper name."

"What happens to them?"

Cenci looked at him searchingly. Did she just imagine it, or was it a look of understanding Mr. Lindley gave her?

"I think Miss Manners drives them away," she whispered. "She hates cats. If one is in the room she says she can tell, even if she can't see the cat."

"Hmm. Have you tried dogs?"

"Yes, sir. But they bark. She doesn't like dogs either. And canaries sing. Turtles run away and goldfish die."

"I see."

There was a deep silence.

"That's why I came today, sir. About Kitty. My last kitty. She was special. I've loved the others, but this kitty was special. All white. The insides of her ears and her nose and the cushions in her paws were pink. White and pink. She was the one that bounced the marble. She was awfully special. Last week—well, last week I couldn't find her when I went to feed her. I *still* can't find her. That's why I came here—I want to put an ad in the paper. I'd know Kitty anywhere, sir. You see, she was blind. Lots of white cats are blind, but people don't always know . . ."

There was no smile on Cenci's face now. Her chin quivered.

Her lips trembled. She put up one hand and kept rubbing it against her lips, so that he wouldn't notice.

"I've got the ad written out," she said, and fished in her purse and produced a slip of paper. He read it carefully: *"Lost, straid or stollen, small white kiten. Blind. A very speshul kiten. Reward. P.O. Box 99."*

"I have the money," said Cenci, reaching in her purse. "How much will it be?"

Seriously he counted the words, took her name and address, told her the amount, gave her back the change.

"The ad will be in the paper next week," he said.

"Not till *next week?*" she asked, dismayed.

"No. You see, the paper just came out this morning. It's only a weekly."

"Oh. Well, good-bye."

She started toward the door. He called her back.

"Yes, sir?"

"You might hear from me before then," he said, "a newspaper office is a clearing house for all sorts of things. If your kitten is found, someone *might* bring it right here."

"Might they?" Her eyes brightened.

"They might, indeed. And by the way, I didn't finish telling you about Nevermore. He's not like ordinary cats in many other ways, too. He eats very strange things."

"What, for instance?"

"Well, erasers. He cut his teeth on erasers."

"He *did?*"

"Yes. And he gobbles up all my old typewriter ribbons, just like Italians eat spaghetti." Cenci looked at him a moment, at the mustache, the big red nose, the bloodshot eyes. He inserted a sheet of paper in his old Oliver typewriter and began pecking away at it.

"Doesn't he ever drink milk?" she asked. The editor shook his head emphatically. "Only ink," he replied, "He practically lives on ink. I have to hide the bottle from him."

Her chin had ceased to quiver. She looked at him again, and the bloodshot eyes gave her a great wink. Then he began tapping away at the typewriter again.

"Are you writing my ad?" she asked with interest.

"No," he said, "I'm pounding out next week's editorial. It's about the slums in Mexican Town. Did you know that about a third of the houses in Mexican Town have been condemned? That they aren't fit for human beings to live in?"

"No, sir," replied Cenci, "I didn't know that."

Brett Lindley seemed to have forgotten all about cats and kittens. He looked ferocious again.

"Did you know," he asked, "that the Mexican children have no playgrounds, no place to play except vacant lots or in the streets?"

"Well, I sometimes play in a vacant lot," she answered.

"I've begun a campaign," he continued, as if he had not heard her. "Every week I write editorials and I have hired people to investigate for me and I've talked to the school board and to the Chamber of Commerce and the churches. So far it hasn't done much good. Nobody seems to care. But in the slums whole families are crowded into one room with only a dirt floor and no ventilation."

Cenci said, "I know. Across the street from where I live is a place like that. It's called a *Vecindad*. It has a *patio* and has rooms all around it and all the families draw buckets of water from the same well in the middle of the *patio*."

"Hmmmm," murmured Brett Lindley, "that's the one on Mesquite Street, isn't it? I have been through some of the hovels there."

"You have?" she cried. "Why, those people are my neighbors."

"Those people are neighbors to all of us," rasped Brett. "All the people in the world are our neighbors."

But Cenci, not noticing his implications, hurried on. "That vacant lot I play in, the one on Alamo Avenue, well, it's kind of fun. I bounce my ball on the adobe wall and there's an awfully cute little Mexican boy named Jesucito that lets me play with him when I can and the boys make kites, sir, the Mexican boys I mean, and they run down the street with them and they fly real high on a windy day."

Brett Lindley leaned back in his chair, "I didn't know that," he said. "I used to make kites myself when I was a kid."

"The Mexican boys' kites," expanded Cenci, pleased to have his attention, "are different from the American boys' kites. They're sort of square. I tried to make one one time but it was too heavy. It got tangled up on the telephone wires."

There was a silence and Brett Lindley looked back at his typewriter and began pounding away again. "Maybe I'll put about the kites in my editorial," he said.

"Is it a good editorial, sir?" she asked timidly.

"Young lady," he replied, "observe this typewriter. Observe the paper in it. Do you see any smoke coming from it?"

"Why, no. No, I don't."

"Then the editorial is no good. If it were any good, smoke would come up from it in clouds. The keys would sizzle. The paper would be scorched."

"Oh, dear! Well, thank you very much for putting in the ad, sir," she said. "Good-bye."

Once again she paused at the door. Once again she smiled. Her smile lighted up her face, the door, the dingy office. For Brett it lighted up the whole world.

At that moment the telephone rang. Cenci waited, listened as Brett yelled into it, "Hello!"

There was a long pause, while somebody on the other end of the wire talked rapidly and with excitement.

"The hell he did," interrupted Brett once, and said hearty words Cenci had never heard before. Finally, "I'll be right over," he shouted, and flung the receiver back on its hook. He ripped the sheet of paper from his typewriter, wadded the paper up and threw it on the floor, missing the big wire wastebasket.

"He hasn't a chance," he muttered, "not a chance."

"Who?" asked Cenci, no longer afraid of the editor.

Brett Lindley stood up, a veritable giant of a man, and started for the door.

"Just a poor Mexican," he said, "name of Pánfilo García or something like that. He was sick and starving and tried to steal some buns from the bakery. It just happened that the sheriff was in there, buying a cake. The Spic got caught and in the scramble the sheriff's gun went off and he was killed."

"Who? Pánfilo?"

"No, the sheriff! I'm going down to the jail."

Without another word he was off, banging the door. Cenci felt as if a violent gust of wind had blown through the room, leaving behind it a vacuum. She hesitated and amidst the clutter of paper on the floor observed the wadded-up editorial Mr. Lindley had cast aside. She walked over to it, picked it up, smelled it, and said to herself sadly, "I guess it wasn't any good. It isn't smoking not one little bit."

As she stooped, the letter she had written to herself slipped out and dropped to the floor. But Cenci did not notice it. Far down the street she could hear the murmur of many voices. There was an angry undertone beneath this volume of sound, and it made her shiver, even though the day was so hot. She had an overwhelming desire to return home, to go *anywhere* to escape that sound of an angry mob. Hurriedly she left the newspaper office and began to run.

Two hours later Brett returned to the office of the *Donde Eagle*. The cat, Nevermore, had disappeared. Brett's huge shoulders sagged, his whole body seemed to sag.

"Pete!" he called, "Pete!"

From the back part of the newspaper office emerged Pete, the printer, a little hunchback. He was wearing a printer's apron; he was so smeared and black he looked like a chimney sweep.

"Yes, Mr. Lindley?"

Brett told him the story about Pánfilo, in angry, jerky sentences. He said to him much the same things he had said to Cenci.

"God-damn it, that Spic hasn't a chance."

Pete said nothing.

Brett opened a desk drawer, drained the last of a bottle of whiskey he took from it, threw the empty bottle toward the wastebasket, missing it.

"That's all, Pete. Get back to your work. Those church bulletins have to be finished tonight, no matter how many poor devils are going to be hanged for stealing a hamburger bun."

"Hanged?"

"Of course he'll be hanged. He hasn't a chance. The whole world stinks, Pete."

Unobtrusively Pete disappeared again. The linotype resumed its clackety-clack. Brett looked at the empty whiskey bottle beside the wastebasket and in so doing saw Cenci's letter, which had come out of the envelope addressed to herself. He recognized the handwriting because of the ad, and he picked up the letter and read it without compunction.

My dear, darling little daughter [he read],

You must forgive me for not writing last week, but I'm so busy and time is preshus as you know because I'm hurrying to get home. To make up for it I kissed your picshure and I new you would understand.

Well, I've also been busy buying you Xmas presents to bring home. Now don't ask what they are!! I've ordered the 4 little Xmas trees, as usual, and some more trimings, so what fun we'll have.

Be a good girl til I come home. I'm sorry about the blind kitty but don't worry. God even takes care of sparrows, so he'll not let Kitty run into things or get hurt. Be patient with Miss Manners. I'll attend to her, don't worry— And remember she has headaches and is sometimes in pane. Don't cry at night when you are lonesum, it does no good and only wets the pillowcase. I'm a grown man, but I'm your father and I get lonesum, too. I'll be with you soon——

Brett read no more. Savagely he sealed and stamped the envelope and put it in the basket marked "Outgoing Mail."

"Poor little kid," he said to himself. He thought a long time about Cenci. Like most newspaper men, he knew a good deal about everybody in the town where he worked. He had often seen her going to the post office, or slipping into the picture show alone. From the very first, he was struck by her look of loneliness.

The facts about Cenci were stark, and if, perhaps, a little unusual, they remained facts. Her mother had died when she was born. Her father had not remarried. He had kept the beautiful and costly house going, had been both mother and father to the little girl. And she had responded with a wealth of love and affection so great it seemed impossible that one tiny girl could love so much. They had been very happy. And then, he, too, had died suddenly of pneumonia.

Her fortune was left in the hands of a trusted family friend, Mr. Graham, who had once lived next door. Mr. Graham was a scientist and the owner of a chain of drugstores of which Stirling's Pharmacy in Donde was one. Nevertheless, Mr. Graham had not himself been in Donde for years. He had never seen Cenci. His associate, a Mr. Derrick, in Austin, attended to her affairs for him. He was honest, dependable, and nearer at hand. Since the death of the little girl's father she had had a series of governesses, who remained a while but usually left after a few months for various reasons. Some of the governesses, as for instance her present one, Miss Manners, realized that the job was a snap. They had practically no supervision; Mr. Derrick was too busy. Miss Manners took advantage of this. The job bored her, and she took frequent trips to visit relatives and friends, sometimes leaving Cenci alone for weeks at a time, with no one to take care of her except the Mexican servants. And they, too, were careless, with no authoritative person to watch their goings and comings. People, Brett thought, usually think only of the poor with pity. But no child in the slums could have been more neglected than this wealthy little girl. For since her father's death, there was but one thing that Cenci needed. That was love.

Brett walked to the back of the office, opened the door to the print shop.

"Pete," he called loudly.

The printer, who was busy locking up the forms containing the church bulletins, looked up. "Yes?"

"How're you coming? Do you think you can wind up this job tonight alone?"

"Sure," answered the printer laconically.

"Okay," said Brett, "I just wanted to know if you needed me. Since you don't, I'm going across the river. I'm going to get drunk."

The little hunchback looked at Brett a moment, started to say something, then changed his mind. He bent back over his work again. A moment or two later, he heard the front door slam and knew Brett had gone.

3

MR. BRONSON and the boys, after their visit to the bridge, dined at the D-Brand Hotel. Dinner over, they went out on the sidewalk again and there across the street, tantalizing and glittering, stood the Montezuma Palace, the movie house they had observed before. The bright lights, the posters and advertisements drew the boys like a magnet. They propelled their father across the street and stood excitedly discussing the evening's program which featured "The Keystone Cops." Mr. Bronson viewed these posters with distaste, but when he saw the sparkling eyes and hopeful looks of the three boys he said, "You have your allowances, boys; if you want to spend your money for this, you have my permission."

"Oh, Father, thanks! But please come in with us. Just this once?"

"No, thank you," said Mr. Bronson firmly.

He had never yet seen a movie. As he had so often explained to the boys, it wasn't that he saw any actual harm in movies, although it was a waste of time and money. To him it would simply not be entertainment. An evening seeing a Shakespearean play—ah, that would be akin to Heaven—but "The Keystone Cops"! Inwardly he shuddered. No, he simply could not do it.

"You boys go ahead," he said gently. "Besides, I must get back to the boxcar. I don't like to leave the animals alone there in a strange town."

Just then three pretty girls, giggling and talking, walked up to the ticket seller and purchased a row of tickets. Instantly

Mark turned away from his father and viewed the girls with frank delight. They in turn stared at him and then disappeared into the movie.

"Come on, Matthew," said Mark. "Let's get going."

Mr. Bronson walked toward the station. He began to look forward with pleasure to the evening before him. He would light the tin lantern and sit in the boxcar and read in peace and quiet. He would meditate. As much as he loved his boys, the long freight trip had been noisy and without privacy. He needed to think. Especially now that he had arrived here and was beginning to see what life here was going to be like, he needed to go over again in his mind his reason for coming to Donde, a reason that troubled him and throbbed like a wound.

He stopped on a corner to wait for a car to pass, and looking up saw the swinging sign, "The Donde Eagle." The door was open and looking in he saw Brett Lindley seated at his desk, reading aloud. James liked newspaper offices. He liked the smell of paper and of wet ink, the hot acrid perfume of melted lead, the sound of the linotype machine, and the roar and rumble of the presses.

The car passed on, but James turned and took a step or two toward the door of the *Eagle*, drawn by the sound of Brett's voice reading aloud. The inflection of each sentence was perfect. The diction was without flaw. It was like a melody with the roar of the presses supplying the chords:

> Little Lamb, who made thee?
> Dost thou know who made thee?
> Gave thee life and bid thee feed
> By the stream and o'er the mead;
> Gave thee clothing of delight,
> Softest clothing, wooly, bright;
> Gave thee such a tender voice,
> Making all the vales rejoice?
> > Little Lamb, who made thee?
> > Dost thou know who made thee? . . .

James went into the office and listened quietly until the poem was finished. Then he said to Brett Lindley, as if he were resuming a conversation begun long ago, "I don't know of anybody who can write about a lamb like William Blake, do you? That passage in 'Tiger, Tiger, Burning Bright,'" he went on, "'*Did he who made the lamb make thee?*' Sometimes I think that that just about sums up everything, or rather in telling about the tiger and the lamb, Blake sums up God."

Mr. Lindley closed the book, looked up at Mr. Bronson with hostile eyes.

"I don't believe in God," he said, and standing up slowly he slipped the book of poems into his pocket. James realized now that the editor was very drunk. He recognized, too, that Brett Lindley was one of those men who appear more sober the drunker they get. The minister had known a man like that in college. When he was sober he was usually merry and jovial but when drunk he became extremely serious. His face would take on a long, pious look and because of that he was nicknamed "The Deacon." Brett Lindley reminded him of The Deacon, the solemn and careful way in which he talked, the cautious, stiff balancing of his body when he arose from his chair and walked across the room. Knowing human nature as he did, a question flashed through James' mind, seeing the drunken editor thus, having heard him read Blake's poem so beautifully. Why? he asked himself, Why? I wonder why? He was drawn to him. He felt not pity for him but understanding. He hoped that when Brett became sober the editor would not dislike him because he was a minister.

"I don't believe in God," repeated Brett and just as he said this the noise of the printing presses died down with a great heaving sigh and the wizened hunchback printer came into the front office carrying a stack of folders in his arms. "Well, at last!" said Mr. Lindley, looking up at the clock. "Three hours late. Pete, we've got to get new rollers for that job press. That's all there is to it."

The little printer looked tired. "Them rollers *is* about wore out," he mumbled through his inky lips. "If you'll wait till I wash up I'll help you fold these."

"No," said Brett, "you go wash up and put on your coat, Pete, and crank up that old jitney and get the hell out of here. Go on. My friend and I will fold them." He turned toward James. "Give me a hand, will you? Say, who are you, anyway? I don't remember seeing you in Donde before."

The minister introduced himself. Brett viewed him foggily, then said, "Okay. Let's get to work, Jim."

The printer disappeared and automatically the newspaper man and the preacher began folding the leaflets.

"Ah," observed Mr. Bronson, "church bulletins."

"Yeah," growled Mr. Lindley, "for the Methodist Church. Look, fold them this way. It's easier."

"You say you don't believe in God," said Mr. Bronson. "What do you print these for, then?"

"For $2.75 a week," answered the newspaper man.

A slight smile quivered at the corner of Mr. Bronson's mouth but he made no comment. In silence the two men finished. The editor picked them up, tied them with a string, and said, "Come on."

He snapped off the light and they stepped out on the sidewalk. Mr. Lindley locked the door and then went to the curb where Pete sat at the wheel of a dilapidated Ford. Brett dropped the church bulletins into the car and Pete roared down the street.

The two men started walking toward the station.

"I don't see," finally said Mr. Bronson, "how you can like poetry and not believe in God."

There began then a debate which lasted until they reached the boxcar. The little stepladder was still there. Mr. Bronson looked at it and then at Mr. Lindley with misgivings, but the editor climbed sedately into the boxcar, complete master of himself. He look around.

"This where you live?"

"Only for tonight," Mr. Bronson answered.

Two double beds had been set up in the boxcar and in these he and the three boys had slept during their journey. They were plain, rather rickety iron bedsteads with small brass knobs at the top of each post.

"Comfortable little place," said Mr. Lindley, sitting down on one of them. "Wish I lived here. Did you buy it or rent it?"

Mr. Bronson looked at the newspaper man thoughtfully. During the argument walking down the street, he had looked forward to digging out some of his books and showing his most prized possession, an old, old Bible, bound in sheepskin. But he saw now that tonight this was beyond question. Brett Lindley planted his elbows on his knees, leaned forward, his head in his hands.

"It's too late for any more poetry," said Mr. Bronson quietly. "Why not let me take you home?"

The editor shook his head.

"I haven't any home, Jim. I live in the hotel. Besides, I like it here. I did have a home once. All paid for. I was a copyreader on the *San Antonio Light*—good job. Nice home, all paid for. Nice wife, name of Rose. Pretty name, Rose. But I lost her when the baby came. Lost the baby. Nothing but a cross now in the cemetery. 'Rose and Little John,' it says. Same cross. Buried them together. Sold my house. Began drinking, helped me forget. Drunk all of the time. Lost my job. Nothing left now, Jim. Nothing left."

Not since he had entered the ministry had anybody called Mr. Bronson Jim. His heart contracted. "You've got the *Eagle*," he said, "the *Donde Eagle*."

"Yes," answered Brett, still holding his head in his hands, staring at the floor. "I've got the *Eagle* and my old typewriter. I've been trying to pound out articles about the slums in Mexican Town. Don't know why I bother. Nobody reads them. The whole world stinks, Jim. Did you know that?"

As he talked his sentences had become jerkier with long

pauses between each one. His huge shoulders sagged and James Bronson said to him gently, "Why don't you lie down? I'll take care of you. We have plenty of beds and I'd be happy to have you stay here tonight."

"Thanks, Jim. Nice home you've got. Thanks."

With Mr. Bronson's help Brett Lindley stretched out and turned his face away from the lantern. "Pretty name," he murmured, "Rose . . ."

Half an hour later James sat alone in the door of the boxcar. He had got out another mattress upon which he had spread a couple of extra blankets. He and Matthew could sleep there. All was quiet in the railroad yards, except for the staccato sound of the telegraph machine in the almost deserted station house across the tracks. Far away on the edge of the desert came the sound of barking, a weird, unholy sound which Fred had told him was the howl of coyotes. He could hear faint strains of dance music coming from somewhere and the sound of Spanish being spoken as two Mexicans came into view and walked off down the tracks.

Strange new sounds, these, different from those to which he had been accustomed, yet sounds which would conjure up this place and this episode in his life whenever he was to hear them again. As he sat there, he heard footfalls, hesitant and uneven, on the cinders between the tracks. He saw that a man was coming toward the boxcar, picking his way through the darkness with a lantern. He recognized Pete, the hunchback printer, his shadow grotesque in the lantern light.

James walked down the ladder, met Pete outside the door. "I suppose you're looking for Mr. Lindley?"

"Yep. Somebody said they seen him around here—I——"

"He's all right," interrupted the minister. "Come, I'll show you. Maybe you can offer a few suggestions. This way."

In the boxcar, by lantern light, the printer took off Brett's shoes, loosened his clothing. He and James did not talk. Pete gave the minister a bottle containing a small amount of whiskey.

"Give him this, when he wakes up," he said. "And don't you go drinking it yourself, neither. He'll need it."

"Don't worry," said James, accepting the flask. "I'm a minister. I don't drink."

"A minister? Gawd!" Peter regarded him inimically, fiercely protective toward the editor. "Well, don't preach to him, that's all I say. He's got a reason for drinking. A good reason. So just don't preach."

"I won't, Pete. Don't worry. I'll leave him alone. All people have troubles. Some solve them one way, some another."

The hunchback looked at him suspiciously. "Okay," he said, "good night."

And with that he was gone. James Bronson hid the bottle, then resumed his post sitting in the boxcar door, waiting for the boys to return from the movie. How strange, he thought, that he had been in Donde only a few hours, yet already it felt like home. And on his first night he already had a guest.

4

SOMEHOW OR OTHER the meeting with Brett Lindley, the editor's brief, yet succinct, account of his life, their discussion of poetry and of William Blake, caused James Bronson to think again about his reasons for coming to Donde. Sitting here in the door of the boxcar, keeping watch over the sleeping editor, James was greatly disturbed. His heart lay sore within him.

On his return from France where he had served as a chaplain during World War I, he felt that the whole world was going to pieces. Before the war, life had been a matter of behaving oneself, of observing the precepts of God, of doing one's duty to family and country and of hoping for a better world after death.

But the futility and useless sacrifice of precious human lives during the war shook his convictions of their foundations. The sudden ending of the fighting did not bring the peace in his heart that it had supposedly brought to the world. He felt, but dared not put into words, that the war had accomplished nothing and profited nothing. He sensed that it was not over. He knew, now, the bitter tragedy of war: *everybody* loses.

Always in the pulpit he had preached a God of love. But now he could not rationalize a God of love who would permit the atrocities and slaughter and hatred he had witnessed, nor the hysterical postwar peace which had followed it. When he preached he felt like a hypocrite. He no longer believed what he had formerly preached with so much sincerity.

Released from the Army, he returned to his comfortable parsonage in a charming little New England town. A substitute pastor had taken his place during his absence overseas. Nora and the children had stayed with her father on the modest farm where he had retired.

Over a period of years, James had greatly increased the church membership and because of his efforts a beautiful stone edifice now housed his flock. He had been rather proud of the job he had done. But now he felt no cause for pride. Just what, he asked himself, did that lovely building symbolize? Nothing. It was merely a well-constructed piece of architecture, just as his sermons were well-constructed. That was all. The church and its members were prosperous and smug. Everything seemed artificial.

About a year after his return he had the unexpected offer of a new position as master of English in a boys' preparatory school in Massachusetts. The salary was not large, just about the same, in fact, as his salary as a minister. It wasn't a matter of money, it was a matter of integrity. He talked the offer over with Nora, showed her the letter. Her usually vivacious eyes became grave.

"James," she said at length, "this is a question you will have to decide for yourself. I believe there exists in most people a small hard kernel, something or other, of—well, I don't know just how to explain it but when I feel indecision on any matter, I let this thing inside of me do the deciding. I can't put this into words, but I just *know*—often my decisions are wrong, I admit, but——"

"I know what you mean, dear," he murmured, "I have it, too. But this time—this time——"

"Of course," Nora interrupted, "there might be an advantage to the teaching position. You're tired. And don't forget that you were gassed in the war."

"Only slightly, dear."

"Yes, only slightly. But since then you've had pneumonia. You catch cold too easily. As a pastor you never rest. Never.

You take upon your shoulders the burdens of all your parishioners. As English master, things would be easier. You would have only the problems of your students. And you *do* get on with boys.

"Also, we would have long summer vacations. But I don't know. Maybe you wouldn't rest even then. You are a burden-bearer, no matter where you are or what you do." She got up, walked over to the chair where he was sitting, took his face between her two hands, kissed his forehead.

"Whatever you decide, James," she said tenderly, "you know it will be all right with me. Never forget that. I'm always with you."

That night he slept little, and in those stark lonely hours he made his decision. He would give up the ministry. He would become a teacher of English. In teaching he would escape the unsolved and sinewy problems of reality. His mind would dwell in the lofty realm of beautiful words, of songlike thoughts, of melodious and mystical ideas. He would teach beauty—only beauty. He would close his eyes on all else.

The next morning he sat down at his study table and began composing his letter to the church council—"In tendering my resignation," he wrote—and then he heard Nora knocking on his door.

"I'm sorry to interrupt you," she said, "but Mr. Graham is here."

"Mr. Graham?"

"Yes, don't you remember? He wrote that he was coming, you know. I forgot to remind you this morning. He just got in from Boston."

"Oh, yes, Mr. Graham. . . ." James vaguely remembered an appointment which had been made by correspondence last week. He frowned in annoyance, looked at the words he had just written: *In tendering my resignation. . . .* He sighed.

"Very well. Send him in."

Mr. Graham was of medium height, nicely dressed, on the

surface giving the impression of a well-to-do business man. He was wearing a gray suit. His hair was gray. He was ill at ease and the first few sentences of their conversation were of no consequence. It was some time before Mr. Graham came to the point.

From an inside coat pocket he took out a billfold from which he extricated a letter. The envelope was in shreds. It was quite clearly a letter which had been read and reread many times. Mr. Graham took the pages out, looked at them a little while, and as he did so, an expression of great sorrow came over his face. Finally he spoke.

"This was written by my son," he said, "Corporal Kenneth Graham." He spoke with great difficulty. "It was one of the last letters he wrote before he was killed at Château-Thierry. I would like you to read it."

James took the letter, adjusted his glasses, and began to read.

I hope you won't be displeased, Dad, when I tell you that one of my friends is our Company chaplain, Major James Bronson. If you were here, Dad, I think you would understand. So many things that seemed important at home don't seem to matter here.

The padre and I have had many long talks. Once we had a short furlough and he and a bunch of us fellows went fishing together. I told him how you and I used to fish and go hunting, and he said he and his sons did, too. We don't always talk about religion, you see. He showed me a picture of his wife. She is beautiful. He said the picture didn't do her justice because she has red hair. He laughed once and said she could have had any man she wanted and he didn't know why she had to pick *him* out, a preacher without any money to buy pretty things for her. I could tell he was awfully proud of her. He's homesick, too, like the rest of us. He must have a swell family. Four sons.

Well, sooner or later, though, we always talk religion. Some of the padres out here are phonies. They make you sick. But

Major Bronson is not a phony, I can tell you that. When we get to talking I believe him. He has made me understand things I never understood before. And after talking to him, I'm not afraid, Dad, like I was at first. I mean, I'm not afraid to die. I'd hate to go back home crippled, or shell-shocked, like some of the fellows. But I'm not even afraid of that, if it would help even a little to put the world on its feet again.

I know I'm not writing this the way I ought to. It's sort of deep, I guess. I know religion irritates you. You have taught me that science explains everything, that there is no God. But —well, I feel that if we could go fishing together again, and could just have some talks, I'd explain better what I'm driving at. Or, if you could get to know this padre, like I do. Gee, Dad, I'd sure like to go fishing with the two of you! Remember that place in the Westfield River? In the Berkshires . . .

James Bronson read the letter through, folded it, handed it back to Mr. Graham. He had a swift stab of remembrance. A slight, fair-haired boy with a sensitive, mobile face. Yet a strong face, too. And eyes that looked straight into his own. Blue eyes, he remembered now.

"Kenny Graham," he said quietly, "yes, I knew him well. He was"—James stumbled over the words—"so young," he said. "So brave, but so terribly young."

"Yes," answered his father, "yes, he was. This letter," he went on, painstakingly putting it back in the billfold, is one of several similar ones he wrote after he met you. I think there were five in all. Yes, there were five."

He had put them away, he said, with Kenny's other things. But the letters had haunted him. He kept going back to them. Mrs. Graham, he said, had died when Kenny was two years old. He had reared the boy alone, they had been very close. They were both interested in science. He himself was a druggist, although his interest in his profession was purely scientific. He had inherited a considerable fortune from his family. Oil wells. But he was putting it all into scientific research. He owned stock in several laboratories and his great ambition had been not only to help save lives but also to prolong the human life span and lengthen man's years of usefulness and productivity.

"But what is the use in doing all this," he asked, "when in other laboratories scientists are working just as hard toward finding newer, quicker ways to kill? Science can build, restore, but also it can destroy. Just what are we going to do with our new-found dangerous knowledge?"

The morning wore on. Nora invited Mr. Graham to stay to lunch and he did so. In the afternoon, the conversation resumed.

"As Kenny wrote in this letter," Mr. Graham said, "you, and the religion you taught him, explained things to him that neither science nor I had been able to explain. You were able to take away his fear of death, his fear of the future, even if he didn't die. I failed him. If it had not been for you and your religion, he would have died just a bitter, frightened, bewildered kid. . . ."

Mr. Graham did not finish. It was almost impossible for him to talk about his son's death. The purpose of this visit, he finally went on to say, was that because of Kenny he felt compelled to *do* something about religion, even though he did not believe in it. But he wanted so much to repay Mr. Bronson for the gift he had given Kenneth to take with him into Eternity.

Mr. Bronson stood up, looked at the unfinished sentence on the church letterhead before him, covered it up with a blotter.

"Mr. Graham," he said, "in that letter Kenny said that I was not a phony like some of the rest of the preachers." He looked piercingly into Mr. Graham's eyes. "Kenny was wrong," he said sharply. "I'm a phony, too." He then proceeded to tell Mr. Graham about the torture of his own doubts, his decision to give up the ministry. They talked all afternoon. Mr. Graham remained to supper, consented to stay the night when he found that Nora had prepared the spare room for him.

A sort of panic came over Mr. Graham. "Don't give up the ministry!" he heard himself begging. "You're tired. You're worried about too many things, you haven't had a chance to think this out. You need a rest. You need a change of climate, a few months of complete relaxation. Take a vacation."

When Mr. Bronson gently reminded him that he had no savings, that his entire month's salary was usually spent by the twenty-third of each month, Mr. Graham had an immediate answer.

"This is where I can help," he said. There was the matter of his son's insurance. . . .

"I—I can't possibly touch it," he said. "I couldn't spend a cent of it on myself, but I can think of no finer use for Kenneth's money than to give it to you."

If it had not been for Nora, James would have remained adamant in his refusal. He did not feel justified in accepting the money. He did not want to be paid for leisure in which to make a decision. But Nora got him off to one side, her brown eyes emitting sparks.

"James," she said in exasperation, "remember the verse in the Bible that says, 'It is more blessed to give than to receive'?"

"Why, yes. Naturally."

"Well," she continued, "there should be a footnote to that saying: 'But *sometimes* it is more blessed to receive than to give'!"

"Just why do you say that?"

"Oh, James! Your ideals are so beautiful, but they are exasperating, too. Have you taken a good look into Mr. Graham's eyes? I believe they are the saddest eyes I have ever seen. He is grieving for his son, but it is more than just grief. He thinks he has failed that son. He—he is trying to bridge the gap, to get back to his boy. He doesn't know how. He feels that if you give up the ministry—oh, James! Don't you *see*? The money means nothing to him, except that it's Kenny's money. Be human! Forget about your own doubts for awhile. Think of Mr. Graham's doubts."

"I see what you mean, but . . ."

Nora went over to him, put her arms around him, raised her face to his. Though she was smiling, he saw that tears were running down her cheeks. "Remember the footnote, James," she said, " '*Sometimes* it is more blessed to receive than to give'!"

"You're right," he said at length, "I have not thought of it from Mr. Graham's standpoint, only my own. It's curious, how selfishness and unselfishness are so close to one another. Almost it would be a selfish thing, wouldn't it, not to accept Mr. Graham's offer?"

"Yes," said Nora, "that's just what I meant."

James continued thoughtfully, "Boys like Kenny Graham—thousands of them, why were they sacrificed? Sometimes I felt myself that in the end these sacrifices will be justified. They *would* be justified, Nora, if the result were peace, peace in men's hearts, peace in every country, unity, harmony.

"Sometimes when I think of it in that light I feel the breath of God's love which brings peace to my own soul but then I look about me and I see that peace has not come yet. I see today's madness which is but the outward sign of disturbed and rudderless hearts and I realize the world is sick. Then God's love deserts me. I feel an evil breath, the breath of illness, and it rushes through my heart." He thought for a long moment. "Crosswinds," he murmured, "the healing sweetness of God's breath coming from one direction and against it, the sick evil wind of a lost world. If I, with my faith and my love of God, feel such conflict in my soul other people must feel it, too. They turn to me, a minister of God, for the answer, yet I can give them no answer because I, too, no longer know.

"This is not peace. There will be another war and perhaps yet others and others. How will it end? Sometimes I think that the problems will be solved only if love can be implanted in the heart of each individual all over the world. But I'm not sure, and until I am sure I cannot remain in the pulpit, not until my own faith and hope are secure and firm. Not until then shall I be fit to lead others.

"Mr. Graham is an atheist. He does not believe in religion, and yet, *he* isn't sure. I think Kenny's letters to him were perhaps that healing breath of God. But I don't know! Crosswinds, Nora! In my heart. In Mr. Graham's. Yes, I shall accept Kenny's insurance and go somewhere, I don't know where, and try to get things straight in my own soul. It doesn't seem right, it doesn't seem fair to take the money which was earned by Kenny's death and yet I think of our four boys. If it had been one of them I would be like Mr. Graham! I couldn't touch the money for myself. I would hate it. I could only spend it in some such way as this. I'm going to tell Mr. Graham that I have accepted." James passed the palm of his hand across his forehead and Nora, looking at him, could not help but think of the pictures she had seen of the Crucifixion. She had never seen such anguish on another's face. She wanted to go to her husband and comfort him but she knew that her comfort wasn't what he needed. Not now.

"I'll go and call Mr. Graham," she said, standing up. "He's in his room, I think. It's best for you to talk to him and tell him the way you feel."

Nora left the study and went to the spare room and stood for a moment beside the closed door. Within she could hear leaden, measured footsteps as Mr. Graham walked from one end of the room to the other, back and forth, just as she had heard him walking during the night. Then she knocked. The footsteps halted.

"Come in."

She opened the door and saw him, his hands in his pockets, and shadows under his eyes. The way the light came in through the window his gray hair looked almost white. He did not give the impression he had given when he came to the house, that of a self-contained, brisk, efficient business man. His shoulders, she saw now, were stooped. She observed on the bureau a picture that she had seen earlier in the morning when she had gone into the room and made up the bed and tidied things up after breakfast. It was a picture of his son, a clean-cut frank boyish face, twinkling eyes, looking right into hers, the lips slightly smiling. "To Dad, my best friend," was written in one corner. Making up the bed a short while ago with that smiling face looking at her she had thought, He doesn't look much older than our twins, and the same thought returned to her now. Mr. Graham saw her eyes on the picture and she turned quickly away. "I am sorry to disturb you, Mr. Graham," she said, trying to control the trembling of her lips, "but I wonder if you'd mind coming into my husband's study? He wants to talk with you again."

"Thank you," he replied, and she stepped aside as he went out the door.

An hour later she heard James calling her. The moment she went into the study she was aware of a different atmosphere. Mr. Graham's shoulders were straighter. James was different, too, in just what way she scarcely knew.

"Your husband has just told me the good news," said Mr. Graham and when he smiled she fancied a resemblance between the smiling face and the photograph of Kenny.

"The question now before us," he continued briskly, "is what spot on this globe of ours you are to choose for your vacation."

Nora sat down, "Well, I would say definitely James should go to a warmer climate, warmer and drier."

"That's what Mr. Graham has been telling me for the last fifteen minutes," said James. "He has even gone so far as to mention a town."

"Yes," said Mr. Graham eagerly. "I suggested the town of Donde on the Texas border. Your husband says he has never heard of it."

Nora laughed. Somehow things suddenly began to seem gay.

"Neither have I," she said. "You say it's on the Texas border?"

"Yes," he said, "here." She saw that a map had been spread out on the study table. With the point of a pencil Mr. Graham indicated the town.

"Oh," she cried. "My, how far away it is! It's far away from everything, isn't it? Right on the border." She touched it and then with the tip of her forefinger traced the length of the Rio Grande River. "My," she said, "way down there! Is this Mexico?"

"Yes," he answered.

"Please don't laugh at me," continued Nora, "but I haven't been out of the United States for a long time. Could we cross over to the Mexican side? Just think, a trip to a foreign country again." Her eyes were sparkling, her happiness was contagious.

"Tourist cards can be easily obtained, I imagine," said Mr. Graham.

"Tourist cards," whispered Nora. "Won't that be fun!" Then studying the map again she brushed a great vast empty area with her fingers. "What's all this?" she asked.

"Desert," answered Mr. Graham, and for the first time since he had arrived he laughed. "Miles and miles of it."

James scrutinized the map. "But why do you recommend Donde?" he asked. "There are warm dry climates much closer. Why such an out-of-the-way spot?"

Mr. Graham hesitated, "I was born there," he said at last. "I lived there for a long time but I haven't been back for twenty years. I keep in touch, in a way. I have a ward there, a little girl, Cenci Thorpe. The families used to be neighbors. I attend to her money and send someone down there three or four times a year to see that she's being well cared for. Her parents are dead. I've never seen the child myself. I still have some real-estate holdings in Donde, too. One house especially, now vacant. I think you would like it but I'm dubious about the neighborhood. It's too close to Mexican Town. But still I think you might like it. It's been empty a very long time." Mr. Graham was looking away from them. He seemed almost to be looking back through the years.

"I could wire ahead and have the house cleaned up and have it put in good shape. I haven't kept it up."

"Oh," cried Nora, straightening up from the map. "That doesn't matter! I'd love it. Is it close to the river?"

"Yes, it's on the river," said Mr. Graham.

"You mean we could look out the window and see Mexico?" asked Nora.

Mr. Graham smiled. "Yes, any time you wish."

"I think we'd better call the children in!" said Mr. Bronson. "I want to talk the matter over with them." He turned in a half-apologetic manner to Mr. Graham. "Since all of us are going, I'd like to tell the boys. We usually talk such things over with them."

There followed after that a lively flow of family conversation. The boys had never been out of the United States. A spell of adventure descended upon them. They looked on Mr. Graham with respect and awe. What a wonderful man, giving them a free trip to Texas and to Mexico if they wished, and a vacation to their father. There were endless questions. Matthew and Mark asked about the fishing and hunting. Nora wanted to know about clothes.

Late that afternoon everything was settled. Mr. Graham said he must get back to Boston. Everybody was greatly disappointed. Already Mr. Graham seemed like an old, old friend. When it came time for him to go, the twins carried his bag to the surrey and *en masse* the family escorted him to the train.

Waiting for it on the station platform Mr. Graham said to James, "Stay as long as you like, eight months, a year, two years. Let's not put a limit on it and I shan't bother you. But please feel free to get in touch with me if you need anything. My associate in Austin, Mr. Grant Derrick, goes to Donde regularly to attend to the affairs of my little ward, Cenci Thorpe. You may call on him in the event of any emergency. I may have to take a business trip to Europe during the winter. I thought if I did I might visit—" He stopped abruptly. "At any rate, I hope while you're in Donde you will rest and relax. Think things over. I shall wait until I hear from you. I have things to think over, too. But already you have made me feel much happier. . . ."

He was interrupted by a shriek from Lukey. "There comes the train," he cried, "and it's my turn to carry your bags."

The boys were in a rollicking mood. The train drew up but only James and Nora saw the look of wistfulness on the face of Mr. Graham as he bade them all farewell, saw the emptiness, the look of sadness in his eyes even when he was smiling and waving good-bye.

Now, far away from Connecticut, far away from familiar surroundings, James sat in the door of the boxcar and was consumed with nostalgia. From his wallet, he took the little picture of Nora, worn and frayed at the edges, the picture he had carried with him overseas, the one he had shown to Kenny. In the lantern light he observed her face, regretting that the camera did not show her lovely hair and milky skin. But the picture held captive her beauty, the strong wide-apart cheekbones, the tantalizing laughing mouth, the vitality. How he missed her! Just then he heard the voices of his sons returning from the movie, and, replacing the picture, he left the boxcar and walked down the tracks to meet them. He had missed them. But all the time he kept thinking of that look in Mr. Graham's eyes. He missed *his* boy, too. Only, Kenny would never come back. Never. And so young—so very young.

5

ON THE FOLLOWING AFTERNOON Cenci sat again at her window, looking out. Miss Manners had not yet returned. The unexpected events of yesterday in the newspaper office now seemed like a pleasant dream, and all day today nothing had happened, and the little girl sat there knowing that today was just like a hundred yesterdays and that tomorrow would probably be like today. She saw some Mexican children playing out in the street and could hear their shouts and laughter coming to her.

She saw an old woman, known as "Old Isabella," mincing down the sidewalk in high-heeled shoes. Although her cheeks were wrinkled they were brightly rouged. Her hair was dyed and she wore a large straw hat trimmed with yellow and red ostrich feathers. Her yellow silk dress was spattered with immense red roses. She wore long earrings, two or three necklaces, and many bracelets on her skinny arms. One could always tell when old Isabella was coming by the jangling of the bracelets, by the heavy perfume which emanated from her, by the rustle of taffeta petticoats beneath her silk dress. Often the children in Mexican Town would jeer at her, sometimes even throw stones at her, but old Isabella held her head high and pretended not to notice.

Once, not long ago, when Cenci had been standing by her own front gate, the old woman had passed by after having been taunted by the children. Cenci had been playing in the garden, had broken off a sprig of cape jasmine which she was holding in her hand, breathing in its rich fragrance, touching its waxy

48

white petals. Impulsively she had run up to old Isabella and had given her the flower, smiling shyly as she did so. To her amazement she saw tears gather in old Isabella's sunken eyes. But the woman said quickly, almost rudely, "Thank you, *niña,* but go. Go quickly. Close the gate. Don't let anybody see you."

Isabella walked on this afternoon out of sight. Just then the little girl heard the clatter of horses' hoofs on the street. Her eyes quickened with interest. At the gate of the house next door, the only house that lay between her and Mexican Town, two horse-drawn drays had drawn up at the gate. They were followed by a vehicle which had no doubt at one time been an elegant surrey with red spoke wheels and a lacy fringe bordering its shiny top. Now the fringe was worn and uneven, the red spokes had been repainted many times, the upholstery mended. It was pulled by a white horse who had also seen his best days.

But Cenci saw neither the carriage nor the horse on that first day. She saw its occupants, a man and three boys. One of the boys had fair hair and blue eyes. He jumped out nimbly when the carriage stopped at the gate, took the reins, fastened them to a horseshoe, and tossed it to the dusty ground. Without waiting for anything more, Cenci crept quietly out of the room, flew downstairs, across the garden, and opening the little gate that separated the two houses, went through it.

For as far back as Cenci could remember, the house next door, known as the old Graham place, had been unoccupied. It was owned by the Mr. Graham who was her guardian. He lived very far away in Boston, and owned two hundred drugstores, Stirling's Pharmacy being one of them. At least, so had Cenci been told. She liked to think of hundreds of nice cool drugstores with people eating banana splits and she thought that Mr. Graham, whose family had been a friend of her family long ago, must be an awfully nice man. Sometimes musing about him on a hot day, she would multiply the number of banana splits she herself had consumed by two hundred. Surely only a *very* nice man could make so many people happy by providing so many banana splits for so many people. She used to think that maybe he might come back to Donde but he never did.

He just owned the house next door, a rambling and haphazard place, to her completely enchanting. It sprawled in various directions with unexpected rooms tacked on here and there. One room had a stained-glass window and a separate entrance with a little white portico. A latticed porch painted green encircled the house on three sides. Next to the room with the stained-glass window was a small one which she pretended was her own. It was such a cute little room. The house was one story high and even on the hottest days it remained cool and dim. Once she had made the amazing discovery that a window giving on the latticed porch had a broken lock. By using a stick she could push the window up and crawl through. After that, whenever she was certain of not being detected she would run through the little gate between her house and the Graham place, step up on the latticed porch, and crawl through the window. Often she would take one of her dolls with her and play house and before she had lost Kitty she had taken her over, too. What fun it had been racing down the long empty halls and through the rooms, Kitty at her heels. The stained-glass window overlooking the Rio Grande had a window seat and she would sit here and look out. She could not make up her mind which she liked the best, her pretend room or the window seat or the pool in the side yard.

In the center of the pool a pink marble baby reclined on a bed fashioned of a large white marble rose. His curly head rested on one fat dimpled arm and his fat little legs were lazily crossed, one over the other, and he had a smile on his dimpled face. There was a circle of white rosebuds around the big rose whereon he rested. One rosebud was broken. Cenci discovered that by turning on a faucet near the porch a fine spray of water came from each rosebud except the broken one, shooting high up into the air and falling back into the pool with a beautiful splashing sound. By thus turning on the faucet, she managed to keep alive the mint bed which grew around the pool. It had

a spicy, tantalizing fragrance. She would pick off leaves of it
and chew them and pretend that they were magic, that the little
room really was hers, and that this was her house and that her
father had come back and that she and her father and Kitty
and Baby lived there in unending happiness.

Sometimes after a dust storm the fat little baby would become
quite grimy and then Cenci would turn on the faucet, fill the
pool up to her ankles, take off her shoes and socks, get into it,
and with one of her own washcloths give him a good bath.
This was fun, only she did wish he wouldn't smile *all* the time
and that after his bath he would close his eyes and go to sleep.
To make up for this deficiency she would chew another mint
leaf and pretend that he had gone to sleep and that he was her
little brother. Whenever a norther would blow up she would
slip over and cover him up with a blanket. He looked awfully
naked and cold out there and even though he was marble, she
couldn't snuggle down in her bed and go to sleep until she
knew that he was covered up, too.

Then one day about two weeks ago, there began a sudden
bustle of activity at the old Graham place. Mexican gardeners
and carpenters descended in hordes. The broken rosebud in the
pool was mended and the whole garland sent up continual shafts
of cool water that fell back on the mint bed like rain. Sprinklers
whirred on the lawn, rubbish was cleared away, and the broken
lock on the window was discovered and repaired. Not until the
day before yesterday did the cleaning women and gardeners
finish their work and depart. Try as she might, she could not
get into the house. All she could do was smell the mint and look
at it from the outside.

But now this afternoon, seeing the surrey and its occupants
stop at the gate, seeing the two drays of furniture, she realized
why it had been fixed up. She had a quick swift pang of loss
at first. She had always thought of the house as hers. Now it
belonged to somebody else but this feeling was followed by one
of mixed emotions. There were three boys and one of them, the
redheaded one, seemed to be about her own age. Maybe even

though she was a girl he would play with her, maybe they would be friendly, like the Mexicans in the Vecindad.

Standing very still by the iron fence, she watched the newcomers as they unlocked the door and filed into the house. Quietly she crept across the lawn and without their observing her, followed them in. The house was clean and smelled of fresh paint and new linoleum. She listened to their exclamations of pleasure and delight as they opened doors and windows, looked in closets, turned lights off and on. Everybody seemed to be talking at once, and through their conversation, like a golden thread which appeared and disappeared from time to time, she heard the word, "Mother." "Oh, won't Mother like this! . . . Mother will want the dining table here. . . . For once we'll have plenty of room. . . ."

Suddenly the redheaded boy almost stumbled over Cenci. "Hello," he said. "Who are *you?*"

"Cenci," she replied. "I live next door. Are you moving in here?"

The boy straightened up proudly. "Yep," he answered. "I'm Luke. Those two guys arguing over there are my brothers, Matthew and Mark. They're twins."

"Which is which?" asked Cenci.

"Matthew is the one with glasses. Mother and Johnny, my other brother, are coming tomorrow and that man over there looking at the stained-glass window—well, he's Father. I'll bet he picks this room for his study. Say," he asked with interest, "have you any brothers?"

"No," she replied, "nor sisters either."

"Where are your father and mother?" he continued.

"I haven't any father and mother," she faltered. "I'm owned by a bank."

"Gee! Hey, Father," he jerked his thumb toward the little girl. "This is Cenci. She came over to help us move in. And she's owned by a bank, Father! Just think!"

Mr. Bronson turned away from the window, came over and

shook hands with the little girl. "How do you do," he said formally. "I was just wishing we had a woman on the place. We want to try to get things fixed up for Mrs. Bronson, my wife, and I've heard about you from your guardian, Mr. Graham —I saw him only recently."

"You *know* Mr. Graham?"

"Yes. He was a guest in our home."

Cenci breathed with contentment. "I've always thought Mr. Graham must be such a nice man!" she said.

"He is."

The little girl's heart swelled with pride. How exciting! Could it have been only a short few moments ago that she had been looking out of the window thinking that today was just like yesterday?

"Ordinarily," explained Mr. Bronson, "we wouldn't move in on a Sunday. But the animals need to get settled, and my wife will be tired when she gets in Tuesday and it is important to have the heavy work finished before she arrives."

"The ox out of the ditch, eh, Father?" called out Mark.

"Perhaps, Son," answered his father. Cenci had no idea what they were talking about, but no matter. She was entranced. "Fortunately," continued Mr. Bronson, "my friend Mr. Brett Lindley was able to obtain two drays for us, even though it is Sunday."

"Mr. Lindley? Of the *Eagle?* How lucky. You see, he's *my* friend, too. You know *all* my friends!"

There followed days of heavy work and great activity. Even a circus, Cenci thought, didn't have many more animals than the Bronsons. And what wonderful furniture! Every chair was different. The dining table had one leg shorter than the other three. It had to have a little plug of paper put under it, to keep it from collapsing. Not in any second-hand shop had she seen such a variety. She was glad that Miss Manners had not returned. She pitched in with broom and dustcloth and by train time the following day she felt as if she already belonged to the Bronsons, and they to her.

6

TUESDAY AFTERNOON, after changing from the Pullman at Yucca
Junction to the old-fashioned chair car for Donde, Nora Bronson
settled herself on the old plush seat and realized how desperately
homesick she was for her children and for James. Actually it had
been only a short time since she had seen them, and she had had
a good visit with her father and had enjoyed the trip into this
new and strange territory.

But knowing that within a few minutes she would be seeing
them all again, her heart beat more rapidly and she wondered
how they had fared in the boxcar and how they had managed
without her. She herself was almost suffocated by the air in the
train, yet she dared not open the window, fearing that John
would fall out of it. The little boy, however, usually so active,
was pale and languid from the heat. His fair hair, damp with
perspiration, curled in even tighter ringlets than usual, and he
nestled against her and fell asleep. She looked out at the desert.
It seemed to her that for an endless time she had seen only
desert, parched grass, cactus, century plants, nothing alive in
sight at all. She worried about James. A hot dry climate, the
doctors had all agreed, would be beneficial, but she wondered
if this heat would be too much. At Yucca Junction she had
looked at the thermometer and gasped in unbelief. It read one
hundred and twenty, but the station master assured her that it
had recently been in the sun. It wasn't really that hot, he said,

not in the shade. Nora kept thinking about James, about his months overseas, and how she had been afraid at the sight of a messenger boy or to hear the telephone ring—afraid of bad news. Then when he had come back, there had been a remoteness about him and he seldom talked about his experiences.

She tried to picture herself as the wife of an English professor, in a boys' school, with James coming and going from his classes, preparing lectures on the poetry he loved so well, having the students in for Sunday tea, meeting with the wives of the other faculty members, listening to lectures, going to chapel, having long vacations at her father's farm. How secure such a life would have been! Had she been right in urging James to come here? Urging him to reconsider before he gave up the ministry? Why was his soul in such turmoil? Why couldn't he go on preaching as he always had? Wouldn't it have been the same, wasn't God still the same as He had been before the war? Then she thought of Mr. Graham and of Kenny's picture. Kenny, she thought. It might have been Matthew or Mark, Luke or even John, had they been a few years older. In spite of the heat, Nora realized that her hands had grown cold. She was filled with a nameless fear.

Johnny, a hot, limp little bundle at her side, stirred and just then the overalled conductor came into the chair car and said, "Want me to take your suitcase off the rack, ma'am? We're gettin' into Donde. Two or three minutes, and we'll be there."

Cenci wanted desperately to go to the station to meet Mrs. Bronson but, just with the family, the surrey would be much too full, so she made no mention of it. Besides, Mr. Bronson had entrusted her with a very great responsibility. Nora, he had explained, would doubtless arrive tired and hungry, much too tired to go to the hotel. And besides, little John might not behave well in a hotel dining room. It would be much nicer to have a good meal waiting for them at home. Mr. Bronson and the boys could not cook fancy dishes. Their type of cookery had been learned on fishing and hunting trips. But there was one meal, Mr. Bronson said, which was *very* easy to prepare and of which Nora was especially fond, a New England boiled dinner.

A New England boiled dinner! Cenci was captivated. She had never heard of one. She had never known any Easterners. But she liked the Bronsons' speech, their precise, clean-cut way of speaking. In twenty-four hours (although the children were not aware of it) Cenci talked like an Easterner and Lukey had acquired an extra-thick Texas accent.

Mr. Bronson dispatched Matthew to a grocery store in search of corned beef, but finding there was no corned beef in Donde, a smoked ham had to be substituted. It had been put on to boil, vegetables had been peeled, whole carrots, onions and potatoes, and a quartered cabbage. Cenci's duty was to sit at the table and put the vegetables in the pot while the rest of the family was at the station. The ham was already done. The vegetables were to go in at an exact time, the cabbage last. The little girl had never felt quite so important. To her it was a matter of life or death to get those vegetables in the pot at the precise moment.

So she did not mind too much being left behind. She looked at the clock at least every three minutes. She went from room to room in the house wishing, as Mr. Bronson had wished, that they had been able to get everything ready. The beds were set up and made, that was one thing. Brett Lindley had helped all day and Pete, whose hobby was wood-carving, had grudgingly whittled out a small block of wood, thus remedying the short leg on the dining-room table.

In the study had been put up Mr. Bronson's table, a long pine one which had once seen service in the kitchen of Nora's father's farm. James said he preferred it to a desk because he needed room for his books. But it looked pretty bare, Cenci thought, without a cover, and she had run eagerly over to her own house and had brought back a Mexican *sarape* with as many colors as the stained-glass window. Its texture was like felt. It made a perfect covering for a study table. Mr. Bronson had been almost on the point of refusing it, when he remembered Nora's words, "Sometimes it is more blessed to receive than to give." The little girl's face had looked so eager. She had seemed so pleased to contribute something.

Lukey had settled the matter by overturning a bottle of ink on it. So Mr. Bronson had capitulated and Brett had placed a blotter over the ink spot hoping to soak up as much of it as possible. The study chair had been put in place and beside it the little round rug, badly worn, which the boys called the "kneeling rug." Cenci did not understand why they called it that, but it had a nice sound anyway. The rest of the floor was bare. Mr. Bronson took his most precious books out of the tin trunk, and arranged them on the table. Later on, he said, he would unpack all of them, put up the book cases, and install the couch upon which he sometimes rested, and the Chippendale chair, still in its crate. How exciting! Cenci could not wait for the house to be completely settled.

She now went into the study, removed the blotter, felt the ink stain with her fingers and, as it had dried stiff, she covered it with a book. Then she went into the dining room. The table was all set for supper. A place had even been set for her. Imagine! That morning there had come a long-distance call from the relative Miss Manners was visiting. "Miss Manners," she had said, "has a very bad headache and a summer cold. Of course she *can* come back but——"

"Oh," Cenci had replied, "she mustn't *think* of coming back before her cold is well." And then she had hung up and had run quickly back to the Bronsons'.

So here was a place set for her at the table and she stood looking at it with a happy heart. She looked at each place and thought about the Bronsons. There was a solidity about the family. They were closely knit, and yet each individual had a great deal of freedom, too. When the boys quarreled and fought, Mr. Bronson let them fight it out. They took care of their own clothes, and all the boys had pressed their pants before going to the station.

"Why don't you send your clothes to the tailor's to have them pressed?" she had asked.

The boys laughed at her. "No dough," they had said. Cenci was impressed. How nice, she thought, to have no dough.

She looked at the clock.

"Dear me, time to put in the carrots and the onions."

She rushed madly to the kitchen and put them in the pot. Next, the potatoes. In another five minutes, the cabbage. Her little face was flushed with her great responsibility. Before the cabbage, she thought, she would barely have time to dash across to her own yard and pick some flowers for the table. Boys, of course, would never think of flowers. Off she went, returning with two white roses. She would have picked more but was afraid she didn't have time.

She took the two roses and put them in a vase, and placed it in the center of the table. No. The roses didn't look right. Such a big table. So many places. She looked at the clock. Time for the cabbage. Into the kitchen she rushed again and dropped the pieces in one at a time, the broth splashing up and scalding her fingers. She gave a great sigh. To the minute, she had done as she had been told. If the train were on time and if old Trojan, the horse, didn't balk, as he sometimes did with a heavy load, the New England dinner would be perfect when Mrs. Bronson arrived. Then she went back to the dining room again and moved the little vase in front of Mrs. Bronson's plate. Ah, that was it. That's where it belonged.

In the meantime, at the station, Luke had been the first one to see Nora as she stepped off the train.

"There she is," he cried and head down, like a small buffalo, he lunged across the station platform bumping into three people on the way.

"Mother!" he shouted and threw his arms around her.

"My heavens, Luke!" she exclaimed, setting Johnny down. "I believe you *are* glad to see me."

Her eyes sparkled and she looked flushed and pretty. At second glance one might observe that her dress was not of the latest fashion and had been pressed and turned and mended many times. Her hat was a joke. Nora Bronson owned two hats. When warm weather came, she put away the brown felt and hauled out the brown straw. Sometimes, in a burst of energy, she would buy some dye and apply it to the straw hat with a toothbrush, or perhaps buy a new ribbon or a flower for it. Sometimes she merely dusted it off.

Luke, having given her a masterful hug, now turned his attention to his little brother.

"Hello, Johnnycake!"

The little boy smiled. Johnny's hair was so blond it was almost white. It was curly and fine and silky. By this time the rest of the family had caught up with Luke. There was a vigorous exchange of hugs and kisses and greetings. Matthew picked up the two shabby straw suitcases which the conductor had set down on the platform. Mark took charge of the lunch basket covered over with a napkin. Mr. Bronson picked up Johnny and they started toward the carriage, all of them talking at once, tripping over one another, completely unaware that everybody at the station was being highly entertained.

"Just wait till you see our house, Mother!" said Mark. "It's the grandest one we've ever had."

"It has a fountain!" screamed Luke. "With a naked baby in it. Pink marble."

"The yard goes all the way through the block," added Mark.

"Father's study has a stained-glass window," put in Matthew.

"It has rooms and rooms and rooms," chanted Luke.

"We've got a boiled dinner almost ready for you," said Matthew. "We fixed it ourselves."

Mr. Bronson helped her into the surrey and soon they were off down the dusty street.

*　　*　　*

Waiting at the house, Cenci examined the dining table critically. The table cloth was on crooked, but she did not notice this. She walked all around it, rearranging the silverware, visualizing where everyone would sit. What lovely dishes. Practically every one nicked. Mr. Bronson told her that his wife had a set of Haviland china, inherited from her mother, but that he didn't dare unpack it. She also had a set of solid silver, including two candlesticks, all heirlooms, but she always carried these with her, for safety's sake. Cenci was not interested in the Haviland and fine silver. She liked these much better. None of the plates were the same size. The plated silver had worn down in spots. But the table looked beautiful. There was only one thing—it did not look proper to have a vase of flowers in front of Mrs. Bronson's place and not in front of his. Cenci did not know quite what it was, whether it was Mr. Bronson's manner of speaking, his gentleness, his kindness, but nevertheless he reminded her of that faint, dear shadow, that dimming memory of her father, the best friend she had ever had. Nora, she was sure, would be tired on her arrival, but Mr. Bronson was tired, too. He had worked awfully hard. He deserved a rose.

Cenci went into the kitchen. The pot was bubbling away merrily. She was worried about the fire, though, so she took off the stove lid and put in several more sticks of wood. She looked at the clock. There would be time, just barely. Again she ran through the gate and into her own garden. Again she cut two roses. But it took her longer than she had planned, for she wanted them to be just as perfect as the other two, and finally she discarded one and returned with the other. There was no time to look for a vase, so she put the flower upon the folded napkin at Mr. Bronson's place. Now everything was *really* perfect.

The New England dinner did not smell the way it had smelled when she had left the house. She went back to the kitchen and anxiously lifted the lid and looked in. Impossible! Why, just a few minutes ago the pot had been half full of water. Now it was empty. She took a spoon and to her horror discovered that some of the vegetables had stuck to the bottom. She pried loose one of the potatoes and looked at it. No wonder it had smelled so strange. She looked about the kitchen wildly, not knowing what to do. Then she took the teakettle and quickly poured in more water until the pot was half full again. Just then she heard the already familiar clop-clop of Trojan's hoofs on the pavement. They were coming! And she had spoiled the dinner. Mr. Bronson had entrusted her with it and she had ruined it.

Cenci had planned to be waiting at the gate on Mesquite Street when they returned, but instead she now ran out of the kitchen and hid on the latticed porch. Here she could look through the openings between the strips of wood and observe the family without being seen. She watched the arrival and then when they were all in the house she moved to an unused room, peeking through the door.

"I suppose, James," Nora laughed, taking off her hat and tossing it on a barrel that had not yet been unpacked, "that you have picked out the very best room for your study, have unpacked all of your books, put them in place, but don't even know where the dishes are."

"Not quite," admitted her husband with a smile. "The study *is* lovely but it is the only room in the house that could be used for a study. It has a separate entrance. When people come to see me they won't have to come trailing through the whole place. You'll like that."

They escorted Nora to the kitchen. She sniffed suspiciously, and quickly went to the stove, took the lid from the pot, and looked in with a practiced eye.

"Something smells funny," said Lukey.

"It smells plain burned to me," said Mark.

All of them gathered around the stove, looking anxious and worried, and Nora's eyes swept around the crescent of expectant faces. She looked into the pot again, moved it to a place on the stove which was not quite so hot.

"It smells wonderful," she said. "It's perfect, absolutely perfect, and I'm starved, too. I didn't know my boys were such good cooks."

The weight of a thousand worlds lifted from Cenci's heart. With one sleeve she wiped the tears that had been gathering in her eyes. Maybe New England dinners were *supposed* to scorch a little, she thought to herself, and thus emboldened she came into the room. Mrs. Bronson *said* it was perfect, she kept thinking to herself, I guess it *is* perfect. I guess I just didn't know.

Nora turned and saw her. "Who is this little girl?" she exclaimed softly. "Did she come with the house?"

James saw the tear-wet cheeks. "I rather believe she did," he answered, and he took the little girl by the hand and drew her forward. "I want you to meet my wife," he said. "This is Mrs. Bronson. Nora, this is Cenci."

"And she is going to stay to supper, too," cried out Luke.

"How lovely!" exclaimed Nora. "I like having company. By the way, where is the dining room?"

Holding her head high and proudly, Cenci led the way.

"In here," she said, loftily. "I'll show you."

Nora looked at the long table, at the crooked cloth, at the white rose on James's napkin and at the vase in front of her plate.

"Did you bring the flowers, dear?" she asked.

Cenci nodded, and then Nora leaned forward and put her arms around the little girl and kissed her. "Thank you," she said. "This is the nicest welcome I have ever had."

After dinner was over that night James and Nora sat out in the side yard beside the fountain. Johnny and Luke were in bed, the twins had gone for a walk to the International Bridge which fascinated them. Cenci had been fetched home by a servant and the noisy hubbub of the household had finally ceased.

The yard was cool and fragrant of mint. The water in the fountain had been turned low, causing only a misty spray from the white marble rosebuds. Once in a while the soft splash of droplets could be heard falling back into the pool. Somewhere in Mexican Town a forlorn lover plucked away at a mandolin and at the intersection of Alamo Avenue and Mesquite Street a group of Mexican children had gathered under a street lamp and were playing, talking in Spanish.

Nora sat back in a garden chair and sighed.

"Tired?"

"A little. It's the heat, I guess."

"You look thin, dear. With the baby coming in January it doesn't seem right for you to be so thin."

"Don't worry about *me!* But it *has* been hot. Is it always like this here?"

"So they say. It gets colder in the winter, of course. They call the cold winds 'northers.' Blue northers are the worst."

The sad mandolin player had ceased his love song, and the Mexican children were now playing a singing game of some sort. Their voices were shrill and sweet.

"How are you, James? That long trip in the boxcar must have been strenuous."

"Oh, I enjoyed it, rather. I made numerous friends."

Nora laughed. "You always do."

They sat in silence awhile. Then he reached over and took one of her hands in his.

"Do you think you can manage here?" he asked. "In this God-forsaken place?"

"With you," she said, "I could manage anywhere! I'm going to love it. I do already."

Dear Nora! James had never quite got over the astonishing and unbelievable fact of her great love for him. They had met by accident on a rainy spring day in New York City, almost seventeen years ago. Nora, slim, gay, redheaded, her arms full of bundles, had dropped into a little restaurant for a cup of coffee and for shelter from a sudden April downpour. All of the tables were full but as she entered she saw a corner booth with a young man seated alone, looking intently at a timetable. There seemed to be more room for her parcels there than in the other booths so she went to it, dropped them on the table with a sigh of relief, sank down on the bench, and said, "Thank goodness, I'm rid of these things." The string from one of the parcels had almost cut her finger. Some of the rain-drenched wrappings had come off and all were in a state of disarray. Nora herself was rain-drenched. Tendrils of soft, curly, red hair clung to her face which was still moist and glistening with water. She flexed her fingers to get the blood circulating and then instinctively put one hand up and touched the top of her hat. "Soaked," she said. "The salesgirl told me not to wear it because it was going to rain but I just fell in love with it and had to put it on."

She took it off and eyed it with dismay. The hat was made of buckram covered with pale yellow silk and adorned with a wreath of blue forget-me-nots and a velvet ribbon which tied under her chin. The starch in the buckram had dissolved to such an extent that the hat was already a pulpy mass without shape. "My Easter hat!" she wailed, and then laughed merrily. "Mrs. Hodges will scold me and Dad will pay for it and tell me to get another." The waiter was now hovering near, with pad in hand and she ordered some coffee and a sandwich and asked him if he could tell her where to dispose of the wrecked hat.

The waiter was a fat little man going bald and he looked at Nora's pretty hair, at the merriment on her face, at the bundles, and he began to laugh, too. "You're not going to throw it away, Miss?" he said. "The flowers and ribbon are still good. I wouldn't throw it away. But I'll take it if you want me to. My missus can use the flowers and ribbon."

All the while James had been sitting there, his timetable forgotten, his eyes drawn irresistibly to the pretty, careless girl who seemed to have been blown in by the storm, bringing with her all of spring's freshness and abandon. As soon as the waiter had departed with the sodden hat James watched Nora rapidly retie the bundles and arrange them in a tidy pile against the wall.

"I'm sorry to have dumped these things all over your table," she said, "but I just had to get rid of them. My finger was killing me." By the time the waiter brought her a cup of coffee, Nora and James were already deep in conversation. She had come to New York for her Easter shopping, she said. She was on spring vacation, and mentioned a fashionable and expensive girls' school. James, a divinity student from Harvard, had also come to New York but not for Easter shopping. He had come on business to see about a pastorate in a small suburban town not far away. He was getting his degree in June and the job he had come to see about was only a temporary one as the current pastor was ill and was going away on vacation.

Nora looked at James with fast-beating heart. His dark suit was neat but almost threadbare. His young face was sensitive and his serious eyes magnetic. Afterwards Nora always told him that people could say what they pleased about not falling in love at first sight but it had certainly happened to her. She had fallen in love with this tall shabby minister at once and made up her mind she was going to marry him. Their brief courtship was a stormy one. James loved her, too, but to him marriage had been something that he had put out of his mind for a long time. His parents were dead. He had worked his way through school. He had nothing, absolutely nothing to offer. There were long sessions between her father, Mr. Abbott, and James in which obstacles to their marriage were piled up like a blockade around her.

Nora was his only child, his darling. She had always been mischievous and willful, impractical, and a spendthrift. Marriage to a poor young minister would bring nothing but disaster, all of them were sure. Nora's father owned a small dairy farm in Massachusetts where they went for vacations although the family lived in New York.

The very day that a sudden spring shower had ruined her

Easter hat and caused her to meet James, Mr. Abbott had lost everything he possessed, except the farm, by an unfortunate business venture. He had not then informed Nora. He was not a young man and could not start over as he might have twenty years before. He had planned to retire to his farm, had hoped that Nora would marry a man who could care for her as he had, but what James did not know, what her own father did not know, was that Nora, deep within herself was neither impractical nor careless just because she had always had plenty of money and had been encouraged to spend it as she pleased. Actually, money meant nothing to her. Her happiest childhood recollections were the long summer months on the farm in Massachusetts. As a little girl she had followed the caretaker's wife, Mrs. Hodges, around like a shadow, helping with the chickens, learning how to cook. One of her pretend games was that Mrs. Hodges was her mother and she even went so far once as to ask her father to let her remain on the farm an entire winter and go to the country school, an idea that had promptly been vetoed. It was, in fact, Mrs. Hodges who stood by Nora in her determination to marry James and in the end Nora won out.

When he took up his duties at the pastorate he had gone to New York to see about the day he met her, James did not go alone. He went with his bride. And in the years that followed Nora was a constant source of surprise and gratification to her idealistic husband. She looked upon money as she did upon rain. Sometimes it fell, sometimes it did not. She could spend it or she could do without it. Her apprenticeship with Mrs. Hodges had not been in vain. She proved to be a good cook, an excellent housekeeper. She could look beautiful no matter what she wore. Her good nature and merriment bubbled out of her irrepressibly. If James had looked the world over he could not have found a more suitable wife. The fact that she loved him seemed like a miracle to him. Once or twice during the first months of their marriage he would say to her, "But what do you see in me?"

In a graver moment she had taken his face between her hands and looked deep into his eyes. "I don't know, darling," she answered. "But sometimes I think that I see God. . . ."

Yes, this was Nora, unpredictable except that James knew she would stand back of him always, more earth-bound than he, emotional, liking beautiful things, and managing to make a beautiful thing out of a marriage which had certainly seemed foolhardy at the beginning. Her father had retired permanently to the farm and he, too, seemed happier than he had been as a Wall Street broker. Mr. and Mrs. Hodges remained on and there was plenty of food but not much in the way of cash. Mr. Abbott became very fond of James, he adored his grandsons, and gave them gifts whenever he could. Even on the farm he maintained his air of elegance, and sometimes Nora, looking at Mark, handsome and spirited, thinking of Lukey and his mischievous ways, and little John's gypsy wanderings, would smile tenderly because in them there was so much of herself and her father. Matthew alone was like James and her love for him pierced her heart.

7

JAMES HAD ELICITED the information from Brett that, although the Methodist Church was the fashionable and thriving one in Donde, there did exist a church of his own faith. It was named the Little Bonne Femme, because of Little Bonne Femme Creek, usually dry, which bounded the property in the back. The church was small. It had no pastor and had had none for several years. The only service held there was Sunday school, which was run by a soldier from the Army Post, a Sergeant Quale, who before joining the regular army had owned a barbecue stand.

The next Sunday morning, James and Nora roused the twins out of bed. "Boys," said he, "for some time now we have had to miss church because we were either on the train, or getting settled, or something, but today we are going to go."

"We had planned to go to church anyway," said Mark, yawning.

"Yes," piped up Luke, already up and dressed. "The Methodist one. I heard that girl tell them."

"What girl?" asked Mr. Bronson, as Mark tried vainly to signal his brother to keep his mouth shut.

Matthew got up. "We just happened to be sitting next to her at the movie the other night, Father," he explained, a slow flush deepening on his slender face.

"Naturally," spoke up Mark, talking quickly, "people get into conversation when they sit next to somebody, and naturally we knew you would want us to go to church, so we asked her about one. So we told her we would be there this morning."

Matthew, seeing a deep frown settling on his father's face, interposed quietly, "We asked her about our church, too, Father, but she said that they don't hold services there. It hasn't got a preacher."

"And naturally," said Luke sticking his hands in his pockets, an impish grin on his face, "this girl was a ravenous beauty."

"Ravishing," corrected Mark.

But Luke was not to be quelled.

"She has a ravishing name, too," he said. "Boy, *what* a name. Delight. Delight Randell. Delight," he began to chirp, hopping about, "Delight, Deeelight."

"Shut up," said Mark. "People can't help what they are named. Besides, everybody calls her Dee."

Mr. Bronson sighed. So! he thought. *This* was beginning all over again. If there were a pretty girl in town, Mark would spot her. He did hope this once that Matthew would not fall for her, too. Matthew was quiet, reticent, unlucky with girls. But Mark, his handsome, frank face glowing with interest, launched forth this morning into an account of how he happened to sit next to this girl and of what all of them said and did. Oh, dear, thought Mr. Bronson to himself. All this business again. Mark had been in love almost from the cradle and he dragged the whole family with him.

"You *should* see her, Father," he said now. "Her eyes are as blue as the sky. Her skin is milk-white. Her hair is golden. Her hands are slim and white. Her neck is like a swan————"

Luke leaned forward, thrusting his puckish little face almost under Mark's.

"Quack, quack," he said.

"Shut up," said Mark.

Their father burst out laughing.

"I am sure Delight is just as you paint her," he said, "but nevertheless you are not going to feast your eyes upon her at the Methodist Church this morning. You boys are coming with your mother and me. Our church may not have a service but it does have Sunday school."

"But, Father," wailed Mark, "Dee told me nobody goes there. Nobody that *is* anybody, at least!"

"That makes no difference," said Mr. Bronson, "get on with your chores now, boys."

Although outwardly a mild man, whatever Mr. Bronson said was law. The boys were disappointed. Nevertheless they did not argue. They might have known that their father would ferret out this miserable little church and make them go to it. Gone were all of their splendid dreams of appearing at the Methodist Church, scrubbed and shining, to dazzle the sky-blue eyes of the angelic creature they had met the week before. In grim mutiny they fed the animals and got themselves ready. Luke, of course, had looked forward to the occasion only so that he could have fresh material for ribbing his brothers.

A few hours later, the Bronson family sallied forth toward Little Bonne Femme, but as it was on their route to pass the Methodist Church the boys looked at it with envy. What a beautiful building! Creamy-yellow limestone, grounds faultlessly landscaped, cars parked all around it, fashionably dressed people swarming about it like bees around a hive.

"Step up, boys, step up," said Mr. Bronson. "I don't want to be late the first morning we are there."

So on they went, with heavy hearts and great sighs which they hoped were not wasted on their parents. Little Bonne Femme Church was so small, so humble, so tightly jammed between two seedy-looking houses that they almost missed it. At some time or other it had been painted gray, but much of the paint had scaled off, giving it a scrofulous appearance. It did boast a steeple, however, and even a bell, which began ringing loudly as they approached. Nobody swarmed in and out of the plain door of this church. Not a car was parked in front. The sun blazed down upon it mercilessly, causing it to stand out naked and ugly.

"In we go, boys," said Mr. Bronson.

And in they went. Up four rickety steps and through the door. At first their eyes were blinded by the sunshine outside and they could not see much. Then the interior became clearly outlined, unadorned, without beauty. A worn hemp carpet, curling at the edges, extended from the door to the base of the pulpit down the middle of the room. The pulpit was badly in need of repair and had a decided list to the right. On each side were tiers of hard benches which possibly may have been painted at one time but had long ago forgotten about it. The windows were so dirty that the sunshine streaming in gave a sickly yellow light. The pulpit was on a platform which contained a high-backed chair with one of its arms missing. Below it and slightly to one side was a little folding organ. From the ceiling were suspended four gaslights, and opposite the organ stood a small table and a chair. An old army saddle lay humped in one corner. As the Bronsons went in, they almost collided with a round, red-faced, middle-aged sergeant who had apparently just completed ringing the bell. The bell-rope near the door was still swaying back and forth. The sergeant beamed, hurried toward the newcomers, and began pumping Mr. Bronson's hand vigorously.

"Good morning, good morning, good morning," he said. "Welcome to our church. Sergeant Quale is the name. And yours?"

"Reverend James Bronson, Sergeant. This is my wife, Mrs. Bronson, and——" Thus James introduced himself and his family, Sergeant Quale grasping hold of each hand, pumping it, and saying good morning, good morning, good morning. When he got to Luke, the little boy's face had a slightly purple look, a definite sign that he could not hold in his suppressed laughter much longer. Sergeant Quale took down all their names in a notebook and then led them to a pew.

"We are just about to begin," he said fervently, and went forward and took his place at the chair in front of the small table. "Let's start, Slim," he said to another soldier sitting unobtrusively in a front pew. Slim was well named. He must have been at least six feet four, and not much bigger around than a pencil, or so it seemed. He had long arms and legs and a great mop of unruly hair. When he unfolded himself from his seat and ambled over to the organ, he looked like a huge spider enveloping an unsuspecting fly. The organ was so small that, in order to pump it, Slim's knees almost touched his chin, and his arms were so long that he had to keep them in an awkward bent position. He gave the general impression of taking the little organ in his lap. In the meantime the Bronsons lined themselves up on a pew, Nora taking care to dust it first.

There were only a few other people scattered about when Sergeant Quale arose and Slim began playing the Doxology. It was remarkable how beautifully he played, Nora thought. Everybody stood, sang, sat down. The sergeant rose again. His red face was glistening with perspiration. He looked very hot indeed in his uniform.

"I'll now read the minutes of last Sunday," he said. And opening a notebook, he began, "Weather fair and warm—August——"

Lukey sitting directly under one of the gaslights looked upwards at its metal pendant. *Weather, fair and warm,* he thought and his mouth became dry with thirst. If only the pendant overhead were a faucet, and cool water might drip from it to refresh him!

"Now, I'll call the roll," went on the sergeant. When he disposed of the few other people, he began on the Bronsons.

"Reverend James Bronson."

"Present," replied the startled Mr. Bronson who had never yet seen a Sunday school conducted in this manner.

"Mrs. James Bronson."

"Present," Nora almost whispered.

"Matthew Bronson."

"Present," said Matthew.

"Mark Bronson."

"Here," said Mark.

"Luke Bronson."

The little boy at the end of the row made a strange convulsive sound which may or may not have been "Present."

"John Bronson."

No answer—Johnny had fallen asleep.

As soon as the Sunday school was over people began to pick up their pocketbooks and straighten their hats, getting ready for departure, but Sergeant Quale once again arose and stood in front of the church facing the congregation. The church was like an oven. Trickles of perspiration ran down from his forehead and down the back of his neck and his face was mottled.

"Ladies and gentlemen," he began, "please may I have a few more words? Today it is our great pleasure to have with us a new family——" He paused and many necks were craned in the direction of the Bronsons lined up in their pew. Then the sergeant went on.

"It has been a long time since a reverend has come to this church. I found today that this little family——" He paused for dramatic effect, then laughed. "This *little* family," he resumed, "has come to live in Donde and be one of us and join our church. Their name is Bronson. They come from Connecticut. They're Yankees. Now, don't laugh, folks. They can't help being Yankee. And we'll forgive 'em because Reverend Bronson is a preacher. It's been a long time since Little Bonne Femme had a real preacher, so now I am going to ask him if he will remain and I'm extending him the honor of preaching us a few words. I hope you won't leave, folks. It has sure been a long time since we had a sermon in this church."

Everybody settled back on their seats, expectantly. James was nonplused. He had not expected this. He looked at Nora, who smiled at him, a twinkle in her eye, and then at the four boys who were fidgeting, embarrassed and anxious to get away. Then he stood up and with his customary dignity walked to the front of the church and looked around.

The congregation was pitifully small: two old women sitting off to themselves in one corner whispering and more interested in each other than in anything else that was going on, a boy and girl of about sixteen writing notes to one another on hymn books and passing them furtively back and forth, a few soldiers, a scattering of civilians. One was a nondescript-looking little woman of indefinite age and of no attractiveness whatever, except for her soft blue eyes.

It was about the most discouraging group that James had ever confronted. He did not know these people. He did not yet know the community. He did not know what they expected. However, he was struck by a strangely pathetic quality in this scene, by the fact that most of the people here were obviously poor. He was struck, too, by the thought, why did they come? They didn't have to come. And as he walked down the aisle he could not help but think, I wonder! Do they have doubts and troubles, too? Are they seeking something, as I am? An impulse to reach across the gulf between them humbled him and drew him to them. He had not brought notes for a sermon. Usually he did, usually he was prepared, but today he had not expected to be called on. When he ascended the pulpit he bowed in his courteous way toward Sergeant Quale and smiled.

"Thank you, Sergeant," he said. "I am a stranger here. I did not expect to speak. It was very kind of you to ask me and kinder still of your congregation to remain and listen to what I have to say." A slight smile came to his lips. "This I can promise, whatever it is that I shall say will be short. The morning is warm. I shall not detain you very long.

"I am not going to preach a formal sermon. I am just going to talk to you. I could not help but think as I looked at your small group of the verse in the Bible that says, 'Where two or three are gathered together in my name there shall I be also.' There are not many of us here, more than two or three, but not many. And yet I wonder if all of us do not feel in this holy place the presence of God? Or, if we do *not* feel it, did we come here to seek it? If you will pardon a few personal remarks I wish to say that I came to this town for my health, which was impaired during my chaplaincy in the recent World War. Also, I came to Donde, not to preach but to think. The heartbreaking things I saw overseas caused me to think as I have never thought before. They have caused me to doubt."

A look of sadness came upon his face as he said this and once again he was conscious of the meek little woman sitting all by herself in the middle of one of the hard benches. He was conscious of the sensitive fingers of Slim resting on the organ. He was conscious of the attention, the full attention of his audience.

The old women in the corner had ceased whispering. The lovers had stopped writing notes and had laid the hymn books aside. Everybody looked up at him with curiosity. But, was it all curiosity? He wondered. He did not know how much education these people had. He did not know the background of any of them and yet suddenly he began speaking to them from his heart. He was remembering one of the poems that he and Brett Lindley, the drunken editor, had discussed the Saturday night he first arrived in Donde. The poem was "The Hound of Heaven," by Francis Thompson, most of which James knew because he had read it so often. And so he said now, "I am thinking of a poem I once read. A poem I reread very often. It, too, is about a man who had doubts, about a man who fled from God and did not know why, and yet in fleeing from him, he was also seeking him. The first lines of this poem apply to me. I don't know whether they apply to you or not but they do apply to many people in these troubled times.

> I fled Him, down the nights and down the days;
> I fled Him, down the arches of the years;
> I fled Him, down the labyrinthine ways
> Of my own mind; and in the midst of tears
> I hid from Him, and under running laughter.[1]

[1] From "The Hound of Heaven," by Francis Thompson; reprinted by permission of The Newman Bookshop and Messrs. Burns, Oates, and Washbourne, Ltd.

James Bronson paused. " 'Of my own mind,' " he repeated. " 'Of my own mind. . . .' " He paused. "As I said before," he went on, "I have doubts. I am sure that many people do not realize that ministers have doubts, but they do. And yet when I think of this poem I keep thinking of this one phrase and of these four words, 'Of my own mind.' Is it in our own minds that doubt exists, that prejudices and hatred are bred? If we could free our own minds from this bondage would the world be different?"

He leaned forward, talking earnestly. He talked for about ten or fifteen minutes and there was scarcely another sound in the room. He observed that the little mousy woman leaned forward and the gaze from her eyes was one of burning intensity. He did not know why he should have noticed her. But it had happened to him before: the singling out of one particular person in a congregation and feeling that he was preaching especially to that one person.

At length he finished. "This," he said, "is not a sermon. It is but a halting talk, a halting voicing of my own thoughts. I do not know you and you do not know me and yet I wish all of you could read this poem and understand it. It ends so beautifully with a note of hope which I, this morning, do not possess. I do not recall the exact words. But I do remember that it says:

> Halts by me that footfall:
> Is my gloom, after all,
> Shade of His hand, outstretched caressingly? [1]

"This, my friends, is the only thought I can leave with you. We have just emerged from a war which should not have been fought. We have sacrificed and I do not understand why nor do I feel that the sacrifice is finished, nor was it justified. I feel that we have just begun to suffer, I feel that something lies in the

---

[1] From "The Hound of Heaven," by Francis Thompson; reprinted by permission of The Newman Bookshop and Messrs. Burns, Oates, and Washbourne, Ltd.

future which none of us can see now. In this small group of people are soldiers who have fought. There are perhaps people who lost loved ones in the war, or who are troubled and lonely for other reasons. I do not know, for you are still strangers to me. But as I look at you I am wondering with the poet, 'Is this gloom I feel yours as well as mine'? And I wish, too, that we had the vision to see ahead as he did and could ask with him, 'Is my gloom, after all, shade of His hand, outstretched caressingly?'"

James ceased speaking. The room was very still. He looked at Nora and then one by one at all of his children and then said reverently, as he did at the end of every sermon, "Let us pray."

After the service the small woman to whom he had felt so drawn as he had preached came up and introduced herself timidly as Miss Ivy Vail. She thanked him for his sermon and he realized he was talking to a woman of education and culture.

"Would it be asking too much of you, Reverend Bronson," she asked in that same shy manner, "for you to come and visit my father? He is old and ill, very ill. I wish he could have heard your sermon this morning——"

"I shall be glad to visit him," answered James promptly. "Thank you for asking me."

She gave him the address and then vanished like a shadow.

It wasn't until they were on their way home that the boys exploded. Why, they said, *that* was not church! The whole performance was a farce. It was all they could do to keep from laughing most of the time. What a way to start in a new town, lining themselves up with an organization like this! Even Nora protested.

"You didn't have to preach, dear," she said with a sigh. "After all, you are supposed to be on vacation."

"Not many more than a dozen people were there, and it turned out to be one of your best sermons, too," said Matthew with indignation. "Wasted. Quite wasted."

"That Sergeant Quale!" said Mark witheringly. "He ought to

be a barker for a side show. And the crack he made about the size of our family. Revolting!"

Mr. Bronson let them all have their say. He always did. That was one reason the family was such a noisy one. When everybody had finished, he said, "Boys, this is our church. Instead of criticizing it, we are going to roll up our sleeves and go to work. The other churches don't need us. This one does. There's nothing in life quite so wonderful as to be needed. And it didn't tire me to preach, Nora. It rested me. I couldn't refuse. You know that as well as I do."

"Yes," said Nora in a strange voice. "I know that."

"And I'm not so sure, boys—maybe we need Little Bonne Femme even more than they need us. Sergeant Quale is—well —not what I'd call polished. But the fellow is sincere. I'd rather be like him than be a snob."

There was a sudden silence. Finally, it was broken by Lukey, the irrepressible, who said, "Well, don't blame me, Father, if I burst out laughing sometime right in the middle of the roll call. I can hold in a long time but not forever."

And suddenly he began walking on his hands, peering out at them and saying, "Good morning, good morning, good morning."

8

IT WAS THE LAST DAY of September and Donde was in an uproar. Pánfilo García, the Mexican who had shot the sheriff in August, had escaped from jail while awaiting trial. Cenci felt as if this matter of Pánfilo was her concern, too. Hadn't she been right there in the *Eagle* office when the news of the shooting came to Mr. Lindley over the telephone? But this morning there was so much confusion she could not get things straight in her mind. Everybody was talking about it and every version differed. Some said that the new sheriff was no good to allow a dangerous criminal like that to slip through his fingers. Many people were terrified. Why, Pánfilo might be hiding anywhere! Lurking in somebody's tool shed or ready to commit another murder if the opportunity presented itself.

Well, Cenci knew that the *Eagle* at least would have the facts correctly. The thing to do was to buy a newspaper and read it for herself. Mr. Lindley always made everything so clear. She hurried down Main Street, stopping at Stirling's Pharmacy to ask for a paper. Sold out, was the reply. She stopped at other places that sold papers only to receive the same answer, so she decided to go directly to the *Eagle* office, and buy a paper there, although she hated to go when she knew the editor would be busy.

When she arrived at the newspaper office, she saw that Mr. Bronson, his back turned to the plate-glass window and the street, was sitting in a chair talking to the editor. Brett Lindley himself was walking around the office talking furiously, kicking up the papers strewn on the floor like a whirlwind. He certainly was making those papers fly around. Cenci entered unobtrusively through the open door. But neither the minister nor the editor saw her, for as she went in, she was shoved aside by a twittery woman accompanied by her homely daughter.

"Mr. Lindley," the woman said hysterically, "I *have* to buy a paper! Can't find a copy in town."

Brett, his feet enmeshed in long rolls of proof sheets, glowered at her.

"Sold out," he said brusquely.

"Oh, dear!" The woman began to wring her hands. "What's this town coming to, Mr. Lindley? Murderers roaming around, escaping from jails. Oh, dear! Do you think it's safe to let my daughter out after dark?"

Brett gave a brief look at the woman's spindly, flat-chested daughter.

"No, Madam," he said, without a change of expression on his face, "I advise you to keep her in after dark and *before* dark, too."

"Oh, dear!" wailed the woman. "Well, thank you, Mr. Lindley, for your advice, but I do wish I could buy a paper."

Cenci stood over in the corner listening, hidden by the tall file rack containing papers from other towns. As soon as the woman had left Brett began kicking the littered floor again.

"Murderer!" he scoffed. "Dangerous! Why, that poor man wouldn't harm a flea. I've been doing a little investigating. Pánfilo's record was spotless. He is an American citizen, just like you and me, and proud of it. He fought in the war, the war to make the world safe for democracy, you know. He fought in the Battle of the Marne but was lucky enough to come back alive, although he was gassed once. Slightly."

James winced.

"Then," went on Brett, "he came back to his wife Lupe and his little son. He got a job and went to work."

"Why did he get fired?" asked James, sitting there thoughtfully.

"Did you ever work in a rock quarry?" asked Brett.

James shook his head in negation.

"No," said Brett, "nor have I. Pánfilo was a little fellow and not too strong, remember. His pay was so inadequate that he couldn't afford the proper food, the proper house, not with the present inflation. It's brutal work. It would have killed either you or me. Pánfilo was fired because he was sick. Because he fainted on the job one day. A murderer! The man who owns that rock quarry is a deacon in one of the churches here. I won't say which one. He passes the collection plate. Is anybody afraid of him? *Who* is the murderer?"

Cenci saw a look of deep trouble come upon the minister's face. "But how do you suppose Pánfilo escaped?" he asked. "A timid little man like that?"

"Oh, I don't know," said Brett. "That moldy adobe jail—no telling. But I know one thing. I'm glad he's gone. And I hope he's had time to get far away from here, or he'll get caught, sure as hell. Even his wife can't be found. I looked for her, thought maybe I could help her out. But she's hiding, too. And there's not a Spic in Mexican Town that will say a word. They're all scared to death, poor devils."

Mr. Bronson said nothing.

Half a dozen or more people came in trying to buy papers. After they had left, Brett lowered his voice, "I hope he got across the river to the other side," he said. "To Mexico. He might have relatives or friends there."

"But how could he get across?" asked James. "The International Bridge is heavily guarded. I've often stood there, watching the sentries, both American and Mexican, marching up and down."

"Has it occurred to you that there's another bridge?" asked Brett. "That ore-train bridge on down the river?"

"Why, yes," answered James, "but it's only a trestle, extremely narrow. And those ore trains are so irregular—I certainly shouldn't risk taking a chance on that."

"Nor I," said Brett, "unless my life were at stake. Poor guy! The cards are stacked against him. I've never seen a case of such rank injustice. The whole world stinks, Jim. I don't care what you preach in your pulpit. If there's one thing I cannot tolerate, it's injustice."

"I cannot rationalize injustice either," said James. "You said just now, 'I don't care what you preach in your pulpit.' One of the reasons right now that I don't know what to preach in my pulpit is this very problem. I can't rationalize the injustice of war, the calling up of young men before they've ever had a future, killing them or sending them back weakened and maimed, the destruction of homes, of innocent children. . . . This thing of Pánfilo, it fits right in and I don't care whether people come to listen to me or not but I'm going to preach about Pánfilo in my pulpit just as you write about him in your editorials. We can work together on this thing, Brett. It's just one case, I admit, one insignificant, pathetic little Mexican but he has a soul, feelings, a heart, he has a family who will be made to suffer. If you and I work together on this, we might accomplish a little something. The way I see it now, the only hope for any of us lies in these small individual attempts to straighten things out. If enough people did them, it wouldn't be small. I had planned to preach tomorrow about something quite different." James rose from his chair. "I'm going home and write a new sermon." He smiled a little, his dry faint smile. "I can't be fired, you know. The worst thing that could happen would be for everybody to walk out. If they do, will you print my sermon on your editorial page?"

Brett Lindley looked at James. "Yes," he said, "I'll print it, but I don't think that people will walk out on you. In fact, I might even come and hear it. I'll print it anyway."

James left the room then, a faraway look in his eyes already, the look of someone trying to compose something, trying to put his thoughts into words.

At this moment Cenci timidly came out from behind the file of papers.

"Mr. Lindley," she said, "what does injustice mean?"

"Hello there! Where did you come from, honey?" he asked. "Injustice," he repeated, "injustice." He walked over to the large dictionary upon which Nevermore was sleeping soundly. Brett picked the cat up and set him on the floor amidst the tangled papers. He opened the dictionary and flipped through its pages.

" 'Injustice,' " he read, " 'want of justice; violation of another's rights; wrong.' That's what injustice means, Cenci. Wrong."

"Oh," she said, and stood there for a moment looking at the editor. She felt very sad. Everything seemed quite clear to her now, and it made her want to cry, but she did not.

Brett looked at her, his face softening as it always did in her presence. "Did you want something, Cenci?" he asked gently. "I didn't even know you were here. Can I help you? Did you come to inquire about Kitty?"

Cenci squeezed her eyes tight. She held her mouth in a firm, taut line.

"No, sir, I only wanted a paper, Mr. Lindley," she said, "but it doesn't matter——"

Brett turned away from her, facing the press room.

"Pete!" he yelled. "Pete!"

When the hunchback printer came at his call, Brett said, "You might as well get the presses going again, Peter. Roll off another hundred."

The printer disappeared and Brett turned again to the little girl.

"I'll send you a paper by Mr. Bronson," he said, "when he goes home to lunch. That is, unless you'd rather wait."

Again in that small, tight voice, Cenci replied, "Thank you, Mr. Lindley, but I don't believe I'll wait. I have to get home."

And then she left the newspaper office and walked down Main Street. But as she walked along, she kept saying to herself, *Want of justice; violation of another's rights; wrong. Wrong. Wrong . . .*

9

SITTING at his study desk one afternoon early in November, it occurred to James Bronson that it does not take long for a pattern to establish itself in one's daily existence. Already it seemed to him that he had lived in Donde for years, had liked it from the first. He liked this house. He liked his study. In this large room its sparse furnishings gave it an almost monastic austerity to which he had become accustomed and which he rather enjoyed. At one end it had a fireplace in which today a small fire burned, for Donde was experiencing its first "norther" of the year. Near the fireplace and not far from his study table stood the only lovely piece of furniture the Bronsons possessed, the eighteenth-century claw-and-ball-foot easy chair which had been left to Nora in her mother's will along with the Haviland china and solid silver. Nora said the chair was Chippendale although her mother could not prove it. She was extremely proud of it and insisted on its being placed in the study because she said the study was used more often than the living room. James thought it did not go with the rest of the furnishings but Nora only laughed and said it would fit there as well as anywhere. Well, it was a comfortable chair, and he liked to sit and read in it.

Next to the table was his old swivel chair which creaked when he leaned back in it. The room also contained bookshelves to the ceiling, a painting of Jesus, the Good Shepherd, and his ancient round-topped tin trunk.

This trunk had a definite purpose, in addition to holding his rare old Bible and the manuscripts of his sermons. When a tiresome guest came who seemed in danger of overstaying his welcome, Mr. Bronson offered him the round-topped trunk. No seat could be designed to create more discomfort to a person placed upon it. One slipped around first to the back, then forward, then sideways, and finally decided that what one had come to say was not very important after all. Although, except for the "kneeling rug," the floor was bare, late in the afternoons the sun streamed in at the stained-glass window, throwing patterns on the scrubbed boards more magnificent than any Oriental rug.

Yes, it was a peaceful, remote room, completely cut off from the rest of the house which was usually noisy. A man could think, in here. Yet since that first night in Donde, James had deliberately tried not to think, except about the immediate pressure of each day.

He had started preaching at Little Bonne Femme more or less accidentally, that first Sunday. He, Nora, the boys, and Cenci, aided by Slim and Sergeant Quale, had given the church a thorough cleaning. Now, the pews were kept dusted. The windows sparkled. The holes in the hemp carpet had been darned. On Sundays a vase of flowers decorated the pulpit.

He and Nora had tactfully reorganized the Sunday school, although Sergeant Quale still remained superintendent, an office he held with pride. The roll call had been discontinued. The Bronson children had been appointed the official janitors and bell ringers, taking turns. Matthew and Mark took one week, Luke and Cenci the next. Cenci loved to ring the bell. Once Lukey had swung on the rope backwards and forwards, like the pendulum of a clock, setting up a terrific clamor. She begged him to let *her* swing on the bell rope, but Lukey, in lordly fashion, had said no, she was only a girl. She had accepted his domination over her meekly. He was the first real playmate she had ever had, except for the marble angel in the fountain and the children in Mexican Town. She *did* want to swing on the bell rope, though, and hoped he had not seen her chin quiver at his refusal.

To everybody's surprise, the congregation of Little Bonne Femme began to pick up. New people came to town. Old residents who had stopped going because there was no pastor started drifting back. Fred came from time to time, when he was in town. Even Brett came, though he took a back seat and slipped out early. Little Bonne Femme, nevertheless, remained poor. The few coins in the collection plates looked lonesome. Most of the people who came there were by no means rich. Thus without exactly knowing how it had happened James again found himself a busy minister. He preached every Sunday. He had conducted one funeral, that of old Mr. Vail, Miss Ivy's father, who had died recently. People began coming to him with their troubles, just as they always had. The friendship deepened between him and Brett Lindley, who came to supper at least once a week and printed church bulletins for Little Bonne Femme free of charge. Sometimes he and Brett and the boys went fishing. Sometimes the two men just talked, disagreeing about practically everything except the poetry of William Blake.

Today, a Saturday afternoon, James was polishing up his tomorrow's sermon and watching over Luke and little John who was taking his nap. Nora had gone to the Army Post to visit the sick wife of a soldier who had been coming to church of late. The twins were working. Mark had a job, Saturday afternoons and after school, as toll collector on the International Bridge. Matthew worked, too, helping Pete, in the job-printing department of the *Eagle*. Yes, thought James Bronson, this is a peaceful afternoon, a peaceful existence. Everything seemed remote from the troubles of the world. He walked to the window and gazed out at the river, thinking about his sermon.

While he stood there, old Isabella, dressed as gaudily as usual, stood in the doorway of her establishment near-by, *La Posada Toronjil,* looking at the tendril of smoke coming from the chimney of the Bronson house. Suddenly she felt somebody tugging at her skirt and she turned and looked down into the bluest, widest eyes she had ever seen, the most angelic face, the loveliest head of silvery-gold ringlets, and a smile that was utterly enchanting and disarming.

"I want to go in there with you," the child said. "I've runned away from home and I want to go in there so they won't find me."

The look he gave her was at once so candid, and at the same time so cunning, that Isabella had a hard time to keep from laughing.

"Why in the world did you run away?" she asked instead, and the child replied without hesitation, "Because I didn't want to take my nap."

"Is *that* all?"

"Oh, no. It's fun to run away."

"Hmm. Don't you get punished?"

"Yes, when I get catched. But you see, even when I get punished I've already had the fun."

Isabella pondered on this a moment. Then she said firmly, "Well, young man, whether you like it or not, I'm going to take you home. Where's your mother?"

"Visiting a sick lady at the Fort. And Father's home, thinking. Father thinks quite a lot. Please let me go in your house with you. It's so pretty."

"No," said Isabella. "Come." She reached out and took his soft little hand in hers, but he pulled it away. "I can walk alone," he said stubbornly, thrusting out his lower lip.

Even in his anger he was so adorable that Isabella was enchanted. She could still feel the softness of his little hand as it had pulled out of her grasp. It had felt like a rosebud, slipping through her fingers.

Up the street they went, the cherubic little boy and old Isabella, the hem of her bright silk dress sweeping the dusty street. Hesitantly she went to the study door and knocked. When James Bronson opened it his eyebrows lifted in surprise.

"I thought you were taking your nap, Son," he said to John, gently reproachful.

"I don't feel like a nap today," answered his son, "I'm too old for naps." He thrust his lower lip out even a little farther. James gazed at his small belligerent offspring thoughtfully. "Come on in," he said, and when Isabella began to retreat he said, "Please. Both of you."

He saw her cheeks flame underneath the rouge.

"Oh, no, thank you," she began, "I can't——" But he waved aside her protest and reluctantly she entered the study. She watched him go to a bookcase and take from it a large book with gaily painted birds on the cover.

"Here, Son," he said, "here is the bird book. Take it to bed with you. If you can't sleep, just rest. Look at the pictures."

The child looked up at his father incredulously.

"But, Father—the *bird book!* I've never been allowed——"

"No, you weren't old enough. If you're too old to take naps, you're old enough for this book. I expect you to take care of it. Soon you'll be going hunting and fishing with the other boys. You'll need to learn all about birds and all the animals——"

The lower lip was no longer protruding. Johnny reached out and took the big book, almost staggering under its weight, "Oh, Father——"

"Run along, Son. It's all right."

As soon as Johnny had gone, James turned to Isabella. "Thank you," he said, "for bringing him home." He smiled faintly. "Johnny has gypsy blood in him, I'm afraid. It's hard to know just how to handle him sometimes. Lukey used to be almost as bad, but he's outgrown it lately, I hope. I'm not sure where he is at the moment, but he was in the back yard awhile ago. . . ."

His voice trailed off. His eye strayed toward his study table upon which he had just placed a teapot, some cups and saucers, a plate of sliced and buttered bread. "I'm having my tea a bit early today," he said. "I wasn't hungry at lunchtime. Won't you join me?"

"But, Reverend Bronson," Isabella objected, "you don't know

who I am! I shouldn't even have stepped inside this door. I—I'm not worthy, sir."

James set out two cups, began pouring the tea. "I know who you are, Isabella," he said evenly. "Do you take cream and sugar? Be seated, will you? As you see," he went on easily, "I have several cups and saucers here. People often drop in."

He handed her the tea with ceremony, even though the cup had a broken handle. Isabella sat rigidly on the edge of the eighteenth-century chair, holding the saucer stiffly. She looked about the room, saw the shabby furniture, the table piled high with books, the stained-glass window, the picture of the Good Shepherd hanging on the wall. Then she became conscious of James Bronson's voice again, speaking to her quietly.

"You said just now that you weren't worthy of entering this room. Did you know that in the Bible it says that men were created a little lower than the angels? That means you, Isabella, as much as it does me. When the time comes when any human being isn't worthy of entering my home, then I'm not worthy of having a home."

It had been a long time since Isabella had cried, except in anger. Now she felt her eyelids smarting, was conscious of a constriction in her throat.

"But you don't understand, Reverend Bronson," she said. "I'm a wicked woman. This is the first time since my childhood I've been asked into a *nice* house." Taking a lace-trimmed handkerchief from her bosom, she wiped her eyes with it.

"To me," continued James Bronson, "there are not bad people and good people in the world, standing apart in two separate rows. No. To me there are just—people. There are bad deeds. There is crime, injustice, suffering, greed. But why? Why? There must be reasons, back of every misdeed. We all make mistakes. All of us."

He sat back in his chair and drank his tea.

"I like tea," he said, "it relaxes me. I was trying to finish a sermon, but my ending was wrong. I kept thinking of other things—would you like another cup, Isabella? I'm going to have one."

"No, sir. No, thank you. I must be going."

He did not press her, but arose and went with her to the door. Once again her eyes surveyed the room, rested on the picture of the Good Shepherd.

"Good-bye, sir," she said, "and thank you. Thank you for the tea, and for the things you said."

He looked at her, saw the tears, the unhappiness in the faded, aging eyes.

"If you should like to talk to me again," he said, "come back. It—it sometimes helps people, you know, just to talk."

"Thank you, Reverend. Thank you."

Then she turned and was gone.

10

AFTER LUNCH that same day, with everybody else in the household well occupied, Lukey had had a left-out feeling. He was envious of his brothers who were old enough to get jobs. He had wanted to accompany his mother to the Army Post, but she had told him the sick woman might have something contagious; he would be better off at home.

The little boy amused himself for a while watching Duchess in the lower back yard. She was really a remarkable cow. With her horns she could turn on the faucet over the water trough from which she and the horse drank. She could turn it on but not off and more than once the entire lower yard had been flooded. She also had a great fondness on washdays of drinking up the bluing water and of eating any soap that might have been left behind. The boys often said they should start a circus. Duchess was definitely a circus animal. They could put her through her tricks and charge admission. But this afternoon Luke soon tired of watching her turn on the faucet, and he was just wondering what else to do with himself when Cenci skipped through the gate separating the two houses.

"Where's everybody?" she asked.

Luke told her, moodily kicking a stone with the toe of his shoe as he spoke.

"Where's everybody at your house?" he growled.

"Oh, Miss Manners has a headache," replied Cenci. "She told me not to bother her."

"I'll tell you what let's do," he said. "Let's run away. Let's take some food and run away and stay out all night and *then* they'll feel sorry. Maybe they'll send a posse out after us. Maybe Matthew and Mark will think I'm dead and *next* time they'll let me get a job, I'll bet. They said I was too young. Maybe," he continued dramatically, "I might get killed and the coyotes would sit by my body and howl and howl, and the buzzards would fly around, and *then* everybody would be sorry."

His eyes were sparkling. Cenci, who also had been feeling forlorn, was dubious about the coyotes and buzzards but the idea of running away definitely appealed to her.

"Let's each one get a bandanna," she said, "and tie some food up in it and put it on the end of a stick like Dick Whittington. . . ."

Suddenly the day had become glamorous and full of adventure. Talking eagerly, the two children tied up their little bundles and in about half an hour set off at a brisk pace down Rio Grande Street. They climbed and slid down the bank of the river until they reached a narrow path which led along the water's edge. Here they walked along, clambering over the rocks, their scheme growing in proportion until they finally decided they would go all the way to New Mexico. The air, however, was chilly and the brisk walk already caused pangs of hunger to assail the little boy.

"I'll tell you what," he said to Cenci. "Let's eat first and then go on to New Mexico."

Thereupon they found a sheltered place beside the riverbank, untied their handkerchiefs, and settled down for a picnic. The norther created small waves on the surface of the water. Across the river, on the Mexican side, the children could see a group of reed huts and miserable houses where the very poor Mexican families made their dwellings. A little farther up the bank they could also see the entrances of caves which had been hollowed out in the river bank. Here, too, people lived. People too poor to pay even the cheap rent of the huts, living in misery and squalor. Faintly from across the river came the sound of people's voices, of a child crying. Smoke could be seen fluffing out of the doors of some of the huts which did not even possess chimneys. Above the sound of the voices came a louder, more raucous noise, as droves of magpies settled on the branches of the mesquite trees and willows that grew on the water's edge, seeking shelter from the wind.

Luke and Cenci ate slowly, talking over their woes, drawn together by the bond of being left out of things. As they talked, the wind grew sharper and New Mexico seemed to get much farther away. The thought of home, of the warm rosy cookstove in the kitchen, of the cheerful little fire in the grate in Mr. Bronson's study became unbearably attractive. Luke did not want to admit it, and was wondering just how he could word it to Cenci so that she would not think that he was a sissy. After all, he thought, the town was probably organizing the posse already, and no doubt by now everybody in the family was thinking of all his virtues, and he had probably made his point without too much inconvenience to himself.

He looked at Cenci. When she was cold her lips got blue, and already she was shivering in her sweater. Yet he knew that she would never be the one to suggest returning. Just then, as he was about to speak, he saw a figure emerge cautiously from one of the caves on the other side of the river. This cave was at a considerable distance from the others, off to itself and almost hidden by the canebrakes and the cat's-claw. The man did not stand up straight but crouched over as if he were trying to hide, looking furtively first to one side, then to another.

"Look!" exclaimed Luke.

As he and Cenci watched, the man slipped noiselessly into the water and began to swim. The children, frightened but fascinated, could not take their eyes from the figure swimming laboriously toward them. They whispered excitedly together.

"Lots of times," Cenci told him, "people swim across when they haven't got permits and don't dare cross the bridge."

"Why haven't they got permits?" hissed Luke in her ear.

"Oh, all kinds of reasons," answered Cenci through chattering teeth. "Maybe we'd better go."

Luke looked up at the steep bank which it would be necessary for them to scale before getting back to the street.

"We can't go without being seen," he whispered back. "That man will see us. Let's just wait here and stay real still until he gets away."

"I think we'd better hide," said Cenci.

Leaving the remains of their supper on the rock, they crept away, finding shelter behind a bush that grew near-by. By this time the swimmer was nearing the bank.

"He's sick or something," whispered Luke. "He almost can't swim."

"The current is pulling him down," sne answered. "Sometimes the current's awful strong."

Horrified, the children watched that desperate figure, battling against the current which was now sucking and pulling him downstream. He was powerless against it.

"He *is* drowning!" cried Lukey. "We've got to help him. Hurry!"

The two children ran from their hiding place and Lukey picked up a long stick which he held out to the struggling man. After several vain attempts, the man got hold of it and pulled himself ashore, grasping some rushes with his other hand. For a few moments he lay there, too exhausted to move. His breathing was rasping and difficult. Finally he pulled himself painfully to a sitting posture and they saw that he was a thin, small Mexican. He was shaking with cold. His wet clothing or what there was of it, clung to him. There was a wild, hunted look in his eyes, but Cenci said to him softly in Spanish, "Don't be afraid. We're not going to hurt you. Are you hungry?"

Going over to the rock where they had been eating, she picked up two thick sandwiches and took them to the Mexican. They were shocked at the way he ate, gulping the food down in a grim hurry, not leaving a crumb. Luke swallowed hard.

"Let's take him home," he said to Cenci. "Father will know what to do. Tell him again not to be afraid. Father will take care of him. Father always takes care of people."

Perhaps because he was so cold and spent, or perhaps because the two children had been compassionate, the Mexican believed them. He followed them along the riverbank, stumbling and falling from weakness, until they got to the edge of town. The two children helped him up the bank when they got to the Bronson house and propelled him across the street. The study light was on. Nora had not yet returned and no one was at home but Johnny who had fallen asleep pillowed on the bird book, and Mr. Bronson who was sitting by the fire, deep in thought. They opened the door with a burst of wind and then brought in the wretched human being they had unwittingly rescued. The man's cheeks were sunken. His hair was matted and filthy. He scarcely seemed human.

"Father," choked Luke and then he stopped, unable to talk.

"We told him *you* would know what to do," Cenci said and then she and Luke disappeared.

The little boy closed the door and leaned up against the house crying. Suddenly he stopped.

"Go on home, Cenci," he said. "And if you dare tell Matthew and Mark you saw me cry, I'll break your arm."

"I won't tell them," she said, sobbing. "I won't ever tell anybody. Not ever! I promise! Not ever!"

And then she turned and ran quickly and disappeared through the little gate.

11

ALTHOUGH Mr. Bronson was not a practical man, his first thought on seeing the fugitive was to get dry clothes on him and something warm inside of him. He took the trembling Mexican to his own room, and, while he undressed, found some clothing. It did not occur to him as he took a suit from its hanger that this was his "Sunday" suit, the one he used to preach in. It was merely the only suit there, so James got the Mexican into it as quickly as possible.

The sleeves and the trousers were too long, but this was a matter easily remedied. James turned up the cuffs. Then he took the man to the study and, as the tea was cold, he made some fresh coffee and after a while the poor fellow's shivering ceased. It did not enter the heads of either one of them what a pathetic and incongruous figure he made, emaciated, unshaven, wearing a suit too large for him, his scrawny neck sticking up out of the collar like a plucked chicken. The Mexican was warm and dry and at the moment nothing else mattered. Also he was extremely tired. He leaned back in the claw-and-ball-foot chair and for a long while said nothing as James paced up and down the floor. Finally the minister sat down beside him.

"You *are* Pánfilo García, aren't you?" he asked.

The Mexican started to deny it, then looked into the minister's deep and honest eyes. "Yes," he said. "You are right, *señor.*"

"Why did you return?" James asked.

In his halting, broken English, Pánfilo tried to explain. He had a cousin in Yucatán, a saddle-mender. This cousin had managed to send Pánfilo a little money, enough so he could go to Yucatán. He had promised to shelter him and give him work, and perhaps in a few years this affair would blow over and he could send for Lupe, his wife, and they could start all over again. Lupe dared not cross the bridge now, and she could not swim, especially with the little boy, Ignacio.

"So I came over to bring them part of the money," Pánfilo concluded simply. "They need it badly. And to tell them good-bye. I could not get anybody to do this errand for me. Everybody is afraid."

"I see. But why did you swim across in the daytime?"

"Because of the river. The current is strong. At night it ees —what you call? *Peligroso. Muy peligroso.*"

"Too dangerous?"

"*Sí, señor.* I was going to hide in the bushes until dark. I did not see the children. But they saved me. They saved my life. I was too weak. . . ."

"Pánfilo," said James, "you are a brave man. You meant well. But it was too risky. I'm sure there are not many people in this part of Texas who would not recognize you. Your picture is everywhere—in the post office, in the town hall, tacked to telephone posts. I know about your history. I know you are a completely innocent man. But in the eyes of the law you are guilty.

"Laws," he continued, "are quite often unjust. And yet, I am sorry to say, they are necessary. I can tell by looking at you that you are a good man. You are not a murderer, a killer——"

"No," whispered Pánfilo, the look of terror coming back into his eyes again. "I do not even know how it happened. It was not my gun. Señor, I could not keel anything . . . my wife Lupe always used to laugh at me. If we had a chicken I could not cut off his head. It was Lupe who had to do it. I could not keel. In the War even, I had to shut my eyes. . . ."

James had heard many versions of the shooting which had

happened on the day the Bronsons had arrived in Donde. Now he listened to Pánfilo's version, naked in its ugly truth.

Pánfilo and Lupe had both been ill for a long time and so had their child Ignacio. Pánfilo had lost his job. They lived in a miserable one-room house with a damp, cold, dirt floor. They ran out of money, first, and finally of food. In desperation Pánfilo got out of bed and looked for work. But he was too weak and ill. Nobody would hire him. All that morning, the morning of the shooting, and the night before he had heard his child crying, *"Tengo hambre"* (I am hungry). Finally Pánfilo could bear it no longer. He went to a bakery in whose windows were displayed cakes, pies, buns, bread, doughnuts, all sorts of mouth-watering food. Surely, he thought, if he went in and asked for just one of the buns the clerk would let him have it.

He went in. The warm crusty fragrance of the bakery was almost overpowering. The shop was filled with people and nobody noticed him. Beside him on the counter, within finger reach, lay a tray of buns, and he did not know what had got into him. He had never stolen before. But it seemed he could hear his child's voice saying, over and over, *Tengo hambre, tengo hambre, Papá.* Everybody was talking and he was quite sure that nobody would see him and, after all, who would miss one of those brown buns? Besides, the clerk was busy and cross. So Pánfilo did not beg, but simply reached out his hand and picked up, not one of those beautiful buns, but three. Hurriedly he put them in his pocket. And yet, quick as he had been, someone did see him.

One of the customers in the bakery happened to be the sheriff, and it was he who saw Pánfilo, and made a lunge for him. Everything became confused. All Pánfilo could think about was to get away from this strong man and to get out of the bakery with the three warm buns. Weak as he was, he suddenly felt possessed of a superhuman strength and he fought back. He saw the revolver in the sheriff's hand, but by now he did not seem like Pánfilo at all, a quiet, home-loving, humble man. He felt like a maniac. He tried to wrench the revolver from the sheriff's hands and neither the Mexican nor anyone else knew exactly how it happened. Women were screaming. And the revolver went off. Pánfilo seemed to be in a kind of walking dream, when he found out that he had killed the sheriff. He had not intended to kill the sheriff. He had not even intended to steal. All of it had happened in just a few minutes. And afterwards when Pánfilo was waiting in the jail, again he had felt that maniacal strength, a slyness, a cunning that was not akin to his nature, and he had managed to escape across the river and to hide on the Mexican side of the Rio Grande, until today. . . .

James leaned over and patted Pánfilo gently on the shoulder. "I know you are speaking the truth," he said. "To me you need no punishment whatever. You have had too much already. Nevertheless," he looked at him squarely, "your being here has placed me in a difficult position. These very laws which are so often wrong are also a protection for me and for my family. For you and yours. Because of that I shall have to give you up to the authorities."

The Mexican said nothing.

"There are two roads ahead of us, Pánfilo," said Mr. Bronson. "One is this: I shall call the police. It will take them, oh— perhaps fifteen or twenty minutes to get here. This house has plenty of doors. I shall leave you alone. If the police arrive and you are gone——" He paused. He wanted to say, "But of course you would be caught anyway," yet seeing the Mexican shrinking into the depths of the chair, he did not.

"The other road," he said, "is for you to remain here and go with the police quietly and obediently. If you do that, it will be easier for you in the end and I promise you my wife and I will take care of your wife and baby. Until you are free we shall see to it that they are fed and clothed and have proper medical care. They can come to visit you every day in the jail."

"Until I am *free?*" asked Pánfilo. "Señor, I shall never be free! They'll hang me. Everything is against me. They'll hang me!"

"No," interrupted the minister. "This is a country where justice prevails. I intend to get a lawyer for you. I shall do everything in my power for you, even if it means going to the governor."

"You are going to see the governor!" gasped Pánfilo. "Just for *me?* Why should you do that?"

"Because," said James, "I do not like to see injustice. Because I know you are an innocent man. There are other people in this town who agree with me. I have a friend, Mr. Lindley, who is editor of the newspaper here. He will help me. We cannot possibly fail."

There was a long silence.

"Please go to the telephone," said Pánfilo at length, "and call the police. I trust you. I shall do as you say. But first the address—the address of Lupe, my wife. She has been hiding, too—she needs this money. . . ."

James got a pencil and pad from his desk, wrote down the name and address. "Mrs. Bronson and I will go to her tonight," he said. "Don't worry."

He stood a moment at his study table. "Before I telephone the police," he said, "may I ask you a question? Would you like me to call a priest?"

Pánfilo shook his head in negation. "Señor," he said, "I am not a Catholic. I am what you call a Liberal. I have no religion. I do not need a priest. Thank you."

James stood there and began turning the leaves of his Bible. "I am a minister, Pánfilo," he said, "the same as a priest. Even though you do not need me, it has been my habit for many years to read something from the Bible, to say a word of prayer before entering into any great undertaking. As a favor to me, would you mind?"

The Mexican looked up at him. "For you, señor," he said, "I would do anything."

"Thank you," said James, and then he brought his open Bible and again sat down before the Mexican, read to him the thirteenth chapter of First Corinthians. When he finished, he closed the Bible and laid it back on his desk.

"Faith, hope, and love, Pánfilo," he murmured. "You already have love, and I think perhaps now you may even have a little hope. But what both of us need is faith. I do not need to ask the Lord for more love or more hope, but for more faith, yes."

When Pánfilo saw James Bronson starting to kneel on the little rug beside his study table chair, he, too, got up and knelt beside him. After the prayer they arose and Pánfilo, Mexican-fashion, shook the minister's hand.

"Thank you, *Padre*," he said. "I did need a priest, after all."

He sat down again in the lovely chair. He even smiled a little. "You may now call the police," he said. "I am ready."

Two hours later Nora returned from her visit and at once started preparations for supper. The cool norther had given color to her cheeks; she looked unusually pretty, and as James absently built up the fire in the cookstove she chattered to him gaily. The soldier's wife, she said, had not been very ill, mostly lonely and homesick. They were from Wisconsin.

"And by the by," she said, "on the way back I had an inspiration. Let's have an 'At Home' for the soldiers once a week, say on Tuesday evenings. Nothing fancy. Just games and conversation, and afterwards something simple to eat, like gingerbread and milk. I'm sure they'd come, James. There is nothing much here in Donde for them in the way of amusement. Except for the officers, of course. They need a touch of home, those fellows."

Absently James agreed with her. The only thing was, he said, it would entail too much work for her. And in her condition. . . .

"In my condition, fiddlesticks!" she exclaimed. "I never felt better in my life! And I'd love to do it."

"Well——"

She now looked at him with apprehension. James spoke as from a great distance. His eyes had a preoccupied faraway look. His face was drawn.

"James! What happened while I was gone? Tell me."

"I—I just sent an innocent man to jail," he replied tonelessly, "that's all."

"James! Who?"

"Pánfilo García."

"Oh! The murderer?"

"He is not a murderer, dear." James then told her the entire story. "I—I—hardly knew what to do," he concluded. "It was, I believe, one of the hardest decisions I've ever had to make."

"You did the right thing," Nora said with conviction. They had moved to the dining room now and were setting the table. Suddenly, holding a plate in midair, she asked sharply,

"James, what suit did you give him?"

He looked at her, frowning.

"Why, the only one in the closet, dear," he replied. "I had this one on."

"You mean you gave him your *good* suit?"

He nodded.

"Oh, James, how *could* you? Are you going to preach in this one tomorrow?"

"I'll have to. My sermon will be just as good. People are not coming to look at my suit."

"But James! Your everyday one was hanging right there on the line! I cleaned it in gasoline yesterday and hung it out so the wind would take the odor out. Why didn't you give him that one? And where are *his* clothes?"

"They—they were just a bunch of rags, Nora, crawling with vermin. Just an old thin sweater and—I burned them up. An innocent man," said James, "and I gave him up to the authorities.

Brett has told me that if Pánfilo is caught, he will surely hang.
I cannot believe that, Nora. I refuse to believe it. If he is convicted I'm going to go to the governor. I shall do everything
I possibly can and Brett will be with me. People in this country
have been horrified by the atrocities in Belgium, by the terrible
conditions that still exist in Europe and yet here right at our own
doorsteps are conditions just as bad. I feel responsible for giving
him up, yet I had to, but having given him up my responsibility
toward him is doubled. As soon as possible we must find his
wife and child and see what we can do for them and then tonight
I'm going to go and visit him at the jail."

Nora looked at her husband standing there in his shabby
second-best suit, patched and mended at one knee. At first
when they had begun talking she thought of the ledger on her
desk, of the size of the grocery bill not yet paid. Now she forgot about them. Yes, she thought, tomorrow James would preach
in this shabby suit. If necessary for him to go to the governor
this would be the suit he would wear, and yet——

Impulsively she went up to him and took one of his hands in
hers, brushed his fingers against her soft lips, held his hand
against her cheek. "I'm sorry, dear," she said. "It doesn't matter
about the suit. Now I must get on with supper. This is the
first cool day we've had since we came here and the boys will be
ravenous. I'll hurry things along and if you want to go immediately to the jail to see Pánfilo I'll go alone to see his wife
or maybe the twins will take me. What did you say her name
was?"

"Lupe," he answered.

"Lupe," she repeated. "Did he give you her address?"

"Yes," answered James Bronson, "I have it. It's on my study
table. It's all written down on the pad with the notes I was
making for my sermon tomorrow. I put it next to my Bible,
Nora, it's right there next to my Bible."

12

TODAY, an afternoon in November, a dust storm was blowing. The wind howled around the Bronson's house, the sun was a jaundiced yellow, and although it was early afternoon it was so dark it had become necessary to turn on the lights. James sat in his study working on a sermon, the one he planned to preach at the midnight service on Christmas Eve. A few scattered notes lay penciled on a sheet of paper in front of him but they lacked inspiration. He did not feel as if he were getting anywhere with it.

From time to time his eyes strayed to the window seat and finally he stood up and walked over toward it. He knew now what the trouble was. Ordinarily on a Friday afternoon a little girl would be sitting there looking at picture books or playing at some quiet game of her own, or trying to sew. Cenci. None of the boys seemed to object to the fact that Cenci was allowed in the study when their father was working on a sermon. They themselves never dared to enter. They did not even dare knock on the door unless it was almost a matter of life and death. But Cenci would sit there all afternoon, even on "sermon days." When she turned the pages of a book, she turned them so softly that he seldom heard her. She did not ask any questions. She did not knock things over and plunge around as the boys did. Working away at his desk, Mr. Bronson would look up and see the slender little figure against the stained glass. Almost she seemed like part of the room itself.

But today she was not here. She was at home in bed with a slight cold and he missed her and could not work. While he sat there thinking about her he heard a timid knock on the outside study door and for once was glad to have an interruption during his writing. He got up and admitted Miss Ivy Vail, the spinster he had noticed at Little Bonne Femme the first Sunday, the one who had asked him to visit her ailing father.

He had never got very well acquainted with her for she was too shy and reticent, yet he had grown accustomed to seeing her in the same pew Sunday after Sunday and always in his sermons he would be conscious of a response in her. He felt that he got closer to her through his preaching than in any other way. After her father's death he was distressed to learn that although Miss Ivy belonged to one of the "best" families in Donde she had been left almost penniless except for her small house.

"Oh, I hope you weren't busy," she said, when she came in today, noticing the scattered sheets of paper on his table.

James reassured her. "No, as a matter of fact," he said, "I was trying to write a sermon and was making no headway with it. I was just sitting here wasting my time. To be quite frank, Miss Vail, I was hoping for an interruption such as your visit to give me an excuse for not working." He laughed in a disarming way, and Miss Vail's face brightened and she smiled. But when he asked her if there was anything he could do for her she said, in a tone of controlled desperation; "Yes. Well, at least I hope so." She told him haltingly and with embarrassment of her financial straits, that she needed to go to work but had been brought up to be a "lady" and so didn't know how to do anything.

James regarded her thoughtfully. No inspiration had come to him for his sermon but suddenly an inspiration came to him about Miss Vail. On the surface the idea seemed completely absurd.

"I know of a position," said James, "I know of someone who

needs help immediately and very badly. I feel confident that you are the exact person for this position and if you wish I shall be only too glad to telephone and recommend you."

He had been in the *Eagle* office that morning and knew that Brett was in need of a society editor on the paper. Since the return of Pánfilo García, the circulation of the *Eagle* had doubled. Brett advertised for a girl and the first one lasted only until the noon hour when she fled in hysterics. What a horrible, messy place to work in! And what a beast Mr. Lindley was, to swear at her. The second girl lasted a week, but when the paper came off the press and she had misspelled the names of ten people she was fired on the spot. The third one had once been an English teacher and had changed the grammar, the punctuation, and a few paragraphs in one of Brett's editorials. He didn't insert an ad this time, just wrote it on the plate-glass window. It wouldn't do any good, he assured James grimly.

"What is the position?" asked Miss Ivy timidly.

"It's working as society editor on the *Donde Eagle*," the minister said. "Mr. Lindley and I are very good friends. He talked to me only this morning asking if I could possibly find somebody to fill the position."

"But I never worked on a paper. I've never worked *any-where*," said Miss Ivy. "And I've heard that Mr. Lindley is so—so——"

Again James laughed. "You've also heard the expression, 'His bark is worse than his bite,' haven't you? I know Mr. Lindley well and he has a very tender heart. Don't let him frighten you. Why don't you go to him right now and while you're on the way I'll call him up? Sometimes if you think things over too much it isn't so good."

Miss Ivy rose, gathered up her gloves and pocketbook, straightened her prim little hat which the wind had blown to one side. "Yes," she said, a note of grim determination in her voice. "I'll go. But I'm sure he won't hire me. And oh, you *will* call him up, won't you?"

"Certainly I'll call. At once," answered James. "Now remember, don't be afraid. Good-bye and good luck to you, Miss Vail."

As soon as the door had closed after her James went to the telephone only to find that it was disconnected, that the dust storm had blown the wires down. He could not reach Brett. He was dismayed and thought first he would follow Miss Ivy and say a good word for her. Then he thought, No, maybe this is a bit of luck. It might be better for her to walk in and get the job without any recommendation except herself. He hung up the receiver and went back to his study table. Odd, he thought, that such an interruption as this should have set his mind to flowing. He began writing on his sermon and soon forgot about Miss Ivy and everything else except the thing he was trying to say.

Twenty minutes later Miss Ivy stood outside the *Eagle* office, bracing herself to go in. It would have astonished most people to know that Miss Ivy was young, or ever had been young. She did not look it. She was thin and angular. She parted her hair in the middle and braided it in long braids which she wore in a big flat wheel at the back of her head, secured firmly in place by sturdy hairpins. She wore no make-up except a little talcum powder. Her clothes were sensible and drab and extremely neat. Since girlhood she had taken care of her father, who, though an invalid, was a tyrant. She had also helped out various brothers, sisters, nieces, and nephews who should have helped themselves but didn't because they could always depend on "good old Ivy." When her father died Miss Ivy was shocked to find that after all the doctor's bills and funeral expenses had been paid there was nothing left except the house and car and a little cash. None of the brothers, sisters, nieces, and nephews whom she had helped came to her rescue when she needed them. In fact, there had been even some hard feeling because the house and car had been left to her in her father's will, instead of to them.

Miss Ivy's house was a narrow, brown little structure, as plain as she was. The garage was also narrow, and so was the cheap little high-breasted Model-T Ford. In fact, everything about Miss Ivy was narrow, her life, her body, her house, her garage, her car. That is, everything that anybody could see. Had people cared to look deeper than the exterior, they might have been astonished to see that her heart was as wide and far reaching as the blue sky, if not wider. And as for her dreams, ah, they were magnificent. But nobody knew about her dreams. If anybody could have seen her at night, bathed and dressed in her nightgown, combing out her thick, shining hair, they might even have found that she was beautiful. Her heavy-lidded eyes were large and soft, a small secret smile hovered around her mouth, her skin was luminous. But of course nobody ever saw Miss Ivy on these occasions, for she was a modest person and always closed the door.

After her father's death, panic seized her. She *had* to do something to make a living. The day she started out job-hunting she was so frightened that she looked even narrower and more pinched than usual. She answered a few ads and became more terrified than ever when her qualifications, or rather her lack of qualifications, were aired and discussed. She was about to give up when she thought of Reverend Bronson who preached such beautiful sermons and had been so kind to her father.

But, oh, dear! Now Reverend Bronson had sent her to Brett Lindley. Of course, he said he would telephone. But when she reached the *Eagle* office she stopped. She simply could not summon the courage to go inside. She read the advertisement which the editor had written with soap in bold letters on the plate-glass window: "DO YOU WANT A JOB?" and all her fears came back in full force. She was mortally afraid of Brett Lindley. She had heard too much about him, about his drinking and swearing, his terrible temper. Why, she had heard that he sometimes threw pastepots and inkwells at people when he was angry! And think of all the society editors he had fired! Even an English teacher.

What Miss Ivy had not heard was the reason back of Brett Lindley's behavior. Nobody except Hunchback Pete, and lately James Bronson, knew what Brett had been like before he came to Donde. They didn't know about the tragedy of Brett's life, which Pete understood so well.

Not too many years ago he had been a happily married newspaper man, a reporter on the *San Antonio Light*. His wife Rose had been both beautiful and good, their existence had been an idyll. The future stretched ahead for them, a bright vision. They had a pretty little garden, they had paid for their house, they were soon to have a baby. In the afternoons Brett would come home early and work in the garden, but he often forgot to put the tools away. Rose would put them away, tactfully upbraiding him for his untidy habits. Once she picked up the rake and said, "Brett, darling, it's dangerous to leave a rake lying like this, with the forks up—one of the neighbor's children might step on it."

But it was Rose who tripped on the rake, one night after dark when she went out to get some clothes from the line. They hadn't been quite dry when she brought in the rest of the washing earlier in the afternoon, but it started to threaten rain so she decided to get them. Such a little thing, tripping over a rake. It was, the doctors said, the manner in which she had fallen. Such a little thing. But because of it the baby had died, and Rose, too.

After that Brett sold the house and put the money in the bank. Eventually he lost his job for he began going on binges that lasted for days. He became bitter and scornful and hard to get along with. His friends at first sympathized with him, then started avoiding him, until finally he had no friends except Hunchback Pete, in the job-printing department. Brett liked Pete and when he and Rose had been so happy they would invite him to their home, especially on Sundays. They were certainly nice to him, and made him feel it was his home as well as theirs, and Rose never treated him as if he were a hunchback, like most people did. Yes, Pete understood. He understood, too, that it was not only grief that tore at Brett's heart. It went deeper than that.

"I killed her," Brett said to him over and over, "she died because of *me*. I was to blame."

Brett didn't try to get a job after he was fired. He moved in with Pete, who had a room over a livery stable. Every week he drew out enough money for his share of their expenses, and for his liquor. Pete took good care of him. If Brett wasn't there when Pete came home from work Pete looked for him until he found him and brought him home. One day Pete found an ad for the sale of the *Donde Eagle,* for a modest sum, as the paper was not doing well. He showed the ad to Brett.

"You need to get away from San Antonio," Pete said, "you've always wanted to own your own paper. I'll go with you. This *Donde Eagle's* about to fold, but you can build her up. The only thing she needs is a good editor."

For the first time in months a spark of interest lit up Brett's eyes. Maybe, he thought, Pete was right. If he could get away from this city so full of memories, if he could just *forget.* . . .

Thus he bought the *Donde Eagle.* His bitterness against life went into the venom of his editorials. He began a campaign against the housing conditions in Mexican Town. He wrote what he pleased, made some enemies and few friends, but Donde read the paper. He worked like a fiend. At Pete's insistence, he got a room at Donde's best hotel, the D-Brand, while Pete took up his abode in a little room back of the press room.

When Brett wanted to move in with him, Pete said, "There ain't no space for two," which was an understatement, "and besides," Pete amended, "it'll look better for the editor to have a good address."

"The hell with how the address looks," growled Brett, "but this room *is* crowded. It's crowded even for one. Why don't you come with *me?*"

"No, thanks," answered Pete. "I feel out of place if things is too clean. I like it inky. Leave me be."

All this, of course, Miss Ivy did not know, as she waited, trembling with fear, in front of the *Eagle* building, a tin-roofed affair, hot in summer and cold in winter.

The dust storm had become worse. Fine particles of grit cut against her face, she could feel it inside the rims of her eyes, in her nostrils, between her teeth. Then she opened the door and went in. Later on she used to laugh and say that the only reason she went in the building was simply for shelter, for a chance to breathe.

Brett Lindley was pecking away at his typewriter, his brow furrowed. He was chewing on an unlighted cigar held fiercely between his teeth, moving it from one side of his mouth to the other as he wrote. All of this Miss Ivy noticed in a flash, the way people do sometimes, unaware at the moment that any impression at all is being made. She also saw, through her dust-reddened eyes, that an underbrush of rusty hair bristled on the backs of his hands and fingers. After she got to know him better, it seemed to her that when he was writing a particularly scathing editorial, this hair seemed to stand on end, quivering like live wires.

The wind blew the door shut when she went in, and she was so choked with dust that she began to cough. A cloud of papers flew up from the floor and Brett Lindley looked up in irritation.

"What do you want?" he barked.

Miss Ivy, still coughing, pointed to the sign on the window. "A job," she managed to say at last, wiping her eyes and blowing her nose.

Brett Lindley looked back with preoccupation at his manuscript, x-d out a word, and then said, blowing the keys of his typewriter, "Hell of a place to live, if you ask me. The keys are so gritty I feel as if I were writing on sand."

He surveyed her without enthusiasm, a wisp of a woman as gray as the fine sifting dust. She was definitely not much to look at. Age, he surmised, about forty-two. Actually, she was twenty-seven.

"Mr. Bronson sent me," she explained in a faint voice. "He said you needed a society editor. He said he would telephone. Did he?"

"No, the wires are down."

"Oh, dear!"

"Why did he send you? Any experience?" Brett asked her.

"No," she replied blankly.

"Can you use a typewriter?" he asked.

"Only with two fingers," she replied, even more bleakly. The interview was worse than she had expected. Why in the world had she assumed she could work on a newspaper? And why had Reverend Bronson sent her here?

"Hmm," growled Brett again. He got up, began pacing the floor.

"Can you spell?" he barked. She brightened at this.

"Yes," she admitted modestly. "I always got 100 in spelling. But I was never good in chemistry," she added.

"The hell with chemistry. Can you write? I mean, do you have aspirations to be an author?"

"Oh, no," she almost whispered, "I wasn't very good in English, either."

Did the frown disappear from his face, or was she just imagining it? He paced up and down the floor again, kicking aside newspapers and curls of paper with his feet. "Do you know anybody in this town?" he asked.

"Of course. My grandparents and parents were born here, and so was I, so naturally I know almost everybody."

"Well, that settles it then, if you can manage on eighteen dollars a week. I need names in my paper. NAMES," he fairly bellowed. "Mrs. K. Vandergier-Stable borrowed a book at the library Tuesday. The Uplifter's Society held a rummage sale in the mansion of Mrs. I. Frown on Thursday afternoon. The net proceeds were $4.89, which will be contributed to the Layette Fund. Mrs. L. Q. Stumpy will entertain the Literary Club next Friday. The subject for discussion will be *Hamlet*. Of course, few of the ladies have read any of *Hamlet* except the soliloquy. But refreshments will be served and the president hopes if there is time a few hands of bridge can be played afterwards. Those present will be—NAMES—that's what this paper needs. And spelled right, mind you. Practically everybody wants his name in the paper, no matter how much he denies it. How about the salary?"

"You mean"—Miss Ivy's lips trembled—"you mean I'm hired?"

"Certainly you're hired! What did you think?"

"The salary is fine. I mean it's more than I expected—without experience."

"I don't want anybody with experience. And you start to work tonight."

"Tonight?"

"Yep. I want you to cover that big wedding at the Methodist Church. Barbaric custom, if you ask me, big weddings. Vulgar. Well, cover it anyhow. Get the facts, and get them right. Church decorations, what the bride wore, what the whole damn family wore, who sang *At Dawning*. And NAMES. If a dog barks during the ceremony, get his name and license number. Do you know these people, by the way?"

"Oh, yes," answered Miss Ivy weakly, "I went to a shower for the bride last week. I went to school with her."

"Good. Bring your stuff back tonight. I'll be here. The story's got to make this week's paper."

At that moment Pete emerged from the pressroom carrying a page proof, still wet.

"Pete!" yelled Brett, nodding to Miss Ivy, "This is the new member of our staff. Meet Miss—Miss—" suddenly Brett burst into hearty laughter. "NAMES," he said, "all I've been yelling about is names, and I didn't ask yours!"

Miss Ivy couldn't quite understand the sudden singing of her heart as she joined quietly in the merriment. "It's Vail," she said, "Miss Ivy Vail. But around town I'm just called Miss Ivy."

"Well, Miss Ivy, I'll see you after the wedding."

Brett walked back to his typewriter, frowned, blew the dust from the keys. "Damned grit," he murmured, and began pecking away. He didn't hear Miss Ivy when she left, softly closing the door behind her.

Miss Ivy had not worked on the *Donde Eagle* a week before she was as much a part of the place as the calendar on the wall. She was appalled at the untidiness of the office, but when she found out that Brett Lindley liked it that way, she let it alone. Except, that is, for her own desk which soon stood out, a gem of neatness and order, amidst the general confusion. She kept it dusted and always knew where everything was. She kept her own typewriter cleaned and repaired, always managed to have a fresh ribbon in it, and covered it up when she left the office with a cover she herself had made out of black oilcloth. She also kept a little geranium plant on her desk, though how it ever grew in that stale air was a miracle, but it grew nonetheless.

A strange companionship grew up between this trio, Brett, Pete, and Miss Ivy. Often when they had to work late at night, Pete would offer her a cup of a brackish brew he called "cawfee," and Miss Ivy learned to drink it, though gingerly, for she had seen inside Pete's quarters and knew how he made his cawfee. He simply added more water and more coffee to the pot on his stove, never bothering to wash the pot until the grounds came to the top. But, Pete complained, when he had to empty the grounds, rinse the pot, and start all over again, it tasted weak. There wasn't no body to it, he said.

Miss Ivy soon found herself kicking aside the papers on the floor as she waded through them the way Brett did on that first day, when nobody was looking. It was fun. Of course, when the mess got too bad, they would have a sweeping-out, and for a day or two the floor would be almost bare. But nobody seemed very happy on those days. The office was something like Pete's cawfee, kind of weak. No body. Nevermore, the cat, walked around sorrowfully and purred less loudly than usual.

Sometimes Matthew Bronson was allowed to join this group,

feeling important and grownup. At present he did only odd jobs about the office and delivered papers, but in the distant future he hoped to be a writer, although he had not confided the secret to anyone yet. His father frequently came to the *Eagle* office, too, but Pete did not like preachers, even though he was forced to admit, reluctantly, that the Reverend Bronson had become fairly adept at folding church bulletins.

So there Miss Ivy was, as firmly established as the floor itself, and as unobtrusive. Brett never praised her, but if she made a mistake he had plenty to say. What none of them knew was that from the moment Miss Ivy had first entered that littered office, she had fallen in love. The ingredients for falling in love, she had found, are not always moonlight and roses. In her case they happened to be a dust storm, the disorder of a newspaper office, the click of an ancient typewriter, a big uncouth man who swore at almost every breath, got drunk on Saturday nights, and whose motto in life was, "The whole world stinks."

When her day's work was done she went back to her narrow little house, cherishing the beautiful, warm secret in her heart.

"It is better to love than to be loved," she had read once, and for the present she was content with that. Loving, she thought, must be like drinking wine (although she did not often drink wine). It is the person who drinks the wine who feels its exhilaration, not the person looking on. She did not aspire to dream that her love might possibly be returned. How could it be? Look at her! Prim and pinched at the mouth and no more exciting than a wisp of smoke. And Rose, Pete had told her over one of his cups of acrid cawfee, Rose had been beautiful. He had shown Miss Ivy her picture in her wedding dress and she was as lovely as her name, dark-haired and dimpled and soft. Oh, no! Miss Ivy never dreamed of replacing Rose.

But she did have one aspiration, one dream that was not beyond the limits of probability. This dream was that some day Brett might drop in and spend an hour or so in her own little house. The house was something like Miss Ivy, drab and dull on the outside, but lovely within. She possessed, from distant and more affluent days, rich rugs and furniture, delicate dishes, fine silver, a good library, one or two beautiful paintings. She had a little gas fire in the pseudo-fireplace of the tiny living room and in the evenings when it was lit things were really quite cozy and attractive.

And in spite of the fact that Miss Ivy had not been very good in English in High School, she loved poetry, although she never mentioned this to Brett. Sometimes, hoping he might drop in, she would put her own well-worn copy of William Blake on the table next to the big chair by the fire. But that, she knew, would be *too* obvious, so she would reluctantly take it away. It was enough just to love.

13

NORA kept the sewing machine in the kitchen. It was bright there, she had the kitchen table to work on, and also when she was cooking something at the same time, she could keep an eye on it. This afternoon, shortly before Thanksgiving, she was making homemade noodle soup.

She loved to sew, and had a knack with the needle, although with four sons and a husband, her sewing had not been much of the inventive or imaginative type. She made all of her husband's shirts, as well as her sons'. And a shirt, she insisted, no matter what you did to it, still remained a shirt. With the current vogue for flashy silk ones, she had had a little more fun along that line, and for the twins' Christmas presents she had recently completed a silk shirt apiece, whose colors would put your eye out. She also made all of the family's underwear. She bought flour sacking and hemmed dish towels. She bought pillow tubing and made pillowcases. She made sheets. The useful things she had learned from Mrs. Hodges on her father's farm had not been learned in vain, she had found out during the years of her marriage.

Near the sewing machine she kept a little rush-bottomed rocking chair which had once belonged to her grandmother, and beside it her basket of mending. Today she was mending, or trying to. In her lap she held the trousers of James's second-best suit, her usually serene forehead puckered with anxiety.

This hole in the knee—definitely it hadn't worn through entirely because of his kneeling upon it. It had been torn, maybe by a nail, though she didn't see how.

Ministers, she thought, with a sigh, are poor in a way in which no other people are poor. They and their families are always in the public eye. They have to have expensive educations and do a great deal of entertaining. If only James had not been so obdurate about accepting the extra money Mr. Graham had offered. Just a *little* more. But she and James did not speak about Mr. Graham these days. She no longer mentioned to him that he was supposed to be on vacation. . . . Well, now, back to that hole in his trousers again.

"James!" she called to him sharply, hearing him in the next room.

I'd better behave myself, he thought as he came in the kitchen at her call, when Nora speaks in a tone like that her redheaded temper is up.

He was quite right. Her eyes were flashing fire as she held up the trousers for inspection.

"Did you want something, dear?" he asked meekly.

"Look at this, James Bronson!" she exclaimed. "Just take a good look. It's all very well and good to give your best suit away to a half-drowned Mexican, and I'm quite sure your sermons would be just as inspiring if you preached them in your nightshirt. However, you might give a thought to the feelings of your family. Matthew and Mark came to me today and said one of their friends had called you 'the rag-picker preacher.' Not to mention *my* feelings, of course."

James viewed the trousers. He was extremely busy today. He did not like mundane interruptions like these, when he was trying to select a text for next Sunday's sermon. However, he certainly had not realized that his children had been hurt, nor that Nora, usually so uncomplaining, had been humiliated. So he replied very gently, "I'm sorry, dear. What do you want me to do about it?"

The fire in Nora's eyes died down. Poor James, she thought, he could not help being a dreamer, and he hadn't even lost his temper, when hers had flared up so.

"I want you to take these to Jacob Stein," she said with a sigh.

"Jacob Stein?" repeated James. "Who's he?"

"He's a Jew," said Nora. "As far as I know, the only Jew in Donde. He owns that fashionable Men's Haberdashery and Tailor Shop on Main Street. I'm sure you've seen it. Anyhow, I've heard that he's an artist at mending, that he can weave back a hole in a piece of wool so expertly that it is unnoticeable. Today is Monday. I wish you'd take these trousers to him and see if he can perform some miracle with them before Sunday. He's terribly busy, and maybe he won't want to be bothered with it. But at least you can try. Better take the coat along, too. He might find some wide seams which will yield a few extra threads for him."

"Very well, dear," James said. And suddenly looking at Nora's anxious face, he reached out a hand and caressed her hair. "Poor Nora," he said, "you *do* have to put up with a lot, don't you? I don't know what I ever would have done without you, all these years. Why you married me in the first place is more than I can understand."

"I married you because I wanted to," she said laughing, "and I want you to stop poor Nora-ing me. Now take this suit quickly and try to be home in time for supper. I'm making some of your favorite noodle soup. Get along."

James wrapped up the suit, went to the back gate, and stepped out on Mesquite Street. He saw Johnny happily at play with a homely little Mexican boy named Jesús de María Ávila y Hernandez, but called by his friends, Jesucito. Cenci was there, too, but alone, disconsolately bouncing a ball against the adobe wall. One entire side of the Vecindad consisted of an adobe wall, without doors or windows, and next to it a vacant lot. Cenci missed Luke who was now, like the twins, also the proud owner of a job, delivering small parcels for Tasman's Grocery Store, which adjoined the *Donde Eagle* on Main Street. Mr. and Mrs. Tasman had joined Little Bonne Femme not long ago. All the boys were diligently saving up Christmas money.

Just why the children preferred to play in the vacant lot of a tenement when they had lovely yards of their own was a mystery James had been unable to fathom. Today, as he stepped out on the street, Cenci spied him and came running toward him.

"Oh, Mr. Bronson! Where are you going? May I go with you, please?"

James had looked forward to doing a little meditating as he walked along the street alone, but seeing the loneliness in the little face upturned to his, he said, "Certainly. That is, if you make me a promise. You see, I'm embarking upon a rather delicate mission, but if you'll promise to keep very quiet and not say anything, you may go with me."

"Cross my heart and hope to die," she said quickly. "I promise. I'll button up my mouth, tight as wax."

They began walking down the street toward town. After an appropriate pause, she said, tactfully, trying to conceal her curiosity, "Did you say you were going on a delicate mission?"

He sighed. "Yes. I'm taking my suit to the tailor's, to see what he can do about the hole in the knee of the trousers. He may not want to do it."

"Oh! Well, it needs mending. That hole looked awful big last Sunday. I think it's spreading."

"Hmm. . . So *you* noticed it, too! Did it embarrass you?"

"Oh, no! I just thought you must have been doing an extra lot of praying lately, to make it spread so."

"So that's what you thought!"

"Yes." She walked along silently for a few moments. Then, "I like to hear you pray, Mr. Bronson."

"Why, Cenci?"

"Well, I don't know. When I pray I ask for—well, special things, like ordering from the mail-order catalogue. Only in the mail-order catalogue, I practically *know* I'll get what I order. But when I pray, I'm pretty sure I won't."

"What do you pray for?"

"I pray for Kitty, the lost kitty. I pray for a father and mother. For brothers and sisters. You see it's an order, ordering a list of things from Heaven. Sometimes, I start off my prayers, 'Lord, God Almighty.' It sounds good and *might* help, or will it? Is it all right to start a prayer, 'Lord, God Almighty'? It has a kind of thundering sound."

"Quite all right."

"But when *you* pray I feel—oh, I don't know. It's different. It makes me feel good inside and I don't mind things so much, like losing Kitty. . . ."

By this time they had reached Main Street.

"To what tailor are you going?" asked the little girl. A tailor Nora had recommended, James told her, a Mr. Jacob Stein.

"Oh! *Him!*"

"What's wrong with him?" asked James, looking down at Cenci severely. "My wife says he's the best one in town."

"Oh, he's a good tailor, I guess. But he's stingy. Everybody says so. And he's as rich as greases, too."

"Croesus, dear, not greases."

"Well, creases, then. He's as rich as creases. He shouldn't be so stingy."

"Has he ever been stingy to you?"

"No. I don't even know him. I've only seen him. He has a funny nose."

"If you don't know him, then, Cenci dear, you should reserve judgment upon him. It isn't fair to say a man is stingy just because you've *heard* he is, is it?"

"No, I guess not. I hadn't thought of *that.*"

"Is he a native Texan?"

"No. Of course I ought to reserve judgment, because I wasn't even born when he came here. But people say he came from New York a long time ago with his mother. For his health, not hers.

Then she died instead of him, and he stayed on all by himself because by that time he was too rich to leave his store. He hasn't got a wife or anything. That's the store, see it? Let's look in at the window."

Stein's Men's Haberdashery and Clothing Emporium was to Donde what Brooks Brothers is to New York. The officers from the Army Post never thought of going anywhere else, nor did the male element of Donde's tight little aristocracy. In the window today stood two dummies, one in a captain's dress uniform, the other in a civilian's evening attire. To the last detail, everything was perfect. Cenci sighed in admiration.

When they went into the shop, however, her face fell in disappointment. Men's clothes, without men in them, were certainly nothing to sigh over. Just racks and racks of suits, both military and civilian, on hangers. Tables piled with dull blocks of folded trousers. Other tables containing enormous bolts of cloth, certainly not very exciting. Nobody was about in the showroom, so Mr. Bronson walked the length of it and entered a small room at the rear, after knocking and hearing a voice say, "Come in."

This back room was a workshop. It contained more bolts of cloth, ironing boards, a sewing machine. It smelled of steam and wet wool. And on one of the tables, cross-legged and busily at work, sat a little gnomelike man with a bald head and—as Cenci had said—a funny nose.

"Mr. Stein?" asked James courteously.

"What you think?" The tailor did not stop to look up from his stitching.

"I have a little piece of work for you, Mr. Stein," went on the minister, "if you are not too busy."

"*Nu?*"

The tailor pushed his glasses up over his forehead, without taking them off, settling them straddlelike across the top of his bald head. Then he looked at the tall, shabbily dressed minister and the little girl who, fascinated, could not take her eyes from his glasses.

"You want I should make you a new suit? By Christmas, maybe. And me so busy I even work by night, and I ain't got but two helpers yet." He paused. "What kind of suit you want?"

"I'm sorry," said James, "but I'm afraid I did not make myself clear." He unwrapped his trousers and showed the tailor the hole in the knee. "I only want a bit of mending done. Here. My wife said perhaps you could weave over this hole. I'll need the trousers by Sunday."

Down came the glasses, as the tailor examined the torn place. Up they went again as he laid the trousers scornfully aside and looked at the minister.

"And for a job like this," he said witheringly, "I should stop working on a hundred-dollar officer's uniform"—he nodded toward the material he had been sewing on when they came in—"which also I should finish by Sunday. The pants ain't worth it."

"I'm sorry," said James, picking up the offending garment and folding it up again. "I knew you were busy, but my wife just thought——"

Suddenly, into the awkward silence, a small vehement voice piped up.

"Mr. Stein!" cried Cenci. "Those are the best pants Mr. Bronson has!" Forgetting her promise to keep quiet, she came to the table upon which the tailor was sitting and holding on to it fiercely with both her hands, she looked up at him almost menacingly. "And do you know why they're his best pants? Because he gave his Sunday suit away. To a Mexican. And do you know why that hole is in the knee? Because Mr. Bronson prays so much. He kneels. He prays for that Mexican. He visits him in that awful old jail and he talks to lawyers and people to try to keep him from getting hanged. That poor Mexican! Mr. Bronson even went to see the governor about him. *In those pants!*"

"So-o-o!" Mr. Stein took his glasses completely off now, put them in their case, snapped it shut, slipped the case in his vest pocket.

"So-o-o!" he repeated, regarding the angry little girl before him, and the minister who was as startled as he at her outburst. "*You* are Mr. Bronson! And ain't I been reading about you in the *Eagle,* even? About how you take trips to governors for a poor Mexican. But I ain't read about these pants, nor about the Sunday suit. Why did you give it to him?"

James sighed. "Because he was cold and ill," he said wearily, and started for the door.

"Please! Mr. Bronson! The pants. I—please excuse, but I also got kind feeling over that Mexican, like you. You want I should mend that hole by Sunday? Comes Friday, the pants will be ready. Good as new—Please!"

"Oh, Mr. Bronson, did you hear that?" cried Cenci joyfully. "Here, I'll put them on the table, shall I, Mr. Stein? And thank you. Thank you *very* much! You're an awfully nice man, Mr. Stein!"

The little tailor smiled, first at Cenci, then at Mr. Bronson. A wistful, dreamy look came into his eyes.

"Mr. Bronson, please. Excuse me, but in the *Eagle* it said you came from the East. Could it be that you are from New York?"

"Well, no," answered James, still not adjusted to the tailor's sudden change of attitude, "I come from Connecticut. But not far from New York, actually."

The tailor leaned forward eagerly. "I hope you are not in a hurry and should do me the kindness to be seated. Will you? And talk a moment? Please. In that chair. The little girl"—he reached out a helping hand to Cenci—"she should sit on the table by me. So-o-o! Thank you. Now! When were you in New York last, Mr. Bronson?"

"Why, about the first of August, I believe. I don't recall the exact date."

Jacob sighed. "What kind of a day was it?" he asked.

"It was raining," answered the minister. "One of those unseasonably cool days that come in August, you know. Foggy. I remember the foghorns were blowing from the river. A miserable day, really."

"Ah!" the little Jew folded his arms and sighed again. "What would I give for one of those muggy New York days!" he said with nostalgia. Cenci sat delightedly on the edge of the table swinging her legs.

"Mr. Bronson," the tailor was speaking again. "Did you see any pushcarts?"

James thought a moment and then said, "Yes, now that I remember it, I did. I was standing on a street corner, and the reason I remember it is because it was filled with furs, and I thought what a funny time of year to see fur."

Jacob shook his head. "Not funny," he said. "They were for the August fur sales. Did you hear a hurdy-gurdy?"

Again James pondered. "No, not that day," he said, "but the day before I heard one. A group of children were dancing around it singing, 'East side, West side, all around the town.'"

An even deeper sigh seemed to come from the depths of Jacob's being. "'The Sidewalks of New York,'" he said, and softly hummed the tune.

There was a silence. Then Jacob asked another question, and still another, until they had talked for almost an hour. Every once in a while the tailor would sigh and repeat, "Oh, for one of those muggy days!"

Cenci, leaning against a bolt of blue serge, listened spellbound, her imagination carrying her far afield. Such lovely sounding names! "The Third Avenue L," "Long Island Sound. . . ." Cenci wondered what kind of sound it was, a loud one or a soft one? And just imagine, Mr. Bronson and Mr. Stein both had been there, both loved it. Once during a lull in the conversation the tailor presented Cenci with a scrap of bright silk, "for to keep," he said generously. She thanked him and folded it into a little square, deciding to make a pincushion out of it some day.

Suddenly, James looked at the clock, arose with haste. "Oh, dear," he said, "I promised my wife I'd be on time for dinner. We're having noodle soup."

"Noodle soup?" asked Jacob. "Chicken? Home-made noodles?"

James nodded.

"Would it have a little garlic in it, maybe?" asked Jacob.

"I'm sure I don't know," smiled James. "She puts *something* in her noodle soup that makes it taste different. Maybe it is garlic."

Standing there, James looked down at the little cross-legged tailor. Straight out of Palestine, he thought to himself, although he calls it New York.

"Mr. Stein," he said, "why don't you come home with me? There'll be plenty of soup and maybe you could tell whether it's garlic or not."

"*Me* go home with *you?*" Jacob shook his head. "Thank you," he said. "It was awful nice of you to ask me. My mother, she used to make noodle soup. Like nobody else. I give you my thanks, but I couldn't go with you."

"Why?" asked James.

The little Jew got down from the table, bowlegged from sitting so long at his stitching, short, homely.

"Your wife," he said. "I don't think would she like it."

"Why?" asked James.

The little man looked up at him. "Because I'm a Jew. I've lived here twenty years, and nobody has yet invited me in their house."

He began picking off little bits of thread that clung to him, brushing himself with a whisk broom.

James said, "I know you're a Jew. Our religions differ, or perhaps, maybe only our interpretations differ. But do you realize that the man I preach about, the man I try the most to be like, whose ideals I keep constantly before me—do you realize that that man, Jesus Christ, was also a Jew? Mr. Stein, my wife, like me, would be honored to have you as our guest. Please put on your coat. Cenci and I will help you close your shop. But let's hurry," he said. "My wife also has red hair and a quick temper." He was smiling now. "And she *might* not like it if we were late."

Jacob picked up James Bronson's trousers and laid them on top of a pile of unfinished work.

"Noodle soup," he said, "like my mother used to make."

He took a fine cambric handkerchief from his pocket and blew his bulbous nose.

"Please, Mr. Bronson. Please, little girl. Excuse. I have not had any from so long."

A few moments later people in Donde were surprised to see the tall minister and the short little tailor walking companionably down the street together, Cenci hopping along between them, holding to one hand of each.

14

PREPARATIONS for Christmas, with the Bronsons, always began the day after Thanksgiving and even then there never seemed enough time. The three boys worked earnestly at their jobs, saving every penny. Packages were furtively sneaked into the house and hidden until one dared not open a closet or drawer or look under a bed. Things became more and more complicated because in addition to Christmas at home, there were the celebrations at the church.

This year there was to be a midnight Christmas Eve service. The carols and music had been turned over to Slim who had managed to round up a male chorus and one or two good solo voices at the Army Post. The service was to be simple: only the music and Mr. Bronson's sermon, for which he had not yet found an ending.

In lighter vein was to be the Christmas play and the tree for the children. Since no fir trees grew in Donde, not even any large cedars, Fred Werck, the cowboy who had accompanied them in the boxcar, having had to take another trip to San Antonio to visit his mother as he had done last August, had returned with two cedar trees—an immense one for the church, a smaller one for the Bronson family.

Fred was immensely proud of these trees and took loving care of them almost as if they were human beings. His friendship with the Bronsons had continued. Several times he had gone hunting with the twins and once with James and Brett as well.

128

He had shown them a favorite spot of his, an abandoned ranch house near the bend of the river between Donde and the ranch where Fred worked.

But when he came to church he usually had an apology. "It makes my old ma feel better," he said in explanation of his presence there. "She sure was surprised when I told her I went to church." On the Saturday nights before Fred attended church he naturally went across the river, so he dozed throughout James's sermons or sometimes slept outright. He would awaken with a jerk and a sheepish smile when the sermon ended and the music began. But after the service he never failed to say to Mr. Bronson, "I sure feel good, Parson, after one of them sermons of yourn. I feel so good I reckon the goodness will last me nigh onto a month. That's strong stuff you ladle out, Parson."

"I'm glad you enjoyed the sermon, Fred," James would invariably reply, shaking his hand with warmth. "With some people, you know, goodness doesn't even last a week, much less a month."

Now with Christmas so near at hand Fred's gift of the trees made things just about perfect. The ladies worked almost night and day on the decorations. They strung popcorn. They made costumes. With yarn they sewed up little square bags of bright-colored mosquito netting, which they filled with hard candy. Each child was to receive an orange and a bag of candy from Santa Claus, after the play.

The play this year was a simplified version of *Hänsel and Gretel,* arranged by Brett Lindley who allowed Matthew to help him. Brett said he would have preferred *Alice Through the Looking Glass,* but the costumes would be too difficult, so he settled for *Hänsel and Gretel* instead. Matthew, he told James, was quite gifted. Maybe next year he'd let him do some actual writing on the *Eagle.* In the meantime the Christmas play took their combined efforts. Cenci was given the rôle of Gretel, Luke that of Hänsel.

Sergeant Quale condescended to become Santa Claus and was

to come down through the fake chimney. Another member, a carpenter, built an extension of the pulpit platform, thereby creating a stage, and a friend of his, an electrician, even put in footlights. Imagine, footlights! One merchant in Donde donated dozens of little candles, complete with holders, for the tree. Mr. Tasman, the grocer for whom Lukey worked, contributed two wooden pails full of hard candy. Somebody else gave the oranges. The coins in the collection plates may have looked lonely, but not much money was needed because everybody gave lavishly of what they had, and Little Bonne Femme prospered.

In addition to these festivities, the high school was giving a party at the Casino to which both Matthew and Mark had been invited. When Nora heard about it she breathed a sigh of relief because the twins' blue serge suits, their first with long trousers, were still good. Her father, for whom they had been named, had made them a birthday gift of the suits last June. She couldn't quite make up her mind about the striped silk shirts, however, which she had made for them. It would rather spoil things to give the shirts away *before* Christmas, and yet, the party at the Casino was—to them—*the* affair of the year. Well, she would think it over. Also, she did not have to worry about the layette for the coming baby, the "Acts of the Apostles," who, thank Heaven, was not due until the last of January. Miss Ivy Vail, beginning to branch out surprisingly into social life these days, had given a shower for her, and Nora had been overwhelmed at the abundance and variety of the gifts. Poor little baby, she thought fleetingly, I feel *so* well, and I'm so busy, I almost forget about it.

In Mexican Town preparations for Christmas were also in full swing. In the large patio of the Vecindad across the way were going to be held the annual *Pastorelas,* every night for a week preceding the Nativity.

Brett Lindley was greatly interested in the Pastorelas, and he and James had discussed them at length. They were, Brett said, somewhat similar to the Miracle Plays of old and had not been changed much for hundreds of years. The handwritten script and musical score, old and prized documents, were kept by the priest and were taken out only once a year. Johnny Bronson was particularly intrigued by the coming Pastorelas because his friend Jesucito was going to be a child angel. Already his *mamá* had made the required white cheesecloth robe and the buckram wings.

James waded through all of these Yuletide preparations the way one wades through bright fallen leaves in autumn when they happen to lie in his path. So much of this, he felt, was too much work. People became overwrought, they worried about money, they ended up by overlooking entirely the true meaning of Christmas. The part of Christmas he looked forward to the most was, in the church, the dignified and holy Christmas Eve service; and in the home, the reading aloud of Dickens's *Christmas Carol*. This year, because of all the other activities, he and Nora decided to have the reading ahead of time. Tomorrow was the high-school party at the Casino, with *Hänsel and Gretel* fast on its heels.

Brett Lindley and Miss Ivy joined them for the *Carol*-reading. Pete had been invited but had declined with ill grace. He hated Christmas, he said. There was some debate as to whether or not to invite Jacob Stein, who—after that first evening—had become a frequent visitor in the Bronson home. They finally agreed to ask him, and his acceptance was immediate and touching.

Fred was also invited, and he came on horseback bearing two gunny sacks filled with mistletoe. If it dried up before Christmas, he assured them, he could get plenty more. The live-oak trees was extry loaded with it this year, he said. For the reading they all made a circle around the hearth in the study but as it was too warm for a fire in the grate Nora had filled it instead with the mistletoe, much to Fred's delight. Sergeant Quale came, too, but Slim, who had also been invited, sent his regrets. Slim was *very* busy, the sergeant explained evasively.

They took turns reading. Brett took the part of Scrooge, and oh! what a mean and hateful and wonderful Scrooge he made. James was narrator, Nora was Mrs. Cratchit; Matthew, Bob

Cratchit; Mark, Scrooge's nephew; Cenci, Tiny Tim; Luke took over various rôles here and there, as did Miss Ivy and Mr. Stein. Fred said he wasn't too good at readin', and reckoned it would be better if he just listened. He was sure a good listener, he insisted. Look how good he listened to sermons!

What fun it had been passing the worn book from one member of the family to the other! How they all laughed when the loose page fell out, as it did every year, and when their father said, as he said every year, "I *must* glue that back in again."

After the reading, each person made three Christmas wishes apiece, which had also become a family tradition. Two of the wishes had to be said aloud, but the third was to be kept secret.

"I'd like to have a Christmas goose just like the Cratchits had," Cenci said for her first wish. "I've never seen a Christmas goose." Cenci looked so pretty that night, her long black hair hanging in a glossy mane almost to her waist and tied back by a pink hair ribbon. Brett kept looking at her, thinking what a perfect Alice Through the Looking Glass she would have made. Well, next year——

Cenci's second wish was for four little Christmas trees, one fastened at each corner of a table. Mark laughed, making fun of her.

"Four little Christmas trees," he said scornfully, "I never heard of such a silly wish. Why in the world did you waste such a chance on a wish when you could have made a good one?"

The little girl's lower lip trembled. "I don't know," she faltered, "but I guess it's because they make me think of my father. I don't remember him very well but it seems like once he fixed a table with four cute little trees, one on each corner and I kind of remember him lighting the candles on them and saying, 'Merry Christmas.' Do people ever have *four* Christmas trees, Mr. Bronson?" she turned to him appealingly, "or do I just think I remember, and is it mixed up with one of my pretend games?"

James Bronson gave Mark a severe look and then closed the book of Dickens' stories gently. "I'm sure it was not a pretend game," he said. "I know of a family once who had that custom."

"Did you?" she asked eagerly.

"Yes, and maybe," he continued, "maybe this year your wish will come true. Maybe you will have four."

Then she smiled and her smile was like a garland of flowers.

The wishes went on around the circle. Fred wished his old ma in San Antone to get well for his first wish and for his second, he wished for an oil well, a gusher. Finally, according to the Bronsons' ritual they were ready for the third wish. This one they made in silence and in unison, all of them holding hands. It was a brief solemn moment full of possibilities and curiosity, and then it was over.

After that Nora served gingerbread with whipped cream flavored with cinnamon, and the evening broke up early. A happy evening long to be remembered. Ah, yes, long to be remembered. . . .

Matthew and Mark had named their room "The Hermitage" and had printed the name on a big piece of cardboard which they tacked to the door. They kept it locked, each boy carrying a key and feeling very smug and superior about it. Nobody else owned a key to the room, except Nora who had to go in to change the sheets on the bed, or on some other necessary errand.

The boys slept together in the chipped enamel bedstead with small brass knobs atop the posts, one of the two beds they had had set up in the boxcar. But they had a desk apiece, separate bureaus, and a favorite chair each. They both had a secret drawer in their desks, also kept locked. Neither of the twins knew the contents of the other's secret drawer.

Mark's contained three fancy silk handkerchiefs he had swiped from three different girls, a batch of love notes he had received at school, and a paper pamphlet entitled *Sex Secrets* which he had purchased through the mails for ten cents—it came to him in a plain envelope. Matthew's secret drawer contained six poems he had written, the beginning of a novel, and also the pamphlet entitled *Sex Secrets,* which he kept hidden although it had been a great disappointment to him as well as a waste of ten cents.

"The Hermitage" was never visited by the younger Bronsons except upon invitation. What an honor! And how tantalizing, too, when occasionally one of the twins misplaced his key or forgot to lock the door.

In this refuge Matthew's desk was neat, just like his father's. Mark's was a mess. He never could find anything. One of their perennial reasons for quarreling was that Mark helped himself to his brother's belongings whenever he could not find his own. It was the same way with their clothes. When the two boys had dates, if Mark got home first he would rush in and take the best of everything. Matthew had to take what was left. Mark knocked things down in the closet. On the floor lay a jumble of mismated socks and shoes, tangled sweaters, tennis balls, bent coat hangers, baseball bats. The hooks on the wall were so overladen they looked hunchbacked.

The boys pressed and cleaned their blue serge suits themselves, but Matthew was more careful of his. He was particularly proud of this suit and it was the only thing he owned which he begrudged his brother. The boys were near enough of a size so they could wear one another's clothes and somehow when Mark needed to be especially well dressed, his suit was always the wrinkled one, the one with a spot, the one a self-respecting young fellow simply could not wear on a date.

Matthew resented this. It was all very well for his brother to take pencils and erasers and algebra books from his desk but when it came to the suit, that was a different matter. He resented also Mark's habit of knocking things down and more than once Matthew had found his suit a heap of wrinkles on the closet floor, after he had meticulously pressed it.

But one day Matthew had a brilliant idea which he put into immediate execution. Since the rooms in the house were high-ceilinged, the closets were unusually tall. The one in "The Hermitage" reached upward almost like an elevator shaft, with a dark empty space at the top. Matthew rigged up a pulley, screwed in a hook near the top, then put his suit on a hanger and up it went, hoisted high like a battle flag and far out of reach. Luke and Cenci, peeping in at the door during this fascinating maneuver, let out a resounding cheer as the suit shot upward. Matthew, having forgotten to close the door, turned around at the applause and scowled.

"Beat it, you two," he said, and closed the door.

Well, there the suit was. It wasn't that Mark was selfish, he was just in such a hurry. His mind was elsewhere. If Matthew's suit was too much trouble to get he would shrug and put on his own. And even then he would sally forth on his date the handsomest boy in Donde.

For some time things went on smoothly between the twins. When the invitation came to the high-school party at the Casino, Matthew was glad that the pulley arrangement had kept his suit in such good shape. Mark had a date with Dee, to be preceded by a little dinner party at Mrs. Randell's. Matthew was going stag. But living as he did, half the time in an imaginary world, he fancied that for this one night he would be the most sought-after boy at the party, stag or no stag. The girls' hearts, especially Dee's, would palpitate at the very thought of dancing with this wonderful dark-haired young fellow in the trim blue serge suit with its knife creases.

A week before the party, he took it down, sponged it off, pressed it with care. Everything, he knew, was going to be perfect. For *once*. Two days before the dance, he found Mark's suit on the floor. It looked rather bedraggled when he hung it up and he spoke to Mark about it. Mark laughed carelessly.

"Oh, I'll press it tomorrow," he said, "I've got plenty of time."

But Matthew was worried about it. He knew Mark probably would not press it tomorrow, that he would put it off. So he himself worked away on his brother's suit one whole afternoon, rubbing off the spots with gasoline, airing it to take away the odor, pressing it underneath a heavy piece of unbleached muslin. Even then, Mark's suit did not look as spic and span as his own.

The afternoon of the party, Mark came home from work early. Matthew had had to stay at the *Eagle* to help Pete with a rush job-printing order. Whistling cheerfully, Mark dashed into the house.

"Matthew pressed your suit for you," said Cenci, meeting him at the door.

"Good," cried Mark, looking at the clock. Then he unlocked the door to "The Hermitage" and stepped in.

"Oh, baby!" he exclaimed under his breath, going over to the bed. For there lay two silk shirts, neatly folded and on each a card in their mother's handwriting saying, "Merry Christmas! I just *couldn't* wait." Mark's shirt had stripes of green, pink, blue, and yellow. Matthew's was more conservative. Mark dashed out to thank his mother, but Cenci told him she was visiting Lupe, Pánfilo García's wife. He hurried back to his room and picked up the shirt.

"Oh, gee! Oh, golly!"

He pranced over to the closet to get his suit, and saw that it was on the closet floor again, a mass of wrinkles. He remembered now that he knocked *something* down in his hurry to get to school that morning, but he had not taken time to pick it up.

He examined it with a sinking heart. It looked terrible. He simply could not wear it, not with that new shirt. And there was no time to press it, in fact he was already late to the dinner party. He shook the suit out, put it on a hanger near an opened window. Maybe in a couple of hours the wind would blow some of the wrinkles out but it certainly could not be worn in the state it was in now. He thought a moment, then stopped whistling and walked over to the closet, unwound the rope from its moorings, pulled down Matthew's suit.

"Well, what the heck," he said to himself with bravado. "He's going stag, anyway. He doesn't even care enough about this party to get himself a date. He won't mind."

He dressed quickly and when he was ready he hastily scribbled a note and pinned it to his own suit by the window. "Hope you don't mind, Mat, old boy. I was so rushed I didn't have a minute to press this. As you're not going to the dinner maybe you'll have time to give it a quick pressing. Thanks a lot."

The party was wonderful. The Casino's decorations made it look like fairyland, balloons of every color floating all over the place. An orchestra had been imported from San Antonio. The scene, the music, the pretty girls, their lovely clothes, his own popularity—all of it went to Mark's head like champagne. He forgot about his brother, did not even notice that Matthew had not come, until one of his classmates said, "Say, where's Matthew? I haven't seen him all evening."

"Oh, he's somewhere around, I guess," answered Mark, but he began to feel uneasy.

When he got home after the party he went quickly into their room, saw his own wrinkled suit still hanging limply by the window, saw Matthew's new silk shirt, unfolded, on top of the bureau. Matthew himself was in bed, apparently asleep, his back turned to his brother.

The next morning on the way to school Mark said, breaking a silence that had lasted between them since they rose, "Why so glum, Mat? Is it about the suit? Honest, I didn't think you'd mind, going stag and all."

Matthew did not answer, and in uncomfortable silence they continued on their way. As the church play was to be that night Mark had got somebody else to take his place working on the International Bridge and came home early. All day he felt depressed. His exhilaration of the night before had completely evaporated. He tried to get rid of his feeling of guilt by saying, over and over, "I'll make it up to him. *Some* way."

His parents and Johnny were at the church, but when he walked in at the back gate he saw Matthew waiting for him on the kitchen stoop, flanked on one side by Lukey, on the other by Cenci. Matthew's face was like stone. None of them spoke a word. When Mark reached the stoop, his brother removed his glasses, put them in their case, and handed them to Luke.

"Put these on my desk," he said briefly. "The door's open. Then clear out, you and Cenci. This is *my* affair."

Matthew and Mark had often fought before, but never the way they did that afternoon. The boys were evenly matched, both were strong, their muscles like steel. They fought out in the back lot, well hidden from both the street and the house by the barn and the carriage shed. Unnoticed, Cenci and Luke crept back and observed the fight in terror.

At length Matthew got his brother down, and sitting on his back twisted one arm, panting as he yelled, "Promise to leave my things alone?"

"Let me up!" Mark answered, still struggling.

Matthew gave his arm another twist. "Promise to leave my things alone or I'll break your arm!" he said.

Lukey, in a strangled voice, whispered to Cenci, "He *is* going to break his arm. I know it. He's strong. He is!"

Cenci could bear it no longer and ran out toward the twins. "Please don't hurt him, Matthew! Don't break his arm! Please!"

Matthew turned on her angrily. "Stay out of this," he said, and with his free arm he pushed her away, sending her sprawling. Cenci got up and brushed the dust from her dress. The way she had fallen her head hit a sharp stone and she could feel a trickle of blood running down her face. She wiped it away with her sleeve. She put the back of her hand against her lips, the way she did when she wanted to cry. But she did not cry.

Matthew turned back to his brother.

"Promise?" he repeated. "Promise?"

Mark, turning his head with difficulty, saw Cenci walking slowly away, her heavy hair swinging from side to side as she walked. His body relaxed. "Aw, okay," he said, breathing hard. "Okay, I promise."

And then Matthew let his brother up and the two boys went into the house, to wash up for the Christmas play.

15

THE CHRISTMAS PLAY at Little Bonne Femme was, in Broadway parlance, a smash hit. The church was packed, clear to the vestibule. People stood in aisles and in the door and even sat in the opened windows, for the evening was warm. Fred's large cedar tree, trimmed with popcorn garlands and lighted by small candles, looked beautiful. He was enormously proud of it.

The evening's entertainment, as might be expected, did not go off entirely without mishap. Santa Claus got stuck in the chimney. And during the play Johnny's tight pants, in his gingerbread costume, burst out at the seams and he had to walk off the stage backwards. And when the oven exploded and the witch blew up into the air, the wire broke and she catapulted into the audience, settling down in the aisle.

But Cenci, as Gretel, was strangely touching. She looked small and forlorn and lost in her ragged dress. When she and Hänsel lay down in the dark forest and were taken care of by the troop of angels, there was not a sound in the little church. Afterwards Brett and Matthew beamed as co-authors and shared curtain calls with the actors. In spite of the crowd there had been plenty of oranges and little colored bags of candy for everybody, and even some left over, heaped under the tree.

The next evening Brett came over to the Bronsons and they all went across the street to see the Pastorelas at the Vecindad. The patio was festive with its gaudy decorations. One entire end of it had been made into an outdoor stage. The Pastorelas, James agreed with Brett, were indeed similar to the Miracle plays of old but were also something like the Passion Play, in that the life of Christ was dramatized. But they were different, too. There was buffoonery in these Pastorelas. There was a Madonna, to be sure, and a Holy Child, and shepherds and angels. But there were plenty of devils. The devils had a wonderful time. Their humor was Rabelaisian. The audience, sitting on rude benches in the patio, howled with laughter, and frequently ad libbed, joining in the fun. Of course in the end, good won over evil and the devils were chased away with gusto.

Nora did not stay through until the end, however. She had been too weary so she slipped away home and went to bed. But from her bedroom window she could hear the music, strange, weird, haunting. Always she would remember this Christmas to the accompaniment of that chanting, blended in with the howling of coyotes and the sound of taps from the Post. It was not like any Christmas she had ever remembered. She heard the family trooping back, talking noisily, but she was sound asleep when James came in at last and went to bed.

As soon as her housework was finished the following morning she dressed for town and started out to do her marketing. The schools were out now. Children were outdoors everywhere playing baseball in the streets, or running about in their front yards. As usual, Mexican Town was swarming. Women sat on doorsteps, gossiping, combing their hair, calling out to one another from open windows. At the wide gateway of the Vecindad Nora paused a moment and looked in.

Today, in the bright sunlight, the decorations looked garish. A slight wind rasped the paper festoons. From the doors of the tenements opening into the patio came the smell of hot *tortillas,* warmed-over beans, and wood smoke. Pigs, dogs, and chickens waited hungrily for scraps of food that might be tossed out to them. A woman was drawing a pail of water from the well. In the vacant lot next to the Vecindad children shrieked and played. Two or three little Mexican girls were washing dolls' clothes and little rags that they hung on a line. They had a tub of water and they splashed and wrung out the dolls' clothes and dipped them in again, just for the fun of dabbling in the cool water on such a warm day.

Nora walked on but when she reached Main Street she stopped and looked in a window displaying Christmas toys. Her eyes had been arrested by the decorations, a hill of cotton sprinkled with artificial snow, artificial icicles, and artificial fir trees. She was overcome by a wave of nostalgia for Connecticut. For real snow. She could feel its cold, sweet breath, could hear the crunch of it under her feet, could see spruce trees against its whiteness, the sharp blue shadows of naked apple trees on its glistening surface.

Here in Donde it was almost hot. Men walked about in their shirt sleeves. Children were bareheaded. She herself did not have on a wrap. It seemed more like the Fourth of July than Christmas, this illusion accentuated by the intermittent pop-pop of firecrackers which she had been hearing lately. It had surprised her to learn that in Texas it was the custom to shoot off firecrackers at Christmas.

Well, she was *not* in Connecticut. Not only was she in Donde, Texas, but in some way her whole family had become entangled in half the affairs of the town. She had hoped so much that James would take a real rest, but instead of that he was working harder than she had ever seen him work before. He had become involved in a controversy over a poor Mexican. He had made many enemies because of it, just as had Brett, but he had also made friends. And the congregation of Little Bonne Femme Church grew larger each Sunday. Pánfilo García was still in jail and James did not miss a day visiting him. He and Nora both frequently went to see Lupe and the baby, Ignacio, gave them food, and enlisted the medical aid of Doctor Ashton. Lupe was getting stronger but still was not able to go out and work. The baby's malnutrition had gone on for so long that the doctor was worried.

This was no vacation, certainly. This was no way for James to think things over, to decide whether or not to give up the ministry. Why, he didn't even have time to think. With the increase of membership at Little Bonne Femme it had become necessary to organize the church more systematically. A board of trustees had been formed and two deacons had been ordained. A Ladies' Aid was also organized. A Young People's Society, a Men's Bible Class, conducted by James on Tuesday nights, prayer meeting on Wednesday nights, choir practice on Thursday. Slim was in charge of the choir.

Standing there at the window, Nora's eyes turned from the artificial snow to the toys. Again she felt a swift pang, this time one of rebellion. Lukey wanted a pair of cowboy boots, but she could not afford them. Prices were soaring. She spent weary hours over her ledger, adding, subtracting, worrying. How wonderful it would be just once, to be able to buy everything she wanted for her children at Christmas!

Usually, seeing her husband in the pulpit, hearing the words of inspiration falling from his lips, she would be lifted away for a while from problems like these. She wondered if perhaps James had not found some great and magnificent secret of living, too deep for her to grasp. She envied him. Sometimes her heart soared with his and she left behind these petty difficulties, but always she came back to earth. He never did. Even in the midst of one of his finest sermons, she would often be thinking, I'll have to cut that sponge cake into very small pieces and make a sauce for it so that it will go around. I'll have to add more water to the stew. I'll have to cut a piece of pasteboard and put it inside the sole of Luke's shoe next time it rains. . . .

Today she was especially worried about a gift for Cenci. The child had everything a little girl could desire, clothes, toys, a library, pocket money, games, a storybook room of her own. Yet they seemed as nothing to her, and she was looking forward to Christmas. Especially this year, since she was spending the holidays with the Bronsons, in the little spare room off the study.

For Miss Manners had finally disappeared into the limbo of all the other governesses. This time her reason for going away had had validity. Her mother had had a stroke and no nurse was available. Nobody regretted Miss Manners's departure, or even missed her much, for she had been away so often. There had been some correspondence between James and Mr. Derrick, while the matter of a new governess was being looked into. In the meantime, Cenci was staying there, until after Christmas, anyway.

Suddenly Nora's quick eye saw in the window a little sewing box, complete with needles, thread, scissors, thimble, and other accessories. Just the thing! The price was out of sight, but no matter. Nora would sit up late tonight and duplicate it at practically no cost.

Excitedly she walked away from the window, planning how she would make it. Dear little Cenci, she thought with joy, I'll make yours even prettier than the one in the window. It will be something that money can't buy. . . .

Nora did the marketing and hurried home. The little Mexican girls in the vacant lot were still happily washing their doll clothes.

Not far from them Cenci and Luke played with a ball. Cenci would toss it against the adobe wall and let it bounce back on the hard ground. Then she would hit it with the palm of her hand, swing one leg over it, and chant in a singsong voice:

> Spanish dancer, do the split,
> Spanish dancer, give a high kick,
> Spanish dancer, turn around,
> Onesy—twosy—threesy—four,
> Spanish dancer, kiss the floor,
> Fivesy—sixy . . .

Cenci played gracefully, bouncing, stooping, counting, pushing her hair from her flushed face when it got in the way. Finally she missed. The ball rolled away from her. Now Luke, who had been waiting impatiently, rushed forward and picked up the ball while Cenci watched, joined by Johnny and Jesucito.

Luke bounced the ball vigorously, shouting,

> Fudge, fudge, tell the judge
> Mother has a newborn baby.
> Wrap it up in tissue paper
> Send it up the elevator . . .
> First floor
> Second floor
> Third floor . . .

He missed. "Kick it out the elevator door," he shouted and handed the ball to Cenci.

> Spanish dancer, twirl your fan,
> Sevensy—eightsy—nine and ten . . .

The children were preoccupied and did not see her, so Nora went on. Like James, she wondered why in the world they preferred to play in that dusty lot in Mexican Town, instead of in their own yards. They said it was because of the adobe wall. They could bounce their balls against it. It had no doors or windows that might be broken. Nora entered her own gate, went into the kitchen, put her parcels on the table, glancing mechanically at the clock, for it was nearing the noon hour and the children would be hungry. James, hearing her, came to the door, an opened book in his hand, his face alight.

"I've finally found a quotation to use in my Christmas Eve sermon," he said. "For the ending, you know. The ending has been bothering me."

Nora put on her apron, poured some potatoes in a dishpan, began peeling them, her eye from time to time on the clock.

"It is this, Nora, from 'The Other Wise Man' by Henry Van Dyke." James Bronson straightened his glasses on his nose, looked down at his book.

"'He took the pearl from his bosom,'" James read aloud.

" 'Never had it seemed so luminous, so radiant, so full of tender, living luster. He laid it in the hand of the slave.

" 'This is thy ransom, daughter! It is the last of my treasures which I kept for the King.' "

"*. . . the last of my treasures . . .*" James Bronson repeated, and somehow, as he said the words, his voice seemed to resound, to become horribly amplified, to blend in with a terrible and ominous roar that filled the room and was at the same time coming into the house from outside, filling the whole outdoors.

"James!"

Nora's face turned white. "The children!" she cried out. "Something has happened! James! Quick! The children!"

Yes, something had happened.

The pre-Christmas tragedy was written up not only in the *Donde Eagle* but in newspapers all over Texas, was even copied in papers elsewhere in the United States. An adobe wall, said the *Eagle* angrily, in the slums of Mexican Town, a building condemned more than a year ago, in a filthy slum with rents fantastically high for the hovels where entire families lived, a wall owned by a landlord too greedy, too indifferent to care. A landlord taking a chance that it would stand, taking a chance that he would not have to spend any money, taking a chance on the lives of children playing out in the Texas sunshine. But the adobe wall had fallen. It comprised one entire side of the Vecindad, a wall without windows and doors. Why waste money on windows and doors? Why waste money on good materials, even for the wall? It might not fall. Worse ones were standing. But this one fell. It had suddenly given way and a group of little Mexican girls had been playing there, washing out dolls' clothes and hanging them on the line.

One little girl, Pepita Gonzales, had been killed instantly, her skull crushed. One child had miraculously been saved. The tub had overturned with her inside of it, the débris piling upon her, and when they had finally dug her out, she was slightly damp and terribly frightened but without a scratch. Other children had suffered broken arms and broken legs and shock and hysteria. All of the children who had been injured where Mexicans except one, an American child, Cenci Thorpe.

She happened to be playing there, bouncing her ball against the adobe wall when it had caved in. Her playmates, Luke and John Bronson, had not been hurt. Only Cenci. Cenci had suffered a concussion and a spinal injury. The doctors did not hold out much hope for her.

Yes, the newspapers played the story up. There were many editorials about it, other than Brett's. There were whispers of possible lawsuits, though poor Mexicans like those had no money for lawsuits. The landlord, however, and other landlords owning equally rotten structures, were pretty worried for a while because the family of the little American girl did have money. *They* could sue—But Nora and James Bronson did not read the newspapers. They did not think about lawsuits. They only wondered desperately whether or not Cenci had a chance to live.

Who is that little girl? Did she come with the house? I half believe so, Nora. . . .

All Nora remembered about those fantastic days was seeing James come back from Mexican Town carrying Cenci's limp little figure in his arms and putting her in bed in the room next to the study. She remembered endless telephone calls, the speedy arrival of Doctor Ashton, of Brett Lindley, the frightened faces of her four boys who went about mute, afraid to ask questions, the weird and terrible wailing in the Vecindad across the street, the tolling of the Catholic church bell for Pepita Gonzales, counting out the six years of her life, the cheap hearse standing in front of the patio gate across the street, carrying Pepita's cheap little blue coffin. In Nora's mind the words, "Rachel, weeping for her children" kept going round and round like a dirge.

Mr. Graham, who was in Europe on a business trip, was notified by cable and replied at length telling James to spare no expense. A brain specialist was summoned from Dallas. He stayed in Donde two days and then went back. There was nothing he could do, he said kindly, nothing that could not be handled by Doctor Ashton. The child could not be moved, she could not stand the trip to the nearest hospital, in San Antonio.

"Do you mean," James asked him, looking at him directly, "that there is no hope for her, then?"

The specialist sighed. "I suppose, Reverend Bronson," he replied, "a doctor should never say there is no hope. There is so much we do not know. I wish I knew more. I wish—" Doctor Ashton had come to the door.

"It's train time," he said. "I'll drive you to the station and we can talk about the case on the way. There are some details I want to go over with you again."

The specialist shook hands with Nora and James and told them good-bye.

Years afterwards, thinking about it, Nora recalled that neighbors and members of the church took complete charge of the house, bringing groceries, cooking meals, seeing about the laundry. She was aware that the machinery of the household continued without her aid while she and James, Brett Lindley, and Miss Ivy took turns at Cenci's bedside. Their efforts to get a nurse so far had been futile. One nurse promised to come next week but now it was too close to Christmas and Donde was so far away from everywhere. Next week . . .

Doctor Ashton came back from the station. He was a quiet, gray, tired little man, conscientious and skilled and beloved in Donde. There were never enough hours in the day for him to take care of his patients, and he seldom got any sleep, and many people didn't pay their bills.

He moved into the Bronson house and stayed in the spare room going out only on emergencies. Then he hurried back, sleeping when he could, acting as both nurse and doctor. Everybody forgot about Christmas. A pall settled down over the Bronson household, usually so merry and haphazard.

On the twenty-fourth of December the unseasonably hot

weather broke. When the day dawned, most of the sky was covered with a great blue-black cloud advancing from the north. A "blue norther," people in Donde called it when icy blasts seemed to spring up from nowhere and the temperature dropped fast, not by degrees, but by tens of degrees. The wind was bitter with alkali, it blew against the houses relentlessly, the dust sounding like sleet against the window panes. People took out their wraps, piled logs on fireplaces, and turned up their gas heaters, but because of the unusual demand, the gas was low and the tiny flames in the heaters gave out little more warmth than match flickers. In Mexican Town the houses were not heated at all. The Mexicans huddled over charcoal braziers in their rags, their faces pinched and blue, and barefooted children would stand one-legged trying to warm one foot by placing it on top of the other, then changing over to the other foot.

The blue norther with its glacial chill blew right into the hearts of the Bronson children. Nothing like this had ever happened to them before. The house no longer seemed their own. Their parents had become strangers, the boys were not allowed in Cenci's room but sometimes when the door opened and closed as somebody came out, they would get a glimpse of a still, gray-white little face against the pillow, and they would hurry away with a strange bleak dread in their hearts. Without being told, the boys dutifully went about their chores. They fed and watered all the animals. They gathered in the eggs and milked the cow and curried the horse. They did not quarrel.

Until now they had had their individual small misfortunes. They had had to do without things. They had had their conflicts and had been punished for their misdemeanors. But they had never experienced tragedy. Life had been more or less of a carnival to them. Almost everything had been fun. But since the accident to Cenci, everything was different. Chores which before had seemed to take forever were polished off in a moment. Duchess had never been so well tended. Trojan's coat had never been so sleek. The dogs and cats were fed until they left food standing in their dishes. Every time a hen cackled the boys almost knocked each other down to rush out and get the egg. Matthew and Mark cleaned up their room without being told. They cleaned out their closet in numb silence. Mark tidied up his desk and pressed his suit.

All the twins could think about was the little girl, Cenci. They hadn't actually paid much attention to her, now that they recalled it. Girls, they thought, especially *little* girls, were a nuisance. In the way. Dust under their feet. Of course, little girls, especially willing ones like Cenci, were quite handy for errands. And now they thought with guilt how they had almost run the legs off her. She was always so eager to please, so desperately anxious to be one of them.

Lukey did not tease his brothers any more. He did not clown around. He tried to make himself useful by taking care of little John, who was too young to realize what had happened. Luke envied Johnny. It was awful to be ten, and old enough to *know*. Old enough to be afraid, longing to go to his mother and sob upon her shoulder, yet too old to do that any more. Too old— He went about with his hands in his pockets, his eyes downcast. He went over to the Vecindad and watched the workmen, already rebuilding the wall whose crumbling had exposed the naked interiors of the houses on that side of the tenement.

He could see the pitiful, inadequate furniture. He could see the people moving around cooking and eating, carrying on their daily existence. It seemed awful to him to think of people living like that, exposed to public view, one whole side of their houses down, their privacy taken away from them. He was only ten but he knew that he was seeing the raw, beating hearts of people which up until now had been covered up. Never again, he thought, choking back great, tearing sobs, could people call him a *little* boy. He was old, old. . . .

16

CENCI'S WISH for a Christmas goose haunted Matthew. He had in his hunting often killed ducks and rabbits and squirrels, but he had never killed a goose. Sometimes he had seen them, warily out of gunshot. Once he and Fred had seen a golden eagle, a thrilling experience. But he was not thinking of golden eagles now. He was thinking of geese. No doubt with this norther blowing, geese, or birds of any kind, would be slow in taking wing. Today, the day before Christmas, he wondered if there might be a chance, just a bare chance, that he might sight a goose.

Since his fight with Mark a painful constraint had lain between the two brothers. Matthew wanted to break it. He wanted to say, "I'm sorry. Let's never fight again." But pride and hurt kept him from it, and now this new thing, this accident of Cenci's seemed to paralyze his tongue completely.

Children are ashamed of grief. They try to hide it. They don't know what to do about it. When their iridescent soap-bubble world suddenly breaks, they become helpless. Sometimes in the face of it they become unnaturally gay. Sometimes it makes them belligerent. Sometimes they simply withdraw into themselves. Thus Matthew. When he would see his mother coming in and out of the sickroom, he would avert his eyes. When his father would call him, he would pretend not to hear.

He had a feeling which he could scarcely put into thought that this thing which had befallen Cenci was God's wrath descending on him because all his life he had been jealous of his brother Mark. This was his punishment.

He felt that if there were something he could do for Cenci it might perhaps exonerate him. He remembered how, when he and Mark had been fighting, Cenci had interfered and he had knocked her down. He had not intended to. He had not realized how small and slight she was, how strong his blow. His fury toward Mark was so overwhelming that he had not even thought about Cenci nor paid attention to her. But now he recalled the hurt and bewildered look in her eyes and he remembered that she did not cry. If only she had cried! But she was always such a game little kid. He recalled the night they had all read Dickens' *Christmas Carol* and what she had said about the Cratchits' goose and how Mark had teased her about the four Christmas trees.

He went to the closet and took out his plaid mackinaw, not as warm a garment as it might have been because it had served him two winters. He put it on, not caring that his arms were too long for it, that his wrists stood out of it, bony and raw. He buttoned it up, counted out a few shells. He examined the gun with misgivings. It was a cheap, single-barrel twelve-gauge shotgun with a hammer that Fred had given them. It did not even have an automatic ejector to toss the empty shell out, and sometimes it missed fire altogether. He was worried about the shells, wishing he could afford better ones. These cheap ones often sent out a dense cloud of smoke, creating a screen between the hunter and his prey.

Tonight was his turn to do the milking. Ordinarily he would have asked Mark to exchange turns, but not today. However, he found Pete in the back yard, chopping wood. Pete, who had refused to come to the *Carol*-reading, had been here off and on since the accident, doing odd jobs. Matthew did not say where he was going, but asked Pete if he could milk a cow.

"What you think?" asked Pete. "I was brang up on a farm."

The matter was arranged, and without a word to anybody else Matthew walked out of the house.

He had no gloves but he thought nothing of it. The norther, cold and biting, blew against him. Fine pellets of dust and sand cut against his face but he was not aware of it. Quickly he left the streets of Donde behind him and went out into the country. With his head bent low, he traversed a stretch of desert and then entered a growth of willow trees that grew along the river. He and Mark had often come hunting here, taking turns with the gun. It was the special place Fred had told them about in the boxcar. This was where they had seen the golden eagle. Once they had made an overnight trip of it, he and Mark, their father, Fred, Brett, and a soldier from the Post.

This was their favorite spot. There was a bend in the river, forming a sheltered little cove. At one time there had once stood an old ranch house here. The house was gone, but there remained many of the trees and shrubs which had long ago stood there, some transplanted. Even the wild ones were thicker and more luxuriant, being irrigated by the river.

When Matthew reached the copse, he forgot about everything except his determination to find a goose. It seemed that his entire lifetime had been centered on this hour, on this venture, that he had lived his fourteen years for this purpose alone, to get a goose for a little girl who had wished for one. He did not consider that he was not warmly enough clad, that his face was bleeding from the whiplash of the storm.

He was not cold, actually. A great fire burned within him. He had a feeling of power, a feeling that by his will alone, like a magician, he could startle a goose from behind some clump of trees, or suddenly, like a miracle, see a whole flock of them flying southward in V-formation, honking, filling the cold air with their thrilling and unmistakable cry.

Matthew was a good hunter. He trod lightly on the leaves and twigs underfoot. He sat motionless, waiting. Once his heart pounded violently when he heard a whir of wings, and he quickly cocked his gun and got ready.

Suddenly, a flock of wild ducks which had been on the river, though hiding from the storm near a protecting bank covered by underbrush, took wing slowly and heavily. He watched them without emotion. Almost immediately they sought the water again and floated down out of sight. He lowered his gun. He could have shot one or two of them, enough for a nice Christmas dinner. But Cenci did not want a duck. She wanted a goose. Like the Cratchits'. He became apathetic, sitting and waiting, listening to every sound.

He looked ahead at a small clearing indented by a marshy pool from the river and fringed by pecan trees and live oaks. It was a beautiful place with the Spanish moss hanging from the trees, being torn into shreds by the wind, almost dipping into the water. And then without having heard it, as if it had risen up from the ground itself, he saw a deer, a magnificent creature wtih great horns and delicately formed legs, standing there, poised, suspicious, listening as Matthew had been listening. Matthew did not move. The deer was only a few yards away from him, but Matthew did not raise his gun. Night after night, before he and Mark had had their big quarrel, they would lie awake and talk about how some day they would go hunting and kill a deer. It was their highest dream. Now was Matthew's chance, but the boy did not move. The deer vanished, almost as it had come. He might have been looking at the picture of a beautiful deer in a book and then had turned the page. He was not interested. Cenci had not asked for a deer.

He was beginning to feel the chill through his thin mackinaw. The winter day was drawing toward its close. Doggedly he remained. I won't go home, he said to himself, until I get what I came for. And then his heart almost stood still. One moment he was looking at the gray Spanish moss, at the black bark of the trees, at little white clouds scuttling across the sky, gray and

black and white, the colors of winter. Then he saw the goose.
He could not believe it. But there it was, the black glossy neck
with its ascot of feathers in the front, the suit of gray feathers.
Gray and black and white . . .

Evidently without realizing it, Matthew had stirred and had
frightened the bird which had been hiding from the cold behind a clump of trees. Like the ducks, the goose arose clumsily.
Matthew raised his gun and with sure and steady aim, fired. From
it arose a cloud of smoke, blinding him, and at first he did not
know whether he had missed or not. He did not wait to reload,
but ran quickly to the riverbank, his eyes burning and smarting
from the smoke and the wind. Instinctively he looked first at the
sky, but it was vacant. The goose was not there. Then his eyes
dropped to the river. Gray and black and white . . .

The goose had fallen into the water. Already it was beginning
to float downstream. In a few minutes the current would carry
it out of sight completely, out of his grasp. He had lost it.

He dropped his gun. Frantically he ran down the riverbank,
not taking his eyes from the goose. He knew he could not
swim with his heavy boots on and all his clothing, even with
the help of the current. He could not possibly swim. But without his clothes, ah, that would be a different matter. Breathing
heavily, running top speed, never taking his eyes from the bundle
of feathers swirling and eddying and floating away from him, he
unbuttoned his mackinaw and threw it to the ground. Still
running he took off his shirt. He paused long enough to unlace
one shoe, afraid for a moment that he had lost sight of the
goose. He swore under his breath at a knot in the laces, but
gave it a savage jerk and broke it in two. Then he threw his
shoe aside. He ran now, limping, with the other shoe still on,
until he caught up with his prey. He came abreast of it and
then stopped, untied, unlaced, and took off the other shoe. He
was stripped. He did not know how far he had run. He was
no more aware of the blue norther than if it had been a light
summer breeze, but slid quickly down the river bank and plunged

into the water, swimming rapidly. The goose was quite far away now, merely a small speck, for it had taken Matthew a little while to clamber down the bank. He kept saying to himself, Take it easy, boy; take it easy, and little by little he gained on the goose until finally he caught up with it.

His fingers were numb. He reached one arm out and took hold of the goose, but could scarcely feel it. Yet he knew he did have it because the bird was no longer floating away from him. Also he could feel its feathers against his bare breast. He turned and made for the shore and climbed up and stood there, lean and graceful and stark naked, holding the heavy goose in his arms, facing the north wind.

I have Cenci's goose! She can have it for Christmas. She is going to get well.

His feet did not feel the earth but it wasn't because they were so cold. Oh, no, it wasn't that at all. He was not walking on the earth. He was way above it. He felt in his heart an elation such as he had never felt before. He knew that after today he would never be quite the same. And as he walked back picking up his garments and putting them on, one by one, he remembered something from the Bible, something his father had told him.

"All things are possible with God."

But also he had another and deeper thought, which filled him with a peace he could not understand. For he knew that even if Cenci did die, now it wouldn't be so bad. Even if she were already in heaven she *must* know at this exact moment that he had not meant to knock her down, that he loved her very much. He had not meant to. If he lived to be an old, old man he would always remember this day. He had grown up. Things would never be quite the same.

All at once he felt terribly tired. The goose was heavy. He would have to walk a long way before he got home and for the first time since Cenci had been hurt he realized he was hungry. He picked up the bird and examined it. Sure enough, a Canada goose, the biggest that comes to Texas. He wasn't sure just how much it weighed but he had never seen such a fine one. The white front of its throat was very white indeed in contrast with the black of the other side. When he got home he would examine it more carefully. He and Mark would talk about it. They would look it up in their bird book and find out all about it. They would weigh it and measure it.

He and Mark. . . . Always in their hunting trips they did this. It came over him like a blow that he and Mark were scarcely speaking to one another, that they were mortal enemies, that the day was past when they could share their secrets and triumphs and their defeats. Suddenly his elation fell away from him. He was consumed with nostalgia for his brother. He felt as if Mark had died. Then in the cold December air he became aware of a sound that he had been halfway listening to for the past few minutes. He could scarcely make out at first what it was, then realized that it was the sound of axe strokes.

Following the sound he came to the same spot where he had seen the deer earlier in the afternoon. Although it was nearly dark when he came within sight of the figure, stooping and rising, chopping away at a little cedar tree, even if he had been half blind, he would have recognized him. Mark! No one else moved with such grace, with such symmetry of action. No one else had hair that exact dark gold, the only bright thing on this dying winter afternoon. Nobody else had a mackinaw like that, with one elbow in tatters, yet worn like a regal garment.

Unseen, Matthew stood for a moment watching his brother, his heart flooded with love and admiration. I should never be jealous of him, he thought. Mark can't help being the way he is any more than I can help being the way I am. We were made that way.

The cedar tree that Mark had been chopping down began to topple. It was not a very big one. In fact, it was more like a shrub, possibly two or three feet high, which had evidently been set out, years ago, when the ranch had been there.

As he watched, he saw Mark lay down his axe, pick up the

tree, and place it carefully with three others he had previously cut, almost exactly like it. And then, as if aware of his brother's presence, Mark turned and saw Matthew standing there with the goose. Across the marshy pool the two brothers looked at one another, wordless. Overhead the wind tore at the treetops, tore at the clouds, which broke and began to scatter. A burst of stars appeared in the opening and were reflected in the pool. The boys said nothing. Matthew took the first step. He walked over to the place where his brother was standing. He laid the goose and his gun beside the little cedars and the axe. There was an awkward moment. Then Matthew said, "Have you got any string?"

Mark nodded. "I brought along a piece of rope. The trees are for"—he choked—"for Cenci," he said. "I made fun of her. At the *Carol*-reading."

"I'll tie them up for you," said his brother, and he took the rope and tied the bases of the four little trees together.

While he did so Mark walked over and examined the goose. He whistled.

"A Canada!" he said. "What a beauty!"

Matthew's heart leaped. He could not speak.

"We'll weigh it and measure it when we get home," said Mark.

Matthew tested the trees to see if the rope would hold them. "We'll have to figure out some way of making them stand up," Mark said. "I think we can do it with a nail and two boards, one tree for each corner——"

He stopped. His voice broke.

"—one for each corner of a little table," he finished. "The way she said."

"Yes," said Matthew. "Maybe Pete will help us fix them."

"Is Pete still there?" asked Mark.

"Yes," answered his brother. "He milked Duchess for me tonight and he's chopping some wood."

"Fred's on the way," said Mark. "I met him when I started off to look for these trees. He was on horseback and let me ride behind and brought me here and showed me where to find these little trees. He would have stayed but I told him that I could get along. He had a tenderloin of venison, frozen stiff. Said it would make good steaks. He said he had to do *something*."

The two brothers stood up. Mark shouldered the four little trees and the axe, Matthew the old gun and the goose. "Are you ready?" he asked. "Shall we go home?"

"Yes," answered Mark, "I'm ready. We'll have to find some trimmings for the trees, though. It'll take quite a lot, for four."

"Some of the stores might still be open," answered Matthew, "and they'll have some leftover trimmings. Cheap."

"I don't know," said Mark. "It's kind of late, but we've *got* to get trimmings somewhere."

"Sure."

The two brothers left the grove of trees with their burdens and headed for the five-mile stretch of desert which lay between them and home.

17

ALTHOUGH the house was full of people coming and going, opening and closing doors, telephoning, gathering in subdued little groups and talking quietly, nevertheless to Luke it seemed emptier than he had ever known it. Matthew and Mark had gone off somewhere, he did not know where. His mother was in the sickroom. The doctor was snatching a few moments of rest. His father was supposed to be sleeping but Luke knew that he was in the study, awake. He could hear him walking up and down.

Luke felt lost. He went from room to room, disconsolately. Scuffing his feet he went out on the porch and in the darkness put his nose close to the Christmas tree which no one had even bothered to put up. *Christmas Eve!* he thought. But it did not seem like Christmas Eve. It was dark and he peered through the window into the study trying to see what time it was, but the clock had stopped. Everybody had been too busy to wind it.

Then he thought that tonight there was going to be the midnight service at the church. He was quite sure nobody else had thought about it. He wondered who would ring the bell, if the twins did not return in time. And in thinking about the bell he recalled with remorse that Cenci had begged to swing on the rope, as he did, but he had never allowed her the privilege. She always dusted the pews for him, and diligently passed around the hymnbooks and did all of the dull, ordinary jobs, so distasteful to him. It made her so *proud,* she often said, to get to be co-janitor, like the rest of them. She did not complain.

Out there on the porch, which was called the "gallery" here in Texas, he began worrying about the bell. He ought to go over to the church and ring it, but he had never rung it at night before, only in the morning. And he was afraid of the dark. Nobody knew this. It was a dreadful secret which he kept carefully guarded, covering it up with bravado, showing off. But when alone in the darkness he expected all sorts of gruesome creatures to jump out at him from behind telephone posts and tree trunks, or to be waiting for him when he turned a corner. Going to church at night with the entire family was different; with such a crowd he felt well protected. And always, on returning, about a block away from the house, Duchess would hear them and moo in welcome, and Flutter would begin barking. Oh, *that* was jolly. But alone——

Yet now was the time for the Christmas service and if he didn't ring the bell people would not come. There would be no service. Probably all the people right now were sitting at home anxiously waiting for its musical sound. If they did not hear it they would say, "The preacher has forgotten. There will be no service. No use to go."

How sad and disappointed his father would be if he knew about it.

Luke took another sniff of the Christmas tree and realized there was but one thing to do. *He must go alone and ring the bell.*

Quickly he went into the house, put on his wraps, and went out the side door, hoping at the last minute that Matthew and Mark would appear, so he could tell them about the situation and they would accompany him. But they had not returned. He ran down the path, opened the gate, and attained the street. Looking back he saw his own house with almost every window lighted. What a beautiful haven it was! How safe! Then he turned back resolutely to the dark street.

He stopped for a moment in front of the gate of the Vecindad.

In spite of the tragedy of the wall, the Mexicans had decided to go on with their pageant, which was basically a religious one, whose climax was to be tonight. In the cold patio the spectators shivered in their inadequate garments. Although they joined in the eerie singing, as they had the other night, now it had an undertone of sadness, of fatalism. The audience did not ad lib as they had before. While Lukey stood there one of the devils pranced out, a regular clown of a fellow. He wore a red skullcap with two red horns which had slipped over to one side giving him an even more ludicrous appearance than was intended. The devil spoke his lines, went through his antics, but nobody laughed.

Not far from the gate Luke spied Jesucito. Under his cheese-cloth costume he wore a ragged sweater and knickerbockers, one pants leg down. The knickers looked so peculiar below the skimpy cheesecloth dress, the wings looked odd sprouting from the plaid sweater. But Lukey did not even smile. Nothing was funny tonight.

He turned away and trudged on. He turned the corner and started down Alamó Avenue, in Mexican Town. Here it was quite dark indeed. Most of the Mexicans were attending the Pastorelas. Only a few windows were dimly lighted. Luke began to imagine things. That devil, for instance—what if he should decide to chase him? And what was that blur of white ahead? An angel, perhaps?

Terrified, Lukey began to run.

At length he reached the church. How dark it looked crowded in between all of the houses which were lighted up for Christmas! How empty! Luke put his hand in his pocket and felt the key, cold against his fingers. He walked up and down the sidewalk, afraid to go in. Maybe, he thought, fairy creatures *did* come out on Christmas Eve. Maybe dumb animals talked. Maybe the church was already filled with elves and goblins, or maybe, Heaven forbid, once he got in he might have a vision, as did the shepherds of old. Maybe real angels would appear near the ceiling, flying around the gas jets, singing *Glory to God, peace on earth.* Luke's hands were wet with cold perspiration as he clutched the key.

"Dear God," he prayed, "don't ever let me see an angel." And then he added, "And oh, dear God, please shove me into that church quick before I get too scared and rush back home."

Then he marched up the steps, clumping his feet loudly. He inserted the key hoping he had got the wrong one but he hadn't. It turned easily. The door swung inward, and his nostrils were filled with that special smell he always associated with churches, the smell of hymn books, of hemp carpeting, of Sunday dresses and powder and perfume and of candles that have been blown out, of the holy pages of open Bibles. To these smells came an added, spicy one, the cedar smell of Fred's Christmas tree and the fragrance of leftover oranges and candy piled under it.

Luke walked in making as much noise as possible. He found some matches and climbed up on a pew and tried to light one of the gaslights but could not reach it. Then he remembered that on the tree were all of those pretty candles. So he walked down the aisle and went over to the Christmas tree and lighted the little candles as far as he could reach. They looked friendly and twinkly. He wasn't quite so scared now as he had been. The lights helped. He was sorry he did not know what time it was, but he decided that he had better take a chance and ring the bell anyway, even if it might be too early. At least people would know that there was going to be church tonight. Then he went back to the vestibule and in the semi-darkness he took hold of the bell rope with both his hands.

Almost he could hear a wistful, pleading little voice saying, *Please let me swing on the bell rope, Lukey. I'm quite strong, really, for a girl.* . . . Luke did not want to hear that voice. He pulled the rope with all his might until he heard the bell's clamor high overhead. He rang it and rang it and rang it. And the sound of the bell almost drowned out the echo of that voice. Not quite, but almost.

Abruptly he stopped. He heard voices outside. Quickly he hid in the curtained-off closet where the brooms and mops and dustcloths were kept. He heard footsteps entering the vestibule.

"I don't see anybody around," he heard a puzzled voice exclaiming, "but that bell sure was a-ringing. I guess they's going to be church tonight anyhow, even if the little girl *is* dying."

The voice belonged to Sergeant Quale.

"Sure we'll have a service," Luke heard in reply and the other voice was that of Slim. "But it's funny about the bell."

"Musta been the norther," said Sergeant Quale. "I've heard tell these Texas northers can do *anything*. Reckon it blowed the church door open and swung the rope and rung the bell."

Slim grunted. "Some norther," he said, "to light the candles on the tree, too. Well, funny things happen on Christmas Eve. Anyhow, we're early enough for our little surprise."

Peeping from behind the curtain, Luke became absorbed as he watched the two soldiers open up both church doors and prop them aside, and then with the help of some other soldiers who evidently had been waiting outside in a truck, they carried a new organ into the church. Luke's eyes almost popped out of his head as he watched them push it down the aisle and place it where the little folding organ had once been. He wondered if maybe Slim had taken the little folding organ and put it into his pocket. Lukey was glad now that he had come, for the church was no longer a place to be frightened in. It was hearty with the sound of men's voices.

One of the soldiers was a young fair-haired boy named Larry who had a sweet tenor voice. He went over to the Christmas tree and picked up an orange and a bag of candy.

"Takes me back," he said softly. "Never could explain why, but it don't seem like Christmas unless I can smell oranges and this-here kind of candy tied up in little colored bags like these."

Luke heard Sergeant Quale call out to Slim. "As soon as the boys get here," he said, "we'll begin."

He and Larry now came to the door and peered anxiously

up and down the street while Slim began going over the keys of the organ, lovingly, tenderly, feeling his way.

"In all the time I been in the Army," said Larry, "I never knowed of a whole platoon to agree to come to church on Christmas Eve and to chip in for a new organ. In all of the time I been in the Army this is the first Christmas Eve I ain't been drunk."

"It's because of the preacher," answered Sergeant Quale, "that's why."

"Maybe," answered Larry. "He sure ain't like any other preacher I ever run acrost. The other ones always talk about saving your soul. They talk about heaven and hell, and the kind of hell they talk about doesn't scare you, and the kind of heaven don't seem as good a place as here on earth. But does this Rev. talk to me about hell and heaven? Hell, no! He says, 'Larry, what do you like to do best?' So I say I like fishing and hunting. So then he says, 'Larry, me and my two boys and a cowboy named Fred aim to go hunting next week. See if you can get a pass. Come along with us.' I feel sorta suspicious but I go. And he don't talk to me about no heaven nor no hell. Him and his boys and Fred and me talk about deer. He don't talk to me about my soul.

"When we come back to his home with a brace of ducks after the hunt, his wife she cooks them and they invite me to supper. How does he know I like fresh buttermilk and homemade bread like my mother used to make before she died when I was ten years old? He still don't ask me to come to church but next Sunday here I am. What a *ronche* trick to play on myself, says I. Why did I come to church when nobody ast me to? If the preacher ast me I'd have been mad at him but he didn't say nothin' so I'm mad at myself for comin' to church. Then he gets up and preaches. I keep waiting for the heaven and hell stuff and for the soul stuff but all I remember is the way he says 'God is love.' So, like a sucker, I come to church again." The soldier paused. "What if they don't show up?" he said anxiously.

"They'll show up," said Sergeant Quale grimly.

And all the time Slim was playing the organ. He was playing the familiar Christmas carols and they sounded good. Luke regretted that he was hiding because he wanted to go and touch the new organ and watch Slim's long, bony fingers playing carols. But if he came out of the broom closet they would ask him about Cenci. So he kept very quiet and remained hidden. He just had to wait to see if a whole platoon really was coming to church. Carefully looking out he watched the soldiers as they dusted the pews and distributed hymnbooks and lighted the gas jets and the rest of the tapers high up on the Christmas tree. It must be time, he thought, to ring the second bell, but he was afraid of being caught. While he was waiting there in the dark closet he thought of the words Sergeant Quale had said when they first came in.

"*. . . even if the little girl is dying.*"

No! cried Luke to himself. No! The sergeant didn't say that. I just heard him wrong. He *didn't* say it! The little boy made up his mind that as soon as he dared he would ring the second bell but would pretend it was Cenci ringing it. He would swing on the rope. He would say, It's your turn, Cenci. This isn't me swinging on the bell. You're strong, awfully strong. It's you. And maybe she would know about it in her sleep and she would get well and everything would be as it had been before.

Then he heard the sound of many voices, the stamping of feet. Ah! The platoon! He did not know what a platoon was. Maybe a thousand men. Maybe more. His heart swelled. Up they came, soldiers from a cavalry regiment with the toughest reputation in the Army. They were talking and laughing and swearing, but Sergeant Quale met them at the door.

"There's hitching posts outside this-here church for all them cuss-words. Hitch 'em there and leave 'em there. And take off your hats."

In they came. There stood the Christmas tree, lovely with its little candles. There was Slim, with the stops pulled out of the organ, playing "Adeste Fideles" with all his might. Silently the men walked in and began filling up the empty pews.

Sergeant Quale got up. "Men," he said, "I sure thank you for coming. I promised you all KP if you didn't come and a good sermon if you did. I'm sorry to disappoint you about the sermon. The preacher ain't here except in spirit. He's in great trouble—him and his whole family. I don't know whether you've heard about it or not. Some of you have, but they's a little orphan girl that lives next door to the preacher and she's just like one of the family. If you read the paper you read about how a wall caved in, in Mexican Town, and killed a little Mexican girl and hurt an American one. That was the little gal, the American one. She's as close to the preacher as his own kids. The doctors they done everything. Went so far as to bring a specialist from Dallas but the little gal is going to die and they can't do nothin'. But we're going to have this Christmas Eve service anyway. I'd like to have been a preacher. Reckon I missed my calling but I can't preach so I'm going to read about the first Christmas, gonna read it strong out of the Bible. Then Slim'll start up a song service and do his stuff on that-there new organ and if any man in this-here church don't say a prayer for that little sick gal he'll get KP tomorrow anyway."

It was a cold night but the sergeant was hot. He took out a handkerchief and ran it around the inside of his collar and wiped the sweat from his forehead. Then he opened the Bible and began to read: *Now when Jesus was born in Bethlehem of Judea in the days of Herod the king, behold . . .*

After the reading, the song service began. What a mighty sound the men's voices made booming out, singing the beloved carols! And how Slim outdid himself with the new organ!

Now, thought Luke, now is the time to ring the bell. They're singing so loud they won't hear me.

Cautiously he slipped out of the closet, took hold of the bell rope, and began to swing back and forth, back and forth. Years afterwards the soldiers spoke of that Christmas service which had been preceded by the ringing of a bell and candles lighted by unseen hands. Some of them even said they heard the bell again above their own voices as they sang, though most of them denied *that*. . . .

You're ringing the bell, Cenci, not me. It's your turn, Cenci. This is you. . . .

Finally Luke dropped the bell cord, tiptoed out of the church door, and crept down the steps. He was not afraid of going home alone. He could not understand why. He was no longer afraid of the dark. Half a block away he stopped, turned, and looked back at the little church. He could see the Christmas tree twinkling through its windows. He could see other people now, men and women and children, going up the steps and into the church. In the still, cold air he could hear Slim playing on that wonderful new organ, could hear the men's voices singing the carol he loved best of all, "O Holy Night":

> *Fall on your knees!*
> *Oh, hear the angel voices* . . .

The little boy turned and slowly started homeward, the sound of the music diminishing in his ears. He did not feel alone any more for by his side a little girl was walking. She was saying, Thank you, Lukey, for letting me swing on the bell rope. It was so much fun! Thank you, Lukey.

18

FOR THE FIRST TIME in his life James could not pray. He had lost contact with God. Until now, it seemed that he and God had had a special means of communication, that there had been a trunk line between him and Heaven, that he and God had been able to get in touch with one another without delay and without earthly interference.

But tonight, Christmas Eve, he could not pray. He sat alone in his study, unaware that the fire in the grate had gone out, unaware of anything except the numbness in his heart. It was his turn to be sleeping while Nora and Miss Ivy kept vigil in the sickroom. He was scheduled to relieve them at twelve. But he had not been able to sleep so he had dressed and come in here.

As he sat there the knocker sounded on the study door. Mechanically, James arose and opened it, admitting Brett Lindley. The editor's cheeks and nose were red from the wind. His eyes were red, too.

"How is she?" he asked, taking off his wraps, and James answered, "The same. I'm supposed to be sleeping, but I can't sleep."

Brett reached in the pocket of his overcoat and produced something white and furry, a kitten.

"I've looked all over town for it," he said thickly. "You'd think it would be an easy thing, finding a white kitten. Well, it isn't. I'd about given up when I found this one, mewing, walking along the river, lost——"

He eyed the kitten with a worried air. It was thin and more gray than white. It was frightened and kept struggling to get out of his arms.

"Not much of a specimen," he said gloomily. "Maybe a little food will help."

Together he and James went out to the kitchen. They built up the fire and Brett warmed some milk, beating up an egg and stirring the mixture together. Then he put it in a saucer behind the stove on the floor and placed the kitten beside it. The sorry-looking little cat put his nose in it, sneezed, drew back warily.

"Too warm," said Brett, "but let's leave him. Cats don't like to eat when they're being watched. He'll be all right. Funny thing, I was walking along the river. I'd given up all hope, and I heard this mewing. It was like a sign or something."

The two men returned to the study. Absently Brett held out his hands to the dead fire, spreading the palms out as if to warm them.

"You say she's about the same?" he asked. James nodded. Brett looked at him.

"Jim," he said presently, "you're a man of prayer. I'm not. I used to pray when I was a kid, but now, I don't pray any more. But you, Jim. You're different. I—I'd like to kneel down with you, right here, if you'd just say a word."

James sat, his hands hanging limply between his knees, his head drooping.

"Brett, I can't pray," he said. "I haven't been able to since the accident. I see now why—why people can't pray at times. When it's somebody you love so much—when it's so close to you—I can't Brett. I've tried. I can't."

Brett sat down. He saw that the fire was dead. The clock did not tick. Rooms, he thought, rooms can die, the same as people. This room is dead. He got up and wound the clock.

He stooped and poked around the ashes and tried unsuccessfully to rekindle the fire. He went out to the kitchen and saw that the cat had lapped up all the milk and was washing himself behind the kitchen stove. Brett put some more wood in the stove, noticed that the woodbox was almost empty. He went outside and brought in more, piling the box high.

There was certainly plenty of wood cut, Brett thought absently. The pile reached almost above his head and he could hear the sound of voices behind the carriage shed so he went to investigate. On an uncut log, in the light of a tin lantern, he saw Hunchback Pete leaning over carefully cutting up some fine kindling, splintering the side of a box with a knife. The cowboy, Fred, was piling it in neat stacks and tying the bundles together.

"The thing about venison," Fred was saying, "it's gotta be cooked right. If a piece of tenderloin can freeze first all the better, but it's gotta be cooked right, same as wild ducks or wild anything, froze or not." He paused, reached over for more splinters. "Reckon that little gal is still alive?" he asked.

"Don't know," said Pete.

"Reckon it would do any good to pray?" asked Fred.

"Nope," said Pete.

"Did you ever hear the preacher in there pray?" persisted Fred. Pete went on shaving the kindling without answering. "Well, I heerd him," said Fred, "on that trip in the boxcar. If I could pray like him it would help. That parson sure can back-talk to God. Not me. Wish I could, though."

Unnoticed, Brett slipped away. And then in the dark he heard the ringing of the church bell of Little Bonne Femme. He had never heard it ring so loudly or so clearly. How strange! He wondered who was ringing it. He looked at the sky, saw that the diminishing norther had swept the clouds away, that the black heavens were studded with stars. It seemed as if the stars were ringing, not the bell. . . . He returned to the study. James sat where he had left him and Brett looked at him and at the familiar shabby room and his heart overflowed with love.

"Jim?" The minister looked up at him. "Jim," Brett said, "I'll pray. It won't be a good prayer, but I'll pray."

The big man dropped to his knees awkwardly.

"Dear God," he said, and then stopped. Beads of sweat stood out on his forehead, he clenched and unclenched his big fists. Out there, looking at the ringing stars, it had seemed easy. Now he did not know what to say. He longed for a typewriter. If he just had a typewriter under his fingers he'd know what to say. Then, incongruously he remembered the words, *"Little lamb, who made thee? Dost thou know who made thee?"* and presently he heard his own voice saying, as if the words were being wrenched from his heart, "Oh, God, you can't let her die! You can't——" and then he got up. "Jim," he said, "that's the best I can do." James looked up.

"That was a fine prayer, Brett," he said softly. "I wish I could do as well."

Little John awoke and sat bolt upright in bed.

"Mama!" he called, but nobody heard him. All day, nobody had paid any attention to him. He had been brushed aside. Lukey had fed him his supper and put him to bed.

"Is this Christmas Eve?" he had asked.

"Yes," Luke answered glumly, "this is Christmas Eve."

"Will Santa Claus come tonight?" he asked.

"I don't know," his brother answered, "I guess he'll be too busy this year. Besides, Johnny, Santa doesn't know where we live. He thinks we're still in Connecticut. I forgot to mail your letter. Honest I did. But I'll mail it tomorrow and I'll write him myself and tell him we live in Donde so you see you'll get your presents, but they'll be late. Next week maybe. Be a good boy and go to sleep. Don't cry now."

Little John had looked back at his brother in fury. "I'm not crying, Lukey! It's *you*. Crybaby! I wouldn't cry for nothin'.

But you told me you'd mail that letter. You promised me."

"I'm sorry. Honest I am."

Luke covered him up and turned out the light and tiptoed out. He looked in a few minutes later and Johnny had fallen asleep.

But now little John sat up in bed wide awake, listening. Not a sound in the house. He peered out the window. Stars were shining and dancing in the sky. It must be quite late, quite, quite late. No doubt any moment now Santa's sleigh would come flying through the sky, the eight reindeers stepping from star to star on their delicate hoofs.

Maybe, the child thought, if I go outside I can catch him. He could stop for just a minute, and I'd tell him we've moved. I'll show him where our house is.

Little John crawled out of bed. He put on a pair of badly worn bedroom slippers and a faded bathrobe that had once belonged to Luke. Of course, he thought, if Santa has been here already I won't need to go out and look for him. So, just to make sure he tiptoed to the study, noiselessly opened the door a crack, and looked in. No, Santa had definitely not been here. There was no Christmas tree. There were no stockings, fat and lumpy, hanging from the mantel. Only his father and Mr. Lindley sat there by the fireplace looking sad and lonely. Poor Papa, thought little John, he is sad because Santa doesn't know where we live this year.

He turned away, walked down the hall. He saw the sickroom door ajar and he went to it and looked in. Miss Ivy's back was turned. She was at a table pouring out some medicine. His mother was writing something down on a pad. Scratch, scratch went the pen in the room. In the dim light John could see Cenci's face on the pillow. She is so sick, he thought. I must find Santa and tell him that Cenci is expecting him, too, and to bring her presents here instead of next door. Then she'd get well, and Papa wouldn't be so sad.

Miss Ivy started toward the bed with the medicine and the little boy moved out of sight and went down the hall. He opened the backdoor and went out into the yard and then to the street. Nimbly he ran toward the Vecindad and watched the play which was almost over. Good was about to triumph over evil and the devils were about to be chased away for another year.

Then Johnny saw a familiar face. The little boy angel Jesucito, his friend, who had completed his part in the play and had sensibly gone to sleep. Longing for companionship, John walked over to where the little Mexican lay on the ground asleep.

"Jesucito," he whispered, "wake up! Come and help me find Santa."

But Jesucito slept on. He had taken off his angel's robe, rolled it up, and made a pillow of it. He had removed his wings and laid them beside him. Johnny picked them up. Oh, what lovely wings! How they sparkled. Johnny viewed them with admiration and respect. If I had these wings on, he thought, I could fly. I could fly up there where the stars are and *then* Santa would see me.

"Hey! Jesús," he whispered to the Mexican boy, "may I borrow your wings? Jesucito, say yes. Please!"

The Mexican boy frowned in his sleep, turned over. Johnny remembered that Jesucito had confided in him earlier in the week that it was really quite a bore to have to be an angel night after night. He did not like his costume and as for the wings, they were a nuisance. He had displayed them to Johnny often, and had even showed him how to put them on.

Johnny now picked them up and put them on and then quickly ran out the gate, the big wings flapping behind him. He didn't feel as light as he had expected to feel, to be truthful. But maybe if he got a good running start down the middle of the street he might suddenly rise, like a kite, and go soaring into the air. The little boy looked about him. The street was empty. The wind fanned his fair curls back from his face. It blew open his bathrobe. Johnny spread out his arms and began to run, faster and faster, straight down Mesquite Street where it dead-ended against a row of houses in Mexican Town.

Sitting on the curb and smoking a hand-rolled corn-husk cigarette sat old Ysidro Gonzales, grandfather of Pepita Gonzales, the little girl who had been killed when the wall fell. Ysidro had played the rôle of one of the shepherds in the Pastorelas. Indeed, he had been playing this rôle for so many Decembers he had lost count. The only thing was that as a young man he had needed a gray wig and a false beard and a costume, but now he just wrapped his faded old red blanket around him and went as he was. He did not even need a staff. He used his own cane, necessary for years because of rheumatic joints and old age. His hair was coarse and white and hung in an uneven fringe around his wrinkled brown face. There was not much of a boundary line to indicate where his hair left off and his beard began.

His part in the Pastorelas had long been over and he had left the scene of forced gaiety and come off alone here to smoke and wait. His joints were like old hinges, rusted and misshapen until he could scarcely move. When a norther blew up the cold crept into him until he felt like he was not held together by joints but by hundreds of pains. Some of the pains were waspish and nagging; others were large, dull ones, ponderous and as impossible to shake off as nightmares; still others were sharp and jagged, the teeth of a ripsaw trying to tear him apart. All of them were cruel.

Now, with Pepita gone, old Ysidro sat gazing down Mesquite Street with tortured eyes. If only he could get warm, just once again! Pepita, his nearest living relative, had lived with him in a dirt-floored cubicle of a room in the Vecindad. Sometimes when they ran out of charcoal for their brazier she would cover his knotty hands with her little ones, warm and alive and soft. Or, she would sit close to him under the blanket and thaw him out with the brazier of her childhood vitality.

But now she was gone. Everything was gone, almost, except his loneliness and pain. There was no charcoal and no money for charcoal. Pepita's funeral had taken his last cent. Of course next month would come the money order from San Antonio. Or

would it? Although it came in his name and he had to sign it
with his X at the post office, the money came for Pepita. As he
could not read, he did not know who sent it, but it always
came. . . .

Suddenly Ysidro was electrified by what at first appeared to be
a vision, straight out of heaven, a small angel floating down the
middle of the street and heading toward him. His dull eyes
blinked open wider and he saw that the small white angel was
not floating, but running at top speed. When he got to the end of
the street his momentum was so great that he could not stop, but
ran directly into a fireplug and fell sprawling and screaming
almost at Ysidro's feet.

Twenty minutes later the old man and the little boy walked
through the gate and into the Bronson's yard, hand in hand.
Johnny knew a few words of Spanish, Ysidro, a few English ones
and thus they had managed to understand one another after a
fashion. Johnny, however, was still worried about Santa Claus.
Every time he asked Ysidro, "Are *you* Santa Claus? Honest?"
The old man replied with emphasis, *"Si! Si!"*

Of course there were the white beard and hair and the red
blanket, but even then, where were the reindeer? And wasn't
Santa fat? This fellow was all bones. Johnny was not at all con-
vinced. Nevertheless he dared not risk losing him so he had taken
Ysidro's hand in his own small perspiring one and dragged him
home.

Once in the kitchen they were engulfed by warmth and com-
motion. Someone scooped the small boy up and carried him off
to bed. Somebody else thanked the old man, gave him a chair by
the stove and a cup of coffee. Warmth! Blessed, blessed warmth!
Ysidro drank the coffee so hot that it made tears run down the
furrows of his cheeks. Then he pulled his chair an inch closer
to the cookstove and held his hands toward it. People buzzed
about him. The telephone rang again and again, but the warmth
had begun to penetrate through Ysidro's pain, melting it. His
cane clattered to the floor and lay there, unnoticed.

The old shepherd was asleep.

19

A FEW MOMENTS after Brett had finished praying he and James heard footsteps in the hall and the door opened. It was Miss Ivy. She was wearing a white organdy apron and looking at her, James thought in a detached sort of way, Why, Miss Ivy is quite pretty. Odd I didn't notice it before.

"Mr. Bronson," she said, taking off her apron and beginning to fold it up, "your wife is *very* tired. And since you aren't sleeping anyway, I wondered if you'd mind taking a turn at Cenci's bedside so Nora can lie down? I thought I'd better go and look for the children."

James stared at her, his eyes glazed. "The children aren't here, you see," explained Miss Ivy hesitantly, "not any of them. Nora is worried."

James got to his feet. "Certainly," he murmured, "certainly. I didn't know they'd gone off. Little John was in his crib the last time I looked. Is the doctor here?"

"Yes. He's asleep at the moment. He said to awaken him if—if there's any change, you know."

"If you don't need me here, Jim," said Brett, "I think I'll go with Miss Ivy. The big boys are all right, I'm sure, but the little ones——"

"Johnny walks in his sleep sometimes," said James, frowning, going toward the sickroom. "But he can't have gone far in such a short time."

"Don't worry, Jim," said Brett, helping Miss Ivy into her coat.

"We'll find them. Your kids are all self-reliant. Cenci is the only one who can't take care of herself tonight."

"We'll take your car," said Brett firmly to Miss Ivy. "I didn't bring mine. The streets are dark as sin. We can drive slowly, and look for the kids. As if things weren't bad enough to-night——"

Brett was muttering angrily when the two of them went out the gate, but Miss Ivy knew that when he was worried it took the form of anger. He cranked the car, swearing with every jerk, then flung the crank on the floor and climbed in, starting off with a bounce that nearly threw both of them out of their seats.

"I never saw such a family," he growled, peering from side to side into the dim fan of illumination spreading out from the car. "One of your lights is out," he said. "I hate a one-eyed car. Why don't you have it fixed? And where the devil shall we go, looking for four lost kids? Little hellions, all of them. Why couldn't they stay home on Christmas Eve, of all times?"

"Well, I guess it isn't much of a Christmas Eve for them," said Miss Ivy timidly. "Everybody forgot about Christmas, I'm afraid, and about them, too. Poor children."

Brett drove around aimlessly, both of them straining their eyes into the darkness. Abruptly he stopped. "I think the globe is loose from the socket," he said. "I'm going to see what I can do with it. Trust a woman to drive around with a half-blind car."

She didn't tell him that the lights had been working perfectly when she had driven over here. She just sat quietly, and while he tinkered with it, above the rattle of the running engine she heard another sound. Quietly she got out of the car and crossed the street, and there, leaning against the wall of a building, in the semi-darkness, she saw the little figure of Luke. He did not hear her. He was sobbing and talking.

"Oh, Cenci," he was saying, "please don't die—please, Cenci. I'll let you swing on the bell every time forever and ever, if you don't die. I swung on it for you tonight. Oh, Cenci! It was *you* swinging it! It was, it was!"

The little boy was trembling with cold and misery. Suddenly he dropped to his knees, and crying and sobbing, he lifted his head and shook his fist at the sky. "Don't you dare let her die," he prayed wildly, "don't you dare, God, you big bully, you big old power-and-the-glory-forever-amen bully——"

"Luke, darling, Lukey——"

The street where they had found him was only a block from where Miss Ivy lived. Together she and Brett gathered him up and took him there. Not once did Miss Ivy think of the accumulation of dust in her little house, of her volume of William Blake. All these months she had kept the place swept and garnished, had dreamed of Brett's coming to it, as her guest. But since the accident she had neglected her own house. And tonight all she could think of was a cold and heartbroken little boy, and it was for Luke, not Brett, that she lighted the gas fire and cooked hot chocolate and made things cheerful.

"You'd better call the Bronsons," she said with authority. "Then Nora can stop worrying and go to sleep," and Brett said meekly, "Yes," and went to do her bidding. When he returned, she was kneeling beside Luke, taking off his shoes and stockings, rubbing his red little feet between her fingers, smiling at him and talking to him reassuringly. "Did you tell them Luke is safe?" she asked, looking up.

"Yes," he answered. "Some strange voice answered the telephone. A woman. Old Isabella, I think, but why Isabella?"

"Maybe she's there helping out," murmured Miss Ivy. "I know this morning she went over and volunteered, so I gave her some ironing to take home. *Everybody* wants to help the Bronsons."

"That's true," answered Brett. "Well, anyhow, whoever it was said Johnny had been found and was in his crib asleep. She said the other boys had just come in, too, and something about a goose and Fred and Sergeant Quale and Slim and Pete's all being there and trimming some trees. Such a family! Is Lukey getting warm?"

She nodded. Miss Ivy had been so busy that she had neglected to slick back her hair and nail it into place with her hairpins. So it was half down, and little tendrils had escaped and lay loosely around her forehead. She had forgotten, too, about her shyness and reserve, because of this heartbroken little boy who called God a big bully, yet had gone out all by himself to ring the church bell when he was afraid of the dark.

Strange, in Miss Ivy's dreams she had thought that if Brett ever did come to see her, he would enjoy her books and rugs and pictures, but now that he was here, he did not see the house at all. He saw only Miss Ivy. He was, actually, seeing her for the first time. He saw that her hair was soft and shining and abundant, that her mouth was tremulous and infinitely desirable, that in the depths of her eyes lay serenity and beauty. And he saw that she was not a prim old maid at all, but young, oh, so very young and dear, and probably nobody had ever told her so, nobody had noticed or cared. Something inside of him seemed to swell and burst, like ice cracking in a frozen river. He reached over and pulled a corner of the blanket over the little boy's shoulder.

"Warm, laddie?" he asked softly. Luke nodded, his eyelids drooping, all the tautness gone from his body. The hot chocolate, the blanket, and the toasting of his feet by the fire and everything had made him sleepy. His eyelids were heavy, and his trip to the church seemed quite faraway and long ago. As he grew sleepier and sleepier he seemed to hear, as from a great distance, the singing of the soldiers, and over and over in his mind echoed the words:

> *Fall on your knees!*
> *Oh, hear the angel voices . . . .*

Yet he struggled against his drowsiness for he knew there was still somewhere else he *must* go tonight, somewhere very important, a fine and wonderful place, though at the moment he couldn't think of where it was. Heavily he lifted his eyelids and looked about. He saw the cheerful fire, the luxurious rugs and draperies, the lovely pictures on the walls. Such a beautiful place and he would like to come back sometime and visit it. He felt his stockings being put on again. Miss Ivy's hands were warm and gentle, and his feet weren't numb any more. All of this was fine. All was good. Through his haze of sleepiness he saw Mr. Lindley helping Miss Ivy with his shoes, and his big hand, red and bristling with hair, reached out and took within it her slim white one, and they both smiled, and Mr. Lindley leaned over and kissed her, and that, too, was good. It was splendid and very fine, and it would be lovely just to lie back and let go, if only he didn't have something else to do, a task left unfinished.

Then he remembered. The austere study. The dead fire. His father's tired, desperate face, his father's voice, "I can't pray, Brett—" His father, who, until tonight, could always pray. Yet tonight, when it was needed most, he couldn't. *Fall on your knees! Oh, hear the angel voices,* that's what the song said.

"That's where I have to go," the little boy remembered, waking up suddenly. "I have to explain to Father. All he has to do is to get down on his knees, like he always does. He just forgot. It's easy to pray. . . ."

"Warm, laddie?"

Mr. Lindley's voice sounded very, *very* far away. And so did Lukey's own voice, when he answered drowsily.

"Yes. But please take me home. It's very important. There's something I have to tell Father."

Then he leaned back in the chair and went to sleep. He did not even awaken when Brett carried him out to the car and they started homeward.

20

AFTER Miss Ivy and Brett left to look for the missing children James went into Cenci's room and Nora rose from her chair.

"Did you get any sleep?" she asked.

"No, dear," he said, "but I'm all right. Don't worry about *me*."

The sickroom had that unearthly look of sickrooms at night. A towel had been thrown across the lampshade, dimming the light, casting unnatural shadows on the walls. The smell of illness lay upon the room and it was so still that Cenci's shallow breathing sounded loud and strangled.

Nora's skirts rustled as she arose and James trod on tiptoe. They spoke in whispers, magnified by the silence of the room, as she told him what the doctor had said. She showed him a paper where she had written down Cenci's temperature, her pulse, her respiration, her blood pressure. The paper crackled loudly in the silent room. Then Nora, weeping softly, went out and closed the door. He studied the chart. He checked his watch, writing down the time on the chart. The pen scratched hard on the paper. He looked at Cenci, so small in the big bed, her breathing scarcely lifting the covers.

Little lamb, who made thee?

James turned away from her. If I could only tell her, once again, how much I love her, he thought. If I could only pray. . . .

Once, long ago, he had had a mystic dream about a little girl.

At that time he had been a theological student, but had had to stay out of school a year and work to earn money to continue his education. Work had been difficult to find, and he had become a day laborer, a plumber's assistant.

In his dream he was coming home after an unusually hard day. He was tired. He was discouraged, exhausted both physically and mentally. He plodded along in his heavy shoes, conscious of his evil-smelling work-stained clothes, of the dirt-crusted look of his big-knuckled hand grasping his empty lunch box, of his grimy fingernails. He felt that not only his body, but his soul itself, was soiled and unclean. Thus in his dream he found himself walking homewards, and presently through the trees he saw the roof of his own cottage and he quickened his steps.

When he reached the gate he saw a little girl waiting on the stoop. She was clean and dainty. Her hair was very fair and quite long and tied back by a ribbon. Her eyes were blue. She was a storybook child, a little princess, a darling. Yet, she was his daughter. In the fashion of dreams he knew that he had expected her to be there, waiting for him to come home, that was the reason he had quickened his footsteps. Observing her bright hair, her clean starched dress, her little red slippers, he was filled with awe. He himself, all the hidden softness and beauty within him seemed to arise from him and leave his earthy and sweat-defiled body behind. He felt radiant, cleansed. That weary clod of a man coming home from work a few moments ago, that was not he. That man was merely a shell, an outer covering for his real self.

The little girl, his daughter, seeing him, jumped lightly to her feet and ran to meet him. Her blue eyes were dancing, a smile of ethereal beauty lighted up her delicate face. As he stooped to kiss her, he felt the softness of her arms encircling him.

"Darling, you'll get your clean clothes all dirty!" he had exclaimed, trying to put her away from him. But she had only laughed and snuggled her head against his shoulder, her bright hair cascading over him like a golden mist.

"You're not dirty," she had said, "you're my own Daddy that I love and I've been waiting for, for such a long time!"

He realized with amazement she was not aware of his grimy clothing. To her they did not matter. He felt purified. And when he awoke from his dream he thought, Hidden somewhere deep within the most wretched human being, there must lie a germ of purity, of radiance, of great beauty. Often it is not visible, but it must be there. No matter what the outer husk, within every human being there is surely something divine.

He did not consciously think of this dream often, only of its symbolism. Yet when he and Nora were married, and after the twins had come, he remembered the exquisite little girl who had been sitting on the stoop waiting for him to come home from work. He hoped if he and Nora had a third child it would be a daughter, exactly like the one in his dream.

He was proud of, though not quite prepared for, the twins' lustiness, their animal-like vigor. Almost from birth, they had manifested strong personalities. They were noisy. They fought. They tore their clothing, wore out their shoes, had measles, marked up his books, and were unduly vociferous on days when he was in contemplative mood or was working on a particularly difficult sermon. Yet he would not have had them different.

Before Luke's arrival, he found himself thinking, a little wistfully, of a daughter. A quiet little daughter with big blue eyes and hair like an angel's, a dainty little girl with small red shoes that never wore out. But Luke's entry into the world was even more belligerent than that of his two elder brothers. His was a breech birth. He defied conventions at the outset. "I," he seemed to say, "am going to be born upside down, just for the heck of it." The long-ago dream became very dim. That quiet little princess of a daughter receded further and further into the realm of all lost dreams, quite blotted out by a pugnacious, redheaded lovable urchin named Luke.

Little John, their changeling child, was something of a stranger to James for he had been born while James was overseas. "Our

Johnny," Nora had written, "is by far our most beautiful baby, silky gold hair, big blue eyes, a dimple in his chin. He is too beautiful for a boy. . . ."

But by the time James returned "Our Johnny" had already developed a tendency toward the wanderlust. He had a flyaway look in his big blue eyes. He was as elusive as a moonbeam. When with him James felt the way men do in the presence of other people's children. The afternoon old Isabella had returned Johnny and James had given him the bird book to look at, brought this youngest son of his close to him for the first time, and the dream of the little girl became but an imagined fragrance, an echo.

Not by the most remote stretch of imagination did Cenci remind him of the child of fantasy who had once awaited him on that mythical doorstep. Cenci was not pretty. She was, truthfully, quite plain. She was plain the way a sparrow is plain. She was like a wildflower in a field of wildflowers, lost and unnoticed.

But James thought tonight of the way her hand felt when, walking by his side down the street, she would reach out and take hold of his. Her hand was warm and trusting and also imploring. It seemed to say, Don't let me go, please. Let me hold to you, tightly, because I've nothing else to hold to, really. Although her eyes were closed now he could see them, large and soft in her little face, fawn's eyes, looking up at him solemnly. He could see her mouth, too taut for the mouth of a little girl, a mouth almost afraid to smile. But when she did smile, such a glory. Such a glory, little Cenci!

It wasn't that Cenci was perfect. He could not have endured a perfect child. She was careless. She didn't like to comb the snarls out of her hair. She left things lying about. She flitted in and out of the Bronson household at unexpected times; one never quite knew when she would be there, or how long she would stay. *Or how long she would stay . . .*

Now he sat down beside the little girl's bed. Afar, as if it were coming from another world, came the sound of the church bell ringing. The midnight service? No, it could not possibly be. He picked up Cenci's wrist and took her pulse. A frail thread of life, beating against his fingertips. Suddenly he felt that he had lost it. A terrible wave of fear cut through him, and in a panic he moved his fingers to another place on her wrist and it seemed an eternity before he felt the thready beat once more. He counted her almost imperceptible respiration again, and got up and wrote everything down on the chart, although it was not time to do so. Should he call Doctor Ashton? He did not know. Maybe it would be better to wait, to let the doctor rest. Anyhow Nora had said the doctor had seen her just before Miss Ivy had gone to the study. Tears were running down Nora's cheeks. The doctor had said he did not think Cenci could possibly live until morning. "It's all in the hands of God, Mrs. Bronson," he had said. "I think you had better call your husband. I'll be near-by."

"But what can James *do?*" she had asked.

And Doctor Ashton had replied, "Only what the rest of us are doing: pray."

James went back to the bed, straightened the covers, laid the palm of his hand on her forehead. How cold it was. He felt her pulse again, lost count completely. In terror he leaned nearer to her, felt her faint breath against his cheek, like a dying breeze. He knelt down, and with her tiny wrist still between his fingers, he whispered through lips of stone.

"Oh, God——"

But the words fell from his lips, stillborn. And kneeling there, he thought about God. God is love, he had often preached, but what did that mean? Who *was* God? As a child he had thought of God as a person, a divine giant to whom one might go when one needed things, or whom it was polite to thank for favors. At other times his conception of God had varied until finally it had crystallized and he had grown to feel that he understood God. Yet when he saw the deeds of men, he wondered. And during the war, seeing the destruction and waste and suffering, he had begun to doubt as he was doubting tonight. If God is love, he thought, why then does he allow things like this to happen? Oh, Cenci! Why? Why?

He laid Cenci's little arm gently back on the sheet and got up and walked over to the window. Within the house, he could hear sounds of people coming and going, the phone ringing, whispered conversations. All of it was remote. He felt that he and Cenci were alone, quite apart from the rest of the world. He had a feeling of detachment, and when he walked to the window he saw that the stars had come out and were unusually close and brilliant. The sense of detachment persisted. Now it seemed that he and Cenci and the stars were alone in the universe, and he began thinking about the stars. Countless stars, countless worlds. Who created them? Why did they, like this small planet, stay in their appointed places? How would they end? How did they begin?

In the beginning, God . . .

James turned away from the dazzling heavens, and saw, in a tumbler on the table, a white rose. Before the norther had struck Donde, roses had still been blooming and somebody had brought one to Cenci. There had been no time to arrange it in a vase so it had been hurriedly put in a tumbler of water. Its fragrance filled the room, even above the odor of the medicine. In the dim light, he regarded the rose, remembering the one on his folded napkin last summer. How, he thought, did flowers begin? People took them for granted, like the stars, yet—like the stars—flowers, too, retained their intricate secret. One petal of this rose had fallen off, had drifted to the table top, and in the semi-darkness, lay there, perfect and a miracle. He picked it up and held it in the palm of his hand. It felt as evanescent as Cenci's pulse. It was heart-shaped and pure, and yet it was not like any other petal. He knew that if he should pluck another one and place it beside this one, the other petal would be different. No two flowers were ever exactly alike. No two snowflakes were identical twins. Who, he thought, had troubled to make them different? What artist had designed them? How long ago?

He heard the ticking of the clock, and thought of sound. The sound of rain. The sound of birds singing, of babies crying, of thunder. James touched the table top, he looked at the hooded lamp and observed not only its light, but also the shadows it cast. He thought of darkness. He took a step and thought of motion. He listened to Cenci's labored breathing, and thought of life. Life. Who had decided that there should be life? Who had created the great beasts of the jungles, the tiniest of insects, the most uncomplicated and lowest forms of animals in the deep sea? He took a few more steps nearer the bed and thought, then, about death. Who, he asked himself, decided that there should be death? Why should flowers drop their petals and fade, sacrifice their perfume and their beauty and then die? What happened then?

Was that the end?

He looked at Cenci's gray-white little face, and thought, just as no two flower petals are alike, so are no two children alike. No other child who had ever been born, or ever would be born, would be like Cenci. No other smile would ever be as radiant as hers, no other small tiptilted nose quite as impudent, no other two eyes quite so direct and brave, no hair so dark and thick and straight. And if that faltering pulse should cease, if that whisper of a breath should become forever still, what then? Would not the Artist who had fashioned her, who had labored to make her different from all other little girls, would not his task continue? Would he throw into the discard a work so divinely begun? Who knew the Power of which she was but one manifestation?

Power . . .

Ah, was that the answer? God is love, yes, but what is love? Is not, perhaps, love but another word for power? And then, prayer. Would not prayer be, not asking, not thanking, but a recognition of this power beyond all human understanding? To pray then should be an alignment, a matter of allowing oneself to be swept into this power, which is God. In other words, to pray is the realization that although man is human, he is also divine. He is not separate from God, but a part of God. And in prayer man's power, which is also God's, becomes manifest . . .

James knelt down by Cenci's bed, overcome by the magnificence of this revelation. He had thought to be a beggar, bowing to some remote King grander than himself. He had wanted to say, Please do not take her from me. She is infinitely dear to me. I cannot do without her. Do not take her away!

But that, he realized now, would not have been prayer. It would have been, merely, as Cenci had once said, an order. That was why he had not been able to pray. But prayer, he knew now, was something far more subtle. Prayer is stars in the sky. Prayer is a white rose. Prayer is the mystery of life and death. Prayer is sound and movement. Prayer is a oneness with the great mysterious Power that motivates everything. Words are not necessary. Thought is not necessary. Only one's self is necessary, the realization that man, too, is divine, that man is a part of God. . . .

James did not know how long it took him to come to this realization. The stars waned in the heavens. The household quieted down. He did not know how long he knelt by Cenci's bed. But he did know that although speech is not necessary, he was, after awhile, speaking. He knew his lips were moving. He was talking quietly.

"You see," he was saying, "I just wanted to tell her once more that I loved her, that I needed her. I felt I could not face life without her. And I was going to tell this to Thee, to beg Thee for her. But I should have known. Thou knowest these things already. Thou knowest how lonely she has been all her life, and that she cries at night, sometimes, and that she is very fond of kittens, and that she needs help with her arithmetic and spelling. I needn't have worried. . . ."

The pale dawn opened the windows. Bells were ringing somewhere. The house had come to life again. But James was not aware of it. He was aware only that the pulse beneath his fingers had gradually but steadily become stronger, that a faint color had come into the drawn white face on the pillow, that for the first time in many days Cenci's eyelids had opened. She looked about the room, puzzled. Then her eyes went back to him. She moved her lips, whispered faintly, "Were you talking, Mr. Bronson? Did you say something?"

Above the happy tumult in his heart, James whispered in reply, "Yes, Cenci, I *was* speaking, I think." He smiled at her, "But I was only talking to the Lord about you. That's all, darling. That's all. I was just talking to our Lord. . . ."

Her eyes closed again. He felt her forehead. It was moist and warm. He counted her pulse, astonished that it was so much stronger. Then he observed that her respiration had become regular and natural, neither too fast nor too slow.

I'd better go and tell Doctor Ashton, he thought. It will be safe to leave her now. He got up, trying to make no sound. However, the movement awakened Cenci again. He saw that she was speaking and he bent over to hear what she was saying. Her voice, very faint, was chanting in a singsong voice,

> Spanish dancer, turn around,
> Spanish dancer, touch the ground. . . .

Suddenly her eyes opened wide. "Where is my ball? Lukey, did you see my ball?"

Then she saw James. Her eyes traveled around the room and back to him. Her mouth parted in one of her smiles. "I must have been dreaming," she said apologetically. "I thought Lukey and I were bouncing our balls. Is it nearly lunch time? I'm awful hungry."

James straightened up.

"I'll go right out and see," he said, trying to keep her from knowing he was choking back sobs of joy. "I'll get you something to eat. I'll be right back. Just lie still, will you, dear? I'll be right back."

He walked down the hall quickly, opened the kitchen door and stopped, aghast. The kitchen was in a hubbub. It was full of people, all of them so busy that they did not at first notice he was there. In the middle of the floor was a table at each corner of which was fastened a small cedar tree. Hunchback Pete was hammering away trying to get one of the trees to stand up straighter. Old Isabella in a purple satin dress was engrossed in putting decorations on the trees. Brett Lindley and Slim were attaching some tiny candles, aided by Mark who kept saying, "Do you think they're going to look all right? Those candleholders sorta sag down."

"Sure, they'll be all right," boomed Brett. "Don't worry, we'll fix everything."

Off in a corner sat Fred plucking what looked like a goose though it was as big as a turkey. Matthew and Sergeant Quale were helping him, piling the feathers up on a spread-out newspaper on the floor. An old Mexican dressed as a shepherd sat close to the stove nodding in his sleep. Miss Ivy was at the sink looking haggard and tired. She was busy filling a hot-water bottle. Some strange woman he did not recognize was stirring something in a saucepan on the stove, her back to him. Then Miss Ivy lifted her eyes and saw James and her face went white. Still holding the hot water bottle she walked over to him, "Cenci?" she asked. "How's Cenci?"

"Cenci's fine," answered James. "She has regained consciousness. She's going to get well." Although he thought he was speaking in a perfectly normal voice there was a sudden hush at his words. He sounded as though he were singing a Hosanna.

"Cenci's better?" asked everyone at once. "Cenci's *better?*"

"Yes! Where's the doctor?"

The dining-room door opened at this point and Doctor Ashton entered the kitchen. His coat was off. He was in his vest and was rolling down his wrinkled shirt sleeves. James had never seen anyone look so tired.

"Oh," James said sympathetically, "did you have to go out on another case?"

"Another case, yes, but I didn't have to go out. It was right here. You are now the father of a new baby son." The doctor pulled out an old-fashioned watch and squinted at it. "Two hours old," he added. "And both he and your wife are sound asleep and doing fine." He lowered his voice. "How about the little girl? Did she——?"

"No!" cried James. "She's better. I came to tell you. I——"

Just then little John walked into the kitchen, drugged with sleep. He was followed by Lukey. "Is it Christmas, Father?" he asked. "Did Santa Claus come?"

James sat down weakly, looked at the calendar on the wall. "Yes," he answered. "I believe it is Christmas. Yes."

"And," added Isabella, fastening a star on one of the little trees, "Santa Claus did come last night, young man, he most certainly did. Just like I told you."

Two hours later Cenci was allowed a look at the great Canada goose which Matthew had got for her and at the little table with its four cedar trees. Then she drifted off to sleep again and the rest of the family had their Christmas. During the long night Fred and Pete had set up the big Christmas tree in the living room and with the aid of Isabella had trimmed it. Stockings had been hung on the mantel and had been filled to overflowing by Slim and Sergeant Quale who had come over to the Bronson's house after the service. Almost every member of Little Bonne Femme, wishing to help, had sent something, no matter how small.

James went in to see Nora who was still asleep, the new baby cradled in her arms. He had kissed her softly and left the room. A great burden had been lifted from all shoulders and all hearts and they gathered around the long dining table for breakfast after having been admonished by the doctor to be quiet. What a crowd! James, four of his five sons, Brett Lindley, Pete, Fred, Isabella, Sergeant Quale, Slim, Miss Ivy, and the woman James did not know, who had come to help during the birth of the baby. Hardly had he finished saying grace when a knock was heard on the kitchen door.

"I'll go see who it is," said Brett, and in a moment he returned smiling broadly. "Come," he said, "all of you."

They rushed to the door and saw that the backyard was almost filled with Mexican children. The morning was still chilly. Some of the little girls were wrapped in blue shawls. As many who possessed them wore coats and sweaters. All were ragged. When the children saw the group at the door they began crying in a singsong chant, *"Creesmas! Cr-e-es-mas!"* holding out their little hands, palms upturned.

It was a custom here, Brett explained, for the Mexican children to go from house to house on Christmas morning, something after the fashion of mummers. They expected a handout and luckily he was prepared. He put his hands in his pockets and drew out new pennies which he tossed into the yard. The children scrambled after them, the pennies flashing like gold in the morning sunlight. The yard was filled with laughter.

As soon as every penny had been pocketed, however, the children did not depart. They huddled together, whispering, and finally shoved Jesucito forward until he was standing on the stoop. The dark-skinned little boy was embarrassed and tongue-tied but the children kept saying something to him and finally, seeing Lukey, he managed to stammer out, "How is the *niña?* How is Cencita?"

Forgetting the doctor's injunctions, Lukey gave a whoop of joy. "Better!" he yelled. "Much better. She's going to get well."

An epidemic of smiles broke out amongst the children. Some of them crossed themselves. All of them said, *"Gracias,"* and then one by one they silently went away.

But at the gate they almost collided with a short, bowlegged little man, laden with parcels and carrying four pairs of cowboy boots, unwrapped. Jacob Stein.

"Creesmas! Cr-e-es-mas!" shouted the children again.

Mr. Stein put down his burdens and—like Brett—dug into his pockets and tossed handfuls of pennies into the air.

"Gracias! Gracias, señor!"

When finally the children were out of sight, Jacob picked up the parcels and cowboy boots and walked slowly toward the back door. His face was furrowed, his eyes and big nose were red. He coughed and cleared his throat, standing there, afraid to ask the question he had come to ask. Finally, "How is she?" His voice broke. "How *is* she?"

James opened the door, went down and helped him up the steps.

"Cenci's all right," he said. "Come on in, Mr. Stein. Don't worry. She's out of danger. Cenci's all right. . . ."

21

YES, Cenci was out of danger. She was all right. She was all right except for one thing. Because of the injury to her spine she could not walk. Her recovery was slow but satisfactory. The specialist from Dallas returned in January and drove her to a hospital there where she remained two weeks. Then he brought her back. She had been so homesick in the hospital, he said, but she was a plucky little girl. No doubt about that. She had learned to walk on crutches. Now she could get out in the sunshine, and there were many things she could do, even on crutches. The specialist had long talks with Doctor Ashton and when he left for Dallas he picked the little girl up in his arms and kissed her good-bye.

"Good luck!" he said. "Remember all the things I told you."

"Yes, sir," she answered. "I'll remember. At least I'll try to!"

He laughed and kissed her good-bye again and then drove back to Dallas.

And now, overnight it seemed, the mesquite trees were beginning to feather out, an unmistakable sign of spring. It was a Sunday morning and the Bronsons were at the church, but Hunchback Pete sat on the edge of the tousled bed in his little hole of a room at the rear of the *Eagle* printing office and looked out the opened window. He couldn't see much except the parking lot back of Tasman's Grocery Store, but in the lot grew a mesquite tree. Weeks ago the silly elms had leafed out, risking a possible freeze, and so had the cottonwoods and the hackberries and pecans, but that didn't mean a thing. Any Texan could tell you that. Only the mesquite trees were wise. They knew when spring had officially arrived. They were patient. Oh, wise guys frequently insisted that sometimes even a mesquite tree made a mistake. But Pete knew they were only blowing their mouths. The mesquite trees *knew*.

This morning, the scrawny little mesquite tree beside his window was clothed in her new dress, mist-green, delicate. A mockingbird swung on one of its branches, singing a love song. So beautiful, so transient.

But Pete knew in another way that spring had come. For within him, his heart lay heavy and bitter. Spring was not meant for him. He, like the mesquite tree, was gnarled and misshapen. But there was a difference. Every spring the mesquite tree frothed out in its pale green gown, dainty and beautiful, covering up its deformities. But Pete could not do this. Nothing made him look any different. He was less fortunate than the tree.

He looked around his miserable room. From his workbench on the floor had fallen sawdust and tiny chips of wood from his wood carvings. There were long proof sheets for the *Eagle,* which he had to take back to the front office. His clothes were littered on chairs. The kerosene stove on which he cooked his meals had gone haywire and sooted up the whole place. The blackened coffeepot and the skillet in which he had fried his egg for breakfast looked unappetizing and repulsive. Ordinarily these things did not bother him but today, in comparison with the beauty outside, it looked sordid, grimy and hopeless.

On a small table in the corner of the room reposed a phonograph with a great brass horn, shaped like a morning-glory blossom. Pete walked over to it and from a box on the floor selected a record, a waltz from *Les Sylphides*. Usually no matter how dispirited he would get, the lovely music from his collection of records was able to raise him above it, but this morning the ballet music was unbearable.

Abruptly he turned the phonograph off, and when he did so he could hear in the distance Little Bonne Femme's church bell ringing. Pete did not go to church. He disliked all ministers. He hated God, who had allowed him to be so malformed.

He had not been born a hunchback. He had been injured in childhood. He had known what it was like to run and laugh and play, to stand straight like the other children. But after the accident, as he had grown older, this great bitterness had formed in his heart. It wasn't fair for most people to be normal, to have all the advantages, and for others to be twisted, ugly and dwarfed, as he was.

This morning when he heard the church bell ringing he thought of Reverend Bronson. Often when James was in the newspaper office with Brett Lindley and Pete was in the back of the building, he would hear them talking. More than once he had wanted to join in these conversations. More than once he had almost gone to James to demand angrily, "If this God of yours is love, then tell me why he ruint my life the way he done. You can't explain. There ain't no explanation."

But Pete remained in the background. His antagonism toward the minister had also become a personal one. Before the Bronsons' arrival in Donde, Pete had been Brett's closest friend. He was fiercely proud of this friendship, of Brett's need for him. He was proud of the fact that he, and he alone, had helped Brett in his time of great trouble.

He was hurt and angered that night last August when Reverend Bronson had happened to stop by the *Eagle* office, had talked about poetry to Brett, had taken care of him in the boxcar. Pete could not talk poetry. He had never read any. He could not discuss philosophy and literature and theology and politics the way the minister did. He was outclassed.

And then when Reverend Bronson had been the means of getting Miss Ivy to work on the *Eagle,* Brett's dependence on Pete lessened even more. Pete liked Miss Ivy. In his honest heart the hunchback knew that Brett needed both her and the minister. That was what cut. Brett still yelled and swore and sometimes got drunk. But not so often. Not nearly so often. Brett was beginning to be happy again, and he needed happiness. Last night he had confided to Pete that Miss Ivy had consented to marry him. The wedding date had not been set, but it would be soon.

It would not have been so bad if Reverend Bronson had been one of those oily-voiced smoothies, like some preachers. Then it would not have been painful to hate him. But he wasn't like that. He did not try to force his religion down people's throats. He lived his religion. This was hard to combat.

After Cenci's accident, it became even harder to combat. In those tense days when the little girl's life had hung by a gossamer thread, Pete's stubbornness had temporarily broken down. Against his will he had gone to the minister's home to help out, if he could. Never, never would he forget that Christmas Eve. That look of despair in Reverend Bronson's eyes. The hours of waiting. Helping Mark fix up the four little Christmas trees, helping old Isabella hang the stockings on the mantel so that Johnny would know Santa Claus had not forgotten them, helping Miss Ivy put Lukey to bed, driving with Brett to bring a woman to assist her and Doctor Ashton at the birth of the new baby, helping Fred and Sergeant Quale and Slim put up the big tree. He had felt himself powerless that night against the troubles of this man. He had felt himself sucked into the love that bound this family together. Nor had it helped matters when on Christmas Day, Mrs. Bronson had said to him, smiling, "I've decided to name the baby Peter, for you. I've always loved the name, and besides, I don't know what we would have done without you these past few days. I *do* hope you'll come to the christening, Pete." But Pete had not gone to the christening.

Afterwards when Cenci was out of danger, he had withdrawn into himself again. People, he knew, did sentimental things at Christmas, and during times of emotional stress. It did not necessarily follow that he should continue to be friendly with the Bronsons. So he had not gone back. The only thing, he could not look James Bronson straight in the eyes any more. He would not allow himself to think of Cenci who had not died but could not walk. Cenci, who like Pete himself, had been left a cripple. She had to use crutches. He tried not to remember how she had always walked so lightly, so lightly. And he knew that the minister was trying not to remember, too.

Since the little girl's accident Reverend Bronson had not been the same. His face had lines in it that it had not had before. The spirit seemed to have gone out of him. He and Brett Lindley, in spite of the disaster, had been unable to better the conditions of the slums in Mexican Town. The adobe wall had been rebuilt but of such inferior material that it could fall again. And Pánfilo García had been convicted of first-degree murder and sentenced to be hanged. Last month Reverend Bronson had made another visit to the governor to no avail. Pánfilo's crime was a clear-cut case of murder. The date for the hanging had been set. Next week. It was final and irrevocable. And Pete could not look directly into the minister's eyes any more. He didn't know why.

Neither could he understand why, suddenly, on this fragile spring day, he decided to go to church when he heard the bell ringing. Perhaps it was because the day was so beautiful, the rebellion in his heart so great that it had become unendurable. He had to go *somewhere*.

Pete washed his face and hands, put on a clean white shirt, his best suit. He polished his shoes and combed his hair. The service would already have begun, but he would be in time for the sermon. That's what he wanted. He wanted to hear just what it was that James Bronson would have to say, for in printing the church notices for the week, he had seen the title of the sermon, "The Pool of Bethesda." Pete knew the story because he had heard the minister and Brett talk about it and argue about it off and on all week.

According to the minister the pool was most of the time just an ordinary pool where people came to bathe and admire the flowers around it and see their reflections in its mirrored surface.

But once a year the pool became different. Once a year an

angel appeared and troubled its waters and vanished. And on that one miraculous day hundreds of people came to the Pool of Bethesda, the ill, the lame, the halt, and the blind. The hopeless ones of this earth. Because on that miraculous day, after the angel had troubled the waters, the first person to bathe in it was cured of his ailment. But only the first. For a long time there had come a man, hopeful of being healed. But he was too crippled to get into the water alone, and he had no manservant. There was no one to lift him and every year somebody else was the first one to bathe in the pool's healing waters. Every year someone else was cured. For thirty-eight years this man had been coming there, each year his heart filled with hope. Each year he returned home, still a cripple. The part of the story which troubled Pete was that this man had no one to help him, to carry him to the Pool. Alone he was unable to get into the water. Pete was alone, too. . . .

So this morning, knowing that the subject of James Bronson's sermon was to be The Pool of Bethesda, Pete wondered just what he would have to say about it. Pete did not believe the story. He knew there was no such pool, no such angel and it seemed unfair to him that even in a story there should exist one man who had no one to help him.

Peter stepped out into the golden sunshine of the street. He walked to the corner where a group of children returning from Sunday school were gathered in a knot, talking over their childish affairs. They were beautiful children. The boys wore their best suits. The girls had dresses with ruffles and sashes, and they carried Sunday-school papers in their hands and little cards with Biblical pictures. For a moment Pete, sensitively aware of all beauty, stood and looked at them. How fresh and pretty they looked, like a nosegay of flowers.

But when they saw him coming, they suddenly began to laugh. One little girl chanted, mockingly. "There was a crooked man and he walked a crooked mile." Some of them called out to him the one word he hated the worst in the English language! *Hunchback*. As he neared them, they wadded up their Sunday-school papers and threw them at him, they pelted him with the little colored cards, and finally ran away, laughing and screeching. Pete lowered his head and walked on. He met other people but could not face them. He knew from long experience that some looked at him with pity, some with revulsion. He felt as if his heart, raw and bleeding, was naked and exposed, only to be hurt again and again. Nevertheless he went on.

When he reached Little Bonne Femme Church, he stopped. He had been by here before. Often he took walks after dark and sometimes he would stop in front of the shabby little structure and look at it and wonder why people came there, and what it was they got from it. And his heart would be filled with hatred because he knew this was the house of the Lord, and the Lord had not given him a fair deal in life.

The singing was over. Everything was very quiet. As Pete walked up the steps, he saw James Bronson arise and stand beside the pulpit. Pete slipped in. Nobody saw him. He stood well over to one side so that even the minister did not see him. He listened to the story about the Pool of Bethesda.

Now there is at Jerusalem by the sheep market a pool, which is called in the Hebrew tongue Bethesda, having five porches. . . . And a certain man was there, which had an infirmity thirty and eight years.

For one blinding moment Pete had the feeling that James Bronson, reading the story from the Bible, was not James Bronson at all, but that on this Sunday morning it was the minister himself who was the crippled man who could not get to the pool in time to be healed. Reverend Bronson's face was gray and lined. It was filled with suffering. After he had finished reading, he closed the Bible and for a long moment said nothing, looking out over his congregation. Then he began. His sermon was simple. It was not very long. Oddly enough, he did not talk very much about the Pool of Bethesda. He talked about beauty. He said that God in his mysterious way had placed beauty in unexpected places. He said there was beauty in suffering, there was beauty in patience, there was beauty in the most humble of tasks.

He said that the crippled man at the Pool of Bethesda was but a symbol. The world, he explained, was filled with men like this one. But deformities, he explained, were not necessarily physical. A deformity might be a great sorrow. It might be hatred. It might be a wrong evaluation. It might be a broken heart. And often, he said, many people, like the man in the story, had no one to help them. Day after day they would seek relief and healing and would not find it, and because they would not find it, their hearts became hard. They blamed it on God. They blamed it on the fact that the Pool was crowded, that there was no one to help them, that even the angel who troubled the waters did not care who was healed and who was not healed. But when Christ came to the Pool, he did not see, really, that the man was crippled. He saw something greater. He saw that the man had been coming there for thirty-eight years, that the man had infinite faith and patience and hope, that he refused to give up. And it was because of this that Christ had said to him, "Take up thy bed and walk." And the man had walked. But long before the day that Christ had come to this pool, the crippled man had already taken up his bed and walked. He, alone, had accomplished the more difficult thing.

"Our great decisions," said James Bronson, "our magnificent moments, are not due to others. They are due to ourselves. To our own faith."

"Christ," he said, "had seen the beauty of this man's life. Deformity, ugliness, illness, suffering—yes, they can be ugly, to those too blind to see the truth. But also they can be the most beautiful things in the world. One might pass an old, wrinkled woman on the street, her life behind her, nothing about her attractive or desirable. And yet that woman might be divinely beautiful because of what lay in her heart. Even Christ himself," concluded Reverend Bronson, "was described as being 'without comeliness.'"

Pete did not wait for the end of the service. He slipped away. But as he walked down the street he was not aware of the taunts of thoughtless children, of looks of pity. He was aware only that the spring flowers were everywhere in bloom, that the trees were budding out, that the sky was as soft and blue as the eyes of a baby. He was aware of a new, wonderful happiness in his own heart. Never, never since his accident had he felt like this before. He felt as if a great anthem were ringing in his ears. He felt as if a magnificent glory surrounded him. Quickly he returned to the newspaper office. He went back to his dingy room and divested himself of his good clothes.

On his workbench lay two blocks of wood. He had been saving them for a long time. Two blocks of African ebony that he had chanced upon once and had been waiting to carve because he knew this wood was not for ordinary purposes. Now, inspired, he picked them up. He turned them over and over in his sensitive hands, feeling their satin softness. Then he took a pencil and sketched a figure on each of them. On one, a man and on the other, a woman. Both of them were old and gnarled and battered by life. But in his sketches, both of them were kneeling. Pete took out his wood-carving instruments, looked them over critically, sharpened the ones that had grown dull.

I will make a pair of book ends, he said to himself, for the preacher. I'll give them to him for Easter. For his study table.

He looked out at the ethereal mesquite tree. He wound up his ancient phonograph and adjusted the tubular record from *Les Sylphides*. Listening to it he could picture in his mind a troop of ballet dancers, gauzy as white butterflies, floating on the air in a flower garden. On his wall, fastened with two tacks, was a picture he had cut from a magazine. The picture showed a stage on which the scenery was copied from one of Corot's paintings. In addition it showed dancers in traditional ballet costumes, poised as if for flight. Pete had never seen a Corot painting, in fact he had never seen a ballet. He was familiar only with the music which now filled his grubby little room and spilled out of the window, drowning even the singing of the mockingbird in the mesquite tree. Pete took one of the blocks of African ebony, squinted at his sketch and then set to work.

"Thirty-eight years," he murmured, and tears rolled down his cheeks. "Thirty-eight years . . ."

He touched his precious ebony as a musician might touch the keys of a fine piano. I want these book ends to be the most beautiful things I ever made, he said to himself, and even then they will be a pore gift to the preacher, a pore thank you, for what he give me today.

22

NEVER, never, thought Cenci on awakening, had there been such a beautiful morning. It was so early in the year that the summer's dust had not yet covered the new spring foliage, the leaves had never looked greener, the sun had never shone more golden. The bird's songs had never sounded sweeter. She got out of bed and looked across the Rio Grande and then her heart seemed to turn to stone. For today, she remembered, was the day that Pánfilo García was to be hanged.

Looking at the river she thought of the afternoon she and Lukey had rescued the Mexican. He did not look like a criminal. She had felt so sorry for him because he was so small and thin and bedraggled and because he was frightened and hungry. He did not look like a murderer. In the movies murderers always had a sly look. They were slick and cunning and the way such movies ended, well, sheriffs with handlebar mustaches, accompanied by cops—dozens of cops with the same kind of mustaches—always chased the murderer who would try to outwit them but never did. After going to a movie like this Cenci would come out devastated with excitement. The chase was always very exciting and if the movie was extra good she would get a little worried for fear the murderer wouldn't be caught although she always knew he would.

But Pánfilo was not at all like this. He was such a beaten little man. And he was so weak that the current of the river had almost sucked him under the water. Then he was so hungry, too. It was awful to see anybody so hungry, like an old stray dog. He was not sly or cunning either but did what she and Lukey told him. Yet Pánfilo was being chased, too, though in such a different way from the movie chases and all along Cenci had hoped it would not turn out the way it did in the movies. But it did. He got caught and today he was going to be hanged. Oh, no! her heart cried. "Oh, no! Lord God Almighty," she prayed, "don't let that little man be hanged! Please!"

James, after a fitful night's sleep in the same jail cell with Pánfilo, awoke early, too. The cot that had been put up for him was hard, the thin mattress lumpy. He had slept in his clothes. For months he had seen the Mexican almost daily and Pánfilo had listened when James read the Bible to him. The scrawny little man talked to him sometimes about his life in Mexico, about the snow-capped mountains. In Mexico he had been a woodcutter, had gone into the mountains riding astride a donkey, bringing back bundles of fat pine wood for which there was always a sale. He would try to make the two bundles evenly balanced on the donkey. He liked the smell of resin. He liked piñon nuts and always brought back a few handfuls as a gift to Lupe whom he was courting. Last night Pánfilo could not eat. He kept thinking of the piñon nuts, he told James, and he wished he could have a few, just a few, to recall the taste, before he died. James had gone to town to find some but had failed. It was a small thing, but he would have liked to do it for Pánfilo. Even in that he had failed. Now James awoke in the damp earthy cell. Outside he could see that the sky was a deep soft blue. He could hear the magpies noisily chattering in the canebrakes on the river. He stirred on his cot and saw that Pánfilo was awake, too. The little man's eyes seemed to have grown larger and James saw that they were beautiful eyes, brown and liquid.

In a few minutes breakfast was brought to them, a basket of good things that Nora and Isabella had prepared, and a pot full of coffee. Neither man could eat, although James drank some coffee. Then he said, "Is there anything I can do for you? Would you like me to pray or to read the Scriptures?"

"No, thank you, señor," said Pánfilo, ever polite. He sat on the edge of his cot, shrunken and apathetic. "You've done everything. You and Mr. Lindley have done everything you could and I wish to thank you. I just beg of you to take care of my wife and child after I am gone. I wish she had been well enough to come to the jail. I wish I could have seen her and Ignacio but maybe it's better this way."

It was a long time until noon and James wondered how they would get through the morning. That night when Cenci had been so ill and he felt that he had lost God yet had found him again, that night was like today. One can find God and find him, he thought, and yet lose him again. God is not here this morning, he said to himself. He is not with me, nor with Pánfilo.

At that moment the jailkeeper who had brought their breakfast unlocked the door and came in. "A vistor for you, Padre," he said to Mr. Bronson. "He's waiting outside."

James left the cell and in the narrow evil-smelling hall distinguished the great hulk of Brett Lindley. After the exchange of a few words Brett handed him a little paper sack. "I managed to get these," he said. "Mr. Tasman helped me. We couldn't get many but maybe they'll help."

James looked in the sack and saw that it contained something that looked at first like small dried beans. He picked one up in his fingers and examined it.

"That's a piñon nut," said Brett. "They grow only on a certain kind of pine tree. It's all I could think of to do, James. Are you coming home?"

"No," said James, "I'll stay till it's over. Tell Nora and the children I'm all right and thanks for these, Brett. I thought about them all night, and I'm sure Pánfilo did, too. Thank Mr. Tasman for me, will you? And you'll keep an eye on Lupe?"

"Yes, Jim. I'll take care of things. Don't worry, Jim. Good-bye."

James took the sack of piñons back into the cell and when Pánfilo saw them his face lighted up and tears filled his eyes and rolled down his cheeks. With his inherent good breeding he first held out the sack to the minister and told him to help himself but James shook his head and smiled. "No, thank you," he said, "I don't like them, you know. I'm sorry. You'll have to eat them all, I fear."

He watched the Mexican as he took the first small hard nut and placed it in his mouth, cracking the shell with his teeth and then carefully taking out the tiny pink kernel and placing the empty shell neatly on a piece of torn newspaper on the cot. Then he put the kernel of the nut back in his mouth and chewed it slowly, making it last as long as possible. When he had finished he smiled.

"They taste just the same. It's too bad you don't like them." Then he put another one in his mouth, cracked it, laid the empty shell beside the other one, looked again at the pink kernel in the palm of his hand.

James looked at the small sack of nuts. He's going to make them last, he thought to himself, he's going to make them last until twelve o'clock. He closed his Bible and put it with his other belongings. He looked through the bars of the window at the tranquil sky. Then he looked back at the growing pile of empty shells. He felt empty like the piñon shells. His heart felt empty. He felt devoid of all feeling yet nevertheless he managed to look up at the sky and to whisper, "Make them last, Compassionate Lord, until twelve o'clock. Make them last."

That day, the day of the hanging, everybody in the Bronson family made it a point to be away from home, for they knew

that James would want to be alone when he returned. The boys
went fishing with Fred. Nora left little John and the baby with
Miss Ivy and Pete, who had lately taken a great fancy to his
namesake. Then she and Brett and Isabella stayed with Lupe,
Pánfilo's wife. The *Donde Eagle* was closed. The phone kept
ringing and ringing in the empty building. Mr. and Mrs. Tasman closed their grocery store and locked it fast. They invited
Jacob Stein to come to their home for noon dinner, an invitation he accepted. He had not only closed his shop but had for
the first time in anybody's remembrance, drawn down the shades
upon his beautiful display windows. Yet although Mrs. Tasman
was a good cook, the meal was scarcely touched. Mr. Stein
apologized.

"Excuse," he said. "It ain't the food. It's me. I got such
feelings over that poor Mexican."

"I know," said Mr. Tasman in a strained voice. "We feel
the same way. And we'll invite you again. Real soon."

Many of the other business men had closed up their shops
like the Tasmans and Jacob. But for the most part business
flourished. There had not been a hanging in Donde for years,
and ranchers and cattlemen had come for many miles. All the
boardinghouses and hotels were crowded, and there was a
lively traffic across the International Bridge. In spite of Brett's
vitriolic editorials and James Bronson's trips to the governor,
the general feeling in the town was one of righteousness and
smugness. After all, the Mexican *had* killed the sheriff, hadn't
he? He had also committed theft. He had escaped from jail.
Such a man was a violent character, a menace to society. The
town and country would be well rid of him.

Newspapermen came from all over the State and feeling ran
high. Brett and Miss Ivy had collected funds enough so that
Pánfilo would not have to be buried in Potter's Field, and so
that Lupe and the child would have a little to go on until she
was strong enough to work.

Only Cenci remained at the Bronson home. After everyone

had left she went to the study and sat down by the stained-glass window.

By now she knew his story well and she could understand how a man would want to get bread for his hungry child. She could even understand about the shooting. It had been an accident. But there were later developments that she did not understand. The prosecuting attorney was going to run for mayor and this prize of a scandal had fallen right into his lap. She could not understand how he meant to get votes by it. She could not understand why a desperate act like stealing three pieces of bread from a counter would stir up all kinds of political issues, nor how because of it, Pánfilo was going to be hanged.

The solution seemed simple to her. If they would only let this wretched man go, and give him a job, and give him and his family a chance! *That* was the solution. She did not see why so many people in the town felt that Pánfilo was a dangerous criminal and a menace. She did not see why there had been so many trials and appeals and why everybody had been so stirred up about it. Nor why the opinions of Mr. Bronson and Mr. Lindley so angered the populace of Donde.

She realized, too, that the solution of Pánfilo's problem had been equally simple to Mr. Bronson, only *he* had tried very hard to do something about it. She had done nothing. Yet, with her sensitive insight, she felt that when Pánfilo was hanged, Mr. Bronson was being hanged, too, and because she loved him so she felt that the punishment was hers as well. All the night before she kept waking up and thinking about Mr. Bronson spending the night in jail. She was sure it would be a comfort to Pánfilo to have him there. No doubt Pánfilo loved the minister as much as she did. Perhaps he would not mind so much to have to step out of this beautiful world today, when he had such a friend to stand by him.

So when everybody else left, Cenci stayed behind. She went into the study. She tidied up his table. No one else except Nora was allowed to touch it and Cenci was proud of this honor. She never threw away even the smallest scrap of paper or anything because it might be important. It might be something that James Bronson needed very badly. It might be a message to him from God. Who could tell?

She straightened all of the books and papers with extreme care. She put a Bible in front and took pains not to put anything on top of it. Mr. Bronson had once told her that other books could be stacked up but that no book in the world was worthy of being put on top of the Bible. So it was always left alone. She found a clean doily and put it over the ink spot. As soon as the table was finished, she took off the cushions from his old swivel chair and shook them out and put them back. They were badly worn. They seemed to have assumed the shape of the minister's body and for a little while she sat upon them. It made her feel closer to him, closer to Pánfilo, closer to all of the people in the world in trouble. Then she shook the cushions a second time, puffing them up.

She wandered about for quite a while and thought about the Easter present she had been making for Mr. Bronson. She had bought a linen handkerchief and had embroidered an elaborate "B" on it. In her imagination the initial was to be very beautiful, with flourishes, delicately padded, absolutely the best piece of embroidery that had ever been done. But as she worked on it, it had not turned out quite that way. It got lumpy. Her fingers were not always clean and the handkerchief was not as white as when she had first bought it. In fact one could hardly tell whether it was a "B" or some other letter in the alphabet.

Nevertheless, she had spent hours on it and had meant to give it to him for Easter, but today, she decided, was a much better day for giving presents than Easter. On Easter he would get many things. Today he would receive nothing. So she got the handkerchief and put it beside the Bible. It did not look quite right so she folded it and refolded it several times, standing off to one side and tilting her head to get a better view. At length she was satisfied. Standing there on her crutches and looking at it, a warm glow came over her. Maybe, she thought, I did a pretty good job on that after all. I am sure he will be proud of it and maybe he will save it and use it on Easter.

The clock ticked loudly in the empty house. As its hands neared the number twelve, the noon hour, she felt a chilling numbness going over her because at twelve, at twelve exactly, Pánfilo was to be hanged. She could imagine the scene, the throngs of greedy people looking forward to a new kind of show. She had seen the gallows. She could picture Pánfilo walking toward it, poor, sick, frightened Pánfilo, and beside him, his staunch friend, James Bronson. The clock struck twelve. A second or so later she heard the clock in Town Hall striking twelve and from the direction of the Town Hall came a terrible and frightening murmur, the murmur of a hysterical mob, towering and receding like an engulfing wave. It reminded Cenci of the sounds she had heard that day in the *Eagle* office, when Brett had rushed out, leaving her alone, the day of the shooting.

Standing there leaning on her crutches she knew exactly what was happening. She looked at the lovely easy chair beside the hearth. She looked at the little "kneeling rug" where he had knelt with so many people in despair. The rug was almost worn through to the floor. Now she looked at it and thought, "Maybe if I kneel there, too, God will make things all right."

She put her crutches to one side and knelt and dropped her head on the cushion. Then she heard a deathly silence coming from the direction of the Town Hall. The silence was worse than the noise had been. She could not stand it, so with her thumbs she stopped up her ears, trying to deafen herself against that ghoulish stillness.

A little later she arose and went to the gate and waited for Mr. Bronson to come back. A block off she saw him walking along, his head bowed, his hands hanging limply at his sides. His face was deathly white. She had never seen him look like this. Opening the gate she hobbled out and went to meet him.

When he saw her neither one of them said a word, but they walked on together and into the house. Immediately he went to the study and for a moment stood there in a daze looking at the room as if he had never seen it before. She touched him tenderly on the arm. The odor of the prison was still about him. She could smell it.

She said, "You must be awful tired. Why don't you lie down?"

She led him to the couch and obediently he lay down and she got a quilt and put it over him and took off his shoes. Then she went to the windows and pulled down all the shades. The study would have been almost in darkness except for the stained glass window. A shaft of glorious light came through it, illuminating the whole room, but she saw Mr. Bronson lift one hand and put it to his eyes, shading them.

Then she went to his desk and took from it the handkerchief she had made for him. She took it out and refolded it into an oblong shape. She laid it upon his eyelids. His hands were cold and she put them under the cover. Then she leaned over and kissed him. She wanted to say something but she did not know what to say. She saw him begin to relax and went away quietly, making as little noise as possible with her crutches, closing the door.

But all afternoon she could smell the prison odor. She could hear that greedy silence from the Town Hall. She would remember it, she knew, all of her life. She would remember the dazed look in Mr. Bronson's eyes. She would remember that a man had been hanged because he had wanted some bread for his starving child.

As soon as she got little Peter bathed this spring morning, Nora hurried to town. In last night's mail she had received a letter from her father which had contained a money order. The money, Mr. Abbott had explained in the letter, was to be used for buying James a new Sunday suit and he hoped it wasn't too late to have it ready for Easter. Nora had sent her father a year's subscription to the *Eagle* and in the letter last night he said he had read every word about James's efforts to save Pánfilo García and about the hanging but Matthew and Mark had written to him things that weren't in the paper such as their father's need for a suit.

If, he wrote, James had attained such prominence and was visiting governors and people like that he certainly ought to be dressed right. It just happened that he had sold a bull calf and had got a fair price for it so as an Easter gift he was sending this money order. There should be enough so that she could buy a length of silk and make herself a new dress, too.

Nora choked up as she read the letter. She knew her father didn't "just happen" to have that much money on hand, that selling the calf had been a sacrifice. Yet a thrill went through her also, at the prospect of getting her husband a new suit in time for Easter. The money wouldn't be enough, however, to include a dress for her as well. Prices were rising, not by the day, it seemed, but by the minute. Well, no matter. A woman could always brighten up an old dress with a new collar and cuffs or something. But a man's suit was a suit. It could not be disguised by a bit of embroidery or a ruffle.

So this morning Nora tripped off blithely to town, humming a little tune and heading for Stein's Clothing Emporium and Men's Haberdashery. She left old Isabella in charge of the house, having first confided the secret to her. Since Christmas Eve old Isabella had stayed on at the Bronsons', but her wrinkled cheeks were no longer rouged. She wore neat house-dresses. She had stopped bleaching her hair which was already beginning to turn a respectable gray at the roots and at the part. La Casa Toronjil remained closed. When Nora told Isabella she could not pay her for her work, the old woman had begged her with tears in her eyes to allow her to remain.

"I've never been so happy," she said, "not since I was a small girl long ago, in the convent. And it isn't me that's helping you, ma'am, it's you that's helping me. You and your family, and your husband, who is a saint on earth, if ever there was one. Please let me stay! I don't need money. I wouldn't take it if you had it." So Isabella had stayed.

This morning as soon as Nora reached the clothing store she stopped outside and waved cheerfully at Mr. Stein who was in the big window, arranging a display of cowboys' leather belts. He beamed at her and said something, but she could not hear because of the traffic on the street and the thickness of the plate glass, so she went inside and met him as he descended into the store. Mr. Stein was in a happy frame of mind. After exchanging greetings with Nora he showed her one of the belts.

"Sooner the cowboys see those belts," he exulted, "they will be crazy for them. Ain't no stylisher belts in Texas. Look!"

Nora gave a gasp of surprised admiration when she took the belt in her hands. Made of the finest leather, elaborately hand tooled, it was further embellished with silver tips and ornaments, and studded with diamonds and rubies.

"Are these jewels *real?*" she asked.

For answer Mr. Stein showed her the price tag. She gasped.

"I had always heard that cowboys are vain and fastidious about their belts and boots," she said, "but I didn't dream they were like this. Do you sell boots, too?"

Mr. Stein's brow furrowed. "I don't know should I carry the boots or not," he said. From behind a showcase he produced a pair of high-heeled boots, almost as elaborate as the belt. "These are just a sample," he explained. "But about cowboy boots I know nothings. About feet, even, I know nothings except they hurt. So-o-o! to add a new line of shoes and boots then should I have to hire a new clerk. I don't know yet. My mind, it is not made up."

So-o-o! Nora thought to herself. Mr. Stein had *not* given the four pairs of boots to her sons at Christmas from his own stock. He had bought them from the leather-goods shop. And they were fine ones, too, Fred said. Mr. Stein now put the sample boots back behind the counter, arranged the jeweled belt in a display case, locked it, and then said, "One new helper I have already. Come."

Her eyes dancing with curiosity, she followed him to the work room. Two Mexican tailors sat cross-legged on the same table where James and Cenci had first met Mr. Stein. A third man, half enveloped in steam, was pressing a suit with a tailor's goose, charcoal-filled. And at the back door, preparing to leave, stood a thin, olive-skinned little woman in mourning, wrapped in a black shawl, her eyes dark and sad in her oval face.

"Lupe!"

Pánfilo García's widow smiled when she saw Nora, and came toward her and shook hands.

"She is my embroiderer," explained Mr. Stein proudly, "Monograms she makes, on shirts, and pajamas and handkerchiefs and" —he paused delicately—"and everythings."

Lupe had delivered some finished work and had returned for more which she had now in a box, under her shawl. Timidly she took out the dozen handkerchiefs she had completed, when Mr. Stein asked to show them to Nora. "Fancy, eh?" he asked.

"Indeed they are!" exclaimed Nora, "I've never seen such lovely work."

After a few more words of conversation Lupe departed and Nora and Mr. Stein returned to the display room.

"Embroidery," explained he, "is somethings she can do at home and at the same time take care of Ignacio. I was meaning to tell you. Besides, she can sew beautiful. She can make lace even. But on men's clothes," he added with a grin, "lace ain't stylish."

"Mr. Stein, you are wonderful," said Nora. "I've been trying to find work for Lupe that wouldn't have to take her away from home, and not too taxing on her strength. The little boy, Ignacio——" she hesitated.

"He still ain't so good?" asked the tailor significantly.

She nodded. "He was neglected too long, I'm afraid," she said. "Still one can always *hope*. . . ."

There was a silence of understanding between them. Then, remembering her errand, Nora told him about the suit for her husband. She opened her pocketbook and laid the money order triumphantly down on the counter.

"And just because you have a bowl of soup at our house once in a while, Mr. Stein," she said gaily, "I don't want any more of your tricks. There's plenty here for a good, readymade suit, without any discount on price. I'd like to surprise him with it for Easter."

"Tricks, Mrs. Bronson?" Jacob was indignant. "I don't play no tricks on my good cash customers like you! Besides, business is business."

There followed a delightful half-hour. Suits were examined and discussed. Price tags were scrutinized. They went into a conspiracy over methods of obtaining the minister's measurements. At length a choice was made. The price was slightly above the amount of the money order which she had made over to Mr. Stein, so she again opened her pocketbook, laid upon the money order a one-dollar bill, a dime, a nickel, and one penny.

"It lacks a dollar and sixteen cents of being enough," she said, and when the tailor started to object she laughed and said, "Business is business," and then walked happily out of the store.

As soon as she had gone, the little Jew walked over to the rack and looked scornfully at the suit she had selected.

"A readymade suit!" he scoffed, "Fer *him!*"

Then he went to a table upon which reposed bolts of fine and expensive material. Between his thumb and forefinger he critically felt the cloth of each one, several times snipping off small samples which he took over to the door and examined by daylight. He made every sort of test known to a good tailor before he finally made his selection.

"Yiss, Mrs. Bronson," he said to himself gleefully, "business is business and you are a schmardt woman. Very schmardt. But Jacob Stein ain't so dumb either. Wait and see!"

23

DURING Nora's absence that morning, while she and Mr. Stein had been selecting James's new suit, a committee from the Uplifters' Society had called at the Bronson home. They were disappointed to find Nora away, for they had come to voice their disapproval of Isabella, a disapproval which had been gathering momentum since Christmas. The Society was interdenominational, was made up mainly of wealthy women who did not have much else to do. Their morals were high. They went about "doing good," packing baskets for the poor at Thanksgiving, making layettes for the offspring of "wayward" girls, helping to send "incorrigible" boys to reform schools.

The committee calling on the Bronsons was headed by the Society's president, Mrs. MacWordy, a short, stout, tightly corseted woman with white, fat hands and piano legs. Mr. Bronson admitted them into his study in his courtly, gracious manner, apologizing because there were not enough chairs for so many, and somehow, as he seated them, Mrs. MacWordy found herself on the round-topped trunk, her feet dangling a full three inches from the floor.

The committee first of all thanked him for his influence in closing La Casa Toronjil. Then it demanded that he send Isabella away from Donde. Why, they said, it was an outrage for her to remain, and doubly an outrage for her to work in the family of one of Donde's ministers. It was unthinkable. A disgrace. And Mr. Bronson the father of five *boys,* too! Think of the influence on *them!*

Mrs. MacWordy did most of the talking, slipping and slithering on the top of the trunk as her indignity increased. Once she almost fell off and Mr. Bronson thought he heard a suppressed giggle from a woman on the seat beneath the stained-glass window. He may have been mistaken, though. The room was heady with the mingled fragrance of so many kinds of French perfume, such beautiful dresses, such fervent interruptions and additions to Mrs. MacWordy's tirade.

At length he stood up beside his study table, looked around at the group which suddenly became quiet.

"Ladies," he said gently, "I'm sure the Uplifters' Society has done a great deal of good in Donde, and will continue to do good in Donde. That, I believe, is your motto. *To Do Good.* Now as far as Isabella is concerned, allow me to say that I could easily find work for her in some other town. In fact, my wife and I suggested this to her because elsewhere she could make more money than she does with us. She is an excellent cook, a good worker. We allowed her to stay, however, because she said"—he hesitated—"she said she was happy here. That she loved us. That we are helping *her.* In other words, ladies, that we—if I may borrow your motto—are also doing good." He paused.

Mrs. MacWordy slipped toward the back of the trunk, almost getting herself wedged in between it and the wall, but finally extricated herself, her face perspiring and becoming red with exertion.

"A moment ago," continued Mr. Bronson, "I said Isabella could make more money elsewhere than she does with us. I was inaccurate. With us, she works for nothing. We cannot afford domestic help, not even of the cheapest. This morning Isabella got up at six o'clock and cooked breakfast for us, eight in all, as the little Thorpe girl is still here pending the arrival of a new governess. While my wife attended to the baby and tidied the house, Isabella did the week's washing. You can see it from here, on those three clotheslines. Then she scrubbed the kitchen floor and this one. Please observe it. At the moment Mrs. Bronson has gone to town on an errand, and Isabella is watching the baby and at the same time baking two cakes for tomorrow night's 'At Home' for the soldiers."

Again he paused while Mrs. MacWordy strained to maintain her perch on the trunk. This time she had slipped too far forward and one of the ladies rose to catch her but sat back down in haste and embarrassment when the Society's president restored her own balance and at the same time, with the toe of one shoe, kicked her rescuer aside.

"Tomorrow," continued Mr. Bronson in his gentle beautifully modulated voice, "Isabella plans to help with the ironing and start washing the windows, make three freezers of ice cream for the 'At Home,' scrub the latticed porch and, I believe, do the churning. My wife will do the cooking and mending, attend to the baby, help with the ironing, and take Lukey to the dentist. As you see, this is a busy household.

"However, if your organization insists on my ridding Donde of Isabella I shall comply on one condition. That is, for one of you to take Isabella's place, beginning at six o'clock tomorrow morning, and take over her self-assumed duties. Your motto is *To Do Good*. In that way you will be doing good, certainly to us for we need Isabella as much as she does us. All of you, I understand, have servants. You have leisure. You are ever seeking worthy causes. I shall find a good place for Isabella and your minds may be set at ease. Do I have any volunteers?"

The silence was appalling. Then one woman sneezed, another blew her nose, and another leaned over and tied her shoe. Nobody spoke. Finally Mrs. MacWordy began angrily.

"Reverend Bronson, we——"

But in her vehemence she lost her battle with the trunk, and this time she did get stuck between it and the wall, her pudgy legs sticking out inertly like the stuffed legs of a sawdust doll.

And this time she could not refuse help. In fact, it took two ladies and the minister to extricate her. Mr. Bronson was extremely apologetic. "I'm sorry," he said. "It seems that we *never* have enough chairs. . . ."

The lady on the window seat laughed out loud. There was a sudden grasping of pocketbooks and gloves, sudden reasons why the Uplifters' Society had to leave. James escorted them gallantly to the door, watched them disappearing down the street, the starch all out of them.

But the starch was out of him, too.

Poor things, he thought, they don't have enough to do. It's much easier to help a bad woman than a good woman.

He sighed and looked at the clock, wondering when Nora would return but glad she had not been here during the visit of the Uplifters.

How nice, Cenci thought, now I have a chance to put another want ad in the *Donde Eagle*. It was fun putting in want ads, and then waiting to see what they looked like in print. The last time her ad had been for something she had lost, for Kitty— that was in August. Today it was for something she had found. Walking along the street she had happened to look down, and there, glittering in the sunshine, lay a ring with a red stone.

She picked it up and looked at it with pleasure. She slipped it on one of her fingers but it was too big and the heavy stone spun around until it practically lay in the palm of her hand. Examining it more closely, she saw that it was not one stone, but a rosette of stones, such a lovely dark red. She slipped it off and noticed that the band was thin, that there were initials engraved on it, almost worn down by rubbing against somebody's finger. She held it tenderly. Somebody had lost it, and without a doubt had loved it very much. She put it in her purse and adjusted her crutches under her arms and hobbled quickly to the *Donde Eagle*.

When she opened the door, she was disappointed that the

room was empty. It looked different, too. Last night it had had
one of its periodic cleanings, and she missed the litter of paper
on the floor, and the overflowing wastebaskets. Miss Ivy's desk
was as neat as anything, and the geranium grew in its pot, the
flowers a pretty red, like the stones in the ring in her purse.
Still, things looked different. However, the office smelled the
same. That was reassuring. And a sheet of paper was in Mr.
Lindley's typewriter, and that was reassuring, too.

It was funny to think that Miss Ivy was Mrs. Lindley now,
that by a few words from James Bronson, they had become man
and wife. She wondered how Brett ever managed to squeeze
himself into Miss Ivy's narrow little house without bursting it.
Well, life was full of strange things, and this was one of them.
Probably today the two of them were out to lunch, so she'd have
to come back. Even the printing press was silent, and the linotype machine, too. Well, anyhow, it smelled the same.

Just then she heard someone coughing in the back. Pete. She
recognized the hunchback's cough. It came from the sawdust
when he was wood-carving. He must not have heard her. She
thought of the lovely ring in her purse with its worn initials,
and decided to go to the back of the office and give it to Pete.
He could take care of it. She went through the room and rapped
on the door.

"Pete! Pete! It's me. Cenci."

"Come in," he called back, and she opened the door and went
in. Pete was sitting on the edge of the untidiest bed she had
ever seen. He held a block of wood between his knees and was
carving it, his brows furrowed.

"I would of opened the door for you," he said, not looking
up, "but this is awful delicate, and if I'd a shifted my position
I'd ruint it. Sit down."

She looked around, and saw nowhere to sit, for the chairs
were piled high, so she remained standing. Anyhow, he was
not paying any attention to her, and she could watch him better
standing up. Pete worked away for awhile, his face puckered

up like a chinaberry. She hoped things were going well, that her coming here had not ruined things. Then gradually the puckers began to disappear and suddenly his homely face broke into smiles and he coughed most magnificently, all the while looking at the block of wood and smiling as he coughed, which Cenci thought quite an achievement. Finally he looked at her.

"Well, little lady," he said, "you must of brang me luck. It turned out fine. Now what can I do for you?"

Since Christmas, when she had found out that Pete had helped the twins fix up the four little trees for her and that he liked little Peter, when as a rule he *didn't* like most babies, she had had a growing softness in her heart toward him. She opened her purse, showed him the ring, told about the advertisement.

"I don't know nothin' about jools," he said, "but I don't think this-here one come from the dime store. I'll ask Mr. Lindley to fix up a elegant ad for you when he comes in. Him and her are out to lunch right now. I'll take care of it, never fear."

"Thank you, Pete," she said, and started to leave. He called her back.

"I see you're still using them crutches," he said, in an off-hand way.

"Yes. I *have* to. I can't walk without them."

"Hmmm . . ."

Pete bent over his carving. "When I was a little shaver," he said, "I was ran over by a horse and wagon. My back was hurt, but not in the same place as yours. Mine was higher up. You're lucky——" He frowned as he examined one of his wood-carving instruments, "This gouge needs sharpening again," he muttered. "This is sure hard wood." He picked up another instrument and went on with his work.

"Well, anyways," he continued, "I had to use crutches for a long time. They was homemade ones, my old man made 'em. I got so I couldn't walk without 'em. I was scairt. We lived on a farm, a seedy little cotton farm. The cotton was so pore we never could get no price for it. One day my old man had to haul his cotton to town, to sell it fer what he could. They was just the two of us, my old man and me. When he left he said, 'Pete, do you think you can milk the cow and tend to things till I get back?'

"I said sure. So off he went. I was a-settin' on the doorstep when he drove off. After a spell, I decided to get up and I reached out for my crutches, but they was gone. I crawled on my hands and knees and looked for 'em everywheres. I was scairt to death. Toward evening the cow begun to bawl, and the horse come up to the pasture gate and begun to whinny. Pa wasn't due back till the next day, and I knowed I had to tend to them animals. And I did. They was depending on me.

"Pa got back the next day, and when he drove in I walked to meet him. Not good walking, mind you, but I was walking. I felt like I wuz leapin' and dancin'. Of course I wasn't. I kept stumbling and falling but Pa didn't say nary a word. He didn't offer to help me none, either. He just unhitched and fed the horses and I follered him to the barn. Every time I fell down, Pa didn't help me up. But all the time he was unhitching I saw him keep rubbing the back of his hand acrost his eyes, and I knowed then that he had hid the crutches and drove off a-purpose. A long time afterwards I found 'em up in the hayloft. They was good crutches. Pa had a knack with wood same as I do. He made 'em, and then he took 'em away. But he never said a word, not then or after."

Cenci looked at him, her chin quivering.

"How did you do it, Pete?" she asked.

Pete blew some fine wood dust from his carving.

"One step at a time, little gal. One step at a time. It was hard, but I done it. I couldn't of let Pa down."

"But Pete, I *can't* walk. Even when I put one foot on the floor it tingles."

"Sure you can walk, little gal. I heard Mr. Lindley telling what the doctors said—Doctor Ashton and this big doctor, too.

Your legs is all right. So is your back. Well, almost, anyways. You can walk, if you want."

"I'm afraid, Pete." She sat down on the cot beside him and leaned over and began to cry. "I'm afraid," she said again. "I dream at night that I'm walking down the street, and it seems so easy, but I wake up and know I can't. But I want to, Pete—awful bad."

"I'll help you," he said. "Me and Mr. Lindley and Miss Ivy has talked it over. You can practice here, and at their house. And Miss Ivy will rub your legs and feet. She has wonderful healing hands. And we won't say nary a word about it to the preacher. You can do it by Easter, if you try extry hard. The doctor will help, too. We ast him. Then on Easter, you can give the surprise to him for a present. To the preacher, I mean. You sure can, little gal. I *know*."

Cenci's sobbing ceased. She smiled.

"By Easter?"

"Sure you can. Easy."

She sat up. "I don't have any Easter present for him," she said. "At least, I did have, but I don't now. Oh, Pete! When can I start? We haven't much time."

The outer door slammed. There were voices in the front office.

"That's them," said Pete, "back from lunch. They sure takes their time, these days. You can start learning to walk right now, honey. Before he gets going on his editorials."

Reluctantly he laid down the piece of African ebony upon which he had been working.

"Now don't forget, little girl. One step at a time. That's all you need to do."

Out of the corner of his eyes he saw her smile, that special smile of hers that lighted up the whole world.

"I won't forget, Pete," she said, "at least I'll try not to."

24

LATE ONE AFTERNOON soon after that, Nora sat at her sewing machine in the kitchen, completing the last of a dozen diapers for the baby, little Pete. All afternoon she had been hemming diapers. She had received so many gifts at Miss Ivy's shower, but nobody had given diapers. People seldom did, at showers. They preferred to give fancy—and often quite useless—things.

Until a few moments ago, Cenci had been sitting there beside her in the rush-bottomed rocking chair, loyally sewing buttons on the boys' clothes, using the sewing box Nora had given her for Christmas. It seemed to Nora that it would be almost heaven to have all the buttons sewed on in place, just once! So this afternoon Cenci, who loved to sew, had fastened on buttons with diligence, a dreary job indeed, but she had stuck to it until she was through. Above the whir of the sewing machine the two of them had indulged in chatter and pleasant gossip. They had talked about weddings. Cenci had been disappointed in the quiet little ceremony when Miss Ivy and Brett Lindley had been married.

"When I get married," she said, "I want a big church wedding with bridesmaids and Mr. Bronson to do the marrying and me to wear my mother's wedding dress with the train."

Nora looked at the eager little face, at the big eyes dreamy with the wedding dream of most little girls, and then at the crutches lying on the floor. She turned away hastily.

The talk went on, companionably. Woman talk. The kind of talk Nora loved, when she was sewing or mending. Finally Cenci finished the last of the buttons and arose to go. She had to go to the *Eagle* office, she said, to see about her ad. Nora hoped she didn't get in the way, especially on press days. She would speak to Miss Ivy about it.

The house was quiet. Isabella had taken Peter and Johnny for an airing, the other boys had gone to a high-school baseball game. James was in his study. A pot of stew was bubbling on the stove, and Nora had an ache between her shoulder blades. With a flourish, she finished the last of the hems, tied the threads, folded the diaper and laid it on the neatly piled stack. She looked at the kitchen clock and frowned. She had made up her mind that today, as soon as Cenci left, she was going to have a talk with James. She had been putting it off, but today she was going to do it. Just then James himself opened the kitchen door and came in. He sniffed the aromatic air.

"Is it long until dinner?" he asked.

"Not long," said Nora.

Resting an elbow on her pile of finished work, she turned in her chair and looked at her husband.

"I was just planning to come into your study," she said. "There's something I have to talk to you about."

She glanced at the work Cenci had been doing, and her practiced eye saw a button the child had missed. Nora picked the garment up, selected a button, threaded a needle, and set to work.

"It's about Cenci," she said.

"Cenci?"

"Yes. For a long time I have felt that we should do something about her. Especially lately. Since the accident."

"What *can* we do?" asked James, avoiding her eyes. He went over to the stove, and lifted the lid from the pot.

"Give that a stir, will you?" said Nora. "But mind, don't break up the pieces of potato."

Absently he did her bidding, his back still turned toward her. "You know what I mean, James Bronson," she went on. "There is one thing to do, and one only. We must adopt her!"

James took a taste of the stew, laid down the spoon, replaced the lid and began walking up and down the floor.

"Nora," he said, "we already have five children. From five or six o'clock in the morning until eleven at night, you work to keep these children fed, clothed, and clean. We have so little money that if it weren't for the chickens and the cow and your sewing, we could not possibly make ends meet. I look at you sometimes, bending over the washtub, and I think of that gay and carefree girl I met in New York one rainy April day. Your greatest concern, then, was the condition of your Easter hat."

She fastened the button, snipped the thread, and stuck the needle in the collar of her blouse. "My greatest concern then was," she said smiling, "not my Easter hat, but how to get a certain divinity student from Harvard to fall in love with me and marry me. But that's neither here nor there. Coming back to Cenci—one more child wouldn't make any difference. In fact, a girl would be a decided help, with so many boys. I've always wanted a little girl. Just today, for instance, Cenci and I had so much fun."

She folded the garment, pressed it down with her roughened work-hardened hands.

"But it's Cenci I'm thinking about," she continued thoughtfully. "Poor, dear, neglected little child! We *must* take her, James."

"No," he said stubbornly. "Her house is a mansion. Her pocket money would keep us in groceries for a week. She has beautiful clothes, everything. It wouldn't be fair to deprive her of these benefits."

"Benefits!" scoffed Nora, her eyes flashing. "Do you call those things benefits? I still maintain she is the most neglected child I have ever known. She belongs with us. Look," she said, getting up, "I want to show you something."

From a high covered shelf, she took a box, but before she opened it, she went cautiously and looked out at all the windows, opened and closed the doors, to be sure no one was around. Then she opened the box tenderly, and took from it a little dress.

"I made this for Cenci. For Easter. It's real taffeta. White taffeta sprinkled with red rosebuds. Jacob Stein told me about the bargain. It was a remnant. He had gone to the department store to look for some material for the lining of a coat, and he ran across this. One end of it was stained, and the remnant wasn't big, so it cost practically nothing. But Cenci isn't very big either, you know, and with a little piecing, there was plenty of material. Look at it," she said, and shook it out and held it up before her. "I could dress her, James, easily. We wouldn't even miss the money, and it would be such a pleasure to me."

James touched the material. "A dress for Cenci," he murmured softly, "a little Easter dress. It's prettier than anything she has. I don't see how you made it."

She folded it and carefully laid it back in the box, and James put the box on the high shelf.

"If she were a waif," he said, "if she were a pauper, I definitely would consider adopting her. She——" he paused. "She is so very—well, I love her so much. Just as you do. But it isn't as simple as that, Nora. Cenci is a very rich little girl. That complicates matters."

"You mean," asked Nora hastily, "that people would criticize us? Would say that we have adopted her just because she is rich? Because we want her money?"

"No," said James, "I hadn't even thought of that angle; I'm not as practical as you. It's this: Our own children came to us empty-handed. It is their fate that they must share with us, that they must do without things. The boys will have to work their way through college, and if Cenci comes to us, she must come on the same terms, without anything. If she is to be a part of our family, she must be poor, like we are. I don't feel it is fair to her, to take away her rightful inheritance. Particularly now, because she is crippled. She isn't strong, like our boys. She will always need money. Not only that, but it wouldn't be fair to our own children if we adopted her and she had more than they. They would resent it. It would set her apart."

"Yes," sighed Nora, "I've considered that problem, too. I'm afraid I've been closing my mind against it."

There followed a silence, broken by James who said, in a worried tone, "Last fall I wrote to Mr. Graham about Cenci. I knew he did not realize that her governess, Miss Manners, was so neglectful of his ward. I didn't tell you about it because with another baby coming and everything it would only have added to your burdens. To my astonishment Mr. Graham asked me if I would adopt the child. Many people had asked for her, he wrote, but he knew they were only after her money. He seemed extremely anxious for our family to have her, how-ever. Of course, Mr. Graham wrote if we took her we would have to take her money, too. He named the amount and I'll have to admit I was shocked by it. Figures, as you have dis-covered, my dear, rather baffle me and the thought that such a little girl had so much money overpowered me. I wrote him that we could not accept it, that it would not be fair to her or to our boys either. He was surprised. He wrote back that it was the first time in his life he had heard of a poor man—he didn't say 'poor' but that's what he meant—turning down a fortune. About that time he had to go abroad on business as you know and Miss Manners was discharged. And then came the accident," he paused. "It's strange," he said, "when I picked up that crushed little body in my arms it didn't occur to me to bring her anywhere except here."

Nora got up, went over to the stove and stirred the stew. "So you want to adopt Cenci, too," she said gently. "Oh, James!"

Out in the yard, now, could be heard the talking and laughing of the boys returning from the game.

"There they come," she said. And then she turned up her face to James, her eyes full of laughter, yet tender, too.

"I sometimes think, darling," she said, "that you don't have the common sense of a gnat. Now go and wash the ink from your hands. The boys will be starved. I'll get things on the table right away."

Cenci sat in the easychair in James' study, industriously knitting a square in an afghan she was making for Peter, her face solemn with concentration. At her side, within easy reach, lay her crutches. From time to time she looked at the study table where James was busily at work. She thought he was writing a sermon, and whenever he was at work on a sermon she kept particularly quiet, even though at times she had so many things to say to him that to keep silent was almost unendurable.

In a distant part of the house she could hear the new baby crying, and she longed to get up and go and see him, but did not want to make any noise. Isabella said he had the three-months' colic. Cenci did not know what that was, but she did know he was absolutely the most wonderful baby in the world. He was bald-headed and smelled of talcum powder and new flannelette, and Cenci wondered what she had ever *seen* in the pink marble baby out in the pool before the Bronsons came.

Of course, the pink marble baby was beautiful and Cenci had heard he had been made by a very famous sculptor but he wasn't soft like Peter. He didn't wrinkle up his face and make funny noises nor did he have the three-months' colic and howl. Besides, Peter had to be bathed every day whether there was a dust storm or not and he was very slippery when soaped and she had not yet been allowed the privilege of bathing him alone. She did help with the drying, though, and the talcum powder and with the dusting on of plain cornstarch in the creases under his arms and under his double chins. It was quite unlike bathing the marble baby. Presently Peter stopped crying, and then the thought came over her that this time tomorrow, even if he did cry, she wouldn't hear him. For tomorrow morning she was going back home. The new governess had arrived. Mr. and Mrs.

Bronson had picked her out, and she seemed quite nice. Her name was Miss Lois Andrews, she was interested in Cenci, was serious about her job, and the little girl felt that she certainly should be grateful to the Bronsons for going to so much trouble to get a good governess for her, after all of the unsuitable ones she had had.

The only thing was, Cenci did not want to go back. She had been in this home too long. She loved it here. Next door did not seem like home any more. The beautiful rooms looked big and hollow and unfamiliar. They did not put their arms around her, lovingly, like the rooms here.

New servants had been hired next door, too. Yesterday Nora and Miss Andrews and Cenci went over the whole place, and things certainly were nice and clean and all ready for her. The garden had been pruned and tended. But all the while Cenci felt as if she and Nora had just gone visiting. She was glad when the visit was over, glad to come back here. Yet Miss Andrews had said, as they left, "Day after tomorrow, then, Mrs. Bronson, we'll be expecting her. I'll come and get her."

So Cenci knew she was not visiting after all. It was the Bronsons whose guest she was, and now the time had come for her to depart.

Cenci laid down her square, and for a few moments sat quietly, aware of the life in this household, listening to it, as a doctor listens to a person's heart. She heard its familiar sounds, now grown so dear. The lowing of the cow, Duchess, soon to be milked, and the murmur of the voices of Matthew and Mark, arguing over whose turn it was to milk her. She could hear Lukey hilariously playing with the dogs. They were barking and yelping, all of them noisy and happy with the joy of living. Cenci could not hear Trojan, the horse, but she knew he was munching away in his stall. He was a very patient old horse, and didn't give any trouble, even though he could not travel very fast any more.

In the kitchen she heard Isabella's fork hitting a dish as she whipped up a meringue for a lemon pie, and accompanying its rhythm she heard Johnny's high piping voice, talking to her. Johnny was Isabella's favorite, and he usually got first chance at licking spoons and dishes when she made pies or cakes. Peter wasn't crying now, maybe he had dropped off to sleep. Maybe he didn't have the three-months' colic after all. She hoped not.

In the study it was very quiet. James had stopped writing and was now reading something. From time to time she could hear him turn a page. Her own white kitten, which she had named Kitty like the others, lay curled up on the window seat, purring loudly. Mr. Lindley had found him for her on Christmas Eve, and by now he had grown quite sleek and proud and beautiful. Well, at least Kitty was hers. Miss Andrews loved cats.

This afternoon Cenci was not only aware of the sounds here, but also of the fragrances. The smell of something extra delicious was coming from the kitchen. She did not know quite what it was. Mr. Stein was coming to supper tonight and she was looking forward to it. He always brought her a little present, usually a scrap of cloth or a pretty button from his shop. He knew she liked to sew. Last week she had made a penwiper for Mr. Bronson to use on his desk and Mr. Stein had pinked it for her with his pinking shears. On the nights he came she would listen spellbound as he and the Bronsons all talked about New York. What an enchanting place it must be! Almost as wonderful, she thought, listening to them, as Paradise itself.

Then there was the fragrance of twilight, coming in at the open window. The smell of the river. The special smell of this study, a smell of books and ink, of worn chairs, the smell —she was quite sure—of goodness itself. She sat there aware in every sense of everything around her, aware of this household. It was more than feeling its pulse. It was as if she were holding its beating heart in the palm of her hand. This was a precious moment. She sat so still she did not notice that James had closed his book, had arisen from his chair. That he had walked over to her very quietly and now stood looking down at her, smiling.

"What are you thinking about, child?" he asked softly. "You've been still for such a long time. I thought you had gone to sleep."

She looked up at him. She could not put into words the thoughts she had been thinking, so she said, "Oh, I was just thinking that tomorrow I have to go home."

He pulled up a footstool and sat down beside her.

"Don't you want to go?" he asked.

"No," she whispered, "I don't want to leave here! Not ever! I know you have lots of children, and that Mrs. Bronson has more than she can do, but I *do* wish I belonged here! I feel as if I did belong to you, and then, when I think, maybe some day you'll all go away——" She paused. "Oh," she cried desperately, "sometimes I wish you had never come to Donde! Then I wouldn't have known you."

"You do belong to us, Cenci," he said at length. "Mrs. Bronson and I have felt that from the very first. We have talked about it many times. She told me that no matter how many children we had, we still needed you. We've both always wanted a little girl.

"If you were poor," he continued, "it would be quite simple. But as it is, there are very many complications. I have written to your guardian about it. But since—since you were hurt, the problem has become even more complex. You see, if we adopt you, we shall have to take your money. You would have a great deal more than our children. It would not be fair, either to you or to our boys. For such a little girl," he sighed, "you have such a lot of money. We have nothing."

"Nothing?" echoed Cenci. "Your family has *nothing?* Why, you have everything. I'm the one who has nothing."

James looked at her thoughtfully.

"You don't realize what you're saying, Cenci," he went on. "My boys are going to have to fight for everything they get, and if we take you as our child you will have to fight, too. You don't know what that means. You won't have much money. You won't have many pretty clothes. You won't have much of anything. Yet if we undertake to bring you up, that's the way it will have to be. You wouldn't be one of us, otherwise."

He looked out the stained-glass window a long time. "Not long ago," he said, "Nora came to me and told me we simply had to adopt you. She said your money could be set aside until you are of age, and that if, by that time, we had not taught you how to use it wisely, it would be our failure, not yours. I have finally almost agreed with her. But not quite. I was not writing a sermon this afternoon. I was writing to your guardian. This is a serious step to take. I want to do what is right. Of course, you will have to go back to your own house for a while anyway, just now, even if we do adopt you. There will be all kinds of legal angles to be cleared up. But," he added gently, "your new governess will let you spend as much time here as possible. I shall still help you with your arithmetic and spelling. Things won't be too different."

He leaned over in a rare gesture, rubbed his cheek against hers. "We do want you so, little Cenci," he said. "And yet we want to do the just thing, too. You're so young! I dare not make this decision in haste, just because of our own need for you. You have enriched my life, but it's *you* I must think about and I have nothing to offer you in return."

Cenci dropped her knitting, heard the needles clattering to the bare floor. She reached up her arms and threw them around Mr. Bronson's neck, burying her face on his shoulder.

"Oh, Mr. Bronson," she cried, "you don't know how much you have to offer. You're the richest man I ever knew. Please arrange about the money with my guardian. You can. I know. The money doesn't matter. I'll go over and stay with Miss Andrews while you're doing the arranging and I'll be good. I promise. But don't ever leave me. Let me belong to you. I *want* to fight for things, like your boys. I want to be like the rest of you. Please let me stay! Oh, Mr. Bronson! I do love all of you, so much!"

25

MARK suddenly discovered that he was getting tired of Dee. She was still the prettiest girl in High School, nobody doubted that, and the boys buzzed around her like bees after honey, and probably always would. But one afternoon Mark dropped into the Montezuma Palace alone and happened to sit down behind Dee who was with another boy. Mark had never considered himself gullible, yet pridefully he had thought that all of Dee's captivating little tricks had been for him alone, his own personal property. But this afternoon in the picture show he saw her using the same charms on somebody else. She flashed her dimples. She leaned her head quite far over to one side, whispering to the other boy so that her lips were not more than an inch away from his. She spread out her skirt so that it lay on his knee. At first Mark was furious. Then, his anger turned quickly to indifference. He had planned to ask Dee for a date that night but he did not do so. Instead, he went over to the Thorpes' to help Miss Andrews in teaching Cenci to walk, a secret everybody knew except his father and Lukey. Lukey was going to be told on the way to the Easter service, but no sooner, or else Mr. Bronson would not be surprised. Lukey never could keep things to himself. Miss Andrews welcomed Mark tonight, for both she and Cenci were discouraged, and he jollied them along and when he left they were both laughing.

The following days, however, he felt restless. Something was missing, and he realized that falling out of love leaves a great void. It is no fun to be out of love. He considered some of the other girls in the High School, but none of them appealed to him. Not one of them was as gay and popular as Dee. For about two weeks he went about depressed and irritable. He wanted to talk to Matthew about it, but he had a guilty feeling about Dee, for, with his customary ease, he had appropriated her from the very first, knowing Matthew had been smitten by her, too.

However, all this time something had been happening to Matthew which he, too, had kept to himself. After the events of Christmas Eve, he had decided that Mark could have Dee. The decision was like a clean piece of surgery in his heart. But it did not leave him depressed. He felt, instead, cleansed and filled with a new, calm happiness. This feeling was augmented by an unexpected incident that had happened in March.

There had been, all these months, sitting at the desk in front of him, a girl named Elspeth Gardiner. She was extremely quiet, a good student, and nobody ever noticed or paid much attention to her. She had fair skin, brown eyes, a high, serene forehead, and she wore her naturally curly brown hair tied back at the nape of her neck with a ribbon. One day, in making an unexpected turn, one of her brown curls dipped itself into his open inkwell. Matthew was embarrassed and apologetic. She was embarrassed, too. He was further humiliated because he did not have a clean handkerchief to offer her with which to sponge off her inky curl. In similar circumstances, he thought ruefully, Mark would have had a clean handkerchief. Mark would have wiped off the curl with gallantry. But all Matthew had was part of a blotter. She had part of a blotter, too. Together they managed to get the worst of the ink off.

The incident itself was of no importance. But going home that afternoon, Matthew could think of nothing else. He thought of the way Elspeth had blushed. He kept thinking of those brown curls, of that high, tranquil forehead of hers. It seemed unbelievable that she had been sitting in front of him since the beginning of school and he had not even noticed her. All he had thought about was Dee. Now, in comparison, Dee seemed silly and artificial. Of course, if Mark liked her, that was his own affair. Matthew thought it was strange, too, as well as a great relief, that for the first time he and Mark liked a different girl.

He could scarcely wait to get to school the next morning. He brushed his teeth twice. He tied and retied his necktie. When he was all dressed, when he was sure no one was looking, he surveyed himself in the mirror. The extra brushing of the teeth, the extra labor on the tie, had made him no whit different. There he stood, thin and gangling, a boy who wore glasses. A boy whose sleeves were never long enough to cover his wrist bones.

Repulsive! he said to himself. That's what you are, Matthew Bronson, completely repulsive and revolting.

For one stinging moment, he felt again that old jealousy of Mark's looks. Mark had everything. Eyes that a girl could simply drown in. An irresistible smile. The talent for always saying the right thing at the right time. Then the jealousy passed. If it had been any other girl but Elspeth, Matthew might have had cause for worry. But Mark liked the Dee kind of girl. The gay ones. The ones that all the other boys liked. Mark enjoyed his feeling of conquest. With Elspeth, this would be lacking. No other boy cared whether Elspeth had dates or not. There would be no competition.

She is *my* kind, Matthew thought, and the knowledge was a sweet and tender secret.

As he and Mark trudged to school in silence, Matthew wanted to tell Mark about her, yet he refrained. He knew what Mark would say, *That* mouse! Well, for gosh sakes, what do you see in *her?*

Besides, this new discovery was something so precious that he wanted to keep it to himself. Walking along, he dreamed of all of the poetic and lovely things he would say to Elspeth when he saw her. His heart raced. His imagination soared. But when he reached school and went into English class and saw her, his mind became a blank. Elspeth smiled at him shyly as she put her books on the desk. Then she sat down in front of him and said, in a stifled whisper, "Hello."

"Hello," he replied, and his voice shot off in one of its embarrassing squeaks, the way it did sometimes these days. He coughed and looked at the clock. In two minutes, the second bell would ring and they would not be allowed to talk. In desperation he cleared his throat and blurted out no flowery speech, but a dismal apology, "Say, I was sorry about that ink yesterday. Did you get it out all right?"

"Oh, don't give it a thought," she said. "I washed my hair last night. The ink came right out. I usually wash it on Saturday."

Then the second bell rang. Matthew had been on the point of telling her that he, too, washed his hair on Saturday nights so it would be nice for Sunday. But he didn't get it said.

She bent industriously over her work and he gazed at her loose curls. For the life of him he could not remember which one had got dipped in the ink. But how beautiful they looked this morning, soft and clean and still faintly smelling of soap. A goldish brown. Her hair was not very curly, except on the ends. She wore it combed back from her face, always tied with a bow at the back of her neck. How in the world he had gazed on those curls day after day, all year, and not seen them was a mystery to him. He thought, too, that now they both had a great bond in common. They both washed their hair on Saturday nights. Stupendous! Today was Friday and he firmly resolved that when school was dismissed he would invite her to go to the movie with him, after dinner. The marrow in his bones seemed to turn to water at the thought.

I'll take my glasses off, he said fiercely to himself, while I'm making the date.

He could scarcely study that day. All he could think about was Elspeth. Although he had been infatuated with Dee, his feeling for her had certainly been nothing like this. He could always put Dee out of his mind at will. His marks remained high. She did not interfere at all with his studies. Elspeth did. He did everything wrong that day, he was a blockhead. And after school he did not, after all, invite her to the movie. He became a weakling. He was afraid she would turn him down. His parents should have named him, not Matthew but Percy. That's the sort of a boy he was. Just a Percy. Repulsive. No good. In a fog of self-damnation, he avoided Elspeth after school and went on home.

The window by which Elspeth sat admitted the morning sunlight. Perhaps it was because she had washed her hair the night before, leaving it so soft and bright. Perhaps it was just the way the light shone on it. Perhaps it was the way she turned her head. But at any rate, on that same Friday morning, Mark happened to turn his head toward her and for the first time he, too, saw her. The way the sunlight streamed in against her hair created the illusion of a halo around her head. She looked like a young Madonna. Mark felt as if a thunderbolt had struck him. All other girls paled in comparison. How stupid he had been to have missed this celestial creature! Yet how lucky he was that the other boys had missed her, too. Perhaps it was Fate, perhaps this exact moment had lain in waiting for him, since the day of birth. Because he knew she was *the* girl. The others had been playmates. Nine tenths of the fun had been in the chase. There would be no chase for Elspeth and Mark was glad. Yet for the first time in his young life his self-confidence deserted him. He became weak-kneed at the thought of any possible competition.

After school, he said to himself, I'm going to make a date with her to go to the movie tonight. Thank goodness I'm not tied up with Dee.

Ordinarily making a date was the least of his troubles. Yet today he began to worry about his approach. Elspeth was different from other girls. She was shy and sensitive. He might say the wrong thing. He began to get cold feet. He tried to study, but could not keep his eyes from her. Once he turned toward the window just as she turned toward him and he winked at her and smiled. To his joy and surprise, she flushed and smiled back.

What beautiful teeth she has! he thought. What a beautiful mouth. I wonder if I dare kiss her tonight? Oh no, not tonight! I'll have to work up to a kiss, gradually.

He saw his brother Matthew, bending over his work, writing on a theme, erasing and scratching out. The sun which shone so divinely on Elspeth's hair also shone on Matthew's glasses, and Mark thought, He's all glasses, poor kid. He doesn't know anything about girls. There he sits, right behind her. But he doesn't know she's alive. Poor old Mat!

And then he winked at Elspeth again, and in a spurt of inspiration began working away on his neglected studies.

Yet, oddly enough, after school, he did not ask her to go to the movie. A girl like that, he argued to himself, must be wooed more gently, with more finesse. He would take his time. She was worth it. He would not admit that he was afraid to ask her. On the way home from school he wanted to tell Matthew about his new love, yet something, he knew not what, detained his tongue. And it was funny, too, that Matthew, ordinarily the more silent of the two, was unusually talkative. After a few preliminary beginnings, Matthew launched forth on the subject of kissing.

"You know, Mark," he said, "I'm not like you. I've never kissed a girl. I've wanted to, but I always keep thinking about my glasses. What's it like, Mark? To kiss, I mean?"

Mark thought of Dee. He said to himself, Poor goof! He's still got a crush on Dee. She'd kiss him any time. She'd kiss anybody.

Aloud he said, "Well, I'll tell you, Mat, there's nothing to it, not a durn thing. Kissing a girl is just like eating cherries—you see how red they are and you think, Gosh how sweet and juicy they'll be. That's all there is to it, Matthew. Forget about your glasses. Go ahead and kiss her. Usually the cherries are sweet. If you do happen to pick up a sour one once in a while, what difference does it make? There are plenty of cherries."

Then Mark began to whistle a merry tune, his head thrown back, the afternoon light shining on his handsome face. His eyes were deep with dreams.

Not this week, Elspeth, maybe not even next, but I'll wait. There'll come a time, the right time. And then . . .

If Christmas had been a great occasion at Little Bonne Femme Church, Easter was to be even greater. For one thing, there were more people. The antagonism of certain members of the Uplifters' Society, the criticism heaped upon James's head because of his trying to get a pardon for Pánfilo for murder had stirred up spirited interest in this apparently meek minister who had dropped into their midst. It seemed that many other people did not like the Uplifters and that a man who makes enemies in an effort toward justice also makes many friends.

The decorations for the Easter service at Little Bonne Femme, the background of greens, especially, had been relegated to the young people. Mr. Tasman, the grocer who had donated the candy for Christmas, loaned them a horse and wagon and the young people were to drive out to the same little grove where Matthew had shot the goose. They were to load the wagon up with willow branches and other greens that grew along the river, perhaps a few oleander branches left there from the abandoned ranch. The young people were to make a day of it, taking their lunch, returning with the wagon well laden. The rest of the flowers were to be provided by the ladies of the church.

Mark had looked forward to this day with wild exuberance. So far he had not yet taken Elspeth to the movies, but he had talked to her after school. Once he had given a little box of candy to her, and he knew that she was well aware of him and of his interest. Sometimes, when she smiled at him shyly, his desire to kiss her had been almost irresistible. She had a provocative mouth, delicate pink, turning up at the corners. It reminded him of a wild rose.

But he knew that a girl like Elspeth would have to be kissed in a very special way. She had been brought up strictly. She might take a kiss seriously. She might even refuse him, unless he could manage to bring it about as if by accident. He thought about it and thought about it, and then, like an inspiration, the solution came to him. For out in that grove the live-oak trees were filled with mistletoe which most definitely was created on earth for being kissed under, and for nothing else. He decided to maneuver until he got her under one of the clumps of mistletoe, alone, off to herself, and he would do it this first time half in fun, and she then could not possibly object. *Anybody* could get kissed under mistletoe.

On the way to the grove, Matthew and Mark sat on the high seat of the wagon, taking turns with the driving. The rest of the young people arranged themselves on the wagon bed, some of them sitting at the opened back, swinging their legs. They sang as the wagon rumbled along: "Pink Lady," "Oh, You Great Big Beautiful Doll," "I'm Sorry, Dear, I Made You Cry," "Come Away With Me, Lucille, In My Merry Oldsmobile," and all the popular or sentimental songs they could think of.

Once, while the crowd was singing, Matthew, who was driving, turned abruptly to his brother and said, "Have you got a date with Dee for the Easter Service?"

Mark shrugged.

"Not yet," he said, adding generously. "Why don't *you* ask her? I don't mind."

"Well, thank you," stammered Matthew, "that's awfully decent of you. But she's yours. I gave up long ago. Isn't it funny how we've had the tough luck always to fall in love with the same girl? It must be because we're twins. In a way we're the same person. Or so I've read."

Mark said nothing.

"Besides," continued Matthew, "I've about made up my mind to ask another girl. I don't think you even know her. She's—he paused—"she's not your type. For once I think we must be two people."

"What's her name?" asked Mark indifferently.

Matthew lowered his voice. "Elspeth," he whispered, "Elspeth Gardiner. She sits right in front of me in English class. She's the girl back there with the pink hair ribbon. I guess you think I'm kind of dumb, asking a quiet girl like that. So you go ahead and ask Dee, I don't care."

Elspeth, riding along in the wagon between two other girls, was in a delicious torment. Since the episode of the inkwell, she had hoped that she and Mathew could become better friends. When she went to class, she could hardly wait for him to come in, his big hands dangling, his wrists sticking out absurdly, his pants too short, his glasses shining in the sun. If only she had the nerve, like some girls, she could have made subtle approaches to him. But whenever she was with him, she froze. She had not been around boys much. She didn't know how to act. Yet she had been so sure, somehow, after the inkwell, that he would invite her to the picture show, or something. But he didn't. If anything, he had acted more remote, almost as if he were angry at her. Maybe he thought she was too forward, that she had planned the inkwell business.

And on that very same day, Matthew's brother Mark had smiled and winked at her not once, but twice. How handsome he was! Any girl in school would break her neck for one of his smiles. And as for being winked at, why, Elspeth was bowled over. No boy had ever winked at her before. In the following weeks, his little attentions had continued. Once he had even given her a box of chocolates. The other girls were always getting boxes of candy, but Elspeth had never had a gift from a boy. She wanted to tell the other girls about it, yet she didn't because she was too timid.

As the Easter Service approached nearer and nearer, she hoped and prayed and dreamed that either Matthew or Mark would make a date with her. She had a lovely new pink dress, and a pink crêpe-de-chine hat like a little poke bonnet. It was a dream of a hat. But the nearer Easter got, the more subdued and distant became Matthew, the more perplexing, Mark. She could not understand it. And although she really liked Matthew the better of the two, she made up her mind that if Mark asked her to accompany him to the Easter Service, she would certainly accept. But of course, he wouldn't! She had never had a date before. Oh, dear! She simply could not waste that beautiful pink hat on a bunch of other girls, also without dates.

When they reached the grove the young people got busily to work cutting down the greenery. Matthew, greatly troubled, had made up his mind that, if possible, he would get Elspeth off to himself though he was not good at such maneuvers, like his brother, Mark. But fortune favored him, and toward the end of the afternoon he found himself with Elspeth, quite apart from the others, near an oleander bush laden with pink blossoms. With constraint they pruned the bush until a heap of branches lay at their feet, and then Matthew laid down his axe and beside it she put down the garden shears she had been using.

"I don't think we'd better prune this any more," he said, "it might kill the bush. Now if you'll just hold out both your arms, I'll pile these branches on them, and then we'll take them to the wagon. I'll carry the heavier ones."

She held out her arms, and one at a time he placed the glossy branches across them. He could, of course, have put them all there at once. In fact, she was quite capable of picking them up and carrying them to the wagon herself. Instead, he loaded her arms very, very slowly. Wordless, they looked into one another's eyes, again and again. Sometimes his hand would touch hers and both of them would tremble. The pile grew higher and higher, almost reaching her chin.

They did not know that Mark, in search of Elspeth, had unexpectedly come upon them. He was standing under a cottonwood tree near-by and could see them though they could not see him. He watched the tender scene, saw that both their faces were flooded with color. To himself he said, And I thought nobody else wanted her!

For the first time in his life he experienced the agonies Matthew must have suffered time after time, when *he* invariably took a girl away from him. The only difference was that to Mark all

of the other girls hadn't mattered. Elspeth did. Now a cold
numbness came through him. He could not move. He was close
enough to hear what they were saying for they had begun to talk
a little. Trite, commonplace remarks. As he watched, he saw
Matthew lay the last branch, laden with waxy pink flowers, just
beneath Elspeth's chin. Their faces were very close. And suddenly he saw Matthew's long awkward arms go around Elspeth.
He saw him kiss her, clumsily, and then both of them laughed
unnaturally, in embarrassment, and she dropped the flowers and
as they both stooped to pick them up they bumped heads and
laughed again. Then he heard Matthew clear his throat and say
in a stumbling and ineffectual manner, "Elspeth, could you . . .
I mean, would you . . . well, I mean, I'd like awfully to take you
to the Easter Service——"

She flushed again and her delicious mouth trembled as if she
were about to cry, but she said shyly, "Thank you, I think it
could be arranged. What I mean is, I'm sure I could go. Thank
you very much. Oh, *thank* you!"

Quietly Mark walked away.

I'm going to find Dee, he said glumly to himself. Guess I'll
have to pretend I really *want* to take her. I owe that much to
Matthew. But I'll never let him know.

As he walked along he kicked a little pebble angrily with his
foot and kept saying to himself, Eating cherries, indeed. Eating
cherries, indeed!

26

IT WAS TWO DAYS before Easter, Good Friday, when the train from Yucca Junction came to its usual spasmodic stop at the station in Donde. It brought but one passenger, Mr. Graham.

"Cab, mister?"

"No, thank you. I'll walk. However, you may attend to my luggage. Here are the checks. The D-Brand Hotel."

The driver of the rattletrap car surveyed the well-dressed stranger with curiosity, pocketed the generous tip, and said to himself, I'll bet he ain't never been *here* before!

As soon as he was alone Mr. Graham looked about him. It was unbelievable that a town could change so little in twenty years. The same single track and the old-fashioned train coming in backwards. The same grubby little station, with the telegraph keys clicking away. The alkali smell in the air. Certainly no town in the United Sstates could be less attractive to the eye, and yet he was swept with emotion when his feet touched the cinders beside the tracks. He had hoped things would be changed, that there would be nothing left, nothing whatever to stir up buried memories, nothing to remind him.

Except for his correspondence with James Bronson about Cenci, Mr. Graham, according to his agreement, had not interfered with the minister. Nevertheless, he had kept up with what had been happening in Donde. At a newsstand dealing in out-of-town papers he had bought several issues of the *Eagle,* had read about

Brett's and Mr. Bronson's attempts to better the slums in Mexican Town, about the trial and hanging of Pánfilo García.

Then he had had a long letter from a Mrs. MacWordy, president of the Uplifters' Society, who had managed to get his address somewhere. Her letter was indignant. She minced no words. Mr. Graham, she wrote, was indirectly ruining the morals of Donde by allowing people like the Bronsons to rent his house. Why, she wrote, people in Donde were not even sure that Mr. Bronson *was* a minister! Nobody paid him a salary. The family, she wrote, had just appeared out of nowhere, like a blight. They had stirred up trouble from the very beginning. Mr. Bronson openly and brazenly championed the cause of a murderer, Pánfilo García, who had killed the sheriff last August. Mr. Bronson had gone to see the governor in an attempt to get a pardon for him, although in this he had failed. What could the Uplifters' Society *do,* she demanded, when a minister (if he was, indeed, a minister!) did not co-operate in their attempts to make Donde a clean decent place to live in? Clearly, she wrote, Mr. Graham had been rooked. He had been away from the town too long to know what was going on.

He should come and see for himself the harm his tenants had done. Why, Mr. Bronson even invited a Jew to his home and common soldiers from the Fort, not officers. His best friend was Mr. Lindley, the editor of the paper and a man who had lost a good position on the *San Antonio Light* because of drunkenness and who had fired a nice girl, an English teacher.

Also, among Mr. Bronson's friends was a cowboy named Fred, a distinctly shady character, who was a friend of the Rogers family, the Mr. Rogers who was hiding in Mexico, a man wanted by the U.S., a "bad man." Mr. Graham simply did not know! It was high time he came to Donde to see the state of affairs for himself and to send the Bronsons back where they came from.

If Brett Lindley's editorials smoked, as he had told Cenci last August, Mrs. MacWordy's letter was an explosion. Mr. Graham, reading it, chuckled and then read it again. He had been wanting an excuse to go to Donde. This fitted in perfectly. He dictated a brief polite note to Mrs. MacWordy and told her that he would attend to the matter she had mentioned as soon as possible and he thanked her for pointing out to him the conditions of affairs . . .

Now Mr. Graham walked toward Main Street and stopped at the *Eagle* office, overcome with nostalgia. For it was here, as a proud small boy, he had had his first job, delivering papers. He went inside and saw that the newspaper office had not changed much either, although there was a different editor, a huge, untidy, bearlike man, pounding away on a typewriter as if he were killing snakes. This must be Mr. Lindley. Across the room was another desk, the typewriter covered up. A little flower pot stood beside the inkwell. But the flower had died. Mr. Graham thought he heard the murmur of voices in the back part of the building, but was not sure. The man at the typewriter scowled at him and barked out brusquely, "Well?"

"I'm sorry to interrupt you," said Mr. Graham, "but I'd like to buy a paper. I just got in on the evening train."

"Hmmmm . . ." said Brett Lindley, "stranger."

He looked over at the desk with the withered geranium. "That new girl!" he said. "Slipped out on me again. Too bad my wife isn't well enough to work here now." Brett picked up a piece of copy paper, folded it over twice, and held a thick blunt-pointed pencil above it. "Okay, shoot. What's your name?"

Mr. Graham hesitated. Finally, "Charles Graham, of Boston, but I wish you wouldn't——"

Charles Graham!

Brett's indifference vanished. He examined the man searchingly beneath his bushy overhanging eyebrows. So this was Johnson's Mr. Graham! It was apparent in every way that this a surprise visit, that Mr. Graham did not want known, yet natural curiosity led him to say, "Why by here?"

Again Mr. Graham hesitated uncomfortably. "I

here," he said, "when I was a little boy. Got my first job here. I couldn't help stopping by. But please don't——"

"Hmmm . . ." said Brett again, adding, "You were lucky to get away. Newspaper work isn't much." Then his eyes went back to the folded paper. "Charles Graham, Boston, Massachusetts," he said, and began writing his notes down in such heavy black pencil strokes that the paper soon looked as if it needed a shave. "Don't know if I'll have room for your item in this week's edition or not," he said. "The paper's tight. Full of ads for Easter clothes. Afraid I can't squeeze it in *this* week."

A look of great relief came over Mr. Graham's face.

"There's a new hotel in Donde," Brett added, "two blocks west on Main Street, the D-Brand. You can't miss it. Welcome back to Donde, mister."

Already Brett seemed to have lost interest in the newcomer and his great hairy paws touched the keys of the typewriter and he began to whack away at it.

"Thank you," said Mr. Graham.

Just then the door leading to the back opened and, to his surprise, he saw a little girl walk out, supported by crutches. Turning to Mr. Lindley, he saw that all the ferociousness had vanished from the editor's face, and as the little girl came up, he said gently, "Well, and how did you get along this afternoon, Cenci darling?"

She sighed. "Not too good, I guess," she said. "I didn't know it would be so hard."

She hobbled over to his desk, looked at the paper in the typewriter critically, wrinkled up her pug nose, sniffed. "It's smoking, Mr. Lindley," she said, "I'd better get out of here. Quick!"

"Maybe you'd better," agreed the editor grinning. "This stranger just got in from the East. Please show him the D-Brand Hotel on the way, will you? I'll see you tomorrow. Goodbye, Mr.—Charles."

"He's in a good writing mood," the little girl explained, nodding toward Brett as she and Mr. Graham stepped out on the sidewalk. "Whenever his editorials are going good, the paper smokes. I wanted to talk to him," she sighed, "but it's always a good idea to stay away when those typewriter keys get hot. But I *did* want to talk to him today."

"What did you want to talk to him about?" asked Mr. Graham. She stopped and looked him over from head to foot.

"Of course I don't know you, Mr. Charles," she said, "but you look like the sort of a man who could keep a secret. I'm so full of secrets right now, I can't hold them in any longer. Would you keep them, if I told you one or two? Here's the D-Brand."

"I'll tell you what I'll do," said Mr. Graham. "If you'll wait a moment I'll register here at the hotel, attend to my luggage, and then I'll walk home with you. You can tell me your secrets on the way. I'm a good secret-keeper. You see, I know a good many secrets myself. They sometimes become an intolerable burden. Then a person needs to tell them to somebody else."

"Gee! Thank you. I knew you'd understand! I could tell by your eyes, kind of. I'll wait right here."

In a few moments Mr. Graham reappeared and they started off down the street. It seemed to him that at every step, almost, somebody spoke to the little girl, so their conversation was often interrupted.

"Well, now," she said, between interruptions, "one secret is that Mr. Bronson is going to have a new suit for Easter Sunday. To preach in."

"Mr. Bronson?"

The little girl's face lighted up. "Yes. He lives next door to me and he's the pastor of Little Bonne Femme Church, and Lukey and them's father and——" She paused. "Pretty soon," she said, "when everything can be fixed up, he going to be *my* father, too. Right now I just have a governess. I'm owned by a bank. This store here," she observed, stopping at a corner, "is the nicest drugstore in town. They make the best ice-cream sodas and banana splits."

Mr. Graham stopped. "What a strange coincidence!" he exclaimed. "At this very moment I was about to ask you about a good drugstore. I have suddenly developed an almost unendurable thirst for a strawberry ice-cream soda. How remarkable."

As Cenci went with him into the drugstore he thought with a pang, It can't be true! It simply can't be true that Stirling's Pharmacy is just as it used to be.

But it was. On one side stretched the soda fountain, ornamented by a huge silver dish heaped up with fruit, flanked by two glass jars, one containing peppermint drops, the other, wintergreen. On the mirror back of the counter, written elaborately by a professional painter, were the names and prices of the various sodas, sundaes, and confections available. On the opposite side of the drugstore were shelves and shelves of patent medicines. At the far end, the prescription department. And there was old Mr. Stirling, not busy at the moment, leaning across the counter, looking out over the store vaguely through his bifocals.

Mr. Stirling had the reputation of being the best pharmacist in the county, if not in the state. It was even said of him that he could weigh drugs accurately by merely holding them in the palm of his hand. His prescription department was immaculate. On each end of the counter stood its two show globes, the age-old alchemist's sign, one red and one green, each one illuminated by a hidden electric bulb that made the bright liquid clear and translucent. In the exact center of the counter stood a mortar and pestle, goblet-shaped, made of fine and highly polished wood. This mortar and pestle was very, very old; it was used merely for decoration. The one Mr. Stirling used for mixing drugs was in the sink at the back.

Behind the counter were more shelves, filled with glass bottles. Long ago, as a child, Mr. Graham had imagined that those glass bottles looked like soldiers. They had tops of old pressed glass embellishd with thumbprint and whorl designs and other traditional pressed-glass patterns. Some of the tops were pointed, others flat. No doubt it was these large tops, resembling heads, that had made him think the bottles looked like soldiers standing at attention in stiff and obedient rows.

Overhead spun two ceiling fans, and as Mr. Graham and Cenci walked in from the hot street they were met by that cool drug-store smell, like no other smell in the world. They sat down together at one of the high, white-topped tables in the rear, and old Mr. Stirling looked right at Mr. Graham and said nothing. There was no recognition in his faded eyes.

Donde has not changed, Stirling's Pharmacy has not changed, thought Mr. Graham with shock. It is *I* who have changed.

Cenci consumed two banana splits, and he an ice-cream soda while she talked. Eating her second one with a long-handled spoon she told him that Mr. and Mrs. Bronson were going to adopt her, but being owned by a bank made it complicated.

"I still call him Mr. Bronson," she said, "that is, in front of people. But by myself I practice at calling him Father, the way his boys do. And I practice calling her Mother."

There came a pause, noisy with the completion of that last drop of ice cream, that elusive bit of crushed fruit that simply *cannot* be left in the dish! Struggling with it, Cenci took up again the secret of the new Easter suit. Mr. Stein, she explained, had got the minister's measurements from an old suit, and no-body else knew about this new one except herself and Nora. She eyed the two empty dishes with sorrow. "Isn't it a shame people can't hold three banana splits?" she asked.

Mr. Graham agreed with her. "It is a shame," he said, "in-deed it is."

They left the drugstore and presently turned down Rio Grande Boulevard.

"Let's see," continued Cenci, "the new suit, all about my adop-tion and practicing on saying Father—that's two secrets. Two nice ones. I know another nice one. I wasn't supposed to know it, but I just happened to hear two of the deacons talking to Mr. Lindley one day and they have decided after the Easter Service to call Mr. Bronson to be the regular pastor. With pay, I mean."

"Hasn't he been getting any pay so far?" asked Mr. Graham in an odd voice.

"I guess not," answered Cenci, "from the way they talked. You see, they're afraid the Bronsons might leave Donde because they're only here on vacation, but people don't want him to leave. Even the ones that got mad at him when he tried to save Pánfilo, even those, well, most of them, want him to stay. Even some of the Uplifters do. Not Mrs. MacWordy, though. What does revolutionize mean, Mr. Charles?"

Mr. Graham tried to explain. "Why?" he asked.

"Because," she answered, "one of the deacons said Mr. Bronson had revolutionized this town. I didn't know whether it was anything good or bad, because revolutions mean fighting. But I was pretty sure it was something good."

"Yes, revolutions are sometimes necessary, I'm afraid. If the cause is just. But there are various ways of fighting."

"I know two more secrets," said Cenci, after a pause. *"Not* good. One is—well, you know Pete has been teaching me to walk. I was going to surprise Mr. Bronson with it. For Easter. But today I couldn't walk. Not without my crutches. Not one step. I *know* I can't by Sunday."

"Why can't you?"

"Because I'm afraid again, like I used to be. Only worse. I just know I can't."

Mr. Graham looked down compassionately at the troubled little girl. His ward! No wonder Mr. Bronson had been so disturbed about her.

"The other thing," she concluded, "is about Mr. Bronson. Ever since Pánfilo was hanged, I've known it. He has been different. He is worried. I wish I could help him, like he helps other people. But I guess nobody but God can help Mr. Bronson, and God acts funny sometimes. He won't help. He just stands off up there in heaven with his arms folded and says, 'Figure things out for yourselves, folks. I've got troubles of my own.' At least, that's what Lukey told me.— Well, here we are. This is my house. And right next door is the Bronsons'. Would you like to go in and visit them? They love company."

"I believe not, thank you, little girl," answered Mr. Graham. "Not today. But soon."

"Well, anyhow," said Cenci. "you can see his shadow. See that stained-glass window? That's his study. He's walking up and down. He's working awful hard on his Easter sermon. So maybe it would be a good idea not to bother him today, after all. And, oh, thanks, Mr. Charles, for letting me tell you all these secrets! Did you ever feel like you were about to explode? Well, that's the way I felt. But it's eased up now. Some."

"Thank *you*," he said ceremoniously, "for confiding in me. And—about that walking. Don't be afraid. Good-bye, my dear."

"Good-bye, sir."

Cenci went in at her own gate and he stood watching her until she entered the door of the big brick house.

It was nearing twilight. He could see the two eldest Bronson boys coming back from the barn carrying a big copper pail full of milk. He heard the horse whinny. Out in the side yard he saw Lukey and John romping around with what seemed to him innumerable cats and dogs. He saw the light in the kitchen, figures moving to and fro. He withdrew into the distance. Again he looked at that stained-glass window, saw that shadow passing relentlessly back and forth. This house, he thought, that window —they have haunted me for so long.

Then he turned and went back to his hotel.

After dining he stepped out again into the street. It had grown dark. He walked first to the river and observed the International Bridge. As a boy, he had thought it the most magnificent bridge in the world. He used to like to watch the sentries marching back and forth. Tonight it seemed to him that there was more traffic on the bridge than there used to be. Then he remembered. Of course, prohibition. The bridge closed at nine, and people were in a hurry to get over there and back before the bridge closed. He noticed one of the sentries, a young boy, who had stopped in his marching and stood looking out over the black water, a look of homesickness on his face. An American soldier . . .

Mr. Graham turned away.

He walked down Main Street again, and saw Stein's Men's Haberdashery and Tailor Shop. The little tailor came to Donde about the time Mr. Graham had left. He and his mother. He was ill and poor, his shop not more than a hole in the wall. But evidently Mr. Stein had prospered, for the store now boasted a plate-glass window which was lighted tonight, displaying a dapper young dummy in white flannel trousers and navy blue coat.

Mr. Graham went on, past the saddle shop and leather-goods store, the two movies, the *Donde Eagle,* the drugstore. Every building, every piece of pavement, every sight, sound, and smell brought back memories almost beyond endurance.

Perhaps, he thought to himself, Mr. Bronson will not be working on his sermon tonight. I *must* talk to him! I believe I'll go back.

So he retraced his footsteps, returned to the minister's house, which had once been his own. Nobody was about, though he heard voices within, heard the sleepy crying of a baby. He went through the gate and into the side yard. Here was the little fountain he had once built for Mary, his wife, with the water splashing into it softly and the mint bed growing around it, its fragrance overpowering. Dimly he could see the marble statue of a baby lying on a white rose in the center of the fountain. He had had the beautiful piece of sculpture made for her as a surprise after the doctors had told her that she must not have a child, with her heart in the condition it had been left after her rheumatic fever. The flesh-colored marble had been imported from Italy.

"Mary," he whispered softly, "Mary . . ."

He remembered the first time he had seen Mary. He was then working at Stirling's Pharmacy as errand boy, although because of his interest in science Mr. Stirling often allowed him to work in the prescription department, cleaning the sink, washing the show globes, polishing the ancient mortar and pestle. Mr. Stirling's profession was his meat and drink, his life, his religion. In slack moments he talked about science to the lad, he talked about pharmacy, about medicines. He loaned books to him. Charles Graham was his eager slave.

On this day Mr. Stirling had entrusted him with the delivery of a prescription for a young girl who was ill with rheumatic fever, Mary St. Claire. And while Charles waited in the hallway of the St. Claire home for the girl's mother to pay for the purchase, he could see Mary through an opened door, propped up in bed. The family was in modest circumstances, the room was immaculately clean but plainly furnished. Mary herself wore a simple, white nightgown, long-sleeved, buttoned at the throat. Her hair was parted in the center and braided in two long braids. But it was not the house Charles Graham saw that day, nor its furnishings, nor Mary's attire. He saw only her face, pale and delicate and illuminated by an inner radiance such as he had never seen in a person before. Always afterwards he was aware of her ethereal radiance. He could not explain just what it was, nor why he was so affected by it.

His own home life had been an unhappy one. His wealthy parents were religious fanatics. Their religion was cruel, sadistic, possessive. When they uttered the word sin they licked their chops over it. They were strict, unbending, self-righteous, and they held the fear of hell and eternal punishment over him ruthlessly, until Charles grew to hate religion and everything connected with it. In the university he became an atheist. Soon after his graduation his parents had died. He had continued with his education, however, and was eventually graduated from a college of pharmacy.

The following year he and Mary St. Claire were married and he built for her the house on Rio Grande Boulevard. Mexican Town had not yet begun to nibble at the fringes of the neighborhood. The house, with its extensive gardens, its costly furnishings, its unimpeded view of the river, was the most beautiful one in Donde, even lovelier than the Thorpe place next door. Nothing, Charles thought, would ever be quite good enough for Mary, that ethereal, frail girl who—miraculously, it seemed to him—had fallen in love with him and become his wife. There was an elusive, baffling quality to her that disturbed him. Sometimes she did not seem quite real. She was a wraith, a spirit, an illusion.

Except for a damaged heart, she had entirely recovered from her illness, however, and he found out that she *was* real, deliciously, temptingly real. She was gay. She loved her beautiful house and the enchanting clothes and gifts he lavished upon her. It was a delightful discovery to him when he found out that Mary was so warmly human. An enchantress, in her own subtle way. The first months of their married life had been filled with an other-world beauty. He had not known what happiness could be like. He looked back upon his grim childhood as if it might have been the childhood of some other person. Or perhaps a nightmare, one of those seemingly neverending nightmares from which he had been rescued by his love for Mary.

Yet in this marriage, even from the first, there had existed one flaw which he had self-confidently expected to correct. Mary was religious. He humored her at first, knowing that in a young girl religion is often transient, a bright flame that quickly burns itself out. During her illness Mary had been close to death and no doubt frightened so she had clutched at religion. But now the danger was past. Soon she would get over it.

Thus at the beginning he said nothing. He allowed her to attend the humble church to which she belonged, Little Bonne Femme, although he did not go with her. Patiently, he waited for her to tire of it. But little by little the insidious knowledge crept upon him that she would never tire of it. Her religion was not a new garment which she would wear out or toss away. It had not been based upon fear, as he had presumed. It was a part of her. He tried to ignore this. He tried to ignore, too, the knowledge that part of the elusive, spiritual incandescence which from the first had drawn him toward her, was in some mysterious way connected with her religion. This thought angered him.

He was jealous of her religion because it was the only part of her which he did not possess. He wanted all of her. He became obsessed with the determination to break her away from it. He fought it as he would have fought a lover who had come between them. He tried to convert her to his own atheism, and it infuriated him because he was not successful. Her God was not a God of wrath and vengeance, but one of love and mercy. Her religion was not one of cruelty and bigotry. It was one of tolerance, of courage. He could not fight that.

He became irritable with her. He picked quarrels with her. He scoffed and made fun of her, and when he saw it hurt her, it gave him a feeling of power and mastery. If he could not possess her, in her entirety, at least he could cause her pain. But the beauty of their marriage was shattered.

She did not tell Charles that a baby was on the way until it was too late. Did she take the risk just because she felt so well and thought the doctors might have been mistaken? Was it only because she wanted a baby so badly, or because she thought a child might draw Charles close to her again? Or did she, perhaps, expect a miracle? Her husband did not know. He only knew that she almost died when Kenneth was born, though she did not die. She lived for two more years. Toward the end she was no longer able to leave the house, not even to sit beside the little fountain she loved so well. One day she asked Charles if he minded if she had a stained-glass window put in her room, overlooking the river.

"If you like," Charles had shrugged. "It's quite a fad these days, I hear. Stained glass for fanlights over doorways. Whole windows. I think it's rococo, myself. But it's your room. Do as you please."

He could see her transparent face now, illuminated by the window as she lay on her couch, day after day, looking over the river. Only once did she bring up the subject of religion, a few days before she died.

"Charles," she said softly, "I want you to know one thing. I'm not afraid. I used to be, but I'm not any more. And I'm leaving Kenny to you, dear. Teach him courage. Teach him faith. I know you don't believe in God, but sometimes, you know, people call God by other names. It doesn't make any difference, just so you bring up Kenny to know that there *is* something greater than the life we see with our eyes, that within our mortal bodies there exists something immortal. Nobody knows what it is. But when you believe *that,* it explains everything. Teach him love, darling, and kindness. Teach him not to hate. Teach him courage. . . ."

But Charles Graham had not taught courage to Kenny. He had sent him off to war, to his destruction, a scared, bewildered boy, a boy with a sensitive, almost spiritual face, like Mary's; gentle, like Mary, and like her, now, through death eternally young. . . .

Mr. Graham got up from the fountain and saw through the porch door the Bronsons filing into the study for evening prayers. He remembered that when he had visited them in Connecticut, this had been a family ritual, after dinner, the reading of a few verses from the Bible followed by a short prayer—Vespers. He could not see James Bronson but could hear his voice as he read:

Now in the place where He was crucified there was a garden; and in the garden a new sepulchre, wherein was never man yet laid. . . .

Mr. Graham left the side yard, and with bowed head walked away.

His feet, almost by their own volition, led him towards Huisache Street. He recalled that the streets of Donde paralleling Rio Grande Boulevard were named after Texas trees, shrubs and flowers, Pecan Street, Cottonwood Street, Magnolia Street, Oleander Street, Cenizo Street, Cape Jasmine Street. He had always thought the names so pretty.

This was Friday night. He had expected to find the church darkened and deserted, but instead it was brilliantly lighted and full of people. After considering a moment he mounted the steps and went in. He had been married here because Mary had begged so. And he had been so much in love. But he had never been inside a church since.

Nobody noticed him when he went in so he stood off to one side, watching. Two men, their faces red from stooping, were laying a new carpet down the aisle, with advice and criticism from various other people who were getting in the way. Women were going from pew to pew, carefully arranging and rearranging new cushions. Other women were busily engaged in decorating. They had stepladders and were fastening wreaths of greens around the plain glass windows.

One woman remarked, "The bluebonnets and the camellias and cape jasmine for the pulpit will have to go on the very last thing on Sunday morning, just before the service. We don't want them to wilt."

Mr. Graham saw a preoccupied man wearing a carpenter's apron, gazing critically at a new pulpit, examining it from all sides. Seeing Mr. Graham, the carpenter said with a worried air, "Does it look all right? At the last minute I decided to add that extra trim, but maybe now it's too fancy."

"It looks beautiful," answered Mr. Graham honestly, as indeed it did. "Did you make it? You are a fine cabinetmaker, if you did."

"Well, thanks. Yep, I made it. The old pulpit was about to fall down. Every time the preacher leaned on it, it rocked forwards or to one side. Made me nervous. You new here? My name is Johnson. Caleb Johnson. Did you notice we'd painted the church? Inside *and* out. Some held out fer gray paint. Others fer white. Some fer brown. So many fights about the color I was afeared it wouldn't get painted at all. I wanted her white. World sure is full of stubborn people, but the whites won. Sure looks pretty."

At this point the tread of heavy feet was heard, and the hubbub of conversation ceased as a group of soldiers marched down the aisle and arranged themselves around the organ. A tall, slim fellow sat down, fiddled with the stops awhile, began pumping and playing a few chords.

"Now tonight, fellers," he said sternly above the music, "give her all you got. Last night I was plumb mortified, the porest rehearsal we've had yet! What will the people think, Easter morning, with everything else nice but the singing? Last night somebody sung a sour note all the way through. Couldn't ketch him. But if I ketch him tonight he'll sure get hell. Here we go now! Ready?"

Such singing! It filled the little church and poured through the windows. The men laying the carpet and the women at their decorating stopped their work, listening. Over the face of the slim fellow at the organ spread a slow and delighted grin. Finally the anthem was finished.

"Nary a sour note," he commented laconically. "That was mighty fine singing. Now the next song." Finally the rehearsal was over. Slim started to gather up his music, making ready for departure, when a young soldier spoke up shyly. Mr. Graham looked at him, remembering the sentry at the bridge, and his heart constricted.

"Let's take time for one more song, Slim," he said. "I have a particular one in mind. I've been honing for it a long time."

Slim was in a jovial mood.

"Name your piece," he said. "I was hankering after another song myself. But it's got to be religious, that's all."

"Oh, it's religious all right," said the young soldier, "only—, well, it's not a Easter piece. We sung it Christmas Eve. It's usually sang at Christmas, but I sure would like to hear it again, even if it ain't Christmas. It's 'O Holy Night.' I sure like that song."

Slim riffled through his music, frowning.

"Don't know as I have it here *now*," he muttered. "Yep,

here it is. In the hymn book. Now listen, men, I'll play it
through oncet. You know it. You sung it Christmas. Then
we'll sing it through all together. First stanza. And *then* Larry
here"—he indicated the young soldier who had asked for the
song—"Larry here will sing a solo. The place that begins 'Fall
on your knees,' and so on. It'll sure sound purty that way.
Now no objectin', Larry. You've got a purely sweet voice. Here
we go."

The organ rolled forth again. And this time, the chorus outdid itself. Mr. Graham's eyes turned to Larry. How young he
looked, how vulnerable. He was a slight boy with a slender
face and blond hair. . . . Mr. Graham could stand no more.
He stumbled out of the church and walked slowly down the
street. Yet outside he paused and listened, just as Lukey had
listened on Christmas Eve. Into the stillness of the night he
could hear Larry's voice, clear and sweet and true:

> *Fall on your knees!*
> *Oh, hear the angel voices . . .*

He remembered Larry's face, and the face of the lonely sentry
on the bridge, and Kenny's face the day the troopship sailed
away to France from New York Harbor——

> *Fall on your knees!*
> *Oh, hear the angel voices . . .*

Mr. Graham stood still. And then suddenly his heart crum-
bled and broke, for he remembered Mary's face, too, illuminated by that radiance whose source, until now, had been a closed
mystery to him. He remembered her smile, and the way she
used to say to him so gently, "Some day, darling, you'll understand, and when you do, I'll be with you. We'll be together
again. For always."

27

JAMES BRONSON had got up quite early that Easter Sunday morning, long before everybody else. He did not notice that the sky was transparently blue, nor that the birds were singing like a heavenly choir, nor that the air was perfumed with the distillation of many flowers.

He went into his study and sat down and read over his Easter sermon. He had never worked so hard on a sermon. He had taken long walks along the Rio Grande, thinking about it. He had read books. He had prayed. Yet there was no divine message in it, no inspiration. It was meticulously written, but he read it over now, and knew it was merely an essay. Any man with education could have written it.

He pushed it aside and sat there in his old bathrobe, his elbows on the table, his face between his hands. He had been in Donde for more than eight months, yet what had he accomplished? What good had he done? None. None at all. Neither this small town nor the world, nor anybody in it, had been benefited by his efforts. He himself had grown no closer to God. The questions and doubts he had had before coming here still remained with him. If anything, his doubts were stronger.

On Christmas Eve, only, for a few brief hours had he felt close to God. That night, praying for Cenci he had had again that feeling of oneness with God which had caused him, as a young man, to go into the ministry.

And when Cenci had miraculously taken a turn for the better he had felt exalted and triumphant but afterwards as the days passed, watching the little girl's too slow recovery, tortured by her pain, he felt as he had felt during the war, angry and rebellious at a God who would allow such injustice. And to Cenci, of all children!

Why should a child be allowed to suffer? Why had she been left a cripple? Her step had once been so light she scarcely seemed to touch the earth. Now for months she had not been able to walk. Why? And thinking about Cenci he thought about Mr. Graham and his son Kenny. Why should Kenny have had to be crucified? Had his death and the combined deaths of all of the other Kenny Grahams made the world a better place to live in?

No! The League of Nations was failing. There was revolution and famine in Europe. Fiume had been seized by the Italians. The United States was being swept over by a wave of lawlessness, of hysterical gaiety, of wild spending. There were labor troubles everywhere. Inflation was growing like a monster. Where would all of this end? Almost with a feeling of prophecy, James knew that there would be another war and he remembered the sadness in Mr. Graham's eyes, and thought with pain, *He had one son, and he gave him. I have five. . . . Are my boys going to the slaughterhouse, too?*

He, James Bronson, had used the insurance money which had been made possible by Kenny's death to come to this remote spot hoping to prove to himself that religion is necessary, that he should remain in the ministry. He had come here hoping that he could recapture the belief he himself had once had, the belief that love is stronger than hatred. Wars, he had found out, wars and suffering and crime are but the fruits of hatred, the fruits of ignorance and greed.

Peace, he had once thought, could come to the world only when it came to each individual heart. To achieve this peace it would be necessary for everybody to forget self, for each individual to purge himself of evil by allowing love to come into his being, until there was room for nothing else.

When he first came to Donde the town had seemed on the surface a peaceful isolated spot where nothing much happened. But never during his ministry had so much happened. The very day of his arrival a desperate man had stolen three pieces of bread for his hungry child and in so doing had been the innocent cause of an accidental death for which he, the Mexican, had been punished by being hanged. This morning he remembered with guilt Pánfilo's last words before he went to the gallows: "You have taught me faith, señor, you have acquainted me with God and I leave this sad world with nothing in my heart but love."

Today, a beautiful Easter morning, he could still see the pathetic little Mexican sitting on the edge of his cot in the cell, eating the *piñones* one by one until he had been taken out and hanged. He had not eaten them all but had saved two. "Take these to my wife and child," he said, "with my love. Tell them never to hate. Tell them only to love." Last week on Palm Sunday, Pánfilo's small son, Ignacio, had died. He had suffered from malnutrition too long and had contracted pneumonia. Pánfilo's theft of the bread for his starving baby had been in vain. Everything was in vain.

The world is sick, said James to himself, God, the Great Physician, has turned his head away. I can preach about him no longer.

He thought of Little Bonne Femme Church. It had grown like the gourd vine. And as its prosperity had increased, its spirituality had decreased. Time after time he had seen this happen. When a humble little church grew until it had to have a newer, grander building, it so often became smug. Lowly people, ashamed of their poor clothes, dropped out. Congregations became proud of "big names," of their fashionable members, of their aristocrats. Jealousies flourished. Rivalry and contention and snobbishness smothered out goodness.

Little Bonne Femme had become just like the rest of them. True, it had not yet attained a new building, but it would have to, soon, at the rate it was growing. There was no longer adequate seating room for its members. For the present, they had had to content themselves by painting the old building and fixing it up. Great efforts had been made to get it ready in time for today, Easter. But the church council had fought about the color of the paint. Two of the deacons, both furniture men, had quarreled about the new carpet. The president and secretary of the Ladies' Aid were not on speaking terms because they had disagreed about the floral decorations. What difference did it make whether he preached a good sermon or not? Who cared? Who would listen to it? People were coming to church today mainly to show off their new clothes. That was all. He remembered the motto Brett used to have: "The whole world stinks." Well, maybe Brett was right. What was the use of trying to imbue people with ideals? They didn't want ideals.

He thought of the Uplifters' Society and its almost demoniacal persecution of old Isabella, a lonely, shattered old woman who had never had her rightful chance in life, but was trying so hard now to become—as she expressed it—"a good woman."

James opened and reread a letter he had received from the boys' preparatory school which had offered him a position last year. The board of trustees, the letter said, was meeting next month. Their offer to him was still open. They would like a reply at once. James took paper and pen, and wrote his answer of acceptance. He had had, he wrote, a good rest. The Texas climate had improved his health. And he had come to a decision. He would accept the position. He would move back to Connecticut and be ready to take up his duties for the summer session.

He did not say in his letter that he had come to Donde, not for his health, but to find God. To try to recapture a lost faith. To seek a solution, just as the whole world—in its various ways —was seeking a solution, to problems too profound for human comprehension. He did not say that this letter was an admission of failure. He merely signed, addressed, and stamped it. He heard the baby, little Peter, crying. He heard the sounds of his house coming to life, the clatter of stovelids in the kitchen, footsteps, voices, but he ignored them. He had one other letter to write, the one to Mr. Graham. That would be hard to do, very hard.

Carefully, he wrote the heading and date and the salutation, "Dear Mr. Graham." Then he sat there, wondering how to begin. Outside it had become bright daylight. Through the open window he could hear the grackles screaming and chattering in the canebrakes along the river. *Dear Mr. Graham——* The ink in his pen dried. He sat there, dully staring at the blank page when he heard a knock on the study door.

"Come in," he said tonelessly, and Isabella, her hair rolled up on kid curlers, opened the door and came in carrying a cup of her fragrant coffee.

"Good morning, sir," she said, smiling. "I hope you'll excuse the curlers. I wanted to keep them in as long as possible. For the Service, you know."

She placed the coffee on the table before him, went over to the window and opened it wider.

"It's a lovely day, sir, isn't it?" she asked. "A lovely Easter."

James looked out, sipped the coffee.

"Yes," he replied politely, "it *is* a nice day. And this is good coffee, too. Thank you, Isabella."

In the doorway she turned. "Breakfast will soon be ready, sir," she said. "I'm making hot biscuits," she added. "I thought I'd have things a little extra nice. Being Easter, you know. Such a lovely Easter."

She closed the door.

Dear Mr. Graham——

He finished his coffee, looked at the clock. It was going to be a busy day. He wouldn't have time, now, to finish Mr. Graham's letter. He would have to do that tomorrow. He crumpled the paper in his hand, dropped it in the wastebasket. But the letter to the board of trustees he propped up against his ink bottle. He would post it this afternoon. Mail didn't go out on Sundays, but it would get off tomorrow, on the noon train. The sooner he mailed it, the better.

Easter is nearly always tricky, thought Cenci. It seems almost as if Nature takes a malicious delight in thwarting the plans of people hoping for a nice day on which to wear their new clothes. In Donde it could be, and usually was, a dry spring. Weeks would go by without even a cloud in the sky. And then, on Easter it would rain. Or, if it didn't rain, there was quite often a dust storm. And on one occasion which the people talked about from one generation to another until it had become a legend, there had been a freeze. A light one, true. But imagine! A freeze at Easter. In fact, a freeze at any time, in Donde!

Nora Bronson didn't usually worry about the Easter weather very much. She simply had her best dress cleaned and put new collars and cuffs on it and that was that. Then she would dig out her spring hat, dust it off with a whisk broom, and perhaps give it a coat of shoe polish, or invest in some new flowers at the five and ten. This year she had made a garland of yellow feathers around the crown, and sewed them on, with advice and help from Cenci, Miss Ivy, and Miss Andrews, Cenci's new governess. It was truly remarkable how lovely it looked. It was the yellow feather, everybody said. The brown dress she adorned with yellow ruching and even after so many babies and everything, she had the same air of style about her which she had had as a girl. No matter what, Nora always looked beautiful. James had been properly impressed by his new suit which had been at his place at the breakfast table. He had been puzzled, however, because Mr. Stein had unexpectedly appeared soon after breakfast and had insisted on James' trying it on.

"I was afraid the pants were too short," he apologized. "I *had* to see."

And then as he had left, Nora laughed and said, "*You* win, Mr. Stein!"

Isabella looked nice today, too, and so different. Her new dress was gray and severely plain. Her black hat covered up the bleached part of her hair, showing only the inch or so of honest gray she was so proud of. She reminded one, somehow, of a nun. . . .

But Cenci was definitely worried about the weather. Oh, dear, she thought, casting a practiced eye on the cloudless heavens, what if it should rain! That would spoil everything. She and Pete and the Lindleys had their little scheme all worked out, to the last detail. Matthew and Mark had gone to church early to collect their dates and ring the bell. Then James and Nora, Luke, John, and the baby had driven to the home of a woman who had volunteered to take care of the younger children during church. The surrey was pretty full as it also contained some potted plants (owing to careful planning on Brett's part) which they were to deliver to various people who were ill. So there was no room for Cenci. Not an inch. She would have to wait, and then James would drive back and pick her up just before the service. Miss Andrews, who had stayed behind to help her dress, said she *preferred* walking, later on, as it was such a divine day. Miss Andrews was awfully sweet but she was still only a governess who might get married or something at any moment. There was no permanence in a governess, even a good one.

Well, surely it wouldn't rain. The day was clear. It was warm, yet not too warm. It was delicious with flower-fragrance. It was drenched with the anthems of birds. It was, really, an Easter Sunday to put all other Easter Sundays to shame, and that was the honest truth.

As soon as the family left, Cenci hurried over to the Bronsons', hobbling on her crutches, waving good-bye to Miss Andrews from the door. Then she went into the minister's house, making sure no one was about, and walked to the little room where she had lain ill so long. It did not have a very good mirror. As a matter of fact, none of the mirrors in the Bronson house were good, but Cenci liked them anyway. She still pretended this room was hers. Here, supporting herself on her crutches, she critically surveyed herself. Her black hair had been brushed until her scalp tingled. She had washed her face with soap and water until it had a glossy shine to it, like polished fruit. She wore a new red hair ribbon, and oh! beauty of beauties, a new hat. Such a hat! A wide leghorn, trimmed with red poppies. She took it off, gave her hair another smoothing, then put the hat on again. Then she looked at her dress, white taffeta, sprigged with red rosebuds. Mrs. Bronson had made it, and Miss Andrews said that not even in New York, no, not even in Paris, could they have found a dress with so much style. It had a red silk sash, wide enough, Mr. Lindley declared emphatically, to insert in his typewriter and use for copy paper, except that of course yellow paper was better for the *Eagle*. Cenci couldn't see the bow of the sash in the back, but she could feel it, heavy and silky and right over the place in her back where her spine had been injured and where it still ached. Brett Lindley had insisted it was not a red bow at all, that it was a pair of wings. Cenci was a little redbird, he said, and if they didn't watch out, she would just fly away and leave them all behind.

Miss Ivy had helped her pick out her Easter oufit, except for the dress, but, for that matter, so had Cenci helped Miss Ivy pick hers. Because when Miss Ivy, from long habit, had been about to buy a beige dress, Cenci had said emphatically, "No. Not beige. Blue. *And* a blue hat to go with it."

"Blue! For *me?* Oh dear, no. My Easter dresses have always been beige."

But Cenci had had her way, and blue it had been. Cenci sighed now, thinking how beautiful Miss Ivy had looked in her blue dress, and how she, pug-nosed, straight-haired little Cenci could never in a thousand years, hope to look like that. Naturally, there was a *reason* just now, why Miss Ivy looked so extra pretty. For quite a while she had not worked at the *Eagle*. Brett had a hard time without her at the office but he didn't mind. He was too happy. He had a new society editor almost every week, and the geranium had died, and the big printing press had finally broken down altogether and the new parts from Dallas hadn't come in time to get out the paper this week. The church bulletins as usual had been printed in the hand press. But Brett didn't mind all of these troubles, he was so extra happy.

Cenci picked up her crutches, and the little package Pete had given her, and went out the back door and sat down on the stoop. She spread her crisp taffeta skirt out like a fan, laid the crutches beside her and stuck out her legs. She wore white lace socks, held up by fancy garters with little red silk rosettes to hide the elastic, and red shoes that must have been made by elves, surely. It did not seem possible that human hands could make shoes like these, so soft and dainty, with two straps that buttoned across each ankle. She thrust out her legs and surveyed the shoes and socks proudly, hoping it wasn't too much of a sin to love pretty things.

She hoped Mr. Bronson would come pretty soon. The sun was getting kind of hot and already the first bell for church had rung. She loved surprises. The only flaw in this one was that she had planned to run out to meet him when he came in at the gate. But she hadn't learned to run yet, only to walk a little. Not too well. And since Good Friday she hadn't even been able to walk. Not a step. She was terrified of falling. She was afraid to let her crutches out of sight.

All yesterday afternoon she had tried to walk but she couldn't. Miss Ivy had rubbed her legs and feet with those soft, yet firm hands of hers. Pete had said, "One step at a time, little gal, one step at a time." And Brett had added, in an unusually gentle tone, "All you need is faith, little girl. Just faith." Nora said, "Just think about your pretty red shoes, darling. Forget about walking. If you can't do it by Easter, why, you'll walk soon. I know you can do it. Don't worry."

But Cenci did worry. She wanted to walk on Easter. Today. She'd planned on it so long. Lukey would be expecting her to walk, as would all the Bronson boys. When Lukey had been told, just before the service, he turned a handspring and let out such a yelp of joy that Matthew had to put his hand over his mouth and Mark told him severely to calm down or he'd get a proper ducking in the fountain. The boys were certainly proud of her. Nothing she had ever done had made them so proud, they said. But they didn't know she was going to disappoint them, that she was too afraid now.

"I *do* wish Mr. Bronson would come!" she sighed.

Her feet in their little red shoes were numb and cold. She kept touching her crutches, afraid they would fall off the stoop. She pulled up her white socks and straightened her garters, realizing that her hands were cold, too, though her face was so hot. She felt dizzy and her spine hurt, under its big red bow.

"Oh, I *do* wish he'd come! I do wish he'd come!"

James was driving back in the surrey alone, to pick up Cenci. In some mysterious way he felt the way he had felt in that dream, long ago, when he had come home from work in his work-stained clothes. Only today he was well dressed in the suit Nora's father had given him. His shoes were polished, his hands clean. Yet he felt again that he was clothed in foul-smelling garments. He felt as if he were arrayed in evil. Discouraged and weary he turned the surrey into Mesquite Street, stopped at the gate and hitched the horse. Then he got out and opened the gate.

"Cenci!" he called.

And then he saw her. He saw her sitting on the stoop, her crutches beside her, her skirt fanned out, her useless little legs in their white socks, her feet in their gay red shoes. The little girl in his dream had been waiting like that. She, too, had been wearing red shoes, and she had jumped up and had come running to meet him, arms outstretched, her face radiant. *Red shoes. . . .*

But Cenci could not run to meet him. She could not even walk. James stood there for a moment, and he thought his heart would break because he knew that when Cenci did arise she would reach for her crutches, and then those gay little red shoes would dangle helplessly as she came to meet him.

"Cenci," he said softly, "are you ready?"

He started toward her, and then he saw her get up, slowly, carefully. She did not reach for her crutches. Instead she put out one small red shoe and steadied it on the ground. Then she put out the other one. She was trembling. Step by step she approached him, not too steadily, not very fast, but proudly, oh! so proudly. He could not believe what he was seeing. And, as in that sweet lost dream, he felt a rush of glory through him, he felt as if he were being baptized anew, washed in purity, cleansed, resurrected.

"Cenci, my darling——"

He hurried toward her then, and stooped and lifted her in his arms, and carried her out to the surrey and put her in the seat. He wanted to say something, but a hard pain paralyzed his throat. He kept looking at her but could not speak. He unhitched the horse and started to get in beside her when he looked back and saw her crutches, lying there on the stoop. He debated a moment, then started to go through the gate to get them, but she called him back.

"I don't need my crutches," she said, and then she smiled at him radiantly, "I won't ever need them again, Mr. Bronson. This was my Easter surprise for you— Pete helped me——"

The minister got in beside her. Trojan started off down the street. "Oh!" she exclaimed, "I almost forgot, here's another present, too. Pete asked me to give them to you. He made them. May I unwrap them now, please, while you drive? I can't wait!"

With his consent she took off the wrappings and showed him the book ends Pete had made, the two kneeling figures, the old man and the old woman, their faces gnarled, wrinkled, tired, yet beautiful with love.

"They're made out of African ebony," Cenci explained, "the very finest wood Pete had. He said nothing was too good for *you* because you—well, he said, you gave him faith. You gave him courage. Courage is being brave, isn't it, Mr. Bronson?"

"Yes, dear. Courage is being brave."

The second bell could be heard ringing and James slapped the reins gently on the horse's back, and the old surrey creaked and began rolling a little faster down the street.

"Isn't it funny, Mr. Bronson, how you gave so much courage to Pete that he had enough left over to give some to me? I guess maybe when you help just one person, you really help *more* than one. Or do you? You see, Pete and I got to be awful good friends, while he was teaching me to walk. He told me you taught him other things, too. Lots of the words I don't remember, but some of them were things like love and beauty and prayer, and all of those."

"But Pete!" exclaimed James. "Pete doesn't like me. He hardly knows me. Why, I haven't exchanged more than a few words with him in all these months, and they were usually about the church bulletins or something like that."

Cenci turned her little face up to him, smiling. "Pete's hard to talk to," she said, "until you get to know him. But Pete knows you, all right. He loves you. You see, he has been coming to church."

"Pete! Coming to church? I've never seen him there."

"I know. He's kind of ashamed, you see. Because he's a hunchback. So he just stands in the vestibule, out of sight. People make fun of him. Some ladies made fun of me, too, once. In a way. They didn't mean to, I guess. But they said, 'Pitiful, isn't she?' and I heard them whispering about me. Pete said not to notice those things, just to try and think of beauty. But it makes him feel bad all the same, and he hides in the vestibule."

"Oh!"

"But," she continued, "you know what Pete said? Well, he said, if I walked for you today, he'd walk down the aisle, full view, like other people, and sit in a pew, and not be ashamed. So I promised him I would. Only right at the last, since Friday,

I got scared and thought I couldn't do it. But when I saw you coming in the gate this morning, and your eyes so sad—I—I—forgot to be afraid. I just loved you so much, I guess and I knew if *you* were with me I could do it. So I did."

The old horse clopped on, the surrey rattled down the street, and Cenci, in a burst of words, told all about how she had learned to walk. As she talked she remembered something Pete had told her about his old man, how he didn't say anything but just kept rubbing the back of his hand across his eyes. Odd, she thought, Mr. Bronson was doing the same thing now. She reached out one of her own hands and rested it on James' knee.

"You know," she said, "you haven't said a thing about my Easter outfit, my hat or my dress, or anything. And especially my shoes." She stuck her feet out in front of her. *"Especially my shoes!* Don't you like them? Did you notice them?"

James took his handkerchief out of his pocket, the one with the lopsided "B" she had embroidered, and wiped his eyes.

"Of course I noticed them," he said thickly, "I noticed them the first thing. I think they're the most beautiful shoes in the world."

She sighed in satisfaction, "I was hoping you would," she said, and snuggled nearer to him and would have laid her head on his shoulder, but it would have mashed her hat.

When they got to the church he stopped the horse and hitched it at the place which had been reserved for him. People were pouring into the little church house. Cars, wagons and vehicles of almost every sort were parked for blocks all up and down the street.

Ordinarily he entered the little side door and went at once to the pulpit, but now Cenci whispered to him, as he lifted her out of the surrey, "I'd like to walk down the aisle, like Pete, *full view.* I want him to know that I'm not afraid, either."

So hand in hand they went in the front door. People were standing at the back of the church, and all along the walls. The windows were clean and sparkling. The new carpet felt very soft under their feet. The interior of the church was like an arbor, so bedecked was it by greens and flowers. And around the new pulpit were hundreds of cape jasmines, camellias and white roses, like a bank of clean new-fallen snow.

Down the new carpet they went, the tall preacher and the little girl, slowly, carefully. He could feel her taut little hand in his, he felt her body trembling, but he held to her hand firmly until they reached the Bronsons' pew. Then she sat down, next to Lukey, in the seat they had been saving for her, and James went on and ascended the pulpit. Slim, at the organ, began playing softly.

From long habit James's eyes first sought those of Nora and he smiled at her and she smiled back. After that his eyes went from one member of his family to the other. He saw Lukey, almost bursting with happiness, next to Cenci. He saw Mark with Dee and Matthew with Elspeth. Then he sought out other faces: Brett Lindley and Miss Ivy, their faces shining, and next to them, Hunchback Pete. He saw old Isabella, in her gray dress. He saw Lupe, wrapped in her black *rebozo,* her soft, beseeching eyes lifted toward him with hope. He saw Mr. Stein ascend the steps, enter the church uncertainly, keeping his hat on until he saw that the other men were bareheaded. Then the little Jew quickly took his hat off and somebody made room for him and he sat down. He saw Fred, the cowboy, strangely subdued yet not sleepy. He wore a black band of mourning around one arm, for his old ma had finally died. James had gone to San Antonio with him last month to conduct her funeral. The minister's eyes traveled from one familiar face to another in the congregation. He looked at the organ and at the beautiful church decorations.

No wonder! he thought. No wonder the women became ill-tempered. They worked too hard, that was all. And no doubt the deacons had had a falling out about the carpet because of their over-anxiety to get the finest one possible. They all love this church, just as I do. They wanted to give it their best.

He saw the men in their good suits and the women in their

new hats and dresses and he thought that that, too, was only human and natural. Flowers bloom in the spring and are not condemned for it. Birds put on their most splendid plumage, but it does not lessen the glory of their singing. God knows there is enough ugliness in the world. It is good to try to be beautiful.

Then he thought of Pete and little Cenci, of their great love and faith and courage. He remembered how Cenci had said, "I guess when you help just one person you help *more* than one. Or do you?"

Dimly, dimly, James recalled the letter he had written to the Board of Trustees early this morning. He knew now that he would never send it. He would never give up the ministry. He couldn't. . . .

A feeling came over him like the one he had had the night Cenci had almost died. As then, he felt, not closer to God, but part of God. He thought of the sermon he had planned to preach today, but knew he would not preach it. He had other things to say to his people, a direct message from God. . . .

I was just talking to the Lord about you, Cenci darling, that's all. I was just talking to our Lord.

James arose from the chair and stood near the pulpit, banked with its white flowers. Slim stopped playing. A silence came over the congregation.

And then, coming up the steps slowly, James saw Mr. Graham. He did not know Mr. Graham was in Donde, and yet, somehow, it did not seem strange to see him walking into the church today. He had the feeling that Mr. Graham had been coming to church here every Sunday all along, that he had been ever present.

Mr. Graham entered softly and joined the group of people who were standing near the door, because there were no longer any empty seats. As he observed them, James thought of the faces of the two kneeling figures Pete had carved for him, faces scourged and tortured by life, yet upon them an expression of infinite love and peace. This same look now illuminated Mr. Graham's face.

> But Mary stood without at the sepulchre weeping; and as she wept, she stooped down, and looked into the sepulchre,
>
> And seeth two angels in white, sitting, the one at the head, and the other at the feet, where the body of Jesus had lain.
>
> And they say unto her, Woman, why weepest thou? She saith unto them, Because they have taken away my Lord, and I know not where they have laid him.
>
> And when she had thus said, she turned herself back, and saw Jesus standing, and knew not that it was Jesus.

James looked out at his beloved flock. People who had been hurt, who no doubt would be hurt again and again, yet must remain indestructible. All over the world were people like these, human, yet a part of God. And all over the world, people were seeking this very God, not knowing He was so near.

Not knowing He was so near . . .

A look of exaltation came upon the minister's face. He took a step forward, his feet quite hidden by the hundreds of white flowers massed at the base of the pulpit. And then he knelt amidst the flowers.

"Let us pray," he said with reverence, and bowed his head.

THE END